"Cousin Drewey came clean out of the Ouachita Mountains, what us Lowdermilks call the Washtaw Mountains, to visit us kin here in Star Valley. His trip was along six hundred miles westbound, and it happened in the summer season a handful of years ago. He crossed Oklahoma then down out of Texas to get here in New Mexico. He came to us on the train; just a man aset in the front car, where the butcher boy sets.

"Cousin Drewey was a lean man of seventy. Those were his years, three score and ten. He packed a satchel, a fiddle and a guitar...."

"... I can personally say that the reason his work is so true to the times, places, and people you'll find in his book is because John L. Sinclair has been there and his books are very largely based on personal experience. His is a major talent, indeed!"—Nelson C. Nye

"John L. Sinclair has again proved himself a master storyteller of those earthy folks who a handful of years ago farmed that sorry stretch of flatness from the Washtaw Mountains of eastside Oklahoma to Star Valley in Eastern New Mexico ... A rollicking good tale ... A beautiful novel."—Frank Waters

COUSIN DREWEY AND THE HOLY TWISTER

BY
JOHN L. SINCLAIR

CHARTER
NEW YORK

A Division of Charter Communications Inc.
A GROSSET & DUNLAP COMPANY
51 Madison Avenue
New York, New York 10010

COUSIN DREWEY AND THE HOLY TWISTER
Copyright © 1980 by John L. Sinclair

All rights reserved. No part of this book may be reproduced in any form or by any means, except for the inclusion of brief quotations in a review, without permission in writing from the publisher.

All characters in this book are fictitious. Any resemblance to actual persons, living or dead, is purely coincidental.

An Ace Charter Book
Published by arrangement with
Columbia Publishing, Inc.
Frenchtown, New Jersey 08825

First Ace Charter Printing: April 1982

Published simultaneously in Canada

2 4 6 8 0 9 7 5 3 1
Manufactured in the United States of America

*And maketh the clouds his
chariot, and walketh upon
the wings of the wind.*

THE HOLY BIBLE

1

COUSIN DREWEY came clean out of the Ouachita Mountains, what us Lowdermilks call the Washtaw Mountains, to visit us kin here in Star Valley. His trip was a long six hundred miles westbound, and it happened in the summer season a handful of years ago. He crossed Oklahoma then down out of Texas to get here in New Mexico. He came to us on the train; just a man aset in the front car, where the butcher boy sets.

Cousin Drewey was a lean man of seventy. Those were his years, three score and ten. He packed a satchel, a fiddle and a guitar. And a hog-leg forty-five single-action revolver. The fiddle rode in its case and the guitar sat on Cousin Drewey's lap; but the six-gun was holstered to his belt, under his coat where no one could see its glory. Cousin Drewey chewed cut and spat ambeer. He hadn't shaved his face for a tolerable spell.

Cousin Drewey got off at the depot. He went up to the agent and said, "Button, where'all will I find them Lowdermilks; 'cause I'm their lawful cousin and I need to know where they're at?"

It was 'round five in the evenin', so Briggs, the agent, figgered rightly how maybe us folks had shed enough sweat in the corn patch for the day. He figgered we'd be settin' on the porch—me and my sister Verbaline Lou, and Maw Maw, and the two hound dogs and the yeller tom cat—listenin' to Pap shoot his big windies, just listenin' to lies of log-size proportions.

"They're mossbacks," Briggs told Cousin Drewey. "You'll know the shanty 'cause it's the sorriest in the valley, 'bout five miles down the road. It's propped up with crossties and the roof waves in the breeze. It's kin to a chicken house. They'll be cookin' supper right now. Hog meat and greens, likely. But you won't smell the hog meat fryin' or the greens boilin' 'cause the Lowdermilks burn old automobile tires for stove fuel, and used rubber ablazin' has a fragrant aroma all its own."

Dadburned if Briggs didn't act the soothsayer from way back, because that's exactly where we were, me and Pap and Maw Maw and Verbaline Lou. The two hound dogs were sleepin' in the yard and the cat was fixin' to go travelin' for the night. Pap was noisy about his windies. He told about a man you can find in 1 Kings 12:25, a righteous feller named Jeroboam.

Cousin Drewey walked the five miles out from Signal Rock depot along the road to us Lowdermilks. And what Cousin Drewey saw 'round about as he headed our way was Star Valley, that sorry stretch of flatness that gave us our farm-dirt and fireside. It's the most open space of territory on the east side of the whole state of New Mexico; where folks think like they do in Texas, where they look like Texans, and talk like they'd come from that good old Lone Star State. Just like us Lowdermilks talk the slash-pine language of eastside Oklahoma, out from the Washtaw Mountains. We looked like we needed curryin' down, to get the moss-roots off our backs.

Cousin Drewey walked all the way, like Briggs told him to do. He didn't hook a ride because there were no rides to hook. He was pint-size, and if any man should call him a Washtaw runt, Cousin Drewey would use his good nature to agree with him. And say how that there

COUSIN DREWEY & THE HOLY TWISTER 3

was *exactly* his nationality.

He wasn't stove-up after his long years on earth, but he was a wearied old cracker after his walk out from town.

Lord, was Cousin Drewey a sight!

"What's your business?" Pap quizzed of Cousin Drewey when that kinfolks walked up. Cousin Drewey had the guitar slung over his back and he packed the fiddle and satchel in his hands, balance-like. Pap was superstitious of all strangers, because men pick up shotguns and women run for the slash pine when strangers walk up back in the Washtaw Mountains. We came years ago to settle here on the dry Star Valley flats. Cousin Drewey looked us over, fearin' how he'd maybe come to the wrong shanty. But he soon made up his mind.

"You're kinfolks, all right," Cousin Drewey said. "You're a mixture of Lowdermilks and Fosters, full-blood. There ain't no argument there. You'alls got slash pine on your faces and sweet-gum rosin on your teeth. I stand here a proud man, proud to call you brethren and sistern."

"You come from the Washtaw Mountains, brother?"

"Straight like a westbound buzzard, first on the Frisco Lines then on the good old A.T. and S.F. road."

"What's your brand of kin?" said Pap.

Me and Pap were alone on the porch, 'cause Maw Maw and Verbaline Lou had run for the house. They'd got themselves out of sight, but their womanly curiosities had them to peek through the board cracks.

"Cousin, second grade," said Cousin Drewey.

"Lowdermilk or Foster?" challenged Pap. 'Cause the Fosters were Maw Maw's tribe and the Lowdermilks Pap's, both breedin' heavy in the timber thickets.

"I'm Uncle Gersh's cousin, first grade," said Cousin Drewey.

Pap snorted, hog fashion. "That don't mean nothin',"

he said. "There's two Uncle Gershes in the Washtaw Mountains, one a Foster, t'other a Lowdermilk. State your kinship, stranger, then we'll welcome you under our roof. We'll feed you a supper of hog meat, greens and cornbread."

Cousin Drewey held his jaw shut for a solid half minute. Then he opened it up to let loose on Pap. "I love hog meat and greens right smart," he said, "but I ain't got no taste for nosey kinfolks. If I say how I'm Uncle Gersh's cousin, first grade, then *that* ought to be my ticket to *your* home-sweet-home. My name is Drewey Stiff and I belong to the rightful political party, though I might be a Lowdermilk and I might be a Foster. And I don't need tell you how I'm a Baptist, Washtaw Mountain variety."

"A Primitive Baptist?" primed Pap, puttin' in a final quiz.

"There ain't no Foster or Lowdermilk what ain't," Cousin Drewey said.

Pap softened his superstitions. But myse'f, I craved to know what category of Primitive Baptist Cousin Drewey was—Foot-washin', Forty-gallon, Holy Bark, or Slab Baptist. But if Pap was fixin' to go hug Cousin Drewey's neck, holler for the womenfolks to come out from behind the bulwarks, and say, "Welcome, dear cousin, to the shelter of our roof," then I wasn't the kind of old boy to pour muddy water in the molasses vat.

Pap whistled for the womenfolks. His whistle had a sweet tune which sang how Cousin Drewey was high-grade in Pap's thinkin', which gave me a happy feelin' deep down where my heart sets. He hollered into the house, "Git out here, you'all kids, 'cause we've got kinfolks come to stay awhile." And he said to me: "Newt," —that's my given name—"step down off the porch and love your Cousin Drewey's neck."

Cousin Drewey saw me comin' so he laid down his

stachel and fiddle flat on the yard dirt. He unswung the guitar from his back. Maw Maw and Verbaline Lou came out of hidin' both redfaced like they had fever. Except they were bashful, nothin' more potent. A natural woman gets snaky on sight of kinfolks, but our women acted brave enough. After me, they took turns at lovin' Cousin Drewey's neck.

Pap and me are slightly proud of our womenfolks. And both together they showed off our pride right smart when they stepped up to Cousin Drewey, with nary a womanly-snake in their frameworks, and gave him smiles before slobbers. Maw Maw shed her Copenhagen dip then looped a fat arm 'round our kinfolk's neck, which set him gigglin' and blushin'. Maw Maw looked like she was no kin to Pap and me. Me and Pap packed lanky frames, both about the same height, except Pap was feisty, always ready for a scrap. I might be lanky but I've got a peaceful nature. And we both carry chin-bristles—just a boy and his Pap. Maw Maw's made of different meat. She's stout and short; and she's carried on legs too big 'round their girth, like she's got an ailment that makes 'em bigger than they should. She once had boobs but they sagged with her years. The work-corns on her hands and sun-crackles up and down her arms gave no hint that there was a heart of gold in their vicinity. She was born with good sense. If Pap had what Maw Maw got from the Lord, he'd be a better man.

I'd whip the tar out of any feller alive if I knew he was thinkin' sinful thoughts about my sister, Verbaline Lou. Like I get when I look at pretty girls in the Sears and Roebuck catalogue, or Monkey Ward or Bellas Hess. Because my sister is the sweetest, prettiest as ever born and come out of Oklahoma. She's slender-built, but corn-fed enough to keep her out from the gut-shrunk tribe of women—and she had sparks in her eyes, and her mouth packed the sense come down from her brain, right size because of her clean, healthy teeth. And she's tall. Not lanky like me and Pap, but more so in height than our short, round-about-the middle, pure country-style Maw Maw. She wore her legs naked, and she fixed her brown hair up to style, down her back and did-up with a clasp, pretty like that. Whenever a man, woman or child came up close to Verbaline he or she felt somethin' warm, and kind, and lovin', and all a girl should be in her youngness.

But don't get me wrong, because she's mossback pure, fed on corn and cornbread, okra and turnip greens, sugar cane sweetenin' and salt from the salt-bog, hog-middlin' and fried chicken, the kind of gut-feedin' that makes us mossbacks glum or bright, heavy or gut-shrunk, smart or foggy-brained; or beautiful like Verbaline Lou.

"I don't aim to stay long," Cousin Drewey said, moppin' his mouth with his big blue-spotted handkerchief after gettin' kissed by the women. "But factways, I've done hear'd so much good talk about you folks who came out here to the West that I couldn't set still 'til I looked you'all in the faces and said a sweet fare-you-well."

"Fare-you-well?" Pap said, comin' off the porch. "Where'all you aim to go?"

"I'm seventy years old last March," said Cousin Drewey. "I've lived five months beyond my allotted time. The Good Book says how the days of a man's years be three score and ten, and if by reason of strength he lives on a while longer it won't profit him much, cause he soon flies away. I figgered my arithmetic down to the digits, back there in the Washtaw Mountains. And the answer I came up with was that I couldn't fly away 'til I saw you'alls kinfolks' faces."

"You don't look more'n fifty-five to me," Pap said.

COUSIN DREWEY & THE HOLY TWISTER

"Me too," said Maw Maw. "You look like you've got plenty livin' meat on your framework, and how the blacksmith couldn't deaden you with a ball-peen hammer."

"I tell you, it won't be long afore I'll be a long-gone citizen," said Cousin Drewey. "If the Good Book says so, a man might just as well pack his satchel and hook a ride to the Pearly Gates. Fact is, dear cousins, I cain't wait to git where I'm goin'. But just plant my leftovers in the Washtaw Mountains."

"You love them Washtaw Mountains, don't you, Cousin Drewey?" said Verbaline Lou. Lord, was she brave for her youngness.

"Best place in the sweet Maker's kindly world for a man's life and leftovers," said Cousin Drewey.

"You look like a musical man," said Pap, eyein' Cousin Drewey's instruments.

"I'm musical and I'm healthy," said Cousin Drewey. "I'm healthy 'cause I cain't go hungry. And a man cain't go hungry if he's got him a fiddle. He can fiddle for a hoedown, or for a hugdance, or on the street corner when he craves to make a dime. A man cain't go hungry if he's got a guitar, if he's got a voice as potent as the one I pack in my glottis. And he won't go hungry if he's got holstered to his belt a hog-leg forty-five."

Cousin Drewey loosened his coat. From off his belt came the shinin' glory. The women stuttered praises while me and Pap gaped.

"We'd be right proud if you'd sing us a song," came Pap's invite.

"Lord, yes!" said Maw Maw. "Come up on the porch, cousin, and set you in a chair. We ain't hear'd 'Big Ole Potato in the Sandy Land' since we came out of the Washtaw Mountains."

"Nope," said Cousin Drewey, "I won't do it for two reasons. One, 'cause a man like me with his steps aimed for the gravehole cain't take no chance with time. I might die on the way to the porch. Second, this is a mighty solemn minute, me meetin' dear kinfolks like you'all. It don't call for hoedown music. But I'll sing you a song while standin' my ground, right here in the yard dirt. I'll sing you the Twenty-third Psalm like old Drewey Stiff sings it, to the tune of 'The Birmin'ham Jail.' "

That's when Cousin Drewey picked up his guitar off the yard dirt. That's when he put his fingers inside his mouth and pulled his tobacco cut from behind his back jaw and laid it kindly on the crown of his hat. He hadn't completely juiced it of ambeer. And that's when he fingered the strings and let his voice sail to the far reaches of Star Valley. His was a song writ by old King David long, long ago; with music rendered by Drewey Stiff.

The Lord is my shepherd
And I shall not want . . .

Lord, was Cousin Drewey a musical man! That old Twenty-third Psalm went flyin' through the air clean over to Old Man Lee Bassett's place and north up the valley where Miss Melody Provine resides.

He restoreth my soul, babe,
He restoreth my soul . . .

But Cousin Drewey had me mystified aplenty. He didn't sound like he packed three-score-and-ten-year-old lungs. He sang like he owned a powerful glottis. He was tuned like a mile-long freight train on the Frisco Lines.

2

Cousin Drewey hadn't stayed with us more than two weeks when he got a wistful look on his face. He'd be up from his pallet under the box elder tree long before sunrise, every day without fail. He was an outdoor man, a barnyard man. There he'd look to the horizon. He knew by sight how six hundred miles buzzard-flight eastward lay the Washtaw Mountains, the Lord's own created green pastures and still waters, the land of restoration for the soul.

"I'd sure hate to die here among you'all," he told us Lowdermilks, "and not git my leftovers buried in the Washtaw Mountains."

Cousin Drewey might have had a mule-size appetite, but we hated the thought of him goin' away. He talked aplenty when he wasn't eatin', but just let him set down to our humble fare and nary a word would come from his soundbox. His jaws moved like they had built in lubrication, his reach was long and he knew where the bowls of vittles sat. He could eat fast and stay with it a long time.

"That dear cousin," Maw Maw said more times than once, "is eatin' us out of house and home."

Cousin Drewey had made right smart of friends in Star Valley. Word got 'round how he was a musical man, one of the finest kind, so folks who'd never come to see us before arrived nigh every day in cars and wagons and trailers pulled by tractors. They came to hear Cousin Drewey tickle his guitar, to watch him saw at his fiddle. He'd render them music on our porch or out by the woodpile. He'd sing them songs like "The Rosewood Casket" or "The Letter Edged in Black," or "The Plot in the Churchyard Grove" or "The Death of Floyd Collins." Or he'd give them that beautiful song called "The Murder of James A. Garfield."

> *My name is Charles J. Guiteau,*
> *My crime I'll never deny,*
> *The murder of James A. Garfield*
> *Upon this scaffold high.*

That's how Cousin Drewey would sing for the neighbors. Or he'd give them that old Twenty-third Psalm, it which led him down to the green pastures beside the still waters, even if he walked through the valley of the shadow of death. And he'd sing them the second chapter of The Song of Solomon, sing it to the tune of "Old Dan Tucker." Or he'd render somethin' he'd made up himself, that song he called "Honeysuckle Candy Woman":

> *Woman, woman, why were you made so sweet?*
> *Woman, woman, why were you made so sweet?*
> *'Cause you're honeysuckle candy*
> *Clean down from head to feet.*

The neighbors would holler praises and Cousin Drewey would switch to his fiddle. He'd saw the strings like his bow had the dancin' spasms. Always between musical selections Cousin Drewey would josh the neighbors and make them bust their guts laughin'. And us poor Lowdermilks would be mighty proud of our kinfolks. But most of all we were tickled because Cousin Drewey had made us good and lastin' friends. Because once those neighbors came 'round to say howdy and get a look at me and Pap and Maw Maw and Verbaline Lou, they figgered how we weren't such sinners after all, even if we were mighty poor. Because there was laughter and joy on the Lowdermilk place, and song, and fiddled tunes.

"I'll swan before Jonah," said Posey Burwinkle's woman, "if that man ain't one full-blood clown from *way* back!"

When I say we were poor, I mean we were poorer than any turkey the prophet Job kept in his yard. Some months of the year we lived on cornbread and beans—no meat but jackrabbit, no nothin' else. We held our shoes together with balin' wire. Our farm was a single-power outfit. We had mostly "one" of anythin' we had, with mighty scant variety. We worked a ten-acre dry-land corn patch with a portion planted to beans and milo maize. The balance of our place was pasture; not of the King David brand, green and grassy, but graveled sand and greasewood, some sage and tumbleweed, just a bunch of salt grass here and there.

That railroad agent was right when he told Cousin Drewey how we lived in a shanty kin to a chicken house, how the rusty tin roof leaked every square yard and how outside in the fresh air that roof waved with the wind like it was the Star Spangled Banner. How it wasn't a pretty house to decorate the valley, how us Lowdermilks weren't a pretty sight for human eyes, except for maybe Verbaline Lou, that is, and how fat old Maw Maw worked herself down to a skinful of sunblisters. And when Cousin Drewey told us all what that feller said about the house, Pap said he wished Briggs would go to hell with the Atchison, Topeka and Santa Fe Railroad.

Because me and Pap built that house soon after we

came in the covered wagon west from the Washtaw Mountains—me button-sized, Verbaline Lou streakin' the floor in wet didies, and Maw Maw a mighty fine woman not yet worked down to ugliness under a sunbonnet.

Pap did most of the house buildin', me and Maw Maw passin' up the lumber and nails and roof-sheets and doors and windows while Pap put them all together. And we made a square house of rough-lumber frame, with two rooms and a kitchen lean-to and a porch along the front. We used the porch a lot, all summer long, where Pap told us his Bible stories, like Solomon, who didn't know his ass from his elbow 'til he asked the Lord for wisdom. Verbaline Lou used one room for herself, because she was in maidenhood and needed nobody pokin' into her boudoir. Me and Pap and Maw Maw slept in the settin'-'round room. And when we planted the box elder tree near the kitchen lean-to door we hadn't any idea how some day Cousin Drewey would need a shelter over his bed. The spreadin' limbs were good enough, except when it rained. It seemed like our kinfolks just didn't give a damn—rain, moonlight or the mosquitoes.

But that old shanty don't confess how we lacked ambition, us Lowdermilks. One day, the year before Cousin Drewey came to us, I was out in the yard with Verbaline Lou, us just messin' 'round with the two hound dogs. Maw Maw came out of the house to get some fresh air, because the cookstove smoked some.

"Where's Pap?" Maw Maw quizzed, for she missed for the minute her lovin' man.

Verbaline Lou said nothin', which told how she didn't know.

"Ain't no tellin' where *that* man is at," I said, because for a truth I couldn't see Pap 'round nowheres.

COUSIN DREWEY & THE HOLY TWISTER

Just then Verbaline Lou aimed her pretty face at the corn patch, out where the green stalks were puttin' on tassels. "There he be," my sister said, and raised her hand in cahoots with her face-aim. "He's out in the corn, and only the sweet Lord knows what he's got on his mind."

Sure enough, we looked in the direction Verbaline Lou talked about, and there Pap walked down a row. And as he walked he used his hands to pet the leaves like he would pet a dog, or like he did to old Jeff the mule when his heart felt kindly. And the way he did it, the way he shook the dust from the tassels, told how he loved that corn right smart. He loved it because he'd planted the seed in the dirt, usin' a hoe, just like he'd used his instrument to plant seed in Maw Maw and make me and Verbaline Lou. Pap loved us kids because we were of his plantin'; he loved Maw Maw together with the earth he called his own. The preacher told Pap, back in the Washtaw Mountains, how Maw Maw was his, his woman to love and cherish, in sickness and health, 'til death do them part. The homestead deed, earned from the government, said how that clean earth out there was Pap's, every pebble and grain of it, to use along with trust in the Lord for makin' us Lowdermilks a livin', slight as it might be. We might have been poor, but Pap's love for Maw Maw and the earth, for me and Verbaline Lou, and for the green-stalked tasselin' corn was more real for substance than all the gold bricks stored in the United States Treasury, sweeter than the waters of Shiloh, softer than silk or satin.

"Let's git," Maw Maw told us kids. "Let's git and he'p Pap brag on that there corn."

We joined Pap when he got nearest us, as he walked down between two rows of that old yellow dent. He came up to us, smilin'-happy. "You know, folkses," he said, comin' up, "you cain't guess what I'm thinkin'. All three of you couldn't guess, even if you strained your think-leaders to bustin' apart."

"Cain't," Maw Maw said.

Me and Verbaline Lou didn't say a goddamn thing. But we looked at Pap so's to tell him to shoot, to get what he had off his mind.

"I'm thinkin' how this brown dirt is some of the bestest in the valley," he said. "I'm kinda proud how we use it to good purpose and raise corn as fine as this here. And we do it with just one old mule that's wearin' out fast, with a set of single harness, with a single-breasted plow and an 1896-model go-devil, and the elbow fuel us four have got tanked up in the bend of our arms. And I'm thinkin', too, how we've got forty acres just like it over yonder beyond the greasewood flat, rich and brown and rarin' to raise corn and pleadin' for me and you'all to clear it, and break it, and plant it to the good seed."

Maw Maw looked at me, and her face told how she thought Pap talked plumb craze. I nodded back to say how my mind and hers worked in cahoots. Verbaline Lou shook her head sadly, but she looked kindly on Pap.

"You're crazy like a drunk skunk," I said to Pap. "How the hell can you break forty acres with one sorry mule and a plow and go-devil? It takes all the sweat we got to raise ten acres. You're dreamin' dreams, Pap, and you're lettin' 'em git the better of you. . . . If the good Lord aimed for mossbacks to have better'n what we've got, He'd put us on green pastures, set beside still waters. Or He'd let us own a team, some good harness, and a full line of farmers' implements. We'd have a wagon with double-trees, not one with single-mule shafts and a seat for prime-poverty to set high on. . . . If the Lord aimed for us Lowdermilks to have more than we got, He'd send us the means to put down a well and set a windmill over it to hoist the water up from down below. He'd give us what we ain't got—the guts and tallow to

COUSIN DREWEY & THE HOLY TWISTER 15

make your dreams come true."

But my words didn't faze Pap one mite. He looked at me like he pitied me, and he said, "Son, let me tell you somethin'. When we planted them little yeller seeds along them rows I had faith inside me how they'd bust open their dents once they felt the damp earth 'round them. When I saw them sprout up to the sunlight I had faith that they'd grow up taller, make leaves and tassels, and ears inside shucks, clean yeller kernels, row beside row of 'em. . . . Son, ain't this the prettiest stand of corn you've ever see'd anywhere in Star Valley?"

"It *sure* is," I told Pap. "But I still think you're dreamier'n a drunk skunk."

"The Lord will provide, son. Trust in the Lord," he smiled at me.

"You bet," said Verbaline Lou, like she'd say when she went to Baptist meetin'. "You bet and *amen.*"

"Praise the Lord," said Maw Maw. "Praise His kindly name."

I craved to say horseshit, but I had no mind to harm the Lowdermilks' feelin's. So I said, "You bet," just like Verbaline Lou.

"Folks," Pap said, and he spoke to all of us. "Some day the dear Lord will send us a means to put that forty acres into crop, and that's when we'all can raise our heads high and be on equal-notch with our feller men. . . . The Lord will send the means out of the heavens, up from the ground, or in the body and soul of some ambassador put in our midst from His Kingdom of Mercy. And maybe that ambassador will show us the way to respect, like the Lord aims for us to be respectable, tell us how we've got the ticket already writ out, right here under our rattley roof, inside our walls, standin' next to us now."

That's when I had to say "Horseshit." I couldn't he'p myself. I saw some wetness come to Pap's eyes, like maybe I'd hurt him, like his own planted son was tryin' to bust down his hopes and dreams.

"While there's life there's hope," Maw Maw said, "that's a fact and that's all there is to it."

Then I saw somethin' like I'd never seen before in all my days. I saw Verbaline Lou walk over to Pap and throw her arms 'round his neck. I saw her sob her wetness onto his shoulder. "Don't worry, Pap," she said, "You'll git your forty acres, sure as there's sky above. You'll git you a well drilled, down deep, and the windmill blades will turn in the wind, the sucker rods will pump the water clean up to its ground. And us Lowdermilks will be able to look our neighbors straight in the face and say how us and them walk on the same level."

"All we need is what it takes for a start," Pap said. "Let the Lord send us the spark, then we'll kindle the blaze for ourselves."

When Verbaline Lou looked up from Pap's shoulder, I couldn't help but think she was the most beautiful girl I'd ever witnessed, before or since.

It takes money to dig or drill a well, so we hauled our water in barrels from a neighbor's windmill four miles away. All the stock we owned was *one* mule named Jeff, a lanky quadruped that we rode bareback or used to pull the wagon, or hook to the plow or go-devil; and *one* cow of brindle complexion that never seemed to find a calf even if she knew by sight all the bulls in the community; and *one* hog that birthed a litter of pigs once a year. We butchered that litter once it got big enough for pork, but like any man knows, meat lasts so long and no longer. We kept two hound dogs and a yeller he-cat; our chicken stock tallied 'round a dozen.

One day, me and Pap and Cousin Drewey were settin' out by the woodpile. Maw Maw and Verbaline Lou were actin' womanly near the kitchen stove. It was toward sundown and there were clouds in the sky.

COUSIN DREWEY & THE HOLY TWISTER   17

"You folks ain't highly stocked with dollars and cents," Cousin Drewey said. "I can see that with my eyes shut. And the thought makes me sad."

"United States currency ain't our shinin' glory," Pap said. "Look 'round, cousin, and you'll see how copper pennies don't breed silver dimes on our sorry pasture."

"Back in the Washtaw Mountains," said Cousin Drewey, "we used to raise pumpkins in the dirt. We paid out big pumpkins for sugar and salt and we got back little pumpkins for change. But I'll confess how a paper dollar in the hand is sweetly soft to feel once in a Christmas or Fourth of July."

"Ain't you talkin' now!" said Pap.

"If I had a few dollars I'd git me back to the Washtaw Mountains. The Lord has spared me to see your kind faces. I've looked and I've had enough."

"You ain't got the train fare, Cousin Drewey?"

"Nope, and I'm too old for hookin' the boxcars and too proud to jerk a thumb at the automobiles."

"How you aim to git?" Pap quizzed.

"The Lord will find a way," said Cousin Drewey. "He never fails to reward a righteous man. I've stayed righteous as best I could, so before long I'll be headin' back to where the grass is wet and the mists hang low over the timbered hills." Cousin Drewey looked up at the sky. His eyes seemed to brighten and a look of joy came to his face. Pap and me looked up at the sky. We both wondered what was pleasin' Cousin Drewey. All we could see were some fluffy white clouds against the big blue.

"You folks ever git any twisters 'round here?" Cousin Drewey said of a sudden.

Both me and Pap thought he meant rattlesnakes. So Pap said, "Hell yes! Big rusty crawlin' ones. When a feller steps near one he gits bit. They ain't got no respect for a man's leg."

Cousin Drewey got so disgusted at what Pap said he

spat ambeer. He aimed at the axe and hit it. "I don't mean them kind of twisters," he said. "I mean storms of the funnel variety, the kind that pick up Ludlow, Oklahoma, carry it across the state line and mix it up with Bloomer, Arkansas, eastbound."

"Never in a lifetime," Pap told him. "This western air is too dry, too sorry, with not enough wetness to carry a cyclone. The wind blows but all it sturs up is dust and tumbleweeds. The Lord says to us like he said to Moses, 'Tornadoes ain't for Star Valley, 'cause they belong to the Washtaw Mountains.' "

"Ain't *that* the truth now," Cousin Drewey said. "They belong to the Lord's country sure enough. I love 'em. When I see 'em funnelin' down on the earth I run out to meet 'em. 'Cause I know that some day a big old holy twister will swoop down and pick me up, me and my fiddle, my guitar and my hog-leg forty-five, catch me with my satchel packed and carry me to the greenest pastures the sweet Lord ever made, the stillest water, and peace of the tastiest flavor. Show me a holy twister and I'll say how it's salvation for my soul. Drop my leftovers on the Washtaw Mountains and let our kinfolks bury 'em deep. But where my spirit goes, Cousin Lowdermilk, the best wish I can give to you is that yours will trail along behind me. 'Cause it will be a mighty wonderful place to dwell."

"We don't git twisters in Star Valley," Pap said.

"Read the Good Book," said Cousin Drewey, and he picked up his guitar as he said it, "and you'll see how good things, even cyclones, will come to a sorry land once in a long century. This twentieth century is almost gone. So I'll look to the sky and sniff at the breeze. Maybe I ain't got the train fare to the Washtaw Mountains or the strength to hook freights or impudence enough to jerk a thumb at the automobiles. . . . The Lord will provide; that's His holy promise."

3

Factful as Joshua, I'll say how Star Valley folks wouldn't leave Cousin Drewey alone. He was a musical man, somethin' akin to a handsome bachelor. It's the women; they can't give a man a rest. Back in the days before Cousin Drewey came to the valley, folks put on a stompdance once in so often. They did somethin' else on Saturday nights, like goin' to the movie-star show in town or somethin' like that. No tellin'. But when they got an ear-taste of Drewey Stiff's fiddle they just *had* to strut the schoolhouse floor *every* solitary Saturday night.

And did Cousin Drewey kick, even though they paid him nary a cartwheel? Hell-fire no! Why? Because Cousin Drewey loved humankind, that's why.

"I never let my left hand know what my big mouth sayeth," Cousin Drewey told Pap. Pap had advised Cousin Drewey to get some sense and charge the folks for his musical services, like the banjo picker and the hoedown caller did. Folks would gladly pay if Cousin Drewey gave them the hint. And Pap said how Cousin Drewey could use the money to he'p pay for the vittles he ate and put by enough to git him to the Washtaw Mountains. But Cousin Drewey just said back at Pap, "Cousin Lowdermilk, when I play music I give alms, and I don't give 'em like Scribes and Pharisees. I give music from my heart. If I oblige with my mouth on

Tuesday I'll tell 'em I'll be there on Saturday night, to saw with my arm and tap with my foot. I'll tell my left hand to he'p my right hand open the fiddle case. All I need extra is a banjo player to set by my side and a man with a glottis to call the hoedown. I'm doin' my alms and I don't need your nose to git stuck in my generosity."

Young Buster Prather was the banjo-pickin' fool and Uncle Posey Burwinkle was the man who packed the glottis. Cousin Drewey liked them both right smart. And it was a fine sight to see the folks gathered together —pure relish for Pap and Maw Maw's weary Saturday nights. Because before Cousin Drewey came upon us— to he'p eat up our subsistence and share our roof—we never went to the schoolhouse dances. We never got to see what our neighbors looked like. Folks came from far and near, and always the name of Cousin Drewey was in their talk. They called him the "bright star over Star Valley." They came out of Signal Rock, that valley big town and trade place. They came from the San Pablo foothills and up from the dry sinkhole of Lava Lake. Old Man Lee Bassett and his woman; the Skinner brothers, Sonny Boy and Clyde, Sonny Boy's wife Lilybelle and all their kids; Orville and Virgie Klingsinger, Jess Henshaw, Shorty Flack. All those good people. Snookie Hapchester and the cowboy named Tobe from Shingle Butte. Mr. Stover the mercantile man, even Reese Blaylock the undertaker. And the fryin'-size attendance showed how Star Valley was playin' up to the Good Book's advice of "Be fruitful and multiply" because towheads ran 'round the room thick like honeybees; while those too little to run, baldheaded and toothless, slid over the floor on their didies. There must have been more than a hundred kids and grownups in and outside the schoolhouse, every one admirin' us Lowdermilks like they'd never done before.

"It don't take much lather to shave the moss off a

mossback," said Old Man Lee Bassett to Mr. Stover. "It just takes a fine cousin like Drewey Stiff to shake the hornet nests out of their hair and scrub the alkali off their hides. There's been some good solid humanity layin' idle in them Lowdermilks, newly sprung to action, and now they're a credit to the community."

Lord! How the folks he'ped the electricity brighten the schoolroom, them in their Sunday attire; they made gladness and laughter by soundin' off their joshin's. The women wore clean print dresses and the men looked starchy in washed shirts and soap-faded overalls. The cowboys and cattlemen showed their difference from the farmers. They stomped 'round in shop-made boots, their belt buckles glistened center of their front middles. They packed more conceit, their brags were noisier.

The big table up against the wall was spread with chuck; pies enough to feed the Israelites, cornbread heaped like bricks, flour biscuits, all breeds of goodies and pickles, potato salad and ice cream, a galvanized washtub brim-full of pink drink, a ten-gallon cream can heavy with coffee. And fried chicken! Lord, how Star Valley loved fried chicken! Factways, it looked like we were fixed to feed the preacher. It was a handsome sight, and it got Cousin Drewey's choppers into percolation, his inside juices primed to digest it all.

Which got us to thinkin'. Was Cousin Drewey a preacher in disguise—Foot-washin' or Forty-gallon? No tellin'. He acted that way when he ate fried chicken. He could eat even more than our local taxi to heaven. I mean the Reverend Sam Hill, him who ran the Signal Rock Souls Redemption Center Tabernacle in town. Our kinfolks loved the breast and hollered double-damnation on any kind woman who accidentally dished him the neck. That's why us Lowdermilks kind of superstitioned how Cousin Drewey might have religion in him somewhere. He could finish a jar of sour pickles at a settin' and massacree a he'pin' of potato salad like the

Comanches did havoc on the settlers of the Pease River Valley. He wasn't a Holy Bark Baptist, *that* was certain. Because the Holy Barks don't like musical instruments —reckon them to be sinful—but he could have been a Slab. After a couple months of Cousin Drewey's sleepin' under our box elder tree he didn't pull himself out of that there mystery. He kept us Lowdermilks guessin', which didn't hurt us none, because a man's business is his'n and not ours.

There was joy aplenty all about, every human kickin' up dust and havin' a good time. Music, hands claspin' hands as legs moved to the square dance. Cousin Drewey sat aset his nail keg, sawin' the fiddle and tappin' his foot. Young Buster Prather tickled his banjo, him on a nail keg too. They both chewed cud while they made music. But Uncle Posey Burwinkle stood perpendicular, because he had to twist his hunkers while he called the dance. He jumped up and down like a man at the racetrack; he cupped his hands to his mouth, givin' sound the push it needed to carry it over the poundin' on the hardwood floor.

First lady to the right;
Swing that man that stole the sheep,
Now the one that hauled it home,
Now the one that ate the meat,
Now the one that gnawed the bones.

Lord, sweet Maker! Did they bow, strut and make circles! Did they sashay left and figger-eight right! Did they make that dance go 'round and 'round!

The high school girls were daintiest of all, them in their youngness and bright trim dresses with their hair tassels fixed up just recent at the beauty shoppey. Fellers who matched them for age smelled of aftershave lotion though they only had fuzz to shave off. Even the cornfed wives had sparks aplenty. Reese Blaylock, the under-

COUSIN DREWEY & THE HOLY TWISTER 23

taker, forgot his mournful trade and wore a smile for once in a week. Old Man Lee Bassett, heavy though he be, sent his poundage into a whirl. . . .

Uncle Posey Burwinkle was the "callin'est" man. He was all that.

> *Wave the ocean, wave the sea,*
> *Wave that pretty girl back to me. . . .*

But there was somethin' about those Saturday dances that made me sad. Because of Verbaline Lou, my sister. There at the dance, and on that *one* particular night, us Lowdermilks sat on the bench that we'd moved against the wall. We sat with the grandpaps and grandmaws and with them too bashful to strut. God almighty, we sure made a row of denim and calico! We sat straight like we had two-by-fours stuck down our backs so's to keep us perpendicular from neck to rump. We looked sour, that cain't be denied. But we were havin' a good time. Me and Verbaline Lou sat together, maybe because we were brother and sister. Pap and Maw Maw were side by side. We're a knit family, that kind of breed.

Our eyesight moved 'round with the whirl of the dance. We watched the feet of the pretty girls, we saw the he-sized cowboy boots go sashay and backprance; I gulped some when the skirts went 'round and wide like open parachutes. Lord! when them legs showed their shapelinesses. . . . And while they danced our ears took in all the tunes Cousin Drewey sawed out of his fiddle, that old up-and-down whine. We caught the sound of Young Buster Prather's ticklin' fingers on the banjo.

> *Swing 'em east, swing 'em west,*
> *Swing that girl you like the best.*

Maybe I'm mossback, full-blood, which means I'm the sorriest kind of nester. But I pack a human heart.

There at the dance I heard the laughter, I saw the happiness. And I ached for the sadness that was there in my sister's eyes. And that sadness told how she'd like to be up there, to be somebody she wasn't. Or maybe to be the somebody she *was,* that somebody hidden inside her who asked only to be let out, to join the fun of her humankind.

She was only twenty years old; four years my junior. Verbaline Lou was pretty, if I say so myself. She was one of the prettiest girls in the valley. Us Lowdermilks and Fosters come from good breed stock; the sunbonnet, clay pipe, hard workin', hickory-hard, oak-solid kind; come down to the Ozarks out of Lee County, Virginia. We're of that kind. Before that we were in this America a long, long time—yonder before memories. We rubbed our blood on Washington's coattails, we moved west in wagons to build up the empty frontier, there to call it home sweet home. We used a scythe to cut a way for the combines, we put our strength to work. We had a likin' for hardwood or soft pine, for the difference between good seed and bad, for a sharp axe and earth so rich you can taste it and love it. But we had an ignorance for steel and concrete, for the brand of education that was invented for to knock a man's neighbor down, to use a feller human for a step up. So we joined the tribe of mossbacks and got ourselves hated. We're superstitious of all men and women who are not our kind. Sometimes we'll take a gun and fire on them. Sometimes we just laugh at them. And always we get poorer.

I remember how Verbaline Lou wore her special dress that night. Maw Maw made it for her out of bits of scrap print material she found God only knows where. Maw Maw made all my sister's clothes. She sewed her underpinnin's—drawers and chemise and such—out of washed-clean flour sacks. She even made her ribbons and tie pretties. And she bound her shoes together with gut when they started to wear out. Us menfolks used balin' wire. I knew all about Verbaline Lou's underpinnin's because I saw them hangin' on the clothesline.

That was the whole trouble, the somebody that couldn't get let out. Her dress wouldn't shine in the square dance, her shoes had too much weight. And her hair wasn't fixed at the beauty shoppey, nor did her neck and wrists glisten with trinkets. It was her poorness, our mossback poorness, that held her on the bench to just set and crave, to work up some envy that wasn't natural with a sweet girl of Lowdermilk make.

"Fellers," Old Man Lee Bassett once said to Pap and me, "let me tell you somethin'. You're as sorry as bat pills. I'm tellin' it for the God's own truth. You Lowdermilks and this here junkpile you call home is an eyesore to Star Valley."

"That ain't for you to say," said Pap, squirtin' juice.

"The hell it ain't," cut back Old Man Lee. "You're wreckin' our reputation. We don't like the automobile tires you burn for stove fuel, just because you're too lazy to go out and cut cedar. We got a timbered mountain just a dozen miles to the west and you've got a mule and a wagon and an axe. And a husky boy called Newt. Your burnin' rubber stinks up an otherwise fresh air community.

"It's only when we run out of stove wood we burn the tires," said Pap. And he said to me, "Ain't that right, Newt?"

I said, "You bet."

"You dress your women like scarecrows," Old Man Lee went on. "Your old woman looks like she's eighty years older than she is. You look like hell yourself. You need some good red meat. All you eat is cornbread and beans, lambs quarters in season and tumbleweed greens. And molasses. You don't know butter, only lard. The thought of what you eat makes me sick. And that girl of yours, Verbaline Lou, she's . . ."

"Newt," Pap said to me, "go in the house and git the shotgun. I aim to shoot this sonofabitch."

Old Man Lee gave Pap's uncomplimentaries no mind. He went on sayin': "That girl, she's one of the nicest anywhere, inside or out of Star Valley. She walks like a graceful queen, she's built slender and trim. How she keeps that way with eatin' so much cornbread I cain't itemize. It's the Lord's doin'. Her face matches for prettiness any anywhere, even them girls that git their pictures took in swimmin' suits in Atlantic City, New Jersey, or somewheres up yonder. And she's smart like a whip. She'll make some man a good wife if you'll let her. She's got cobwebs tangled up in her tresses; she's got an outer layer of Lowdermilk dust. All she needs is to git combed and dusted. It ain't for you to do it, Pap Lowdermilk. It's for some up-and-comin' young bachelor here in the valley. And I ain't lyin' when I say there's a bachelor or two with the same opinions as me."

"Who'all?" bristled Pap. "Name one and I'll thank you kindly."

"Young Clyde Skinner, for one," said Old Man Lee. "Folks have hear'd that feller talk out of his heart. And once folks hear a feller talk out of his heart, the neighbors cain't waste time to gossip about it out of their mouths."

Pap put his head back and laughed. He laughed so hard that the ambeer made slick brown over his bristles. It shone like dewdrops.

"You're crazy like a drunk jackrabbit," Pap said.

He said that 'cause he knew young Clyde Skinner. He knew him for a high-muckety squirt of the nigh-gentleman variety; a bachelor, still wet behind the ears to the ways of this wide, weary world. Clyde shaved his whiskers every day. He wouldn't be caught with a rumpled shirt when he went to town. He ate out of a paper sack, like his brother and sister-in-law. He liked store-bought vittles 'cause of his school education. Pap

Lowdermilk packed a mightly low reckonin' for Clyde Skinner, 'cause Pap was a mossback and couldn't he'p hisse'f.

But Star Valley folks thought different. And I thought different, and Maw Maw and Verbaline Lou thought different. Us except Pap knew the Skinner brothers—Sonny Boy and Clyde—to ramrod one of the sweetest cow outfits up against the San Pablo foothills. For age, Clyde carried twenty-seven years; Sonny Boy was four years his brother's elder. They lived in a house, neat, kept that way by Sonny Boy's wife Lilybelle. Man and wife, they'd birthed three kids—two boys and a girl. A windmill pumped water for the corrals and a galvanized pipe carried enough to the house to irrigate the garden and wet the kitchen sink and fill the bathtub and keep the Skinners clean from the scalp down. Pap said they owned the bathroom 'cause they were too tender to get out in the cold, too high-uppety to make a trail to the brush. They cooked with gas out of a bottle; they made enough money to buy a refrigerator.

"Lord God Almighty!" said Pap when he talked about the Skinner's. "What a sorry kind of life them poor folks were born to live!"

Or when me and Pap went to Signal Rock to hunker down and spit cud juice front of the pool hall, we'd hear cattle bawlin' over by the stock pens and somebody would say, "That's them Skinner boys shippin' calves. They've got three carloads goin' to Kansas City. Young Clyde has got his satchel packed and he'll ride with 'em all the way, him sittin' pretty in the caboose."

That kind of talk made Pap disgusted. "Them Skinner fellers git paid for what they *know*," he said. "They let the balance of mankind sweat out the things to *do*. They're sinners in the sight of the Lord. They're educated fools. They're too smart for their britches."

Or like one day in the summer—of which Verbaline Lou told me herse'f—how she was walkin' out by the black-top highway, just a girl alone and killin' time. Along came Clyde in his pickup. "You goin' somewheres, Miss Lowdermilk?" he said—and when he called her "Miss" it was the first time in her life she'd been called that category. Verbaline Lou told me, and made me promise not to tell Pap or Maw Maw, how right then while she looked at Clyde in his pickup truck that somethin' went bounce in her heart, and her veins tingled like they never had before, and she knew her eyes were brighter than diamonds. She said, "Thank you kindly, but I'm headin' home. I like to walk. It's good for my constitution." Clyde would have liked to have taken her where she was goin', given her a ride in his pickup truck; or better still, to drive her out to his ranch and make her acquainted with Lily belle and the kids, and with Sonny Boy, and to show her his fine whiteface cattle, and turn on the radio set. But Clyde knew too good that if he did that, then Pap Lowdermilk would meet him with a loaded shotgun the next time he ventured off his boundaries. So all he said to Verbaline Lou was, "Maybe I'll see you at the schoolhouse hoedown next Saturday night. I'd sure like you to know my sister-in-law, Lilybelle. I think she'd like you right smart."

And Verbaline Lou said, "Maybe." That's all she said.

There at the woodpile, where me and Pap sat on our hunkers listenin' to Old Man Lee Bassett sound off on romance, we had time to think a little for ourselves—Pap in his fashion, me in mine. I thought then how handy it would be to have Clyde for a brother-in-law, and we be kin by marriage to Sonny Boy and Lilybelle. Maybe they'd give me a job ridin' 'round their pastures, he'p fix fence and put a little U.S. currency in my pocket. Maybe they'd he'p Pap and Maw Maw come out of the rawhide, he'p them live like most folks do this day and time. But I looked at Pap's face and figgered the category of his mind.

"I got a daughter," Pap said, "and I got a twelve-gauge shotgun. I got a full box of buckshot shells, of which I need only one. 'Cause my aim is the best west of the Cross Timbers, bar none, none plus. If that young whippersnapper ever comes 'round my holy house acourtin' my girl with a handful of flowers or a boxful of chocolate candy, I'll pepper his blossom like it had the chickenpox. I'll make it itch. I'll put him on the run. I'll feed him buckshot 'til he cain't set down for twelve days after Christmas. That's what I'll do, kind neighbor, and I swear my purpose before Jonah. When a man swears before Jonah he'll need to keep his word, 'cause Jonah ain't got no respect for romance any more than me."

Old Man Lee Bassett said back at Pap, "You ain't got a lick of sense or civilization, Pap Lowdermilk. You're so silly you cain't see the treasure pile you've got at your elbow. You won't use your wealth because you're too blamed lazy. You're . . ."

Pap got up off his hunkers. He rizz up from the stump to look down on Old Man Lee, to shake his fist in front of our kindly neighbor's face. "Me got a treasure pile!" he hollered at Old Man Lee. "Look 'round; and if you can find aught but poverty on the Lowdermilk homestead I'll give you my daughter; and you can take her to Clyde Skinner and tell him to git wed with her. But he'd better do it before I take down the shotgun off the hook."

"You've got more wealth than you'll find in the First National Bank."

"Lord God!" Pap said, "I do believe this dear neighbor is plumb craze!"

"You've got salvation, which is better'n cash," Old Man Lee said.

"Salvation! . . . Me and mine won't git salvation 'til we git to heaven."

"You've got Cousin Drewey. He's your salvation."

"Hell-fire! Cousin Drewey ain't nothin' but a crusty

old mossback, like me," Pap exploded like a charge under a tree stump. "He eats too much."

"Maybe so," said Old Man Lee, "but he's a fiddlin' sonofagun."

I thought back on that talk when I sat next to Verbaline Lou on the bench at that Saturday night dance; while I watched her face and saw the wishfulness on it, while I saw Pap set sour and Maw Maw look like she was waitin' for the Battle of Armageddon. I thought of that talk while the dance went 'round and 'round and the whine from Cousin Drewey's fiddle made the steps to promenade, to circle left and how-dee-do.

*Swing your partner, pat her on the head,
If she don't like clabber give her cornbread.*

And while I sat thinkin', the music came to a sudden stop. I saw the dancers mill 'round like cattle, short-breathed and sweatin'. They joshed each other, the young fellers howled like coyotes, some crowed like roosters just to make noise. And among all those good Star Valley folks was Clyde Skinner, him in his shinny cowboy boots and his tan-colored pants with the crease down front, his western-style shirt and a bow necktie. All the sweet girls had their eyes on Clyde. And Sonny Boy was there, too, and Lilybelle, their clothes tellin' how their ranch wasn't no liability.

I said to myself, "Hell-fire! There ain't nothin' wrong with these neighbors. There ain't one what needs fixin'." I said it, then I heard Uncle Posey Burwinkle shout with his iron lungpower, "Everybody eat!"

That room broke into a roar. Folks pushed each other toward the big table where the chuck was laid. Then I saw Cousin Drewey go high nigh to the ceilin' as two husky men lifted him on their shoulders and packed him toward the fried chicken. "You'all feed Cousin Drewey," I heard a woman shout, "'cause he's a dose of the Lord's manna dropped down from heaven."

COUSIN DREWEY & THE HOLY TWISTER 31

All the grandpaps and grandmaws deserted the bench, left us four Lowdermilks asettin'. Pap didn't move, nor Maw Maw, neither did me nor Verbaline Lou. We watched everybody load up their paper plates; and me, me alone maybe, saw some sadness cloud my sister's face. She stared ahead, like somebody was movin' hands in front of her eyes, hypnotizin' her, doin' like the carnival man does on a woman dressed in tights . . . Then her eyes brightened and Verbaline Lou turned into the most beautiful woman in the world.

Of a sudden, a tall man stood in front of us. His belt buckle shone like the silver it was, and he bent down toward us like a gentleman from way back. Clyde Skinner said, "I couldn't tell what you like best, Miss Lowdermilk, but I thought some chicken thighs might have the most meat on 'em. And potato salad and pickles. Lord, I sure hope you like potato salad."

Verbaline Lou took the plate. It was loaded like a flatcar with all colors of tasty chuck. "Thank you kindly," she said. And she said it out of a glottis that told how she'd met her man.

Clyde took Pap by the coat collar. He lifted him up off the bench like Pap didn't weigh nothin'. "Let's you and me git over to the table where you can fix your wife some vittles, Pap Lowdermilk." I saw how Pap was kind of mad, but he was too bashful to say anythin'. Clyde said to me, "Newt, you come along too. There's enough fried chicken over there to fill all the deacons with a twice-time he'pin'. Your pretty appetite won't faze the supply."

I saw Pap trail behind Clyde to the vittle table, meek like a collie dog. I knew then that he'd just shot off his loud mouth to Old Man Lee Bassett that day at the woodpile. I saw how his mean brag didn't pack substance. He couldn't pepper Clyde's blossom with the shotgun no matter how best he tried. He might have a good aim, but he couldn't hit nothin' so handsome as that.

4

No matter how potent Star Valley folks loved Cousin Drewey, how much they craved his presence in their midst, Cousin Drewey mourned to get back to the Washtaw Mountains. He hoped to the Lord how he wouldn't die of his three-score-and-ten years here among us Lowdermilks before the train fare came whistlin' in his direction.

"If you'll use your head as well as your fiddle," Pap told him one day, "you'll pass 'round the hat next Saturday night. You'll pray for a contribution. There ain't a human bein' in that crowd what won't drop in a dollar or two. And if I know the A.T. and S.F. and the Frisco Lines correctly, they love nothin' better'n givin' a man a ticket if he's got the price."

So Cousin Drewey used his thinker come the followin' Saturday night. He took off his hat after he'd fiddled a 'round or two, spit in it for good luck, then hollered to the folks for to shut up their noise. He said he had an announcement to make. The folks clapped their hands, then listened to Cousin Drewey; they stood politely while our kinfolk told how he was takin' up the collection so's to buy his way back to the Washtaw Mountains on those old Frisco Lines. He told about his three-score-and-ten years, and said how he hoped the dear Lord would spare him 'til after he'd changed trains at Hugo.

COUSIN DREWEY & THE HOLY TWISTER

That's when he got to walkin' 'round with the hat; he held it brimside up in front of every livin' soul. But when he did that, doggone if that livin' soul didn't turn his back on Cousin Drewey and dropped nary a dime in the yawnin' felt.

"It ain't that us folks here in this valley be of a miserly pack," Old Man Lee Bassett told Cousin Drewey. "It's just that we watch our investments mighty close. It stands to sublime reason that to buy *you* a train ticket, one that will take you far away from us, is like investin' good money in Misery, Incorporated."

"Doggone!" said Cousin Drewey, tickled silly, when he went back to his fiddle. "These here folks love me so much they won't put a dime in my hat. They won't let me desert them for the Washtaw Mountains. They *sure* hate to think of me findin' eternal rest in the green pastures, next to the still waters."

"That's the pure solid truth," said young Clyde Skinner.

So long as Cousin Drewey fiddled in the schoolhouse he seemed to forget his crave. So long as he sawed out "Sweet Betsy From Pike" or "Jerry, Go Oil That Car" he didn't suffer any. But once he got back to our place he got to thinkin' how sweet a hunk of red-gum rosin would taste in his mouth, and how his appetite called for a scoop at the glibs on the bottom of a molasses vat. That was his prime trouble. Us Lowdermilks would have loved to he'p him out, but we were too poor; and every day in every way Cousin Drewey was makin' us poorer and poorer. Nights found Cousin Drewey so miserable, so homesick he couldn't sleep. So he got out of bed and picked up his guitar. He sang songs about our poverty, how we didn't feed him like his constitution craved, how he really could masticate some fresh red meat. He sang of turnips and cabbage and a mess of okra.

*Cousin, cousin,
Why don't you bake them ribs?*

Next mornin', 'round sun up, me and Pap found Cousin Drewey settin' on his stump at the woodpile. Maw Maw told us to bring Cousin Drewey in because she and Verbaline Lou had breakfast ready—just cornbread and coffee and nothin' else. She told Pap to give our kinfolks the sad tidin's before we brought him in, that the day had come for the hog meat supply to run out. We had roastin' ears and turnips; not many but some, down in the dugout where we kept them things away from the frost. We had enough corn meal and dried beans, a little salt but no sugar. We had enough coffee for a week. Factways, Cousin Drewey's vittle intake had been mighty hard on us Lowdermilks.

"Well now," Cousin Drewey said—and he said it after Pap told him about the shortage—"then it looks like this kinfolks of your'n had better git out and use his hog-leg forty-five. There's meat awalkin' that needs adressin'."

The thought of red meat made Cousin Drewey exercise his choppers. He sat there on his stump lookin' as if he had a hunk of fried hind quarter back of his teeth where his cud mostly sat. We could see how he was thinkin' hard.

"Your personality is a boon to mankind," Pap said, "but your digest juices is the wreck of the Lowdermilks. You've ate us out of house and home, sweet cousin."

Cousin Drewey opened his coat. He pulled the hog-leg forty-five from its holster. He held it up for us to admire. We could see how it had six shells loaded in the cylinder.

"Where you aim to go git your meat?" Pap quizzed him.

"Cain't tell so early in the day," Cousin Drewey said,

"but before sundown the sweet Lord will show a way."

"You can take old Jeff, the mule," Pap said, "and you can ride up into the San Pablo Mountains. If you git up there you'll find the deer runnin' aplenty; up there you can skin yourself a buck."

Cousin Drewey shook his head. "Nope," he said, "it ain't legal season."

"What's that matter to hungry folks?" Pap said.

"I ain't only hungry," Cousin Drewey said, "but I'm godly. It's sinful to kill deer out of season. Them deer belong to the state game department, and the department belongs to the good people of the United States of America. The department ain't never done me no harm, 'cause the wardens never caught me. The folks of the United States never done me no harm, 'cause they don't know me from the next man on the street. When I go kill some red meat, Cousin Lowdermilk, you can bet your last cabbage how it will be off some critter what belongs to a man who's done me harm. A man who's made me feel bitter and I won't sweeten 'til I pay him the same harm back."

That same mornin' me and Pap and Cousin Drewey walked the five miles into town. We figgered we'd hunker down front of the pool hall and chew cud. We'd talk about the men who passed us by and admire the pretty girls' legs. It was the best way to spend a day out of the country.

We walked down Main Street, we passed by Veryl and Peryl's Limp In-Leap Out Garage and that man and wife hollered us a howdy. We saw Reese Blaylock outside his funeral home polishin' his hearse ready for business. He waved to us and we waved back. Nigh everybody on the street recognized Cousin Drewey and seemed plumb tickled silly to see him. Everybody was so friendly that it made us feel good.

"Doggone!" said Cousin Drewey, stoppin' on his

tracks to look up at heaven. "I just *love* mankind. . . . I *love* people plumb to death."

But he said that there before we came up front of the First National Bank. He said that there before the sweet Lord showed him the way to red meat. He said that there before he saw and heard Fats Recknagel, the rich cattleman.

We came up front of the brass-glass door of the First National Bank. Cousin Drewey walked moon-eyed, kind of dizzy for his load of good will. He stumbled on the sidewalk, then righted himself correctly. We fixed to move on, but we heard a voice say like out of nowhere, "Pick up your feet, clodhopper, this ain't the turnip patch."

That voice made us stop on our tracks. We looked 'round to find where such uncomplimentaries came from, and what we saw churned our blood to buttermilk. We saw Fats Recknagel standin' next to the bank door. He chewed on a short stogie like is common practice with men of his sorry breed. His ice-cream-colored pants were stuck in his short-topped cowboy boots, the diamond in his belt buckle shone like the bright and mornin' star. We saw the nasty look he wore on his face, 'round about his sneerin' mouth, under his pig eyes. Mostly he packed that sneer for the whole world, but that minute he aimed it special for Cousin Drewey and us Lowdermilks.

We saw the short fatness of him, the bulk of his mighty paunch. He was meanness from boot heel up to the crown of his cocky John B. Stetson hat. He was the richest no-count in the valley. There ain't no crime to richness, only to the way that richness is won. Fats won it to the cost of honest folks, folks that had heard his loud mouth tell how they could profit and better their lot by some proposition he packed in his mind, by his sublime know-how. But when he got folks' land, or folks' cash in hand, or the sweat of folks' labor, he'd go to his lawyers because he craved to hold it for his own. Lawyers listened to men like Fats; they don't listen to dirt farmers. He lived on cotton and rice, he had wheat in Montana, he owned cattle outfits in Texas and Colorado and Star Valley. He ran sheep in Utah, raised apples in Oregon. And oil in Oklahoma. The love of money was Fats Recknagel's pride, the root of all evil which the Good Book had a heap to talk about.

Fats came from that part of Texas where most rich men come from. He recognized only three eternities: Heaven, Hell and Houston—and of the three, Houston was the best. He was always near a telephone, hand so's to call the ranch and ask his wife how the stocks, bonds and company shares were doin'; how the banks were loadin' up with Recknagel profits, what the lawyers had on their minds about knockin' an honest man down.

The Fats woman had her mouth pasted at the telephone too. She talked with the managers and stockbrokers, showed how she and Fats were lovebirds of the same feather. Folks told how Fats couldn't kiss his wife unless she had a dollar bill stuck on her cheek; which didn't matter, for she wasn't of the kissin' category.

The sight of Fats made us sick, like we'd poured too much fried meat grease on our greens. There he stood at his favorite place, next to the bank. He grinned 'round his jowls, like the uncomplimentaries he'd pitched did him a heap of evil-good.

Cousin Drewey just stood. Me and Pap tried to pull him along before Fats could think of somethin' more to say. Our kinfolks might have been slight sized, but we couldn't make him move.

"Who'all's that feller?"

"He's got a name," Pap said, "but it ain't worth tellin'." Pap talked that way while he he'ped me get Cousin Drewey unstuck. "Come on, Cousin Drewey," I said, he'pin' Pap. "This ain't no place for a righteous man, 'specially for a man who wears a hog-leg forty-five." We got Cousin Drewey into motion; we pulled him off his stance, but it was like pullin' a stump. We got him travelin' so's Fats Recknagel couldn't hear what he had to say. We got him headed back to our farm. We were halfway down the block before he could say his speech.

"That feller there," Cousin Drewey said, pointin' back at Fats, "has done me a heap of *harm*. He didn't sweat to do it, 'cause he just said it out of his big fat mouth. Cousin Lowdermilk, let me tell you this: I pack this hog-leg forty-five special for fellers what do me *harm*."

Pap wrestled Cousin Drewey along but I looked back toward Fats. I saw Fats bent over. He laughed off some of his grease. He laughed like he'd said somethin' funny, somethin' mean, somethin' harmful to a feller-man's feelin's—the only kind of somethin' he figgered worth laughin' about. He looked like he was fixed to go inside and tell the bank president about it, and have him laugh too; and the vice president and the cashier. And all them jellybeans stuck inside their cages, and the girls done up in powder and paint. Have them bust their guts. Then I looked ahead again before the sight of Fats Recknagel made me sicker.

Cousin Drewey said naught most of the way back to the farm. Only once did he stop to quiz us. "Cousin Lowdermilk," he said, "what does that feller make his livin' from mostly, here in Star Valley?"

Pap said, "Cattle. He's got the prettiest Black Angus herd anywhere to be found in this valley or in the republic. He's got four or five, maybe more, tough cowpunchers to ride after them. He'll be shippin' some prime beef next month or the month after."

Cousin Drewey said nothin' to that. He just walked on beside us, talkless but deep in thought. He had a smile on his face, like he'd solved a problem. He got

COUSIN DREWEY & THE HOLY TWISTER 39

spry, took long strides. It was hard for me and Pap to keep up.

Verbaline Lou was sweepin' off the porch and the breeze was wavin' the roof; it looked like the props were holdin' up the shanty. Maw Maw would be inside bakin' cornbread 'cause smoke came from the chimney. We passed the chicken house, then the corral where old Jeff nosed at some fodder. Next we came to the dugout where we kept our potatoes, cabbage and carrots. It was six feet down in the earth, a room lined and ceilinged with rail-ties, not big but enough. It had a heavy timber door and the roof was a four-foot thickness of tamped dirt.

"What'all you keep in there?" Cousin Drewey asked asudden.

"Any vittle what needs keepin' cool," Pap said.

"Sweet land of the Jebusites!" Cousin Drewey said, like he'd had a prime idea; one like us Lowdermilks had never thought up. "Do you know, dear kinfolks, how that there dugout can make you a sweet cyclone cellar for you and your loved ones if a holy twister ever comes funnelin' in your direction?"

"We don't git twisters in Star Valley," Pap said, "the air's too dry."

"That ain't for you to say," Cousin Drewey said, sniffin' deliciously at the smell of bakin' cornbread in the air. "If it's the Lord's will to blow me and you Lowdermilks back to the Washtaw Mountains, then He'll send us transportation. He'll send a twister here to Star Valley, eastbound. And that twister will be a holy one, sanctified by the angels, the biggest ever to blow. It'll reach the terminal apuffin' and ablowin'. It'll set us down gently, easy—me and you'all—on the green pastures that stretch out next to the still waters."

5

Anytime Cousin Drewey wasn't fiddlin' for the dances or walkin' into Signal Rock with me and Pap he'd be spendin' his time out by the woodpile asettin' on the sawed-off block, it next to the axe; and he'd look wishful and chew cud. He sat like he craved to get home to the Washtaw Mountains right quick, like he feared he might find a gravehole here in Star Valley. He set squonched and miserable, like a buzzard on the peak of a fence post. He'd face east, because that was his favorite direction.

Me and Pap, Maw Maw and Verbaline Lou, all us Lowdermilks, said more than once how we figgered Cousin Drewey could sweeten his existence by doin' somethin' else for a change. He he'ped in the corn patch some. He chopped out weeds along the bean rows, but he talked his philosophies more than he cut with the hoe. He ate his vittles like a hungry hound dog, he slept sound like a dead skunk, and when he chewed cud he could spit farther and hit the axe better'n me and Pap. Whatever Cousin Drewey did he did like nobody's business, but we all would have been proud if Cousin Drewey hadn't sat so much on his hunkers.

So it stands to reason how Pap smiled pleasantly when he called me out to the porch one day and said how I was to look toward the corral. "Doggone!" said

COUSIN DREWEY & THE HOLY TWISTER 41

Pap. "Doggone if Cousin Drewey ain't got up off his royal-rusty and he's out there in the corral actin' friendly with old Jeff. . . . If I know old Jeff then I know how he likes to git his neck rubbed and for some human bein' to tell him what a fine mule he is. . . . Newt, just look at your kinfolks there. If he ain't a mule lover then I ain't never seen one before in my livin' days."

What Pap said was the deacon's truth. Cousin Drewey was out in the corral. He forked out some fodder for old Jeff to chew on and old Jeff was lettin' Cousin Drewey handle him like he wouldn't let anyone else. Our kinfolks would rub Jeff's neck, and tickle him under the chin, and run his hand forward and hindways along Jeff's backbone. He even lifted Jeff's hooves and looked to see how they were shaped, hind foot and front. Jeff let him do all that without kickin' Cousin Drewey clean over the fodder stack. If me or Pap tried to get *that* friendly with Jeff we'd feel somethin' hit us right smack and we'd quit actin' kindly to mules. It was a miracle we watched, one clean out of Matthew—or Mark, Luke or John. After that Cousin Drewey got even more familiar; he'd put the bridle on old Jeff and ride him bareback 'round the corral. He'd do that because us Lowdermilks owned neither horn nor cantle of a saddle.

When he wasn't playin' like that, just him and old Jeff, Cousin Drewey would be back again on the sawed-off stump. There he'd set, shootin' ambeer comets at the axe. He was clean shed of that wishful look because he'd handle his hog-leg forty-five; hold it with love, and talk to it like it had ears. He'd feel it like a man does the skin of a woman; he'd rub it 'til the cylinder, the barrel and even the walnut grip got shiny like a flowin' river. He'd turn the gun 'round in his hand, give it sunlight for better admiration. Sometimes he'd rod out the barrel, make it slick for an out-travelin' bullet.

That's what Cousin Drewey was doin' that evenin'

when me and Pap went out to the woodpile just because we hadn't nothin' better to do. We pulled up beside our kinfolks, lowered ourselves down 'til our hunkers met our heels. We pulled out our plugs for to cut off some sweetness, us fixed to gas awhile. That's when Cousin Drewey opened his coat and put the gun back in the holster.

"Cousin Lowdermilk," he said to Pap, and his eye packed that wishful look again, "what'all do folks call that horse's ass? What *is* his polite name?"

"Which horse's ass you talkin' about? Star Valley is full of horses' asses. We got more'n the Kentucky racetrack."

"I mean that prime sonofabitch."

"We're stocked up on them varmints too. They run like hound dogs in Tennessee. Except our kind is worser; our kind is human and the bite is poison."

"I mean that bastard."

"If you aim to hunt a bastard, you'd best go to the First National Bank."

"Now you're gettin' closer to what I mean. I mean that fat-pork what told us fellers to lift our feet and not act the clodhopper, him with the diamond in his belt buckle, that hog-eyed no'count who harmed my feelin's," Cousin Drewey went on.

Pap parted his teeth but only to shoot ambeer. He hit the axe.

Cousin Drewey said, "When I git my feelin's harmed I crave to do some vengeance, Cousin Lowdermilk. I cain't he'p myself. It's the hardness in me, or maybe the softness, only the prophet Amos knows which."

Lord God, was Cousin Drewey mad!

"Fats Recknagel," Pap said, "that's the name of your meat."

Cousin Drewey was wet 'round the mouth. He'd got that way because of the ire he had stored inside. His hands shook, 'specially his right hand, it which he used to grip a gun. His eyes glistened sparks like they saw the target, but what he packed in his brain was only his to know.

"He did my feelin's harm," Cousin Drewey said. "I aim to shoot me some vengeance. I ain't got no vengeance for the game department; I ain't got none for the good folk of this world. But I got aplenty to give that full-blood no'count of a sorry human bein'. . . . I'll make my hog-leg forty-five talk spitfire language. . . . I'll tickle the trigger. . . . I'll give it a twice-time rooty-toot-toot."

6

Cousin Drewey was back to his old happy self come next Saturday hoedown. He'd left his vengeance behind, out by the stump-block next to the woodpile. So Cousin Drewey showed up with us Lowdermilks, with his fiddle and his smile, to set alongside Young Buster Prather, front of Uncle Posey Burwinkle.

There was chuck aplenty on the table that night; like pink drink by the ten-gallon canfuls. On the floor there were feet fixed to skip 'round. Everybody hoorawed and laughed. They joshed and they rawhided. They hollered for the music makers to get on the high horse. They milled 'round like cattle in a pen. They were primed, except for Sonny Boy Skinner who came jouncin' in on crutches.

"Doggone!" hollered Old Man Lee Bassett. "Look at Sonny Boy! Folks, there slides a prime lesson in the ways of holy matrimony. Most times Lilybelle aims to bust her man's neck, except this time she aimed the crowbar too low." The folks nigh bust a gut laughin' at what Old Man Lee had to say, which put them to joshin' about Sonny Boy on his crutches.

It seemed like that cowman had sprained his left ankle right smart. He told how he'd been practicin' in his own corral for the calf-rope contest at the Signal Rock rodeo,

COUSIN DREWEY & THE HOLY TWISTER 45

it comin' up. He had a nice little bay pony, trained for calf-ropin' like only Sonny Boy can train him, and both together they were foolin' 'round. Sonny Boy built a loop in his rope, choused the calf a-high-tailin' and sent that loop to catch him 'round the neck. Sonny Boy's saddle-horn held the rope's end while the horse stood sweetly. Caught, the calf danced conniptions. Sonny Boy dismounted in a hurry, like calf-ropers always be; his left ankle turned when it hit the ground and Sonny Boy went over like a rock had hit him. He said his foot hurt mighty bad. Some feller turned the calf loose while Lilybelle helped Sonny Boy into the pickup truck. She drove it to town with Sonny Boy cussin' his damned luck. Sawbones Doc Ramsbury bandaged the ankle and gave him the crutches. Sonny Boy said, "Hell-fire!" The doc said how the sprain was a bad one but how Sonny Boy had a long time to live—too long for the good of the world. Talk like that made Sonny Boy rawhide Sawbones Doc Ramsbury back. But when they talked seriously again the doc said how Sonny Boy couldn't compete in the Signal Rock rodeo but there'd be a heap more that Sonny Boy could ride in after the foot got well.

Us Lowdermilks, like always, sat on the bench along with grandpaps and grandmaws. Pap and Maw Maw kept Verbaline Lou in between them so's they could lock her tight. They feared to sit her on the outside, next to somebody who might any time get up and dance, leavin' the bench-room vacant. They feared how young Clyde Skinner might see the space sitless and come to court Verbaline Lou and ask her how she was gettin' along this day and time. They didn't need some single man who needed a woman to come plunk his royal-rusty down on the bench next to Verbaline Lou. They feared that like they did the hour of judgment. So we sat to behold the dance, us Lowdermilks, like we were made of concrete and had steel bars for backbones.

Uncle Posey gave a coyote yell, long and mournful; Cousin Drewey pulled a steady saw at his bow. Like always, that was the signal for the dance to begin. And when it begun, it went 'round and 'round. They pranced and circled, they tapped some, while the ladies parachuted their skirts. They acted polite as hell. They scattered the sprinkled corn meal that was put on the floor to slicken the polished oak. They thumped, they howled, they made noise. And when they got done with a set so's to swallow some breath, that's when they'd huddle in bunches to gas about things, about doin's of the times.

There was woman-talk—about kids and puttin' up preserves, about Paris fashions, and how to please the menfolks.

Man-talk—all about fields and pastures, horses and cattle, tractors and the cost of keepin' them runnin'; the scarcity of rain, baseball, how to work and love and how to please the bankers and womenfolks.

There was one small bunch up close to where the musical men rested their instruments, next to where Uncle Posey Burwinkle was coolin' off his glottis. That bunch was made of Sonny Boy Skinner, standin' on crutches, and his brother Clyde in his ice-cream pants. They were shootin' off their big mouths to Snookie Hapchester and two other fellers, cowboys both. Sonny Boy was mournful about his crippled foot and said so out loud. Clyde told how the Signal Rock rodeo was to be the best in valley history. One of the meanest buckin' horses out of Oklahoma was contracted for, a chisel-head named Double Decker—lightnin' on the hoof, pure suicide for a man to straddle. Clyde said how ridin' that bronc was like askin' the State Warden to dust off the electric chair, then to get out of the way so's a man could sit down. Kindly pleadin' for the electrocution-gents to turn on the sparks. Double Decker was *that* kind of death. And to hear Clyde talk, that four-legged cyclone gave the wildest ride since Casey Jones gunned Old Ninety-Seven down the grade to Danville.

That's how the Skinner brothers talked while us Lowdermilks listened and didn't shift our rusties off the bench. Pap looked at Clyde like he didn't trust him a mite. He feared how Clyde might come courtin' Verbaline Lou, like give her an invite to get up and dance. Maw Maw looked at Clyde, too, with an eye that told how she wished to God he would. And Verbaline Lou looked someplace else. She was plumb scared of Pap. She figgered how if Pap caught her lookin' at Clyde he'd see how she packed love in her heart, how she itched to hug Clyde's neck. Me, I just combed the room with my eyesight watchin' everybody have a good time.

No matter how or where us Lowdermilks looked, the Skinner boys kept on talkin'. They were mighty loud. And they would have kept on talkin' about old Double Decker 'til Uncle Posey Burwinkle called for to get ready for a new set, but they had to quit because of Cousin Drewey. That kinfolks came alive all asudden, because he didn't like what the Skinner fellers had to say. He didn't like their opinions. Cousin Drewey came off his chair like he was settin' on a red-hot rail spike set perpendicular. Every eye shifted in his direction. He was up on his feet, wavin' the fiddle like a man does the Stars and Stripes. He yelled somethin', but what'all he yelled nobody could tell. He mouth-blubbered like a Pentecostal. He was *that* much on the prod. Factways, we wondered if he hadn't caught a dose of religion.

"Hell-fire!" Cousin Drewey shouted, nigh crackin' his soundbox. "I ain't never hear'd such goddamn horseshit spoken about in all my days. Never since my maw gave me natural dinner."

Cousin Drewey's talk made the ladies blush. But Lord, was *he* on the prod! He picked up a chair and hauled it to the middle of the floor. He told some kids to get out of his way. Then he mounted it like a politician, cleared his throat like a deacon, spread his arms like a buzzard takin' flight. High up on the chair Cousin Drewey looked like he had somethin' to say.

"Kind folks and ladies," Cousin Drewey said, and the way he said it told how he'd talked off a pedestal many times before in his life. "I'm up here to make a solemn declaration and to say how you've got in your midst two fellers that don't know their twin-hunkers from their bended elbows."

Everybody clapped their hands and shouted wisdom. But they soon rested their soundpipes to let our kinfolks have the platform.

"Them fellers were born with names," Cousin Drewey went on, while he hoisted the fiddle high, while he waved the bow to the tune of his talk. "But I'm shamed to name them, 'cause they're citizens both and ought to have better sense."

The Skinner brothers blushed slightly; they knew how Cousin Drewey was accusin' them. Pap leaned over and said to us Lowdermilks, "If our dear cousin don't watch his opinions that young Clyde Skinner will git up there and knock him off the roost. Clyde ain't on crutches, and I hear tell how he's got ticklish feelin's. Cousin Drewey's fixin' to git plumb insultin'."

Cousin Drewey didn't pay Pap no mind because he was too far away to hear what was said. Instead, he fixed to get insultin', just like Pap prophesied.

Cousin Drewey said: "I just hear'd 'em talk about a horse, a buckin' horse, a horse what they think in their sad misguidance gives the wildest ride of any vehicle since them old reckless Bible days. . . . Folks, let me tell you about the Washtaw Mountains. That's where we don't ride buckin' horses, or velocipedes, or anythin' gentle as them. Sure enough, we ride mules, but I don't

COUSIN DREWEY & THE HOLY TWISTER 49

class a mule ride among the wildest the Lord can provide. . . . When us folks of the Washtaw Mountains call for excitement, we ask the sweet Maker to make us a cyclone, one that we can straddle and ride to Arkansas, one that'll make us grip leather and hold on the best we can."

That got the congregation to hollerin'. They clapped and they stomped, and then shut up so's they could hear some more.

"Let me tell you how I was settin' out on the porch of my house one evenin' back in the Washtaw Mountains," he preached from his pedestal. "It was the sticky month of June and the bugs were bitin' mighty sharp; up in the sky the clouds were colored gray-green, they were collidin' with each other. A big black funnel was comin' hell-bent toward us in the west. . . . I said to Uncle Gersh . . ."

Pap leaned over against me. He said, "Newt, which Uncle Gersh you reckon Cousin Drewey's got in mind? Uncle Gersh Lowdermilk or Uncle Gersh Foster?"

"Ain't no tellin' which," I said to Pap, "could be either one."

Now that Cousin Drewey had Uncle Gersh in mind he got hog wild. He hollered, " 'Uncle Gersh,' I said, 'Have you got your satchel packed, 'cause it looks mighty like us'ns are goin' for a ride? There's a holy twister headin' our way; there's a seat reserved for you and me in the smokin' car, up front where the butcher boy sets.' "

Talk like that and the thought of twisters put Cousin Drewey on his high-horse. He nigh touched the ceilin' with his fiddle and bow, he swung them both 'round while he prevaricated the wholesome truth. He told how he and Uncle Gersh went out and looked at the oncomin' funnel—eastbound. It was black and wicked, pure-Satan dancin' over the earth. Cousin Drewey told how he said for Uncle Gersh to go on the porch and fetch two chairs, because a cyclone don't have no cushions for the passengers. Uncle Gersh got hold of the chairs just in time, just before the air turned black and cold and mighty wet and Cousin Drewey felt himself travelin' kind of perpendicular. He went in circles like a crazy mule in a corral. He went so fast that he had to whoop like the Comanches.

Once in so often Cousin Drewey saw Uncle Gersh settin' in his chair, holdin' on for the dear life in his bones. Next they were joined by a house, barn, windmill and tank; which Cousin Drewey recognized as belongin' to Old Man Spence, a neighbor to the east. Then along came Old Man Spence himself. Cousin Drewey didn't ask him how he was gettin' along because they weren't on speakin' terms. Next came a chicken house with the door and window shut, but the twister got so fierce it made kindlin' of the woodwork and the chickens came out to crow and cackle and scatter their feathers. When Cousin Drewey looked down he saw how they followed the Washtaw Mountains, northeast toward Fort Smith. They were gettin' close to Howe, Oklahoma, where the Rock Island Railroad crosses the Kansas City Southern. So Cousin Drewey hollered at Uncle Gersh, "Uncle Gersh, that must be Howe down there below, 'cause I can see a freight train switched off the main track at the depot." And Uncle Gersh hollered back, "I reckon you're right, Nephew Drewey, 'cause they're always loadin' or unloadin' freight at Howe."

Uncle Gersh had no sooner said those truthful words than the freight train came up to join them. It went circle like the wall of a roundhouse; the engine stank of oil, soot, cinders and hot iron, and the boxcars were colored red, yellow and green. The tender followed the engine, all right, but it was goin' so fast a feller couldn't see the name of the line writ on the side. It wasn't 'til the train crew got off that Cousin Drewey eased his curiosity.

"What'all kind of fellers you be?" Cousin Drewey asked a brakeman. "Are you Rock Island fellers or Kansas City Southern fellers?"

The brakeman smiled at the engineer and the conductor winked at the fireman. Leastways they smiled and winked the best they could under the circumstances.

"We're Rock Island fellers," the brakeman said. "We wouldn't be caught in hell workin' for the Kansas City Southern."

"You'all got any coffee in the caboose?" Cousin Drewey quizzed.

"Did," the conductor said. "We had a full pot down on the sidin', but when we got to goin' it spilled over."

"When you reckon we'll git to Little Rock?" Cousin Drewey said.

"Mighty soon," said the engineer. "These twisters make notches."

And no sooner had he said those prophet-size words than they all looked down and saw the big dome on the Arkansas State Capitol. They saw the Arkansas River twistin' and crawlin' across Pulaski County—they saw the bright lights of Main Street lookin' like a ribbon of stars, they heard the automobiles honkin'. Then the twister laid them gently down—the chickens at the packin' house, the freight train in the yards, Old Man Spence in the county jail, the train crew in front of the beanery, and Cousin Drewey and Uncle Gersh in the hall outside the governor's office. When the governor came out he shook their hands; and the next day they stole a ride on a Frisco Lines gondola back to the Washtaw Mountains.

When Cousin Drewey got done talkin' about the cyclone, he shut his mouth and lowered his fiddle and waited for the Star Valley folks to say somethin' pleasant. He craved for them to holler like they were glad the twister didn't eat him up—make hash of his meat, bones, fat and gristle, him and Uncle Gersh, and Old Man Spence, and the Rock Island train crew. He waited, silent, but he didn't have to wait long.

"Doggone!" yelled Old Man Lee Bassett. "If that ain't the wildest ride I ever hear'd tell of. If *that* ain't made sweet ice cream with coconut toppin' out of that mean bronc named Double Decker then I ain't never hear'd the Baptist-truth spoke before."

Everybody hollered congratulations at Cousin Drewey while Sonny Boy on his crutches and Clyde of the big-mouth just stood blushin' for shame. Cousin Drewey's ride had bested them by two hundred miles of horizontal flight.

Cousin Drewey got down off his chair. He took his set-piece back next to Young Buster Prather who was ticklin' his banjo into tune.

Uncle Posey Burwinkle's noise got the folks back to attention. "Folks," he was shoutin', "we'll dance one more set and then we'll go massacree the fried chicken."

So Cousin Drewey sawed the fiddle, Young Buster Prather tickled his banjo 'til it squealed, and Uncle Posey Burwinkle cupped his hands to his mouth.

> *Chase that rabbit, chase that squirrel,*
> *Chase that pretty girl 'round the world.*
> *All hands up and circle 'round,*
> *Don't let the pretty girls git out of town.*

The set ended all asudden. "Let's eat!" hollered Uncle Posey and everybody moved over to the table. Everybody but us Lowdermilks, who tied our rusties to where we were settin'.

I saw Pap's face turn hard like hickory. It told how he just waited for Clyde Skinner to come packin' a dish of fried chicken over to Verbaline Lou, to act the gentleman like he'd done before. Pap's look told how he'd take that plate and bust it over Clyde's face if he dared do it again. He would for sure.

I saw Maw Maw's eyes tell how she wished that fine man would get up guts; wished how the girl she'd birthed would get the chance like any other sweetness in the valley, chances that were slung 'round by fine young gents nigh every day of the year. She'd like to see Verbaline Lou get her man. That's all.

And I saw the sparkle in my sister's eyes, just wishful and maybe trustin'. I saw how she couldn't dare look to where Clyde was talkin' to Mistress Lee Bassett over by the big canful of pink drink. She feared lest he'd go over and fill up a plate for her. She was feared for Clyde because of Pap.

And then I saw what I didn't expect. I saw Clyde walk toward us, stridin' in his handsome cowboy boots. He came up in front of Verbaline Lou, stretched out and took her hand in his—lifted her clean to her feet, by golly!

"I'd sure like you to eat fried chicken with me, Miss Lowdermilk," he said, just before he led her off. "Mistress Bassett says how *really* and *truly* it's plumb delicious."

I watched Maw Maw smile the happiest she'd ever rendered in her life. I saw Pap scowl worser than any time before. I could tell how he wished for his shotgun so's to shoot Clyde through the navel—make doublehash of that spot. He looked 'round, hopin' how maybe he'd brought the weapon along. But he found how he hadn't. And because he hadn't there was nothin' to do but set and scowl. A man's scowl never hurt anybody. It didn't keep Clyde and Verbaline Lou from eatin' fried chicken together, out there in the middle of the floor, under the big hangin' lamp, where all Star Valley could see how they made a mighty sweet couple.

7

The next day was Sunday. Us Lowdermilks were up before sunlight and fixed to do up the chores.

"Newt," Pap said to me, "I got somethin' devilin' my mind."

Me and him were walkin' out toward the corral. We'd just stepped off the front porch. Maw Maw and Verbaline Lou were cookin' up a breakfast in the house; they fried the very last of the hog meat, they baked a stack of cornbread. The coffee made itself smelt out of the old black pot and the Lord was willin' that we had plenty of molasses and fried-meat grease. We weren't starvin' or near it. Cousin Drewey hadn't gotten up out of his bed of heaped tow-sacks under the box elder tree. Cousin Drewey never got up 'til he knew how the womenfolks had the breakfast cooked and me and Pap done finished up the chores. It was his personality.

"What's devilin' your mind, Pap?" I quizzed.

"It devils me to think how Cousin Drewey has ate up all our hog meat."

"He sure is a hog-meat-eatin' fool," I said.

"He's more'n that. He's the eatin'est man. He eats up everythin'," Pap said, and I could see by his face how he was riled right smart.

I grunted an agreement. But there was nothin' to be

COUSIN DREWEY & THE HOLY TWISTER   55

said that could pull a brake on Cousin Drewey's appetite. His paunch was kin to his personality.

"It ain't what he eats, Newt," Pap said. "It ain't *that* what's devilin' my poor mind, 'cause I'll give a man my last crust if he'll he'p me out. But our kinfolks won't he'p us with the chores. He sleeps 'til he cain't sleep no more, 'til the flies crawl and wake him up. We give him a hoe and tell him we'd sure love his company in the corn patch. He he'ps, all right, but he talks more'n he chops; then he lays down his hoe and heads for the house. He comes back with his guitar and he sets down and sings us a song. I don't need his music 'cause his sweat is good enough for me. Music ain't never chopped out the careless weeds, it ain't never made hash of the thistles. It ain't never put vittles on our kitchen shelf, it ain't never pulled us up from the stony ground."

"That ain't what Old Man Lee Bassett says," I reminded Pap. "Old Man Lee says how Cousin Drewey is our salvation. He says how that kinfolks was sent by the Lord, to lift us up afore we drowned ourse'fs in our own no'countness."

"That old man ain't got a lick of sense," Pap said.

We'd been standin' still to auger out our opinions, now me and Pap walked on toward the corral. "You might go over and git Cousin Drewey out of the towsacks, Newt," Pap said. "That ain't askin' too much. He can he'p us with the chores, then we can all go in and eat some breakfast."

"You bet," I said. But I kept on walkin' and Pap knew the reason. He knew I'd go over and holler Cousin Drewey awake, sooner or later, but he also knew that first I'd have to go over to he'p keep the lower plank of the corral from gettin' dehydrated.

"Doggone!" Pap said.

I looked at his face which had shed itself of any concern over Cousin Drewey. I could tell *that* and didn't need to look twice. Then I looked into the corral and saw for myself what Pap was talkin' about.

"Newt," Pap said. "Where's old Jeff? I wonder where that old mule is at."

Sure enough, the milk cow was up next to the fodder but the mule was somewhere else. Pap looked, then he said to me, "Newt, you button your fly, then git out under the box elder tree and see if Cousin Drewey is in the tow-sacks. I might be wrong, but I kind'a think our kinfolks has gone for a ride, bareback, him and his hog-leg forty-five."

Pap thought correctly. Cousin Drewey was up out of the tow-sacks. But he wasn't 'round. I went to the house hopin' to find him eatin' up the last of the hog meat, him not carin' if us-balance starved to death. But the womenfolks said how they hadn't witnessed his hair or hide. I looked to the wall, up where his guitar and fiddle hung. They were there like always. I went to the corner of the room and there rested his satchel. It seemed like Cousin Drewey had just he'ped himself to old Jeff and had ridden off somewhere. Pap said how Cousin Drewey had ridden off to do himself some mischief that might harm us Lowdermilks.

"Newt," Pap says, "let's fix these here chores quick 'cause we'd better git into town afore Cousin Drewey shoots the hell out of Fats Recknagel with his old hog-leg forty-five."

We fixed the chores and ate some breakfast; we made the five miles to Signal Rock Main Street in strides like nobody took before. We came across from the First National Bank and there. . . . Sure enough! There stood that mean cattleman up against the big brass and glass door with his hands in his pockets jinglin' coin. He had his mind on how he could bleed a poor man out of some more.

* * *

COUSIN DREWEY & THE HOLY TWISTER   57

The bank was closed, naturally. But Sundays didn't faze Fats a mite. He still liked to stand outside the big brass and glass door and think about all the money he had stocked in the big vault. He stayed there most of the time, happy to know how his wife was faithful to him out on the ranch, settin' at the card table where the telephone was, callin' up Houston to ask how much richer they were gettin' hour by hour. Banks was Fats's favorite territory, not only the Signal Rock First National but any bank in the world.

Sometimes he and his wife craved to go sightseein' in their Cadillac-car. They'd do that mostly in the summer or fall, when the countryside was green or when the mountain trees were golden-bright before sheddin' their leaves; when the evenin' air was clean and fresh and Christian folks could feel the sweet Lord God all 'round. Did they admire the scenery made by the Lord's lovin' kindness and the farmers' sweat? Did they watch the birds fly from here to yonder? Did they stop and park and love each other's neck, them alone in the cool light of sunset? They did like hell.

Because what they had in mind was the feel, sight and smell of money. So they'd pick out a bank somewhere within a hundred miles of Signal Rock. They'd be happy as a couple slopped hogs as they rode along, and when they got to the bank they'd stop to look it over. They'd always take a picnic lunch along for to eat on the steps outside. Then they'd go inside and hunt up the president and ask him to show them 'round. They'd talk "big money" with him, and Fats's eyes would brighten when he saw all the stacked money. He'd sniff at the open vault and let the tasty perfume go down his pipes clean into his framework. They'd paid respects to all the banks in a hundred-mile circle, and they always wished for a new one to open up. All the bank folks held high respect for Fats and his woman and they told Fats so out loud. Which pleased him mightily because nobody else in the county reckoned Fats to be higher on the human scale of integrity than a snake's belly.

And sometimes Fats and his woman would talk and figger on a high old fling, on somethin' profitable enough to pay the gas and oil. Did they go for a session at the Country Club where the high moguls hang out? Did they attend the movie-star show? Did they act civilized that way? Not on your britches, inside or out.

Because they'd hunt up a Bingo game somewhere. They'd set at the Bingo table lookin' like twin buzzards, movin' the do-funnies 'round and thinkin' kindly about dollars and cents. The Bingo games in Star Valley always played for money.

Or sometimes they'd fly off in an airplane, like anybody else in need of a long trip to see the world. But it wasn't the Grand Canyon they'd fly to, or to Niagara Falls, or Washington, D.C. Never fail, they'd buy a ticket to Las Vegas, Nevada, so's to jerk the slot machines and make some money. If they lost it didn't matter, for the pleasure of handlin' money was good enough. They didn't give mind to the pretty girls or the bright lights, because the brightest face in Las Vegas was on a slot machine. Fats often said how he was ashamed to say so and hoped the good Lord would forgive him, but he reckoned how the look of a ten dollar bill was prettier than a twenty; he figgered the Mint people ought to get some sense and make it vice-versa.

Fats and his woman were pure Texas folks. They came from a sweet land. But they weren't sweet.

Which was natural. So it stands to reason how Sunday didn't matter with Fats any more than Wednesday. The cows were calvin' and the rice mills were grindin' and the oil wells were pumpin' barrels. That's why he stood next to the bank even when the big brass and glass door was closed. That's how we saw him there, jinglin' coin and lookin' mean.

COUSIN DREWEY & THE HOLY TWISTER 59

"Cousin Drewey ain't killed him yet," Pap said.

"I don't think Cousin Drewey aims to shoot Fats Recknagel," I said to Pap.

"Why not, Newt? The sonofabitch needs shootin'."

"Let's git home," I said. "Cousin Drewey has gone somewhere else. I think how maybe Cousin Drewey and old Jeff, them and the old hog-leg forty-five, are somewheres in Fats Recknagel's pasture. And I think maybe, too, how us Lowdermilks will have some beef for supper. Maybe not tonight's supper, but Monday's or Tuesday's. I see the handwrit on the wall, like Daniel saw it in the dinner-hall of Belshazzar."

If my Pap ever had compassion, he showed it then for Fats Recknagel.

"Newt," he said, "we'll just go over there next to the bank and tell Fats how Cousin Drewey ain't up to no good in his pasture. I don't like that horse's ass, as you well might know. But I respect his property, 'specially them registered Black Angus cattle. We'll tell him to let loose his cowpunchers on Cousin Drewey and old Jeff afore Cousin Drewey kills a beef and gits hisse'f and us Lowdermilks in trouble."

I followed Pap across the street. But before we could get close to Fats Recknagel that big paunchy cattleman saw us comin'. He took on a fresh load of hate to his face, he put the sparks of meanness in his eyes, his look dared us to walk up beside him.

"Mister," said Pap, gettin' close as he could, "me and Newt here would *sure* like a brotherly word with you, 'cause . . ."

Fats spat words like a rattlesnake spits poison. "Git, clodhopper!" he scowled at us Lowdermilks. "Git before I call the sheriff. I ain't got hospitality, and I ain't got a dime for you. You don't need a cup of coffee, because all you need is to git out of my eyesight."

Pap turned to me. He said, "Newt, that sonofabitch has done harmed my feelin's. Let's me and you git out of his eyesight and don't say a damn word about what we know."

So we got out of Fats's eyesight. Halfway down the block Pap stopped. He said, "Newt, there's nothin' I'd love better for tonight's supper than a fried beefsteak, and for tomorrow's dinner a beef heart stuffed with cornmeal and onion dressin'. All I can say now is Lord bless Cousin Drewey, him and old Jeff and the hog-leg forty-five. May he pick a fat one; may his gun speak a twice-time rooty-toot-toot."

So we walked on home, Pap actin' like a man pleased with himself.

But he acted that way only for a short time. . . .

Up to the time when Maw Maw met us on the porch.

8

"Woman," said Pap, "what's feedin' on your mind?" He said that because he saw the same as me: the worried look on Maw Maw's face, like she had somethin' itchy to tell Pap. She wrung her hands, her complexion was slightly pale. She stuttered in her talk, she sounded Pentecostal. We couldn't make it out.

"He'pmeet," she said, comin' out of her stutters, "it's Verbaline Lou."

"I reckoned as much," Pap said.

"I *do* believe we've lost her forever."

"What the hell?"

"I couldn't he'p it," Maw Maw said. "Right after you fellers left for town, soon after you went 'round the bend, that there Lilybelle rode up to the yard in the Skinner pickup truck."

"Where was Verbaline Lou?"

"In the house, here. We was both in the house, actin' godly."

Pap's madness hit the porch roof. It skidded off and echoed out by the hog pens. He stomped *that* much and hollered *that* loud.

"I knew it, I knew it!" he said with tolerable noise. "It was bound to happen sooner or later. Where's our gal now?"

"Done gone off with Lilybelle, them in the pickup truck."

"Where, you reckon?"

"To the Skinner brothers ranch, likely."

Pap danced 'round like he had to go leak. "That there Clyde, the sonofabitch, had got too much ambition in his pants. He ain't got no Christian love in his head, he ain't got no respect for poor folks in his heart. He's got our sweetness up at the ranch right now so's he can violate her modesty. It shocks me to think what she and Clyde might be doin' now, lovin' necks, maybe. Lord God, what a burden for Baptist parents to bear! What did Lilybelle say when she got out of the truck, when she met you in the yard?"

"She said, 'Howdy, Mistress Lowdermilk. I sure hope the world is treatin' you okay today.' That's what she said, walkin' up to the porch."

"That's harlot talk," Pap blustered. "That's pure-D sportin' house language. That's what the lady says to us gents when we ring the bell in Tulsa; when she asks us in to set while she brings on the girls."

Maw Maw said nothin', but she took Pap's talk for the deacon's truth.

"Hell-fire!" Pap said. "Why didn't you git down the shotgun and pepper her rusty? It's the best bull's-eye in the valley, all wrapped up in silk."

Maw Maw's glottis must have got hung up because she said no more. Myself, it wasn't my business. I reckoned how it was Pap and Maw Maw who worked to make Verbaline Lou together, and they didn't need me talkin' opinions about their manufacture. So I held what I thought inside my head. But my thoughts were kindly to Lilybelle. Everybody was noiseless on the porch except Pap.

"You needn't talk, woman," he shouted, "you needn't tell me nothin' 'cause I know all about it, I know how our sweetness went. . . . That Lilybelle went up to her and she said, 'Verbaline Lou, I sure would love you

COUSIN DREWEY & THE HOLY TWISTER   63

to come out with me now, 'cause I'm headin' for the ranch. I'd like you to see how us high-grade citizens live, 'cause me and Sonny Boy aim to give you a treat. We'll feed you some light bread, you can listen to our radio.' That's whorehouse talk, woman, and that's the way it happened. That's when Verbaline Lou got in the truck and rode off to sin and destruction. Am I right or ain't I?"

Maw Maw nodded a you bet. She mourned like Verbaline Lou had died.

Pap kicked the side of the house. "She might ride out, but she ain't ridin' back," he said. He didn't calm down a mite. " 'Cause I'm headin' out for the Skinner ranch myse'f, awalkin' with the shotgun in my hands. And after I lay out Clyde for dead and make Sonny Boy wish he'd never been born, I'm goin' to pick up my girl and head for home. If I need to tell the sheriff all about it, he'll need to come here, 'cause I'll have done enough travelin' for the day."

Was Pap angered! Lord, Lord!

He pushed me aside and nigh bowled Maw Maw off her feet. He kicked open the door and stepped inside the house.

"And there ain't nothin' this side of the devil's red hell as will stop me," he hollered, walkin' to where his shotgun hung on the wall. "I won't eat, and I won't drink, and I won't lay my weary head on a piller. I won't do nothin' 'til I've made out of Clyde Skinner somethin' to haul off in a sack."

Me and Maw Maw followed him inside, we saw him take down the shotgun. He spit on the barrel and rubbed it with his hand; he bent the breach to make sure it was loaded. He went over to the drawer where he kept his box of shells, then he fixed to bid us a sweet fare-you-well.

He eyed the door.

But he didn't get near it.

'Cause on the way his glance caught the table, there amiddle of our settin'-'round room. And on the table, plumb center of a fancy platter, sat a great big old chocolate-covered cake, the biggest and highest we'd ever witnessed in our lives.

"What's that?" he quizzed Maw Maw.

"It's a cake," Maw Maw told him. "Lilybelle left it here. She said she made it herse'f. She put it there as a gift for us Lowdermilks."

Pap looked down at his shotgun, then he walked over to sniff at the cake. He bent low so's to pull the chocolate smell into his nose. He licked his lip-bristles like a hound dog licks when he dreams of eatin' a dead rabbit. Then Pap turned 'round and put the shotgun back on the hook. He pulled a chair up to the table and got out his knife.

Pap got so sick from eatin' too much cake that he went to his bed. He wasn't awake when Verbaline Lou got back. Factways, us Lowdermilks had never eaten of such tasty bake-stuff; that's why Pap got sick. Because all the sweetness we ever got was cornbread mixed up with hog grease and molasses; except for the chuck folks took to the Saturday-night dances. But at the dance we were all too bashful to eat like our hunger called for. We wished we could eat vittles like that under our own roof, with nobody but us Lowdermilks 'round to watch us eat it. It didn't last no time, and that's how come Pap got sick to his guts.

Maw Maw said how she'd *sure* love to know how to mix somethin' like that, and I told Maw Maw how I'd *sure* love to know someone who could. That pleased Maw Maw right smart. We both figgered our girl had hit the right track. Maybe Lilybelle would show Verbaline Lou how to mix cake. Maybe Verbaline Lou would learn how to do all sorts of things if she kept goin' to the ranch.

COUSIN DREWEY & THE HOLY TWISTER 65

* * *

Maw Maw was gettin' supper ready when Verbaline Lou came home. Lilybelle let her off from the pickup truck out in the yard. Verbaline Lou packed a big somethin' wrapped up in paper and string, the sweet Lord only knew what. She took it into her room where she slept. Me, I looked at that package and hoped it was somethin' to eat. Then Verbaline Lou came out of her room and stopped next to me and Maw Maw. She was shed of the package. It was nothin' to eat or she'd have hauled it in for supper.

"Your Pap's madder'n a drunk skunk," Maw Maw told her.

"About me?"

"I reckon."

"Where's he now?"

"In his bed, sicker'n a horse. He says you committed worser'n sinful. He was fixed to git down the shotgun and go hunt you and Clyde up. But he saw the cake and it stopped him."

I itched to know so I asked Verbaline Lou, "What'all you folks did out at the ranch all day?"

"Me and Lilybelle, we tried on dresses. We fooled 'round the sewin' machine. Me and her looked at ourse'fs in the mirror. She gave me a pair of shoes, the right kind for next Saturday's dance."

"What else?" I quizzed, thinkin' of the package.

"What else ain't your concern," she told me back.

"You crave some supper, gal?" Maw Maw said.

"Cain't," said Verbaline Lou. "I ate too much dinner."

"You and who?" I spoke up, thinkin' of Clyde.

"Me and Lilybelle and the kids. We had roast meat and white potatoes, and all kinds of green-colored things. And gravy—Lord God! And apple pie and milk, and coffee and ice cream, and she had a bowl full of apples and bananas set on the table."

"Clyde wasn't there?" Maw Maw said.

"No, him and Sonny Boy were off somewheres. Sonny Boy went off on his crutches and Lilybelle said how Clyde drove the car. Them both together. No tellin' where they went, to the pasture maybe."

"Didn't Clyde know you was goin' to eat dinner with 'em?" I said.

"Hell, yes. . . . Has Cousin Drewey got home yet?"

"He ain't," Maw Maw said. "Pap reckons how him and old Jeff will stay out tonight. At first Pap thought how maybe he's gone back to the Washtaw Mountains; but if he aimed that'all, he'd have taken along his satchel, it and the fiddle and guitar, 'cause Cousin Drewey's a musical man. So we all reckon how he's gone out to kill one of Fats Recknagel's critters, and may the sweet Lord forgive his sinful ways."

"What made Pap sick?" said Verbaline Lou.

"The cake."

"It was the best cake ever mixed."

"Sure thing, but Pap ate too much."

"Lilybelle says she's goin' to show me how to make one like it," Verbaline Lou said.

"Hot damn!" I hollered; because myse'f, I like cake.

"I'm goin' back with Lilybelle come Wednesday," Verbaline Lou said. "She's goin' to fix up my hair pretty. She says I've got right-nice hair if I'll wash it out with some stuff she'll buy at the drug store. I don't know what it is. It looks like whiskey in the bottle, but when you shake it it makes foam."

"Pap will git down his shotgun," Maw Maw said, "he'll be over his sickness by then and there won't be no cake to stop him."

Verbaline Lou smiled at Maw Maw. She looked sweet, all right. Then she bust out laughin' like her guts were fixed to ache, like we'd have to put a stitch in her tubes. "Hell-fire!" she called. "Maw Maw, and you too,

Newt! Cousin Drewey will be home from Fats Recknagel's pasture by Wednesday. He'll be here in the house, the Lord's blessin' on us Lowdermilks. By that time I'll have told him all about my day at the Skinner boys' ranch, and about my good time with Lilybelle. I'll have told him about me puttin' on the prettiest dresses in the world and how Lilybelle said to look at myse'f in the mirror, the prettiest girl in all Star Valley. I'll tell him how I'm headin' off to git the dirt washed out of my hair, to make of myse'f a girl fit to be loved. I'll tell him how I love Clyde Skinner and aim to marry him like he aims to marry me. Pap won't take down his shotgun 'cause Cousin Drewey will be there. If Pap gets rambunctious, then Cousin Drewey will make him sit down, tell him to cut hisse'f a piece of cake. 'Cause Cousin Drewey has been sent to us Lowdermilks by the Lord; he's our salvation, and you won't need to read the Bible-prophets to find out he's that breed of blessin'."

9

Pap and me were out walkin' toward the corral early next mornin' like always. We had to do up the chores even if Cousin Drewey and Verbaline Lou had sinned in our midst, each in his or her own way. We tried hard not to think of them for the time bein'. It wasn't easy. Pap had got over his cake-sickness; he'd slept it off like a man sleeps off whiskey. He was good tempered, which was rare like payday for Pap.

"Newt," Pap said to me, with a deacon's smile on his bristly face, "I'm goin' to dedicate this happy day to good works and forgiveness. When Verbaline Lou gits up out of bed, I aim to love her neck and tell her how her old Pap ain't mad because she messed 'round with Lilybelle. I'll tell her how she's still my sugar-tit gal, the legal daughter by me and Maw Maw's crotch-labor. We made her with the Lord's he'p and we ain't sorry we did it together that night, or maybe it was daylight back of the barn. And as for Cousin Drewey, I ain't got nothin' but sweetness for him, 'cause he's kinfolks, Foster or Lowdermilk and I don't care a damn which."

Lord, was Pap Lowdermilk the good-natured Samaritan!

"Blessin's on our prodigal kinfolks, cousin and daughter," he said as we made tracks toward the corral.

COUSIN DREWEY & THE HOLY TWISTER 69

We hurried, because the lower plank was hollerin'. We both had just got up. We're only human. But in spite of our tryin' to keep our minds off Cousin Drewey, just for the sake of Christianity, his picture kept lopin' in. We couldn't keep him and old Jeff and the hog-leg forty-five out of our heads; we visioned him packin' in a fat carcass of Black Angus beef, shot in the head with its throat cut.

That'all might have been dream stuff, but when we arrived at the corral we knew for sure how Cousin Drewey was back with us again. Because there stood old Jeff next to the milk cow. He stood next to that old brindle that could never find a calf, that cow what kept us Lowdermilks from drinkin' milk. They stood together chewin' on the fodder we'd forked onto the ground the night before. It was proof enough that Cousin Drewey had come home from his travels, how he'd dismounted from old Jeff sometime in the night while we'all slept in the house.

Pap looked at the mule bug-eyed. He was right pleased. "Newt," he said, "I *do* believe our kinfolks is in the tow-sacks sleepin' off his ride. Maybe you'd better go over by the box elder tree and see if he's where I think he is."

I did just like Pap said; and sure enough, I could see how the sackpile was humped like somebody was wrapped up in it. It couldn't be none other but Cousin Drewey. His trousers dangled by their galluses up on the limb above his bed. And next to them was hung his old hog-leg forty-five on the holster belt. Aside the sack-pile was his coat, his hat, his socks and his shoes. I wouldn't see his shirt and drawers because he never failed to wear them to bed, winter or summer, cold or hot. Cousin Drewey was a sight for sore eyes when he got fixed for crawlin' into the sacks. But what *really* counted that minute was how Cousin Drewey was home again from

Fats Recknagel's pasture. That was a truth no lawyer could fight to deny.

Lord, did I feel good! It was good to know how Cousin Drewey was back with us again. I figgered if I looked 'round I might have some *real* tidin's of joy to tell. So I walked back to Pap, who was messin' in the corral; I walked by way of the dugout cellar where we stored our potatoes and turnips. By that I mean I went by the roofed-over hole in the ground that Cousin Drewey reckoned would make a sweet cyclone shelter should a twister ever come funnelin' down on us Lowdermilks. I mean that there which Cousin Drewey said how it would make the best place in God's world to keep freshly butchered meat away from the flies and the eyes of the sheriff.

All the proof of meat bein' already down the cellar was there on the outside. First, there was old Jeff's hoofprints, showin' how he'd come to a stop. Second, there was a dent in the dirt that showed how somethin' heavy had been pitched off that mule's back. Third, there was bits of black hair lyin' 'round, like a carcass has been skinned. There was pure tell-tale of nefarious doin's. And the two hound dogs were sleepin' on the roof, both content like they were full of guts. The cat mewed up behind them, full like a blood-blown tick. And me, I visioned a whole carcass of cut-up beef hangin' on the hooks down in the dark.

"Pap," I said, when I got back to the corral, "you're right like Bible-wisdom. Cousin Drewey is rolled up in the sacks. I could hear his snores, I could see his pants ahangin' and his old hog-leg forty-five up on the treelimb. I came back by way of the dugout, and it looks mighty like Cousin Drewey came back with a load of plunder."

Pap's face brightened for thoughts of fried liver, but he darkened it with a frown come all asudden. "You didn't see no hide hangin' up, did you, Newt? We cain't let Cousin Drewey hang the hide up on a limb for the sheriff to see."

"I didn't see no hide," I told Pap, "but Cousin Drewey sure left black critter-hairs front of that cellar door. It looks like he's done skinned some meat."

"Dadburn that silly sonofabitch!" Pap said. He limbered. He came over the corral boards like a bat out of hell. "Let's me and you git to that cellar quick. What's hangin' inside is Cousin Drewey's business, but them there black hairs is yours and mine to pick up. We'll need to sack 'em and burn 'em, son. If the sheriff comes after Cousin Drewey, like he well might, we don't need no black critter-hairs 'round. And most of all we don't need a black calf-hide with Fats Recknagel's brand on it, cause if the law finds it, it's pure evidence against Cousin Drewey. It's proof of his sinful ways. 'Thou shalt not steal,' the sweet Lord said to Moses. And the same applies to Cousin Drewey, even if he ain't an Israelite."

Pap and me went to the cellar, outside. We didn't dare look inside. We got us a burlap sack and picked up all the black hairs that Cousin Drewey spilled.

"Newt," Pap said, "let's me and you plant some potatoes."

So we got us a shovel apiece and dug up the ground all 'round the cellar. We dug a patch twenty feet each side of that there roofed-over hole in the ground; and when Maw Maw yelled from the house how the breakfast was ready, we called back to say how we were busy and how we'd be there directly. Me and Pap were all sweat when we finally walked to the house.

"We'll git some potatoes planted before noon," Pap said. "You cain't beat potatoes for coverin' up rustled meat."

Maw Maw and Verbaline Lou were both settin' at the table when me and Pap got in. We washed up at the basin and took each an end of the towel to dry ourse'fs of wetness. We flushed out our mouths with the dipper, then sat down next to what the womenfolks had cooked up.

"Cousin Drewey got home last night," Pap told the womenfolks. "He got home mounted on old Jeff."

"Praise the Lord," Maw Maw said. "We'd better let him sleep."

"If you'all find potatoes sproutin' 'round the dugout," Pap said, "just let 'em sprout. They're growin' there 'cause Cousin Drewey spilled some Black Angus hair front of the door. If the sheriff comes 'round he ain't gonna snoop in the potato patch. 'Cause you cain't find red meat among the tubers."

Cousin Drewey stayed in the tow-sacks most of the day. If the sun beat down on him, he didn't seem to care. If the flies tried to devil him, he just had to cover his head with a sack and not let his bare feet stick out. Me and Pap worked like mules 'round the cellar, diggin' dirt and puttin' potatoes in rows. Maybe it wasn't exactly the best time to plant potatoes, but like I said to Pap: "What the hell!" We were workin' for the sheriff, not for ourse'fs.

Every once in a while Pap would set down his shovel and go over to the dugout door. He'd put his nose to sniffin'. "Newt," he said, "I *do* hope Cousin Drewey's got some liver hangin' up in there. It makes my mouth go yum-yum anytime I think of liver cooked in hog grease, covered up all slick 'til you cain't see the meat for white onions. If he's got that kind of redness hangin' up down there, then I'll pray sweetly how the Lord will forgive Cousin Drewey. Then I'll beg Cousin Drewey to bring it out for Maw Maw and the gal, so them doggone women can fry it down for tonight's supper."

We had the ground dug up and the potatoes planted by noon, as Pap prophesied. We went to the house when the sun was directly above; and sure enough, Maw Maw had vittles on the table waitin' for us. Beans and greens. The greens were lambsquarters which Maw Maw had picked out next to the patch; they boil down soft in salt and grease. Them and beans are all right for a man's dinner.

Maw Maw and Verbaline Lou were in the settin'-'round room, gabbin' woman-talk. My sister had her package open on the table, but she covered it up when me and Pap passed by into the kitchen. Like it was nothin' for our eyes to see. Maw Maw had a prideful look. Both us men could see that. We sat down to the beans and greens and played like we weren't givin' the women no mind.

"And then what did she say?" Maw Maw said to Verbaline Lou.

Pap was too hungry to listen, shovelin' down forkfuls like a man naturally does, but I cocked my ear toward the settin'-'round room. I sure loved to know what was in that package.

"She said she'd like to civilize me," I hear'd Verbaline Lou tell Maw Maw. "Lilybelle said how it's hard to scrape the moss off a mossback, but claimed I was born a lady and all I need is to git the fuzz pulled out of me so's the lady will show."

"*Do* tell," I hear'd Maw Maw say.

"Lilybelle said how she bought them dresses special for me, and for me to wear 'em, for me to show off how pretty I am. She says by next Saturday night's dance she aims to give this here Star Valley a surprise like they never got before. . . . I don't aim to wear the dresses 'til it's time to git slicked for the dance. But Lilybelle said how I'd better start wearin' the panties right now. It might take some time to git used to the elastic band, and the lace trimmin' 'round the bottom is likely to tickle, but just at first."

"That sounds like good sense to me," Maw Maw said.

"And Lilybelle said how I'll have to wash 'em every day and hang 'em out to dry, 'cause that's what the girls do in the city. She said just wash 'em and hang 'em, then I'll always have nice fresh undies."

"Undies?" Maw Maw said, perplexed. "What's them things?"

"Like we see in the mail-order catalogue."

"Ain't that the truth now, daughter. Many's the time I looked at them in pictures and wished I didn't need sew drawers no more out of flour sacks. Now the sweet Lord has sent you a pair by way of Lilybelle."

"Six pairs, Maw Maw," said Verbaline Lou. "Lilybelle says how I need that many if I aim to wash 'em every day and hang 'em out on the clothesline."

Maw Maw clicked her tongue for admiration. "Doggone," she said, "if high-up folks like Lilybelle ain't smart for their looks! Them Skinners are kindly, right smart."

"That's why I washed out the first pair this mornin' and hung 'em up," Verbaline Lou said. "That's why I've got the second pair on and four more settin' in this here box. They're light and flimsy and pretty as hell."

Pap ate like he'd suffered hunger for eighteen nights. I knew he hadn't paid mind to womanly talk. But *I* had, because I'd caught every word. . . . I feared! Lord God, how I feared! . . . I knew what Pap would say and do if he saw them flimsies hangin' out on the line. I wished how I could tell Verbaline Lou to go hide them away before Pap finished his greens, before he wiped the bean smears off his chin-bristles. But I was frozen to my chair 'til Pap got up.

"Pap," I said, "there's some molasses here. You ain't had molasses poured over your cornbread. It ain't right for a man to have dinner and not git any sweetness on his cornbread."

COUSIN DREWEY & THE HOLY TWISTER

But Pap looked like he aimed to stay up. "I've had aplenty."

He went to the water bucket and picked up a dipperful. He sloshed it 'round his mouth, then went out the back door so's to spit it out on the rose bush Maw Maw had growin' there. Then I heard him holler bluehell.

"Newt! . . . Damn it, come here! . . . Come atrottin', 'cause I cain't believe my eyes." That's the kind of talk Pap hollered. I got up off my chair, quick.

"Look!" he said, pointin' out to the clothesline. "Am I seein' ha'nts, or is it the sunshine what's turned pink? What's them two things hangin' on the rope?"

"That there on the off-side," I told Pap, "is a pair of panties. And that on the near-side is what the mail-order catalogue calls a brass-seer."

Pap whooped like a Comanche down the Pease River Valley, and his whoop wasn't for joy. I could see the two flimsy things hangin' in the bright sunshine. To the back of them was the box elder tree, where Cousin Drewey snored deep down in his tow-sacks.

"What's a brass-seer?" Pap said.

"Damned if I know," I told Pap. "It's woman-truck. It's got somethin' to do with Verbaline Lou's globes."

Pap whooped again. He kicked a bucket and sent Maw Maw's broom high in the air.

"Hell-fire and pesky damnation!"

He turned 'round and took to the house. I didn't follow because I knew he'd be back as soon as he got his shotgun. Maybe he looked at the table, I don't know, hopin' for a cake to stop him. But he was out back beside me before I could count eighteen. He bent the gun, opened the breach and saw how there was a loaded shell in each barrel. I heard Verbaline Lou scream; I heard Maw Maw holler to the Lord, beseechin' the Lord that Pap wouldn't get violent.

First, Pap aimed at the panties; he pulled the trigger to send the pinkness high in the air over toward the box elder tree.

Then he pulled on the other barrel, and the buckshot caught the brass-seer.

Then we heard Cousin Drewey holler. A shower of leaves was fallin' down on his pile of tow-sacks, because any human bein' knows how women's flimsies can't hold buckshot back. The shower must go somewhere, so Pap's just went on to hit Cousin Drewey's box elder tree. Maw Maw and Verbaline Lou were behind us. Maw Maw held my sweet sister while she sobbed for her grief. But what took our eyesight mostly was Cousin Drewey, who had come up like a bat out of hell out of the tow-sacks and into the daylight.

He came toward us dancin' like he had the black-demon-shakes, or better still like the sheriff was after him; barefooted, but the stickers didn't faze him a mite. His drawers were wrinkled 'round him and his shirt-tail was wavin' in the breeze. His hair was toozled and his face was wild.

"What you firin' at me for, Cousin Lowdermilk?" he hollered as he leapt the ground. "You'all'd better save your buckshot for the sheriff. Are you craze, or ain't you?"

Truly, Cousin Drewey was a sight for sore eyes.

10

Verbaline Lou spent most of the day in her little room. She lay face down on her bed; there she wept her eyes to wetness. She'd mourn 'til they dried, then she'd bust loose and wet them again. Hers was a soul in misery.

Pap was likewise. He seemed plumb shamed for what he had done to wound the heart of Verbaline Lou, his one and only sugar-tit girl. He wished the Lord would take off his trigger-finger so's he wouldn't do some innocent loved one a heap of harm. So he went out to the stump by the woodpile. He sat there with his head drooped, whittlin' on a stick and chewin' cud. The evenin' was hot and the flies mighty bad, but Pap felt nary one of them torments. He was too far gone with a dose of misery.

Cousin Drewey went back to the box elder tree. He got into his pants and shoes, then he strapped on his hog-leg forty-five. Maw Maw put out his dinner of beans and greens and while he ate he quizzed Maw Maw as to why Verbaline Lou grieved so much. Maw Maw confessed everythin', about how that girl had spent Sunday with Lilybelle and how Pap got sick on cake. She told how Pap shot the panties off the clothesline because he didn't admire silk or pinkness. They were highup society stuff in his mind. Cousin Drewey ate on his dinner;

he loaded up, too, with all Maw Maw had to tell. Then he felt how he'd had enough beans and greens. He craved no more cornbread sopped in bean juice. He got up and flushed his mouth out with the water dipper. He didn't say nothin' to Maw Maw. But he had a kind'a look in his eye which was half the wisdom of Confucius and half the wrath of Moses. He walked outside and over to the woodpile to join Pap, to he'p him chew cud and spit at the axe.

He sat down on his hunkers. He said to Pap, "Cousin Lowdermilk, I've done made an opinion of you. I think you're a silly sonofabitch."

Now here in Star Valley those kind of words make fightin' language. But Pap took the accusation like he deserved it. He whittled and he chewed and he didn't look up from the ground.

"What'all did you have to go and make that happy girl miserable for?" Cousin Drewey said. "Your own flesh and blood, gentle womanhood for a fact. You ain't fit to have her love; somebody ought to whip you on the ass with a dead rabbit."

Pap spat, he hit the axe. "You're right, Cousin Drewey, I ain't fit for love, hers or anybody else's. I wish the Lord would take off my trigger finger and just leave me the balance of my anatomy. That is, leave me the limbs and carcass that cain't do nobody no harm."

"While the Lord is takin' off your trigger finger," Cousin Drewey said, "He might git thorough and pull the meanness out of your heart. He might disintegrate the silly notions you've got cached in your head. If He takes off your trigger finger and still leaves you with a mean heart and a silly head, then you'll use somethin' else you've got handy to harm your brothers, even your sistern in mankind. You'll just lose your head again. You'll go to kickin'. You'll git to pitchin' rocks."

Pap looked up. He said: "What'all you think of that feller?"

"You mean Clyde Skinner?"

"I don't mean nobody else."

"He's a man of virtue, Pap Lowdermilk. He raises them blessin's like hogs. He owns a heap of 'em."

"Name one."

"Kindly, I'll name his chief virtue. The one I reckon blue ribbon."

"Name it."

"He loves your daughter right smart," Cousin Drewey said. "I can see that when I look at him. I can tell how he'd like to wed; and I know when I look at him how no other woman but Verbaline Lou could fill the bill. And say, Cousin Lowdermilk, did you ever catch the spark in your gal's eyes when she looks at Clyde? There's love there, there's respect, there's trust, there's hope that she'll come out of her mossback shell, that she'll shed the toughness put there by the kind of life you and Maw Maw birthed her to live. It says how once she steps into the light that's fillin' her heart now, even in the goddamn shanty she's got to call home—which you in your ignorance think is good enough for anyone—like I say, when she steps out so that light can surround her like a mist, give her joy to breathe and the respect of the whole valley to wear with pride. . . . Well hell, Pap Lowdermilk, that's when the finest thing ever will come to your life. It will be the *first* step up for you in the congregation of solid mankind. It's the congregation that thinks wisely, what does things to show the worth of the Lord's given salt. Right now, cousin, you ain't got wisdom. You ain't got no salt. But your girl has. That Verbaline Lou, she's got salt aplenty. She's got enough to build a statue of Lot's feisty wife."

"Lot's wife was Bible-truth," Pap said. "Your talk is plumb horseshit."

That kind of talk couldn't faze Cousin Drewey. "You cain't condemn truth, Cousin Lowdermilk, and you cain't praise horseshit for bein' sweeter'n rose petals.

You might plead with the Lord to pull off your trigger finger, but it won't do no good if you've got a mind to hurt somebody some other way. Prayin' for yourse'f and censurin' another feller ain't Christian neighbors. They don't habitat the same tongue, they cain't git sung off the same breath. Even if you think you're the mightiest Baptist alive, even if you think you've got more of the deacon's sweetness than Saint Paul of Tarsus."

"I ain't got no deacon's sweetness," said Pap. "What I got is Pap Lowdermilk sweetness. It's the best brand of sweetness this side of the cross timbers."

"It's one or the other," Cousin Drewey went on to tell. "I'll bet my hog-leg forty-five agin' your double-barrel shotgun how Verbaline Lou will wed up with Clyde Skinner. I'll wager how the preacher will caution that girl never to look on you again through all her wedded days, 'til death do them part. He'll caution her for two reasons: first, 'cause you're common as bat-shit, and second 'cause you ain't got good sense. The preacher will give Maw Maw some advice too; he'll tell her to drop you like a hot spike and go join the old folks' home. And the sooner you git yourse'f dead like a mule, the better you'll be for yourse'f and the world. You ain't no good alive."

"What'all you know about Clyde Skinner, cousin?" Pap said.

"Slightly but enough," said Cousin Drewey. So he told Pap how Clyde was an up-and-comin' young feller, though he couldn't vouch for him bein' any better than most of the human race. Cousin Drewey figgered out loud to Pap how a girl with Verbaline Lou's statistics will need to be satisfied with the "good enough" and leave the "bestest" to the girls in high society. And to never lose sight of the fact that this is a cruel world.

"What the hell would a girl like Verbaline Lou want with the 'bestest' anyhow?" said Pap. "She's a mossback. She was born in a shanty; if she's been picked out by the Lord for livin' her life and dyin' her death next to a radio set, or sleepin' with a man in a bed laid with them fancy sheets, or birthin' her kids in a hospital, just actin' the sonofabitchin' lady, it's the Lord's will. Praise the Lord! If that's the kind of will He packs, then it's good enough for me."

That was Pap talkin', but he craved to know more about Clyde Skinner. So Cousin Drewey went on to say how Clyde was a bachelor, the right kind of kindlin' for a girl to use when she strikes a light to the fire of matrimony. That was Clyde's prime specification, his very top notch. The second notch down was that he was partnered with his brother on one of the sweetest ranches in the valley. Marry him, then Verbaline Lou wouldn't starve to death, her kids would always have milk. And third notch down—mighty-main in Cousin Drewey's opinion—was that Clyde didn't go messin' 'round the rodeos like his brother Sonny Boy. He stayed home and mostly tended to ranch business. He didn't ride the fool-broncs in the arena, he didn't contest his calf-ropin' capabilities. And he didn't end up with a sprained leg; he didn't show hisse'f at the hoedown on a pair of crutches. Sonny Boy, Cousin Drewey reckoned, was a married man, coupled to Lilybelle like Adam to Eve, and he ought to respect his responsibility. No chisel-headed bronc or high-tailin' calf would respect it for him.

"Them rodeos is gonna git Sonny Boy in trouble, worse trouble as ever put him on crutches," Pap said to prophesy.

"Cousin Lowdermilk," said Cousin Drewey, "you talk the wisdom of Balak, King of Moab. You're a soothsayer from way back. You'll live to see your prophecy come to pass. And no man's troubles ever done me or you any good."

11

Wednesday mornin' came 'round bright and early. Pap walked with a cheerful temper; he'd been that way since he'd talked all about Clyde with Cousin Drewey out next to the woodpile. Now we'd done up the chores, fixed them up right. Cousin Drewey was still bedded in his tow-sacks, nobody givin' a damn whether he woke up or not. Me and Pap had a hoe apiece, we were out in the patch choppin' weeds from the pinto beans. Pap talked like his tongue had the Pentecostal; he told me what he reckoned about the Resurrection.

The mostest thing that had pulled Pap out of his meanness into Christian love—love for everyone in the valley, even Fats Recknagel—was the happy fact that *that* same evenin' after those two cousins had talked all about Clyde out next to the woodpile, chewin' cud, that Cousin Drewey went down in the dugout and came up with the entire beef liver for Maw Maw to fry. She cut it up and smothered it with white onions, she sprinkled it with salt and black pepper, and it made a stack on the platter big enough to feed the Israelites. Pap said out loud how that was a mighty charitable thing to do for Cousin Drewey to bring up the beef liver, and he told that culprit what he figgered St. Paul of Tarsus would say if he preached 'round Star Valley—because charity had top notch in that apostle's mind, more so than faith or hope.

Lilybelle pulled into our yard about mid-mornin', aset in her pickup truck. Verbaline Lou was shamed to tell her what Pap had done to the panties and brass-seer. But it stood to reason that she'd be pleased to relate how Pap tolerated them on the clothesline the day after that, lettin' them hang pink in the sun. Me and my sister figgered to ourselves—until Maw Maw stopped us—how Pap feared Cousin Drewey; how if Pap caught a spasm and took his shotgun to the flimsies then Cousin Drewey would seek revenge and make hash of Pap's drawers with his old hog-leg forty-five when Maw Maw hung 'em on the line to dry. That's what Pap feared. But Maw Maw had different politics to holler about. She said how, really and truly, Pap was gettin' hisse'f civilized and the category was showin' outside of him as minute after minute rolled along. We were a happy family of Lowdermilks, my sister the smilin'est of all. And it came about because of Lilybelle and the beef liver.

When Pap saw Lilybelle step out of the pickup he rested his hoe and whistled admiration. "Newt," he said to me, "do you see that pretty girl? Do you see that girl with the naked legs, with her royal-rusty awigglin', all wrapped up in blue?"

What Pap meant was that Lilybelle walked over to our shanty barelegged up to her blue shorts, and for a fact she wriggled her rusty some. She wore tan-colored slippers and a kind'a pullover shirt that was striped like the Star Spangled Banner. She had her blonde hair pulled tight on her head, tied up pretty in the back like a horse's tail. Her legs were whiter than any me or Pap ever saw before on a woman. And now she walked careful so's not to trip. She didn't aim to spill that big old somethin' covered with a white cloth what she carried in her hands. Verbaline Lou met Lilybelle on the porch.

They loved each other's neck like they were sisters long departed but come back.

Pap licked 'round inside his mouth. He made like he was pure-hungry. "Newt," he said, "that girl makes a pretty picture for my eyes. If some feller, maybe a year ago, told me how a pretty girl like that'n would step inside our shanty, I'd tell him he was a dad-blamed liar, how he couldn't prophesy worth a damn and didn't know his ass from his elbow."

"That Lilybelle is all right to look at," I agreed.

"Newt, do you reckon what I reckon?"

"Ain't no tellin' what you reckon, Pap."

"I kind'a reckon how she's packin' in another of them cakes with the white meat and the brown hide. Maybe I'm wrong but that's what I reckon. If it's what I think, then I won't be choppin' these pesky weeds no more today. 'Cause just as she gits goin', her and our gal, that's when I'll make tracks for the shanty. I aim to git me a dose of sickness today. . . . That Lilybelle makes the best cake in the world, so the Lord will forgive my iniquity if I git drunk on it. . . . So praise the Lord; thank them Skinners for their kindly natures."

We didn't hoe weeds. We just watched the shanty and soon we saw Lilybelle and my sister drive off in the pick-up truck bound for the Skinner brothers' ranch. Pap threw down his hoe, spit on his hands and high-tailed it across the patch.

We found Maw Maw all alone in the shanty; and sure enough, there smack in the middle of the table sat a big chocolate-covered cake. Pap howled for joy. He gave a quick glance to where his shotgun hung on the wall, but he didn't take it down. He got out his knife instead. When he got *really* close to the cake he howled like he'd never done before.

"Woman!" he hollered at Maw Maw. "Newt!" he yelled at me. "Damn it to hell!" he squawked at both of us. "Don't you'all see what I see?"

"I ain't blind, neither is Newt," Maw Maw said. She halfway chuckled like an old hen. "For a fact, it's a most delicious cake, but Lilybelle figgered how you'd like what's writ on top."

Pap couldn't read much, because he'd never gone to school. But book-ignorance couldn't faze Pap—he *sure* could make out what Lilybelle said in white icin' atop that chocolate-brown cake. Because the words said: FOR PAP.

"Goddamn the sonofabitchin' hell!" Pap shouted. "Them's the prettiest words I ever sawed in all my life."

He danced slightly while he fixed to cut the cake. "This is *my* cake, folks, 'cause Lilybelle writ how she made it for me. But I aim to give you some, just to let you know how good it tastes. When Lilybelle comes back again, that's when I'm goin' to kiss her neck. I'm gonna pat her blue-rusty if it's the last Christian act I do in this here life."

Pap said that, all right, but Maw Maw and me knew how it would take a heap of days for Pap to get up bravery enough to meet Lilybelle face to face. We knew how when he'd see her comin' he'd hightail it for the patch, or go hide behind the shed. And we knew too, me and Maw Maw both, that he wouldn't come out of hidin' 'til she'd drive off in her pickup truck.

"I'd sure love to have that girl for kinfolks," Pap said. He was eatin' cake like a hog while he said it, he had chocolate smeared all over his chin. But Pap was the kind of man who didn't give a damn. So he quizzed Maw Maw. "Woman, do you reckon how Clyde will commit matrimony with Verbaline Lou today? Do you reckon they'll git to be man and wife by sundown? Or do you reckon I'll need wait 'til I'm past my prime before I can take that sweet Lilybelle on my lap and call her my own daughter, second to Verbaline Lou, 'cause Verbaline Lou done married up with Clyde?"

"No, I don't think they'll git wed today," Maw Maw said after she'd cut her some cake. She acted pure-sow when she got it in her mouth.

"What about you, Newt? What do you reckon about our girl and Clyde?" Pap asked. He was a man hell-bent to be enlightened.

"They won't git wed-up today," I told him, "or tomorrow or the next."

I told him as best I could with a mouthful of cake and hoped for Pap to understand. I went on to say, "They got a heap of things to do before they can go honeymoonin' off somewheres, before Clyde can sleep in the same bed with Verbaline Lou and not have the sweet Lord hollerin' down from heaven about their sinful ways. First, Clyde will need to propose to Verbaline Lou, then she'll have to say yes, and then . . ."

"She'll say yes as sure as I'm eatin' cake," Maw Maw said, cuttin' me off. She had the chocolatest-lookin' mouth of any woman alive. She was sow for a fact.

"You're damn right," Pap said. "Then they'll need to git a license, and Clyde will buy hisse'f an ice-cream suit, and Verbaline Lou'll git one of them gowns what brides wear, all fluff and white as her virginity."

"I'm proud to say how's she still got *that*," Maw Maw said, "which is more'n can be said for most of the female tribe." Maw Maw figgered how Lilybelle might have been that way, too, when she wedded up with Sonny Boy, still had that there thing.

"Where do you reckon them two will commit matrimony, Maw Maw?" Pap quizzed. "Do you reckon they'll go to the justice of the peace or to the Reverend Sam Hill? Will they head for the county courthouse or for the Signal Rock Souls Redemption Center Tabernacle?"

"They won't git the judge to marry 'em up, not if I know Verbaline Lou," Maw Maw said. "She'll git a

Christian preacher, a Baptist like the Reverend Sam Hill. And she don't need no courthouse, 'cause our Verbaline Lou is more Christian than she is legal."

When Pap got done eatin' most of the cake he said how he'd better get to his bed, because pretty damn quick he'd be catchin' a dose of sickness. But he had no more said the words when Cousin Drewey came in through the back door, out of his tow-sacks and up for a day of livin'. But he wasn't the same old Cousin Drewey. He didn't have that calm look he mostly wore when he came in for breakfast. He looked kind'a worried and wild, like he'd seen a ghost.

"Folks," he said, "hold on a minute. 'Cause I've done got somethin' to say. But before I say it, please foller me out to the front porch.

Us Lowdermilks followed Cousin Drewey to the front porch.

"See what I see?" he said, pointin' to the road outside our front gate.

"I *sure* do," Pap said.

"I ain't blind," I said.

"Me neither," said Maw Maw. "And I can see the hand-writ on the wall, just like in Daniel 5:5. Folks, the hand-writ is fearsome to behold."

That's when Cousin Drewey smiled like he wasn't afeared. "I can take care of *them*," he said.

What we saw out by the front gate was two men. They'd come up ahorseback but they were both dismounted and studyin' somethin' on the dirt of the road.

"They're cowpunchers," Cousin Drewey said. "They work for wages paid by Fats Recknagel. What they're doin' there is studyin' some muleprints at the gate, the same prints as they caught out in the pasture. They've foller'd 'em clean from there to here. They've come to the end of the line. All they need now is for old Fats and the sheriff to come. . . ."

Cousin Drewey stopped his talk. He stopped because

his soothsayin' had come to pass. For right then a big Cadillac-car came up beside the cowpunchers and on its front seat sat Fats Recknagel. Next to him sat the sheriff. They got out and saw what the cowpunchers had to show them. Fats pointed in through the gate where old Jeff's tracks showed plain, clean up to the dugout; it where the meat hung inside. Then Fats and the sheriff got in the car. They drove away. The cowpunchers mounted their horses, whipped the butts with the bridle reins and were out of sight in a cloud of dust.

"Like I said," Cousin Drewey told us Lowdermilks, "I ain't feared a mite. I ain't feared of Fats or the law, or of any cowpuncher alive who wears a saddle-pounded royal-rusty 'cause I know how to handle sonsofbitches like them. The law needs a search warrant to come inside that gate, to go down the dugout and look at the beef. Now listen to me and do what I say.

"When I found that there calf in Fats Recknagel's pasture, he was fat and sassy, a full-blood Black Angus, registered. He belonged to Fats Recknagel, that was his nationality. But as soon as I fired a shot from my old hog-leg forty-five that calf turned color, he wasn't a citizen of Fats Recknagel no more. *He was Lowdermilk beef, and as Lowdermilk beef he hangs in the dugout today*. Remember that fact like you remember the eighth commandment . . . and leave all future negotiations to old Cousin Drewey Stiff who can scratch the sheriff like Job scratched his boils."

"What about the hide?" said Pap. "First thing the law will ask you is where the hell is that there hide. If you ain't got the hide you'll git in trouble. If you bring out the hide and it's got Fats Recknagel's spade brand on it, then you'll git behind bars like a cooped-up rooster. They'll ask you where's the Lowdermilk hide, branded, so's to prove your innocence and there ain't so much thing as a Lowdermilk brand. Cousin Drewey, we're in trouble up to our crusty necks. We're all that and more so, or I don't know the law."

Cousin Drewey laughed. "I ain't never hear'd a better speech like that before, Cousin Lowdermilk. You don't know the law and you don't know your ass from your elbow. You're so damn foolish you forgot to brand your calf, that which I butchered last Saturday night so's we could all eat beef. Fact is, I buried that Black Angus hide out where no man can find it, all except for one teensy piece of skin and hair. *And I ate it.* I ate it so's I wouldn't git caught tellin' a lie. It was plumb delicious, so delicious that the thought makes me hungry. Right now, folks, I'm rarin' for breakfast. I just thought I'd tell you how ignorant you are; how you don't know nothin' about beef hides. But you've got sense aplenty if you shut your mouths like lockjawed mules and leave the talkin' to old Drewey Stiff."

12

By what Verbaline Lou told us Lowdermilks, she did a heap for herse'f out at the Skinner ranch that day. We were eatin' supper when she got back, just me and Maw Maw and Cousin Drewey. Pap was still in his bed, laid out with his cake-sickness. He snored like he had somethin' gummed up in his glottis, whistlin' and growlin' kind'a, and we could hear him clean into the kitchen. We figgered how he'd likely stay in bed all night.

Us Lowdermilks are Christian folk, so it was the Lord's own sweet plan to keep Clyde Skinner alive when He laid Pap down sicker'n a horse. 'Cause if Pap had been up and eatin' supper when Verbaline Lou got home he'd have got up and reached for his shotgun. He'd have done that, cake or no cake, even if it had sat with FOR PAP writ on the top, 'cause it was Clyde Skinner *hisse'f* who rode Verbaline Lou home in the pickup truck. When Verbaline Lou bid Clyde a sweet fare-you-well for the night, that's when they held hands a long time before Verbaline Lou turned and stepped up on the porch. Before Clyde gunned the pickup out to the road like he was tickled silly about somethin'.

When Maw Maw saw how it was Clyde outside and not Lilybelle, she said, "Lord God, it's a heavenly blessin' how Pap is down sick like a horse. Th mighty reckless for Clyde to come packin' our girl home, them not havin' Lilybelle for a . . . what d'you call them things?"

"A chaperoney," Cousin Drewey said.

"That's what I mean. They oughtn't to be ridin' together alone, not 'til they commit matrimony. Myse'f, I don't care. It's just Pap."

"Pap gits pretty reckless with his shotgun," I said, me eatin' meat.

Cousin Drewey laughed my words down. "Hell-fire!" he said. "All that old saw-horse has used his shotgun to is bits of pink flimsy hangin' out on the clothesline. He couldn't hit a jackrabbit standin' still. He cain't go out and pack home the game, far less make target of a human-man. He's like the sorry hunter and the constipated owl; the hunter could shoot but he couldn't hit, and the owl could hoot but he couldn't . . ."

"Cousin!" Maw Maw hollered, 'cause she aimed to shut off his mouth. "That ain't no way to talk at a Christian table! Like I was sayin', the Lord ain't done paralyzed Pap's trigger-finger, not yet. If Verbaline Lou's got any virtue left after ridin' alone with Clyde Skinner then Pap will shoot to keep that virtue in her britches. Mark my words, that's what he'd do. But praise the Lord for His unboundful mercy! Praise the Lord for makin' Pap sicker'n a horse!"

Verbaline Lou came in carryin' another package for us to guess about. Like before, she took it to her room, passed the table by, not to give us a howdy. We took time off from eatin' meat, packed looks that said what the hell! We were *that* perplexed.

We noticed mostly the package when our girl passed the table by. But when she came out of her room to have supper with us that's when we truly gaped for surprise.

Maw Maw yelled, "Good God Almighty, daughter! What'all has done happened to your looks?" All I could say was "Goddamn!" Cousin Drewey didn't say nothin'.

We couldn't he'p ourselves. Verbaline Lou was a sight for sore eyes. She caught a chair and sat down at the table. "It's Lilybelle. It's what she did to my hair. It's called a shampoo. Ain't it pretty?"

"No," Maw Maw told her. "It ain't pretty. It's pure Jezebel. It's heathen doin's and I don't thank Lilybelle a mite. Times are sinful enough without a girl gittin' her hair washed."

"Have some fried meat, gal," said Cousin Drewey, pushin' the platter over our girl's way. "Here's some Lowdermilk beef, that's its born nationality."

"Where's Pap?" quizzed Verbaline Lou.

"Down," said Maw Maw. "Weakly with sickness, like the last time when Lilybelle came over."

Verbaline Lou laughed. "Lilybelle ain't that bad, is she?"

"Ain't her," said Maw Maw. "It's the cake. Pap likes cake too much, that's all. He's hog, full-blood."

I looked up at Verbaline Lou's mouth. "What's that redness?"

"It's lipstick. Girls use lipstick these days. It's modern."

"Is it sticky?" Maw Maw said.

"No, it's pretty."

"It ain't pretty smeared over your chin," Maw Maw said. "And it ain't pretty what I'm thinkin'. How come Clyde took you home, not Lilybelle?"

" 'Cause that's the way things are workin'," Verbaline Lou said. She smiled like she'd said somethin' smart. Cousin Drewey laughed out loud but didn't say a damn thing. Myse'f, I had my mouth put to chewin' meat.

"Daughter," said Maw Maw, "you still got that there thing?"

"What thing?"

COUSIN DREWEY & THE HOLY TWISTER 93

"Down in your britches."

This time Cousin Drewey *really* bust a gut. He laughed 'til he choked, 'til he drank some coffee for relief. "That ain't none of your damn business, cousin," he said to Maw Maw. "If Verbaline Lou lost what she owned, that's her business—and Clyde's—not yours or mine. And it ain't no concern of that silly sonofabitch what got hisse'f sick on cake. If she lost it to Clyde, she lost it legal, 'cause Clyde is fixed to be her lovin' man. She didn't lose it in the ditch and she didn't sell it in the cathouse. If she gave it away in the back of Clyde's pickup, then it ain't the first time in history a pickup was used for that kind of freight. If the Lord is smilin' on them two lovebirds now, then you and me and Newt ought to do the same. That cake-sick old bastard on yonderly bed don't know how to smile. He ought to git whupped, whupped on the ass with a dead rabbit."

"You got your virgin-bud?" Maw Maw asked Verbaline Lou.

Verbaline Lou chewed on some meat. She slid some grease potatoes into her plate. She didn't seem to pay Maw Maw no mind.

"It's *her* bud and it's private," said Cousin Drewey, talkin' up for Verbaline Lou. "Leave the girl alone, then think back to your own fryin'-size years. There's talk 'round the Washtaw Mountains. Folks tell how you wasn't no gal to let the fellers be, 'cause you horsed aplenty and craved stud. Maybe it was, but likely it wasn't Pap Lowdermilk who took you for the first time in your maidenhood, 'cause the grapevine said in them days how you had more sparks than a powerline; how one sunny day, bedded down among the daisies up the sawmill branch, you and Deacon Hightower . . ."

Maw Maw turned red. Her face got that way for a fact, and all because her mind packed memories. She yelped like a kicked dog, hollerin' crazy, and her noise nigh woke Pap off his bed. . . . But not quite.

When she got quiet again she said, "Daughter, you can tell us here what you did today. Did you have a happy time?"

Verbaline Lou said, "You bet." Then she told all about the goin's-on at the Skinner brothers' ranch, all about she and Clyde and Lilybelle, all about Sonny Boy and the kids, about the cattle and horses out in the pasture.

"After Lilybelle washed my hair," Verbaline Lou told, "while the doodads were holdin' my curls together, me and Clyde went out to the pasture. We went in the pickup truck."

"Just you and him alone?" Maw Maw quizzed. It was that old superstition comin' back to her mind.

"No," Verbaline Lou said. " 'Cause me and Clyde just sat the seat, Clyde drivin'. Sonny Boy laid in the back so's to stretch out his ligaments. He had the crutches layin' at his side. Them fellers wanted to show me the stock, specially the quarter horse stock. Sonny Boy's mighty proud of his horses. He's got eight breedin' mares, all registered. They're the prettiest horses I ever seen in all my life. And Sonny Boy is bleedin' with sorrow. He's that way 'cause he cain't git a stud-horse to find them mares some colts."

Maw Maw caught a better frame of mind. It was Sonny Boy's horses that did the trick. Like me and Cousin Drewey, she was takin' in all Verbaline Lou had to say. If a man owns quarter horse stock, that man is rich. He's got money and he needs the best grass to graze them. If a man's got quarter horse stock he's got everythin'. Because there's no horse on God's earth that makes a better mount than that kind of manufacture. No other mare can be matched for breedin' like the eight pretty ones Sonny Boy owned. They're slick, packed with sense, so nimble as to turn on a dime, they're fast on the

COUSIN DREWEY & THE HOLY TWISTER   95

foot like a double-jointed greyhound—and, most blessed of all, when they get sold they bring money enough to buy out the mail-order catalogue.

"How come he cain't find a stud-horse nowheres?" Maw Maw asked.

Verbaline Lou told all what the Skinner boys told her. "To git the kind of blood his mares need, to do 'em right with a stud-horse, Sonny Boy said how he'd need to go clean to Texas, eastbound. I don't know what, but it has somethin' to do with the register-certificate. There ain't none in this state fit to do what a Texas stud can do, and there ain't none what Sonny Boy can hire in Star Valley. That's the truth, that's the deacon's fact."

"Too bad there ain't any," Maw Maw said.

"But that ain't the truth," Verbaline Lou said. "There's the bestest stud right here in our midst, just the right horse to find Sonny Boy's mares some colts. But Sonny Boy cain't git to use him. He's tried to do business with the feller who owns that stud. But the feller told Sonny Boy to make tracks when Sonny Boy offered a price. Sonny Boy went back and back again, 'til the feller said how he'd git the sheriff if he ever had to look at Sonny Boy's silly face one more time. He said it out loud."

I kind'a grinned over my greased greens. Cousin Drewey looked at me.

"Who's the feller?" Maw Maw asked. "Who's the feller who won't hire the stud out to Sonny Boy?"

"Fats Recknagel," Verbaline Lou said. "He's got the prettiest stud you ever saw, but . . ."

"But a man cain't hire that stud-horse's weapon for no price on the docket," Cousin Drewey said. He looked like the thought made him mad. "He cain't rent the service 'cause it's Fats Recknagel's horse's weapon, 'cause it don't belong to nobody else. That silly bastard! And I ain't talkin' about Sonny Boy."

"Fats told Sonny Boy how he has the best quarter horses west of the Texas state line, and how he aims to keep 'em that way. He said if he let the Skinner boys use his stud, no matter how much money they paid him, then he'd have competition. Then he'd have a neighbor who had just as good quarter horses as him; maybe better, 'cause he hadn't seen Sonny Boy's mares, only hear'd tell about 'em, and Fats didn't crave to be equal or second to anybody. He *had* to be the best. That's when he told Sonny Boy to git goin'. Fats said how he loved nothin' better than to sic the sheriff on his neighbors."

I looked over at Cousin Drewey. "What'all you think about that, Cousin Drewey?" I said. "Don't you reckon there's some way Sonny Boy can git hold of that studhorse, so's to use the weapon on his mares?"

But Cousin Drewey didn't pay my quiz no mind. He seemed to be thinkin' deep; he didn't chew Lowdermilk beef, he didn't fork greens into his mouth. Because his visions seemed to be somewhere else. He was thinkin' harder than a man does when he works on a Bible psalm; he was tryin' to figger it out.

He looked up and he said, "Sweet gal, where'all does Fats Recknagel graze that stud-horse? Does he keep him in a shed and pour the grain and hay to him, or does he let him run out on that irrigated grass inside the high fence next to his house? If I just knew as to which was which, then I think I can make of Sonny Boy the kind'a feller he ain't."

Verbaline Lou looked at me. She seemed kind'a leary of what she should tell. I winked at her; I told her by that wink how she'd better tell Cousin Drewey as to which was which, because Fats Recknagel was sorry meat, just a man who deserved the worst of hell.

"He keeps the stud in the shed all winter," she said. "Leastways, that's what Sonny Boy reckoned. But when summer comes 'round he lets him run out on the pasture."

"Day and night?" Cousin Drewey said.

"I reckon," said Verbaline Lou.

Cousin Drewey got up off his chair. He went to the wall and looked at the calendar. "It ain't winter yet," he said. "And it's the Lord's blessin' it ain't."

When he came back to the table we could all see how he hadn't had enough supper. He just he'ped himself to more. He wore a contented look on his face.

Verbaline Lou squirmed uneasy. "You won't git Sonny Boy in trouble, will you Cousin Drewey?"

"Nope. I just said I'll make of him what he ain't. I'll make of him the owner of the best horse-stock in Star Valley; a man fit to spit in Fats Recknagel's eye."

"What you got in that package, sister?" I asked Verbaline Lou.

"What package?"

"That which you carried from the pickup to your room."

"It's female stuff. It ain't none of your concern. But you'll watch it struttin' 'round come next Saturday's dance," Verbaline Lou said.

"I don't like what Lilybelle did to your looks," Maw Maw said. "I never thought I'd call my daughter Jezebel."

"You might call her more'n *that* someday," Cousin Drewey said to Maw Maw. "You might tell her how she looks like a prime lady when she gits all dressed up. Right now the Skinner folks are just curryin' a mossback; and the best way to curry a mossback is to start with the head and work down to the toes. I hear tell how the finished product is gentle enough to meet up with New York society."

13

It stands reasonable to believe how us Lowdermilks never gave mind to drapin' our natural frames with cloth and leather 'til Clyde Skinner and his sister-in-law Lilybelle came into our lives to show us how it is done. Even Verbaline Lou didn't care none for dollin' up pretty 'til she got matrimonially inclined. She didn't give a damn how her hair set, or how her skirt swished 'round, or how her shoes weren't full-blood kin to each other. Vanity troubled her nary a mite, because that's the kind of girl she was raised to be, the Washtaw Mountain variety, manufactured by Pap and Maw Maw, and the way wives and husbands like Maw Maw and Pap raise daughters into womanhood is somethin' to behold. And me, I never cared if the seat of my pants was torn. I never cared if my ass shone out like the sun shines over the palmy deserts of Arizona.

So it stands to equal reason how Pap and Maw Maw, and me, folks loyal to the ways of the Washtaw Mountains, stood gapin' for the sight that walked up in front of us that Saturday night early. It was just before we were all fixed to go to the big dance. That's when Cousin Drewey came into the house from under the box elder tree.

Lord God, if that kinfolks wasn't oiled up for the prance!

COUSIN DREWEY & THE HOLY TWISTER 99

We were standin' next to the hot cookstove in the kitchen leanto. Just me and Pap. Maw Maw was in the settin'-'round room gettin' into a print-material gown and puttin' on clean shoes. Nighttime didn't call for a sunbonnet so she'd put a crease down the middle of her scalp and built a bun up behind. She looked like a woman, all right. But she looked nothin' like she was kin to Verbaline Lou. Me and Pap didn't doll up none. We were men. We stank of the farm and aimed to stay that way. Our overalls were dirty, our shirts packed some grease stains, and Pap's chin was stubbly like a barley field done harvested. Cud-juice and pot-likker had dried on his chin. The stains told how he was a tobacco-chewin' man, how he'd had greens for dinner that day. And me, I'd shaved and doused my face. But I hadn't put my heart and soul into it. I couldn't just *couldn't*.

Me and Pap warmed our rusties at the cookstove, toasted 'em and then turned 'round to comfort our bellies. We were doin' that'all when Cousin Drewey walked into the house.

"Good God Almighty," Pap yelled, on sight of our kinfolks.

Maw Maw heard Pap make his flabbergasted noise; that's when she ran in on us to see. She stood bug-eyed for a solid minute.

"Cousin Drewey," she said, agape like Pap, "what'all have you done to your natural looks?"

Cousin Drewey beamed. He looked us straight in our faces, then turned right so we could admire him from that angle. Then to the left. He aimed to show us how he'd become a gentleman all 'round.

"If that sonofabitch turns his back on us . . ." Pap said, "if he does, I'll use my foot to kick him smack in the ass. He's made me mad by showin' us his looks, and I don't need citified meat like him shelterin' under my roof."

But when Cousin Drewey turned 'round, to let us marvel at the back of his shirt, Pap didn't move to kick him in the ass.

"I got the makin's of all this from Clyde Skinner," Cousin Drewey said. "He brought it in a box and put it on my pallet under the box elder tree. I figgered he aimed for me to wear it to the dance. It's the right fit, boots and all, so I put 'em on and here I am." He made more circles for the admiration of our eyesight.

"He's dressed up like a cowpuncher," Maw Maw said.

Sure enough, there was Cousin Drewey shinin' in a glorious light. He'd shed his baggy overalls, he'd hung his blue shirt on the tree limb, he'd changed his socks and laid aside his canalboat shoes, them soled by himself over and over with automobile tires. He stood in tight striped pants, a purple shirt with a wide yellow trim, a belt buckle big as a steer's head, and green boots with high heels, them built to upboost his rearworks. Atop his head was a hat, high crowned with spangles on it, wider brimmed than a man naturally needs. Cousin Drewey had done turned himself into a Hollywood cowboy; he'd faked himself, and us Lowdermilks stood flabbergasted, shamed to call him kinfolks.

Pap tried to say somethin' but couldn't. I tried, but couldn't he'p out. So Maw Maw had to open her mouth and say somethin'.

"Why, Cousin Drewey!" she said, "ain't you old enough to know better?"

That tickled Cousin Drewey's funnybone. "Better?" he said. "Why, sweet cousin, this here get-up makes me feel like I'm just turned twenty-one, prime-peckered, with a young man's appetite for good looks. That's how I feel, though the good Lord knows I've hit the three-score-and-ten notch on our civilized calendar. I done hit it long since. I feel that good old button-sized itch again, and I aim to hunt me some calico before midnight. I'm gonna spend a dollar in the Busy Bee Café on Signal

COUSIN DREWEY & THE HOLY TWISTER 101

Rock Main Street and tell the hasher to go bring me some brains and eggs. I'll tell her to make the order double, 'cause I'll have my sweet fluff of calico on the seat beside me, us two in the Busy Bee Café. And we'll daub ketchup on our brains and eggs. Then we'll go back to the dance; and we'll hug-stomp some 'til we git to itchin' down yonder, and that's when we'll head for the outer reefs of Star Valley, where it's lonesome enough for poontang. And after we've had poontang, my calico fluff and me, we'll take back to the dance, lookin' drooped. Because my name is Young Drewey Stiff, of that wild band called the Border Stompers. I don't ride a horse, I don't fix fence, I don't pound my seat in the saddle. But I tickle a guitar; I sit up on the bandstand with the boys and I make my fiddle talk mountain language."

"He ain't a cowboy," Pap told us after he'd got wind. "He ain't even a Washtaw Mountain man no more. I try, but I cain't think what he can be. He's nothin', goddamn nothin', *that's* what Cousin Drewey has turned out to be."

But Maw Maw showed how she was on Cousin Drewey's side, *for* him full-blood. "He's a musical man," she said, "he's all that and more so. He's our kinfolks out of the Washtaw Mountains. I don't see his clothes, I just see his meat. He's kinfolks, and back in the Washtaw Mountains kinship is thicker'n . . ."

"Piss," cut in Pap. Pap was rude, because he'd shut Maw Maw up.

Cousin Drewey heard what Maw Maw had to say. He didn't care what kind of liquid Pap added to the complimentary soup. So as to show his appreciation to Maw Maw he let out a coyote yell, like any Young Drewey Stiff is likely to do. Or Roy Rogers, high up on Trigger. But he said nothin'. No words, he just yelled.

Cousin Drewey's cowboy drapin's weren't the kind we're used to in Star Valley. You see the striped pants and the green boots, the purple shirt with the yellow trim, you see 'em all on the movie-star-show cowboys. But you don't see 'em on the grass of the wide-away flats, or down the draws and canyons where the cattle shelter from the wind. Our kind of cowpunchers go for simpler clothes. They're workin' boys, not musical men. Their boot-heels are worn down, their pants-seats get thin from saddle-poundin'. They're mostly freedom boys; they don't wash much, and they smell slightly like bachelors. All bachelors, all widowers smell slightly, leastways in Star Valley. They ride a lot, dawn to dark, and for that reason they're dosed with the piles. Nigh every cowpuncher suffers mightily from the piles. And he never can keep his shirttail down his pants, because that thing rides up, always hangin' out. And he don't pack a lick of romance; he cozies up to the whores—he's the proud owner of a dose of clap. He talks a lot, but he's ignorant. He's prideful—he brags on himself, nigh most of the livelong day. He's mean to horses and dogs. And he's liable to stay a bachelor all his life, unless he's got salt enough to block up a ranch for himself and trade 'round with cattle. That way he can build a herd and get the ladies to like him.

But we handed Cousin Drewey our forgiveness. We knew for a fact how Clyde Skinner was aided and abetted by Sonny Boy's woman. She was behind the way our kinfolks looked. What they aimed was to have Cousin Drewey look like a movie-star-show musician, the kind who tickles a guitar and sings smart words out of his wide mouth. Clyde and Lilybelle craved Star Valley folks to drizzle compliments on Cousin Drewey's looks. And that's *exactly* what Star Valley folks did in the schoolhouse that Saturday night.

I might say now how that dance which the folks put on that Saturday night was the prime spectacle for that

COUSIN DREWEY & THE HOLY TWISTER 103

year. It was a gala event to outdo the county fair. Word got 'round that Old Man Lee Bassett and his woman were the artists responsible for the decorations. Strong women waxed the floor to a slickness fit to break any man's neck; and they'd sprinkled cornmeal to make feet slide easier than regular. All the light sixtures were fancied up with red, green, blue and pink crêpe paper; streamers ran thisaway and that across the big room, down from the ceilin' slightly. The streamers were of paper, too, with colors enough to chouse the monotony. It wasn't Christmas, it wasn't Easter, it wasn't the Fourth of July. It was just a Saturday-night dance at the Star Valley schoolhouse. And when Star Valley women set out to do somethin', they do that somethin' right.

I sat with Pap and Maw Maw on the bench against the wall. Everybody else was up and 'round, doin' somethin' smart. They acted neighborly, they openly congratulated Cousin Drewey for his cowboy outfit. They told for the fact how it made him look forty years younger.

"Forty years ago," Cousin Drewey said, back-joshin' the folks and thankin' kindly them who bragged on his looks, "I was a man in my prime, just thirty years old. I was the pride and passion of the Washtaw Mountain women. In them days I acted stud. I was hung like a Clydesdale, the lily of the valley, the bright and mornin' star. I didn't need clothes to make my beauty shine. I could eat like a dog. I never scowled at a bowl of greens. I gnawed on hog-jowl to beat hell. I never lost a cartwheel at stud-poker . . . and as for whiskey, home-stilled or bottle-bought, it took more'n a quart to warm my gullet. I preached the gospel just to he'p the preacher out, and when he needed sinners I rounded 'em up with my hog-leg forty-five. I told 'em what I knew about Joshua, I told 'em all about Rahab the harlot; I told 'em all that once I got 'em to the mourner's bench. For *pure* everyday wisdom I was excelled by no man; I knew my digits, I savvied my isms, I respected the laws on the dockets. I always had a coin or two in my pocket. But where I shined (and I'm talkin' about myse'f, Professor Drewey Stiff) was when I stud-horsed the womenfolks. When I employed my Clydesdale propensities, and the physical attributes thereof, and when I came off the perch I felt like I'd befriended society. Like I'd he'ped the husbands out, them of the Washtaw Mountains from the Red River east to Bradley County, from Tulip southbound to the Louisiana line. They were polite, they thanked me kindly for he'pin' them out. So don't call me names, you Star Valley husbands, don't call me forty years younger. Because you're just tryin' to patronize my conceit. You aim to make me feel like a man again. Maybe so, but you'll need to incarcerate your wives. You'd better put 'em in padlocks. Because I might just exercise the history I'm proud of, me and my Clydesdales, me and them studs. In those days I liked pretty scenery; I liked the lay of the land."

That kind of talk made the ladies go turkey-red, and they'd walk off shamed because Cousin Drewey's talk was entirely too raw. But the men would hold ground and laugh their bellies out at what our kinfolks said. They'd back-slap Cousin Drewey, they'd prod him hard for to give out more Washtaw Mountain slash-pine-cracker josheroo. And when Cousin Drewey saw how the menfolks were pleased, he'd open his mouth and confess to his poontang-doin's some more.

Us Lowdermilks sat silent on our bench against the wall. We were all there except Verbaline Lou, who was up at the Skinner ranch with Lilybelle and her kids—shamelessly with Clyde and his brother Sonny Boy. But we knew she'd be down directly. She'd be dressed in finery, all that Lilybelle had bought her, to show off before

Christians, knowin' how the Lord don't pack admiration for vanity. It seemed like the Skinner folks loved nothin' better than to dissipate their substance on riotous toggery, to dress folks up, even to a silly old fart named Cousin Drewey. Pap, me and Maw Maw, we sat like three pillars of salt—Genesis 19:26. We sat still and tended our own business, lookin' at folks havin' a good time.

Pap's gaze was aimed at the celin' where crêpe paper pretties hung on streamers from wall to wall. Everywhere, never more than three feet apart, dripped bloody hearts, like you see 'round about on Valentine's Day. They were cut out of cardboard and painted red. That's what caught us Lowdermilks guessin'; we tried to figger out what'all and what the hell. Sure enough, there were Valentine dances held every year in the very same schoolhouse room. But Valentine comes in February not like it was then, the tag end of summer.

"How come?" I quizzed Pap. I whispered low so's not to come out of our Lowdermilk pride.

"Romance," Pap whispered back.

"Who'all you reckon, Pap?"

Pap said back at me, "A nasty little chippy-bitch who don't pack sweet thoughts for old folks. She might be legal age, but she'll pull our proud name through hogswill in the troughs. I hate to think it; she's done joined up with high society."

"Name her, Pap," I said, knowin' dog-good who he meant.

"Cain't," said Pap.

"Why cain't?"

" 'Cause she's my own spit, me and Maw Maw's flesh and blood. She's the meat we dressed out of ten minutes poontang—matrimonially legal. But I don't own her no more, she ain't my big girl, she ain't my sugar tit, she ain't fit to wear the name of Lowdermilk."

That brand of talk was educational; it told how Pap meant my sister, who was shamin' herself with Clyde Skinner.

"It's what you call *love*, Pap," I said, actin' in defense of that poor girl. "She *loves* Clyde, and Clyde *loves* her back. They might be sinful, but they're *love*-sinful. It's *love*, like you've got for Maw Maw, what Maw Maw's got for you."

But Pap said nothin' agin my talk for Verbaline Lou. He didn't say nothin' about how pure love would be announced to everybody at the dance that night, how maybe those kids were married up already. Legal, preacher-finished. Or maybe they still walked unhitched and this night they'd make their intentions clear. Lawful as the world spins 'round. But the guts of the cardboard hearts was love. That's what they hung for. . . . Love. . . . That there. . . . *Love,* and nothin' else. . . . But I knew dog-good what Pap thought about love. He reckoned it to be a word with four letters in it. And more times than once, when Pap talked about love, he'd holler without shame a half-dozen other words, each with four letters, what he claimed meant the same thing.

The music hit the ceilin' all of a sudden. It circled 'round and bounced off the walls. Cousin Drewey was high on his perch. He sawed the fiddle and his purple shirt shone like a springtime iris. His boots were as green as the jungles of Africa. He sawed the dance and tapped his foot; he chewed tobacco, he spat straight and hit the can. Young Buster Prather tickled the banjo, Uncle Posey Burwinkle had his hands cupped to his mouth—he called that old "Yellerhammer Right, Jaybird Left" —and the folks stomped to keep the pine floor hot.

I didn't give a damn. There was too much noise. The folks couldn't hear, so I spoke loud at Pap. "Pap," I said, "I'm your blood-kin boy. You've told me more'n once what's wrong with this nation, how its politicians ain't doin' the people right. And just as often you've handed me your thoughts on the Resurrection and how we'll get hoisted to the Pearly Gates, that's if we don't act the sorry sonofabitch down here below. Now you've got 'em prancin' in front of you. Look 'em over, Pap, scrutinize their earthly ways, and tell me what you reckon about them fellers and womenfolks, and all them kids."

"Newt," he said, and he had his finger pointed at the circlin' congregation, "I'm lookin' at 'em, I've got their digits down pat, I know their isms, and they cain't fool me by hidin' their ignorance away from my eyesight. Son, ask me again. Ask me what I think of human-kind, and I'll tell how they're common as bat-shit, even that old tolerably-alkalied bastard standin' by the door yonder."

"That's Old Man Lee Bassett," I said to Pap. "He's been standin' there like the warden of the State Pen, welcomin' with a handshake all Star Valley folks what come to the dance."

"He ain't moved way all the time we've been here. He's feared he'll miss a victim; and it strikes me plumb-clockwise how he's waitin' for somebody special, like maybe your sister, maybe my sugar-tit gal."

"And Clyde Skinner," I said to Pap.

"You notice somethin', Newt? You notice how Lilybelle and them kids of her'n ain't here?"

"They ain't here," I said, "that's a fact."

"They ain't here because they're doin' bridal honors, all them Skinners, even Sonny Boy, that pistol-prick on crutches."

"You reckon Verbaline Lou's done wedded up with Clyde, Pap?"

"I reckon."

"Made that way by the justice of the peace?"

"Likely."

"That'll break Maw Maw's heart," I said. "She don't believe in folks gettin' wedded by no justice of the peace. Folks need to get wedded by the preacher, in the Lord's house, 'cause matrimony is the Lord's business. A preacher naturally speaks for the Lord. It's somethin' about matrimony. It's love, that's what it is, Pap."

"I don't need no love-talk," Pap says, "and I don't need it out of my own flesh and blood. Love is a four-letter word. It don't rhyme with shit but it means the same thing."

I couldn't keep my eyes off Old Man Lee. All I saw was him and that big black hole in the wall, the open door. Then I saw Old Man Lee turn and he went outside to scrutinize the situation, because the headlights of somebody's car was brightenin' up the schoolyard. Its light showed up all the cars and pickup trucks parked there.

The music went 'round and the dance turned wild and furious. Cousin Drewey sawed his instrument; his foot tapped, keepin' time, and his jaw moved as it chewed cud to the action of his bow.

Old Man Lee came back in, but he wasn't alone. He was handpumpin' and backslappin' to beat hell. Somebody new had come, in fact two of 'em. They both wore John B. Stetson hats; not the movie-star kind like Cousin Drewey's. But the pure-D John B. They were Western men. They had gimlet eyes and they didn't smile. One was little, the other big, but the six-gun revolvers they holstered on their belts looked like they talked a fiery kind of language. And the badges pinned to their shirts glistened in the lamplight. They handpumped with Old Man Lee; and they pumped because they were politicians. They backslapped because they were *that* make of toad.

"You see what I see, Pap?" I said.

COUSIN DREWEY & THE HOLY TWISTER

"I ain't blind."

"It's the sheriff, come to the dance."

"Reckon he aims to arrest somebody?"

"Likely, but who'all?"

"You reckon he's here to arrest Cousin Drewey, Newt?"

"He couldn't arrest nobody else. It was Cousin Drewey who acted sinful. He's meat for the jailer because of rustled beef."

"Well hell, which one you reckon is the sheriff, Newt?"

"The little one."

"And who's the big one?"

"That's his piss-ant deputy."

14

There's somethin' truthful said about a sheriff—any sheriff, anywhere—a fact most potent in boondocks counties, like the one in which Star Valley stretches north and south; and myse'f, I find it easy to believe. And that fact is that any sheriff elected on the ballot is secondly a "law," and first and primely a goddamn "politician." I've looked the situation over myse'f and hear'd the neighbors agree with my philosophy. A sheriff is a man who spits on his badge to keep it clean, shines it to a polish—and many sheriffs have principles of the same bright glisten. And equally as many, like our symbol of law and order, have characters as black as the scum in a stagnant water hole.

Pap Lowdermilk hates politicians. He hates them worse than he hates bankers, and that's sayin' plenty. I've suffered Pap's opinions like a dutiful son should, and to this day can't figger exactly *why* Pap should hate a politician.

Only once in my sorry recollection did Pap come nigh a gun-feud with a man appointed to public office. That was when he committed a nuisance of himse'f and was loaded into the Signal Rock jail by the town constable, a sorry bastard to use the mildest designation. But the fuss was kindled by a goddamn high-mogul of the First

COUSIN DREWEY & THE HOLY TWISTER 111

National Bank in Signal Rock.

Pap's hate of bankers started maybe four or five years ago, when the frost caught the bean crop and left us nary a healthy pod. Beans make our winter livin'—for breakfast, dinner and supper—and without beans we can starve to death as easy as a cat in a mouseless territory. Us Lowdermilks were on the brink of starvation. The winter comin' up would be cold like winters never fail to be in Star Valley. If we couldn't find no automobile tires thrown out somewheres we'd have to chop stovewood or freeze into ice. And believe me, third to hatin' bankers and politicians, Pap hated exercisin' an elbow with axe, sledge and wedge. The neighbors might complain about the stink of burnin' rubber, but Pap didn't give a damn. Us Lowdermilks were wastin' away in poverty, and that's all there was to it.

One day of asudden we had a visitor; it was Old Man Lee Bassett, and he looked 'round and felt sorry for our plight. When Pap told him about the bean crop, it gone to the realm of no return, Old Man Lee whistled his Christian sympathy.

"It ain't only the beans," Pap said. "We need money to buy a ton of old, worn-out automobile tires from the wreckin' yard. If we don't get some stove fuel we'll freeze like the beans, and there ain't no death more painful."

We were sittin' out on the porch—me and Pap and Maw Maw, while our kindly neighbor-visitor was hunkered down next to the step. Old Man Lee had some snuff in a little can and gave us a dip all 'round. We were plumb out of chew-tobacco.

"I *sure* wish you wouldn't burn them automobile tires, Pap, and I speak for the whole valley," said Old Man Lee. "There ain't a stink worse than that burnin' rubber come out of your chimney-pipe. You ought to hate it yourse'f."

"I hate huntin' stovewood worser," Pap told Old Man Lee.

"A fire built of cedar smells sweeter," Old Man Lee said.

"I don't smell sweet myse'f," Pap augured, "so I don't ask my chimney to be what I ain't. It's easier to trade beans to the wreckin' yard man, but we ain't got no beans to trade."

Old Man Lee heard what Pap had to say, so he bent his head in thought. He acted pure-Methodist; he aimed to do us charity; he craved to he'p us out. After a minute he raised his head; he opened his mouth and said: "Folks, I got an idea. You own this land—you've got the deed and it's good land."

"That's a fact," Pap said.

"You've got collateral," Old Man Lee gave us to know.

Pap looked at me and I looked at him—then we both looked at Maw Maw. In a flick we turned our heads and all three looked at Old Man Lee Bassett.

"Is it catchin'?" Pap quizzed.

I'd never heard that word before; I knew Pap hadn't, neither had Maw Maw. We let our Copenhagen drip, and I wondered if that jawbustin' word had to do with the wastin' disease. . . . But we didn't stay ignorant for long, because Old Man Lee figgered we were mossbacks and needed education.

"Hell!" hollered Old Man Lee, "that ain't no ailment. It's a big word the bankers use. It means you can go to the bank and tell the presi*dent* how you need some money so's to keep you and your woman and your two kids from starvin' to death. You can tell him how you're a good farmer—which you are—and how it was the frost that killed the bean crop. Any good farmer loses his bean crop to the frost now and then. The banker will understand, 'cause he knows farmin' and farmers, and it's his business to he'p 'em out when they need it. He's got the money, and all a farmer has to do is ask him for a thousand, two thousand, or maybe five thousand dollars."

Pap whistled for the sound of all those dollars. "The hell you say!" he shouted.

"That jaw-bustin' word," Old Man Lee went further to explain, "means you've got security enough to pay back the note. That is if you don't go ahead and let the frost ruin your bean crop next year, and you ain't got the cash to pay the banker back. The banker, then, can take your land for the payment and the Lord will bless you both. But I know you, Pap Lowdermilk. I know how you won't let the frost make hash of the beans next year. I know how you'll go to the First National Bank and ask for Mr. Wilbur Pruitt, the cashier, and tell him you need some money. I know you'll do that there, tomorrow or not later than next week, and how you'll take Newt and Maw Maw and Verbaline Lou with you. How you'll all get dressed up in your best overalls and calico, and how if you've got a necktie you'll put it on. I know how you'll ask Mr. Wilbur Pruitt for the loan of enough money to feed, shelter and warm you for all this winter, and have more left over to buy a team of mules and farm implements, enough to break another forty acres to bean crop, borrow enough to civilize you and make you into farmers and banish your mossback category for all time to come. You can even ask the banker for some extra spendin' money, to get a prime radio set, maybe a pressure cooker for Maw Maw."

So when Old Man Lee told us more about that big word called "collateral," and even said how we could use his name for a high recommendation—if we'd only quit burnin' them stinkin' automobile tires—it was all it took to put us in a financial frame of mind. Us Lowdermilks, right there and then, pledged ourse'fs to go to the First National Bank of Signal Rock and ask for Mr. Wilbur Pruitt.

"We cain't go tomorrow," Pap said after Old Man Lee Bassett had rode home in his pickup truck, " 'cause I'll need time to look through the mail-order catalogue and see what we need. But we can go see Mr. Wilbur Pruitt next week and ask him if he'll let us have five thousand dollars, 'cause the frost done ruined the bean crop."

My sister Verbaline Lou is the smartest of us Lowdermilks, so Pap had her he'p him with the mail-order catalogue. He asked me what I craved most, so I told him a motor-sickle. Pap asked Verbaline Lou to find a motor-sickle in the mail-order catalogue. She found a sweet outfit called Number R28-A-9438-N, which cost $259.95, and it weighed 172 pounds. The next page of the catalogue showed a special kind of hat, boots, belt and leather coat to go with it—all black—made to look handsome on a feller ridin' that red motor-sickle. When Pap asked Verbaline Lou what she needed, she said how she'd like an electric guitar. So we all hunted an electric guitar, and doggone if we didn't find one on page 1300. It cost $194.95; it had triple pickup and there was a 120-watt music-power amplifier to go with it, for an extra $239.95, and the shippin' weight of both wasn't as much as my motor-cickle. That's when Pap said he'd buy them for his sugar-tit gal, and maybe she'd sing her way to fame and fortune, just like girls do in the movie-star romance magazines.

"Kids," Pap said, "I know what I want—'cause I want a prime radio worse than a widderwoman needs relief from her pangs. I've already got it writ on the order blank. . . . But what we got to find out now is what Maw Maw craves; and she don't need to tell me, 'cause I know that woman like I do the back of my hand. We'll get Maw Maw a pretty electric washin' machine, and an

COUSIN DREWEY & THE HOLY TWISTER 115

electric pressure cooker—and what she needs, too, is an electric sewin' machine."

So we filled out the order blank just like the mail-order company said to do, and it added up to a tolerable financial statement.

"Pap," I said, tryin' to get his attention while he danced 'round like crazy for the pure joy of gettin' $5,000 all asudden.

"What, son?" he said, slowin' down from dancin' like crazy. "You got somethin' on your mind, somethin' else you need out of this mail-order catalogue?"

"Pap," I said, "we ain't got no electricity. We cain't run my sister's guitar. And Maw Maw's outfits won't run without sparks. So I don't reckon we'd better get 'em just to set 'round doin' nothin'."

Pap thought a minute. Then he spried up.

"Folks," he said, "listen to me, to the ramrod of this family. Just listen to what'all I have to say. What we'll do is get Mr. Wilbur Pruitt to string the wires this way. It won't cost him much. I need them sparks for my prime radio set. I need them in the worst way, and Mr. Wilbur Pruitt will thank me for the business."

"It's more'n a mile to the highline, Pap," I said. "It'll cost more'n this farm is worth to bring the wires this way."

"You shut your silly mouth, Newt," Pap said back to me. "You don't know sparks from silver moonlight. I'm feelin' good; we're all feelin' good and we don't need your sass or your snide remarks."

I felt sad all the while I harnessed old Jeff, the mule, to the single-shaft wagon and then I put the old automobile seat in the back-bed, for me and my sister to sit on. Pap acted sillier as I've ever witnessed before. He got us all seated down for the ride to Signal Rock, then stood up to make us a speech.

"Lowdermilks," he said, "Lowdermilks, just let me give you a word. Just let me advise you'all before we tackle this high-up executive business. First place, none of us, except me, knows how to talk with bankers. It takes special kind of talk. You've got to watch your Ps and Qs 'cause we all know a banker packs a gimlet eye."

He stopped for breath. I knew if I said somethin', like tellin' him to hush and get goin', he'd try to hurt my feelin's. So I said nary a word; I just let him act the goddamn fool.

"Any human bein' with a hound-dog's reason knows how to act 'round bankers," Pap went on. "First thing, most of all, a banker admires a pure-D Christian. If a man ain't got a lick of Christianity inside his mind and frame, even if he don't know Boaz from Belshazzar, he'd better make out how he does. Folks, once we get inside the bank I'd be highly proud if you'd keep your talk down your windpipes. There ain't *one* of you what's got business sense. So just you let *me* do the talkin' with Mr. Wilbur Pruitt, and I'll promise you how some sweet sundown, next week or the week after, just soon as the mail-order house can ship us the plunder, we'll all be feedin' our ears on the radio set, 'cause we'll just get Mr. Wilbur Pruitt to string the sparks our way."

That's when Pap sat down, took up the reins and guided old Jeff off to the highway that led to Signal Rock.

To look at us Lowdermilks you'd think we were headin' for the Reverend Sam Hill's Signal Rock Souls Redemption Center Tabernacle; like we aimed to drop a dime in the Reverend Sam's hat instead of haulin' $5,000 out of Mr. Wilbur Pruitt's till-box. Because Pap was dressed up slightly like Sunday. He wore his jellybean hat and a necktie, and the necktie showed a kind of shiny green above the bib of his clean overalls. Maw Maw was clean draped in never-worn-before cotton print. Verbaline Lou had on her print dress with the big bow tied on her back-hip, and Maw Maw had done up that girl's hair with a bun, just like her'n. Except a man could tell how Verbaline Lou was naturally pretty, and all it took was somebody (like Lilybelle) to put her out of the mossback. Verbaline Lou couldn't talk much, because Pap made the noise 'round the shanty. But when Verbaline Lou *did* say somethin', she said it softly with plenty sense. She didn't sound like us'ns.

Pap drove the wagon 'round the block four times before he jerked the lines on Jeff and pulled up front of the bank. He fixed it so Jeff's head would droop over the fire hydrant, so's to loop the lines 'round-about that instrument and hold that mule there while Pap and us balance went inside the bank to talk Christianity and high finance with the mogul hisse'f. On either side were two automobiles, but spite of 'em, we had room to get down. I saw how one big automobile was the Cadillac-car that belonged to Fats Recknagel. The other was just as fancy —a Lincoln, I reckon—that must have belonged to Mr. Wilbur Pruitt. You know how those bankers do, they park their automobiles outside the bank.

Folks looked our way as we got down off the wagon. They sort of said to each other: "Look at them Lowdermilks, will you! They're all dressed up to talk highmogul business. They're headed for the First National Bank."

It taxed Pap's strength to push open the big brass door. That door was shiny-slick, polished by the janitor. But there's no door anywhere that can faze Pap. So he led the way inside. We looked 'round, and all the bank flunkies looked up from their desks. They scrutinized us out of their cages, or out from behind glass-paneled doors.

"Howdy," Pap said, and he said it to every human bein' in sight.

The bank stank of money, the stinkin'est commodity on earth. It stank of paper and typewriters and glue and scissors, and it stank of perfumed women and of men in jellybean suits. It wasn't no kin to the farm, because inside that bank the frost couldn't get the beans. But there was salvation there for us Lowdermilks that comin' winter. That is if Pap would just talk sense to Mr. Wilbur Pruitt and not make a goddamn sonofabitchin' jackass of himself.

"Where'all will I find Mr. Wilbur Pruitt?" I heard Pap ask a pale-skinned jellybean in a white collar and dark blue suit, just a boy aset in a chair next to a desk.

The boy said nothin'. He just cocked a jerk of his silly head yonderly toward a glass door that had CASHIER writ on it. He looked on us Lowdermilks with sympathy, like we didn't pack good sense. But that's the way jellybeans are made; they've got good sense for themselves so long as they walk on concrete and keep in the shadow of big buildin's. But put the man in the jellybean suit out somewhere 'round where the Lowdermilks live, out where the sun shines on God's dirt, where there's lonesomeness; where the rattlesnakes coil and the coyotes wail their kin, where there ain't no he'p 'round when the countryside makes war on slummers out of the city because the land is foreign, and off the concrete the city man sits he'pless on the cushion of his car. The city man needs support, like concrete hard as hisse'f. That's why I felt sorry for that blue-suited, milk-white sonofabitch next to the desk who dusted us Lowdermilks out of his way, off to the cashier's door.

Me, Maw Maw and Verbaline Lou followed Pap; and we came to the door, and it was open. Mr. Wilbur Pruitt sat at his desk, his feet hoisted high on the top, sittin' comfortable. A big fat cigar made smoke 'round his face, and his bald head shone with the light come down from the ceilin'—and through the cigar-smoke haze we

COUSIN DREWEY & THE HOLY TWISTER   119

could see the blue-steel of his gimlet eye. He was talkin' to four or five cattlemen, all smokin' cigars. Some were fat, a couple lean—but there was an extra fat one that packed an eye kin to Mr. Wilbur Pruitt's, and his name was Fats Recknagel. Inside the bank, Fats was twin-brother of God Almighty; outside, as public sentiment told, he was common as bat-shit.

Salvation!

That's right. Pap told us balance to stand silent while he borrowed $5,000, and the best way to get $5,000 from the likes of Mr. Wilbur Pruitt was to crack his hard kernel with a little Christian love. So we entered the office; we stood sayin' nothin'.

The banker and the cattlemen quit their talk; they looked at us like we'd come to rob the bank, like we looked like nothin' born on this man's earth, like we had no business to be alive.

Salvation!

"Brethren," spoke up Pap, usin' his financial know-how, "have you'all been saved?"

I looked up at the ceilin' to ask a little he'p from heaven. I saw the big white light up there, it that shone down on the shiny desk; and I looked 'round the room some. Factways, I was slightly ashamed of Pap. There were green-colored cabinets; I figgered they must hold dollar bills. I saw a big picture of the President of the United States, and next to it drooped an American flag. I smelled the cloth of the carpet, it and the woodwork polish, but most of all I smelled the cigars of the high-moguls. I clenched my hands, and felt how they sweated for dread. And after I smelled and felt and dreaded, I knew for a fact how us Lowdermilks were in Mr. Wilbur Pruitt's office. I took a turn at lookin' again, and this time I saw the banker's eyes turn from gimlet-blue to granite-gray, then to fire-red. They were made that way because he was mad as hell.

Mr. Wilbur Pruitt took the cigar from his mouth, he pulled his feet off the top of the desk; he quit settin' back easy in the big desk chair; he braced himself, like there was somethin' mighty important he aimed to do.

"You'all git!" came the shout of an angry man.

Lord! The sound of it made pure shambles of peace and good will.

"Vacate this bank, you no'count white trash!"

That's what we heard Mr. Wilbur Pruitt holler at the top of his lungs. I leaped for the open door; I felt somethin' warm and human right behind me and knew how it was Verbaline Lou. Maw Maw was makin' exit on the heels of us kids. The speed we made caused every soul in the bank-lobby to look our way, because the dear Lord knows we were cuttin' notches. Pap wasn't with us. He'd stayed behind with Mr. Wilbur Pruitt. We wished he'd catch up and meet us outside. All we craved just then was for to get back in the sunshine out on the sidewalk. We'd just wait for Pap to come out with the $5,000, and maybe with Mr. Wilbur Pruitt's promise to string the sparks from the highline to the prime radio set in our house, after Pap had bust the granite with some brotherly love. Hope doesn't cost folks nothin'. We'd wait in the wagon, where old Jeff drooped his head over the fire hydrant. But like I said, we didn't need to wait long. That was, for a fact, the speediest business transaction ever experienced in the gilt-edged, blue-chip history of the First National Bank.

We made notches through the lobby like all hell was givin' us chase. And there was a big noise in back of us. It was Mr. Wilbur Pruitt, hollerin' the howls of an anguished man. But some of the noise came off of Pap, too, 'cause Pap can truly deafen a man's ears when he tells what he reckons about the Resurrection. That's when I saw a guard in gray uniform—a stiff dick with a badge and gun, with a pair of handcuffs danglin' on his belt—that's when we saw him high-tail in the direction of Mr. Wilbur Pruitt's office. He was just doin' his duty, 'cause us Lowdermilks were in the bank. He'd hear'd his boss yell for he'p, so he just ran to see what'all.

"Newt," Maw Maw said, when me and her were outside and up on the wagon-seat, when Verbaline Lou was back on the cushion behind. "Son, what you reckon will come of all this mess."

"Maw Maw," I said, "I *do* believe Pap won't get his $5,000."

"That man don't look like no Christian, Newt."

I said back at Maw Maw: "He don't pack a lick of I Corinthians, 13:1."

"I don't thank Old Man Lee Bassett none for gettin' us into this'all, Newt," Maw Maw said.

"Me neither, Maw Maw," I said. "Old Man Lee will never get a mess of gratitude from me. I don't reckon how he'll get the thanks of any of us Lowdermilks."

Just then we had to back the wagon out on the street, away from the fire hydrant, clear of the door of the First National Bank 'cause the feller in the blue suit came out to tell us to make room. Down Main Street we hear'd the wail of the city police car. We saw the red dome light makin' flickers. And we saw it comin' at us, just as we backed old Jeff and the wagon out on the street away from the front of the First National Bank. We saw the town constable aset in the driver's seat. Lord, did that police look mean! He stepped on the gas, he made notches. 'Cause he had Pap Lowdermilk on his mind. He came hellbent; and he didn't stop his siren-howlin' 'til he pulled up at the curb where Jeff and us Lowdermilks had most recently been. Then they led Pap out of the bank—a pitiful sight to behold—handcuffed like a criminal, like worse than a murderer. He looked like he hadn't paid his taxes.

"It's like the publicans said to Nicodemus . . ." he

said, hollerin' at the boy in the blue suit, and at the crowd that had gathered to see what'all.

That's when he got hisse'f jostled by the bank lobby-guard, and sneered at by the boy in the blue suit when the town constable got out of the police car so's to he'p put Pap on the cushions. And when they had Pap pitched in by the coat-neck and the seat of his pants, that's when they hauled him off to jail. And that's when the balance of us Lowdermilks, with me drivin' old Jeff, made our sad way back to the homestead.

The next day, bright and early, Old Man Lee Bassett came by for a visit. He was in his pickup truck, and next to him on the seat was Pap. Old Man Lee had paid out Pap's sentence for solid cash, because cash on the barrel talks powerful language. It talks that way with horse's dicks that wear badges danglin' on their shirts. He paid Pap out for $250, the price of the crime of incitin' riot. But when he had Pap safely inside the house, with the balance of us Lowdermilks standin' by, he told us how he had a load of goodies in the pickup truck, like sacks of beans and corn meal, and coffee and salt and cans of lard. And there was a mighty-sized slab of salt hot-back there in the pickup truck.

Old Man Lee asked me if, directly, I'd he'p him pack all that plunder into the house, so's Maw Maw could stack it where she aimed. Then he spat his quid into the stove-grate; it looked like he'd need a clear mouth for some mighty serious talk. He proclaimed how we were about to negotiate a financial conference, takin' up where Mr. Wilbur Pruitt left off. Cudless, he opened up, sayin' if we needed any money for the hard, cold on-comin' winter, all we'd have to do is whistle. And come spring, he told us, that's when he'd bring us seed for the corn and bean crops. He'd give us the cash we'd need for puttin' the seed in the good fruitful earth.

"Hell no!" Pap hollered, lookin' to the wall for his

shotgun. "We ain't askin' for charity. We don't need your charity. I thank you kindly for gettin' me out of jail, but I'll thank you kindlier if you'll git off my land and don't come back no more."

Sadly, Old Man Lee shook his head at Pap. "It ain't charity, Pap Lowdermilk, because it's pure-D common-sense business. I ain't givin' you nothin' for nothin'. I'm *loanin'* it to you. I'm deliverin' the goods and the cash, and I'm takin' no risks. Besides, I'm chargin' you five percent interest—steep, maybe, but fair for us both. I got you in the mess of goin' to the First National Bank, where you don't belong—where a *heap* of good folks don't belong. I'm makin' my atonement. You might be mossback, your house might have cooties, but you're the best farmer in Star Valley because you and earth and seed and rain and sunshine know each other, respect each other, one givin' bounty to the other. I'll collect the principal, plus the five percent, next fall. It's not charity. *I'll* profit by *your* harvest."

"That's different," Pap said. "And I might add how your manhood is mighty different from that of Mr. Wilbur Pruitt."

"Ain't you talkin' now!" Old Man Lee said back. "Different; physically, psychologically, spiritually and morally. And I thank my sweet Creator for the privilege."

And that's exactly what us Lowdermilks did the next fall—we paid Old Man Lee back his kindness, *plus* five percent. But that business transaction at the bank did somethin' to Pap. It got him a hate for bankers. From then on he packed an unbecomin' opinion of all jellybeans wearin' blue suits, for perfumed blondes and dark-haired jezebels inside the tellers' cages. And as for bank-lobby guards with guns and handcuffs stuck to their belts, with badges danglin' at their shirt pockets, his hate was most potent.

"If you're lookin' for a sonofabitch," Pap said whenever he was given the chance, "you'll find him in the First National Bank."

Which satisfied Pap a heap. But me, and Maw Maw and Verbaline Lou, all us three, remember with sadness that minute when we sat in the wagon and watched them haul Pap out of the bank and throw him in the constable's car. And how after that sad sight I flicked old Jeff on the rusty with the lines-end. How with tearful eyes we headed back to the homestead.

Maw Maw, that old gal on the wagon-seat, her beside me, all asudden said: "Doggone! It ain't right to have pained that sweetness." And she said that because we heard Verbaline Lou, my sister, Pap's sugar tit, her sobbin' girl-tears on the cushion in the wagon-bed.

15

It seemed a compliment to have the sheriff of the county come to play pretty at our Star Valley Saturday night dance. It was sweet to have him there; Hank Hudgeons, the law himself, along with the deputy-law. They brightened the shindig with the glitter of their badges. The stocks on their six-guns looked out from the holsters. They gave the dance a cozy feelin', like if any poor neighbor, or even some kinfolks, should trip out of line. . . .

The law gassed some with Old Man Lee Bassett before they walked 'round to mingle with the folks; and they stayed clear of the center floor while the dance was goin' 'round.

When Uncle Posey Burwinkle called quit to that "Yellerhammer Right, Jaybird Left," when the folks milled 'round like cattle, joshin' and hoorawin', that's when the sheriff moved to the floor middle so's to act sociable. There'd be a couple more rounds of dance, more fiddlin' out of Cousin Drewey, more hollerin' from Uncle Posey Burwinkle's glottis, more stomp and racket before the women would line up at the tables and play the hasher with fried chicken and potato salad. Or deal out pie and cake and pink drink. So while the folks just rested up before the next dance, that's when Uncle Posey Burwinkle came over and plunked his rusty on the bench next to us Lowdermilks.

"Well," he said, like we didn't know, "it's mighty like

law and order has done come to our Saturday-night dance. We'd better watch our language. We'd better mind our good manners and our Ps and Qs. We'd better act innocent like newborn babes or we'll be committin' a misdemeanor and that political sonofabitch'll haul us off to jail."

Pap said nothin' because he thought the same as Uncle Posey. Maw Maw dipped Copenhagen, otherwise she kept her mouth shut. But me, I couldn't hold a rein on my opinion.

"Maybe he's huntin' somebody," I said.

Uncle Posey smoked on a pipe. That way he was different from us Lowdermilks. He didn't chew cud. His pipe was a corncob, seasoned black with streaks of yellow. And the way he punched tobacco into the bowl, sayin' nothin' to my opinion, showed how he was thinkin' right smart. But I figgered he'd open up when he'd thought enough. I waited for him to say what he reckoned. So I gave my eyesight to the sheriff, who strutted 'round, him and his deputy. Them, the small-sized bantie-cock and the overgrown piss-ant. The sheriff back-slapped, hand-pumped and showed his good nature. And by the way they both laughed out loud, bendin' double because of what some old country boy said, you'd know how the laughs rode upward from their deep guts.

"No, Newt, I don't reckon he is," Uncle Posey finally said, openin' up, a man with philosophies strainin'. "Maybe he was up to Signal Rock, maybe 'cause of some poor unbecomin' bastard. Maybe some old boy committed a nuisance against some old lady's fence. No tellin'. Old ladies like to whistle for sheriffs, innocently thinkin' how the sheriff wouldn't piss on the same spot along the same line of fence if he got the chance. He's a politician and I hate politicians. I hate 'em worse'n a hound dog hates a rattlesnake."

"What you know about politicians, Uncle Posey?"

COUSIN DREWEY & THE HOLY TWISTER 127

"Newt, I come from Texas, don't I?"

"Likely."

"It's my nationality."

"You might be proud, Uncle Posey."

"Well, any time you want to hunt a politician, Newt, the best place to catch one is Texas. I was born in the Blacklands—Bell County. I was raised on the richest, most crop-givin' farm in the world and my paw and maw saw that me and my buds followed the Christian road. That road ain't got no chug-holes in the pavement, and it's never dark, even after the sun goes down. Us Burwinkle kids was learned to love the Lord. We packed law-abidin' habits. We all got the same middle name— H. H stands for Honesty. Ask me my name and I'll tell you. It's Posey H. Burwinkle.

"The way was narrow but I kept it straight. I didn't diddle the calico, and there was plenty 'round about. We tended the preacher's meetin' every Sunday, we read the Good Book every night. I had a brother named Deacon H. Burwinkle. That's a Texas name, and he sinned. Jesus Christ, did that feller sin! He was plumb stud. You won't believe me, but he quit us the night before his weddin' day. He left the gal alone to fret, with her folks and with the burden she'd caught out of Deacon's poon-tangin' 'round. He just ran off and the Lord only knew where. Later, we hear'd how he was drivin' a street car in Houston. But the balance of us Burwinkles followed the Lord's golden path.

"Later, we hear'd how Deacon was servin' time in Huntsville, that big pen, and how holdin' up a store clerk next to a cash register was his satanic crime. But all my sisters were virgins, they kept their buds. Later, we hear'd how Deacon had got let out of Huntsville, how he'd gone to San Angelo then to Dallas. Factways, he was on parole. He wore a diamond stickpin set in a butterfly necktie; his pants were striped, his hat was a derby. And he went nowheres without his gold-headed walkin' cane. But the balance of us Burwinkles kept droppin' dimes in the preacher's hat, which bought our way to heaven, whenever that sweet time comes. . . . Later, we hear'd how Deacon had done it—he bought hisse'f a little old pearl-handled pistol, and doggone if he didn't shoot a man who sat across the poker table! So they took Deacon to Huntsville, and this time they set him down in the electric chair.

"Deacon was mean all right, but the balance of us Burwinkles was kind'a saintly. We were bags of solid righteousness, sanitary packed. . . . Factways, every citizen of Bell County was like us Burwinkles, upright, perpendicular. All were the right brand of citizen, except poor long-gone Deacon. . . . Deacon and that silly sonofabitch you see yonder, him who's kissin' the babies."

"You mean the sheriff, Uncle Posey?"

"That's right, Newt, I mean the sheriff."

"Did he come from Bell County, Texas?"

"He came here from Bell County, Texas, Newt, 'cause that's his natural habitat."

"How come he came way out here?"

" 'Cause he ain't no good, Newt."

"Is he dodgin' the law?"

"You bet."

Uncle Posey was one of my favorite human bein's. He gassed a lot, told windies of the most monstrous proportions. To this day I don't believe he had a brother named Deacon; or, if he had, that brother never got treated to sparks at Huntsville. Uncle Posey was slightly kin to Cousin Drewey when it came to windies; he told them without blushin', he told them for the solid truth. Maybe he believed them hisse'f, just like Cousin Drewey.

I looked 'round the dance hall. Lord, were Star Valley folks havin' a good time! Yonder was Orville Klingsinger chasin' his own kids 'round, playin' with them like a dutiful father should. He tickled their little sides for pleasure. There was Virgie, his woman, gassin' about female things, aset with other calico on the benches. Old Man Lee Bassett was talkin' wild to three good farmers who chewed cud while they listened. And yonder walked that man from Bell County, the sheriff, and now his tracks were aimed toward Cousin Drewey. Our kinfolks stood next to Young Buster Prather. He was he'pin' Buster talk to two pretty girls. Buster was a button, so girls held high-priority interest in his mind.

And yonder was the sheriff, stridin' in that direction, makin' tracks for our kinfolks, toward Buster and the girls. The heavyweight deputy followed behind, like he played bodyguard or somethin'. Lord! I held my breath for dread. Because Cousin Drewey was a sinner. . . .

And the sheriff *knew* Cousin Drewey was a sinner.

"Howdy, Hank!" That's what I heard Young Buster say, most joyously. "What'all you doin' up in Star Valley this bright moonlight night?" And he held out his hand for a shake with the sheriff.

"Buster," said he, "I've come here to strut some, to whirl the gals, swing 'em 'round and 'round, to enjoy a session of the 'Josie Do.' And to chit-chat with the best folks in the world."

He said more, but I couldn't hear because of the dance-hall racket. I saw him shake hands with Buster and act fatherly to the two girls. He pulled his arm 'round their necks and nuzzled his nose in their hair. The silly bitches, they didn't know he was a bastard, but maybe girls love bastards. No tellin'. I saw him act the damn fool then I saw him face Cousin Drewey. But the noise of the folks drowned out for my ears anythin' he said.

Lord, I felt better when I saw him reach out, take Cousin Drewey by the hand and slap him on the back like a good-natured pistol-prick, because sheriffs don't act *that* neighborly to any sinner they aim to haul off to jail.

Cousin Drewey nearly bust a gut; he had Young

Buster Prather and the two girls in stitches. I heard Uncle Posey say somethin' to Pap, but Pap didn't pay him no mind. Neither did Maw Maw, she paid him not a lick. Because them two Lowdermilks had their eyes fixed, not on Cousin Drewey or the sheriff, but up to the ceilin' where the red hearts hung from the streamers. Maw Maw dripped Copenhagen down her chin. Pap's cud took a beatin'; they were both sad of heart and didn't feel nothin' else. They just wished our girl would take sick, or somethin', and not show up at the dance. But they figgered too, how that dance was for her honor, and for Clyde's, so wishin' a plague would be too much to hope.

Uncle Posey Burwinkle pulled himself over to stand where he stood when he called the dances. But we knew, like it always happened before, how the folks would yell at Cousin Drewey and threaten to shoot him dead if he didn't sing them a song. They'd crave a song of his own make—pure Washtaw Mountain—and they pleaded kindly if he'd pick some on his guitar. That's when I saw Cousin Drewey leave the sheriff with the girls and he and Buster get up high on the stand. When he picked up his guitar, when he cleared his glottis, that's when the world would know we'd get "Honeysuckle Candy Woman":

> *Honeysuckle Candy Woman,*
> *Where did you git them eyes?*
> *They're mean like a cat's,*
> *And they match your mouth for lies.*

That's the kind of song the folks would get when they stomped and hooted for Cousin Drewey to get up and sing. They'd get that kind when Cousin Drewey felt ungodly, but most times they'd get a Bible song, because Cousin Drewey liked to show his equal to the preacher. A man knows by readin' The Book of Job how that prophet of Uz claimed the Lord afflicted the righteous,

COUSIN DREWEY & THE HOLY TWISTER 131

and he couldn't catch the reasons why. The way the Book told, and how Cousin Drewey sang it, was that Job was given the damnedest dose of boils any human bein' could get, whether he lived in B.C. or A.D. He was miserable, and all he could do was set and groan and wish he was dead. But he had three buds, three good old boys—Eliphaz the Temanite, Bildad the Shuhite, and Zophar the Naamathite—Hebrews sure enough.

The Bible didn't say so, but Cousin Drewey's song *did,* and said how they made the right hand for a game of stud-poker. But Job had one hell of a time holdin' the cards 'cause of those boils. The Bible didn't say so, but Cousin Drewey sang how they *did* and he sang how they kissed the dice and shot craps. And all the while they talked religion, told what they reckoned about the Resurrection, and had it all writ down in the Bible. And what was writ in the Bible made a song for Cousin Drewey, a sweet song called "Job's Boils."

> *Old Job, a prophet of Uz,*
> *That was his native land.*

And Cousin Drewey would sing the song so sweetly, and strum the guitar so tenderly, that every listenin' ear would sort of reach with the hands and seek relief from the imagination.

> *He scratched and he scratched*
> *But they wouldn't come loose,*
> *'Cause the Lord done put 'em there.*

Pap and Maw Maw's focus was up at the cardboard hearts. I knew for sure how they were thinkin' about Verbaline Lou. It wouldn't be long now. Then the girl who used to be my sister would come stompin' in with all the tinsel of Delilah draped 'round her, with bracelets and such, flimsy stockin's held up by garters, her ass padded in silk. And holdin' her hand would be the man she loved. Clyde Skinner, in new boots and slicker's pants, a bow-tied shirt, a prime ornament, topped with a John B. Stetson hat. That's when Star Valley folks would holler praises, 'cause children of the Lord's manufacture were fixed to take on matrimonial life. And, too, that's when Pap and Maw Maw's hearts would break for sure.

Cousin Drewey finished his song, Young Buster Prather took up his banjo, Uncle Posey Burwinkle hollered how the next dance would be the Ocean Roll. Folks stomped, clapped and whistled; they were mightily pleased with Cousin Drewey. The sheriff jumped up next to Cousin Drewey, to shake his hand and pound his back. The piss-ant deputy was nigh in tears after hearin' about Job's misery.

And I said to Pap, "What you reckon, Pap?"

Pap took his eyesight down from the red cardboard hearts; he turned his head my way. "What?" he said.

"What do you reckon about that sonofabitch?"

"Don't reckon nothin', Newt. If he aimed to domicile Cousin Drewey in his buggy jail he'd have done it by now. Cousin Drewey sinned; look at Cousin Drewey, and there you'll behold a sinner. But I don't like the way that sheriff is kissin' all the babies, and goosin' and feelin' 'round the women. If he comes over here and puts a hand on any of my womenfolks, I'll shoot him dead. That is, if I had my shotgun."

For a fact, there he was, the sheriff, t'other side of the room, kissin' babies. He'd set Pomona Hobbs's littlest— a big boy in didies named Earl—on his arm while he talked pretty. He quick gave Earl back to Pomona, and Pomona figgered how she'd better change the didies.

Old Man Lee Bassett was over by the big entrance door. It looked mighty like he was expectin' somebody, and those somebodies held high priority in us Lowdermilks' minds.

"You reckon Verbaline Lou will get here, Pap?"

"You bet."

"When?"

"Directly."

"What you reckon about them hearts?"

"They're a Bible-parable, clean out of The Book of Luke," Pap said. "Newt, they tell us about the prodigal daughter, about a Christian girl who left her sweet parents to go sinnin' in the household of Herod the Tetrarch. She put on silk, she put on bracelets of silver and gold, and through the silk a feller could see all she's got. The parable tells how she lies abed with that Hebrew king. They're sinners of the worst kind. Old Herod don't give a damn, he don't respect her virginity. He acts stud; she acts the chippy bitch and they make them old bedsprings squeal. But sooner or later, sure as snow in December, Herod's love cools off. Because some fresh calico shows up in Jerusalem—maybe blonde, which Verbaline Lou ain't—and Herod takes on a change of pasture. That prodigal daughter weeps salt tears, but it don't do no good. Herod won't look at her no more. So she packs up her war-bag and heads for home. She's got Herod Junior ridin' on her arm. She asks forgiveness of her pap and maw maw, and bein' Christian folks that pap and maw maw give it gladly with their hearts. And after she's ate her supper and given Herod Junior his titty-dinner she claims how a mess of Star Valley greens taste better than all the champagne and roast duck in Jerusalem. And, Newt . . ."

"What, Pap?"

"We've got a Herod in this valley called Clyde Skinner. He might be rich, he might have a mighty spread of a ranch, and maybe he's got honorable intentions about our girl. . . . And that's what them red hearts stand for—bloody, drippin' scarlet."

16

Most times when I'm alone and idle, when I get to thinkin', it strikes me potent how this world of mine is made up of three wide scopes of territory. They're mighty real to me; they're peopled with folk I know like I do the back of my hand. I sit out on the woodblock, maybe, or on the bare ground when I go ramblin' some. Maybe I'll have Pap's shotgun, out to get me a rabbit for us Lowdermilks' supper. That's when it ain't nobody else's business, when I can think of the *extra* people who inhabit the earth.

The three scopes go thisaway: like the Territory of Music, where you'll find Cousin Drewey residin', and us Lowdermilks, and the likes of Uncle Posey Burwinkle. The next scope is that of the ugly politician—the Hank Hudgeons Territory is its rightful name. Then next and final comes the Territory of Love, where you'll find my sister, Verbaline Lou, and her lovin' man, Clyde Skinner.

That last, as I see it, is a long string of peaks, and these peaks split apart two wide, rollin' stretches of dirt. They run north and south, like a mighty cross-cut saw, teeth up. That's Verbaline Lou's territory, all right, hers and Clyde's. They're lovers, and they've got neighbors. To the east of that sawtooth range lies Cousin Drewey's

COUSIN DREWEY & THE HOLY TWISTER 135

Territory of Music and to the west of the mountains is the stretch that ain't so pretty—the Hank Hudgeons Territory. That's where you'll find our sheriff and his piss-ant deputy, that's where you find them both, surrounded by all the slimy politicians on earth. That's where you'll find Fats Recknagel, and Mr. Wilbur Pruitt, the bank-flunky in the blue suit. There, too, you can hear the police car siren howlin' like a lonesome coyote, there's the land where you'll see the dome blinker flashin' red.

Factways, there doesn't seem to be any north or south to the dream-world I keep in my mind. The mountains are there, high and long, and to the east and west lie the two flat scopes—the ugly and the beautiful. That's the lay of the land I cultivate when I'm alone.

First let me tell about the Hank Hudgeons Territory, because it's somethin' to deal with in a hurry and cook to a frazzle quick. It's big prairie without grass or runnin' creeks; and what water there is, is still as death and hot and has green slime all over its thick body. To drink it biles up your guts; you'll wish to hell you'd gone thirsty. There's cattle there, but they're weak and gaunt, gut-shrunk with their ribs makin' ridges on their poor red sides. They're hungry, 'cause that's the way the politicians run their businesses, and 'cause their land is the worst land ever made of the Lord's seven-day creation. The sky above that sorry territory is bright with sun, but too much sun; there's no trace of cloud, no promise of rain. Crops fail and die. Which don't matter too much, 'cause men of Hank Hudgeons's caliber don't care for crops, or grass, or whether their cattle suffer or not. They work in courthouses, and in state capitols, in long halls where spittoons line the way. There's thunder, but it ain't the brand made by God; there's lightnin', but it's the kind made to kill. And the eternal racket deafens a feller's hearin', 'cause it's the noise of politicians hatin' each other, cravin' to take away each other's jobs, callin' names at each other, makin' promises, stealin' and lyin' and nestin' for themse'fs a bed in hell; embezzlin' the county collection, jailin'-up when they themse'fs should be jailed—and all the while the spittoons in the state capitols and in the county courthouses get ranker and ranker. *That's* no land for a Christian soul to inhabit, and most times I try not to think about it. Even the Lord couldn't tie me up and haul me to the Hank Hudgeons Territory. I respect the Lord, 'cause I know He's all-powerful and most times merciful. But when it comes to Hank Hudgeons the Lord can get unreasonable, just like a mortal man. . . . 'Cause what us Lowdermilks know about Hank Hudgeons, that county sheriff shouldn't hold office.

Hank's land lies west of the Love Mountains; it's the ugly side.

But east side of the Love Mountains is the Territory of Music, different for a fact, *mighty* different. It's the scope where Cousin Drewey is presi*dent*—Presi*dent* Drewey Stiff, that's that chief executive's name. It's a place of green pastures where cows feed and never fail to find a calf. They wear bags of milk; and there's sheep on the grass, and it's every bit like it was in the Book of Psalms, where David made music on his harp. And there, next to the green pastures, the streams run black and heavy with catfish. Good water, deep and clean. Out of the rich dirt grow slash-pine and gum, and all kinds of hardwood like hickory and beau d'arc, and the fields are planted to corn and cane. There's hogs on pasture, big old gruntin' hogs, with rings in their noses so's to keep them from rootin' up the pretty land.

In that scope of territory there's always the promise of rain. The barns bust their sides, filled with hay and fodder; and in the yards there's sorghum cookin', bubblin' in the vats. There's where kids hang 'round so's to get a taste of glibs. Folks are kind in the Territory of Music; they never fail to give the kids a taste of glibs. And the kids are healthy, full of sass. They never have to go to school. The air is full of slash-pine essence, and of milk-cows grazin', of sorghum cookin', of fish in the clear runnin' creeks—all that, and plenty cud-tobacco on hand. . . . Lord, Lord! What a blessin'!

From out the kitchen lean-to comes the sweet smell of supper. Inside, good old gals like Maw Maw are up 'gainst the cook-stove, fryin' hog-middle, shakin' the meat in the skillets. In the pots the greens are boilin' soft, soakin' in the taste of pot-likker. And cornbread. They bake cornbread in the Territory of Music in pans two feet long, eighteen inches wide, three inches thick out of meal homeground with plenty of grit. It's Washtaw Mountain fodder, it ain't no Yankee Johnny Cake. It's so slick with hog-grease you can almost hear the grunts.

There's religion in the Territory of Music—Bible-readin' every night, savin' souls on Sundays, movin' down to the mourners' bench, dunkin' in the creeks, hollerin' praises, droppin' dimes in the preacher's hats. In that blessed land the preachers put on a show. They act up better than anywhere else on earth, they kick wilder, tear up things to teensier shreds, put their deafenin' might to a congregation's ears, shout with a bloody vengeance and consign all competin' Christian denominations to the worst kind of fiery hell. That's Canaan, it's God's chosen land.

The wagons roll in the Territory of Music; they just move along down the brown-dirt lanes, slow and steady like a lazy river. And on Saturdays, soon after noon, we hitch the mules and take off to town. We take out, then come back with plunder; like fellers do who go out to the thicket with guns and a hunger for venison. Or maybe some kind of a furry supper-varmint. A roast porcupine is good anywhere, but his taste is sweeter in the Territory of Music. Once come to town we head for tradin'—our wagons are empty but they yawn for cargo. Mostly, we go in empty, but sometimes we're loaded; and that's when we exchange plunder for plunder. We never pack much cash—no weight in dollar bills, damn few nickels and dimes, and we *never* look at twenty dollars in all our spanful lives. But we've got plenty pumpkins, plenty jugged-up sorghum; we're worth our weight in hog-meat, *it* and home-rendered lard. At the mercantile store we pay out pumpkins, big pumpkins; the feller there is our breed of man, so he gives us little pumpkins back for change. And when we get the tradin' done, on those blessed Saturday evenin's, there in the Territory of Music, that's when we gather 'round the loaded wagons and gab some language to our neighbors. There we meet kinfolks. There we hear about wrongdoers in our midst, about their sins and trespasses. And there, too, we get learned of saintly acts perpetuated by the Christians among us.

Lord, Lord, that heaven-kissed land, its sights and smells, and the sounds that mix with the pine-tanged air! Hogs gruntin', mules brayin', preachers rantin', women singin' praises—but the sweetest sound in the Territory of Music is that come off the instruments, off the cat-gut strings and the sweeps of the bow.

That's where the fiddlers fiddle, and the likes of Cousin Drewey are at their prime. Some are dirty—just dirty, drunken fiddlers, good for nothin' else. Don't trust 'em, they're lazy and they steal. Don't let your kids get near them, 'cause they use nasty talk; their talk ain't good for kids to hear. They'll talk the same in front of your womenfolks, and you'll have to reach for your shotgun and tell 'em you'll have to pepper their rusties if they don't change their speech to the good manners of civilized human bein's. And there's no such thing as a

COUSIN DREWEY & THE HOLY TWISTER 139

teetotalin' fiddler, alive or dead.

When the sun's high, and the clock's at the hour when it shines the hottest . . . well, sir, that's when you're on the cultivator. Or maybe you're navigatin' the go-devil. Or plowin'. Or middle-bustin'—dancin' over the furrowed-up sod. You're behind the mules and you catch the sweat drippin' off your balls. It's mid-mornin'; you wish it would come dinner time. Or better yet, quittin' time. 'Cause your earthly travail is too damn hard and constant. You say to the mules—likewise to the goddamn plow, or even to the cultivator—you say, "To hell with this! Why did the dear Lord make us farmers of the land, farmers so doggone kin to the land? Why did He made us manflesh, or mule-flesh? Why did He make our implements of such hard iron? Why does that sweet Maker make us toil so hard for a livin'? Why didn't He make us aristocrats like He did the fiddlers, them lazy, idle, no'count fellers?"

And you think of your womenfolks, even your cousins and your mothers-in-law, and while you dance the furrows you think of their hard toil 'round the cookstove, it blazin' in the lean-to. And you think of those poor female kin, stirrin' greens, bakin' cornbread, tossin' meat in the skillet, gettin' the coffee hot and brown and too thick to drown a rat. And you think to yourse'f, "Why did them sweetnesses have to get born women? Why didn't their Creator fix 'em different 'round the crotches? Why didn't He make us all fiddlers so we could sleep out sun-high hours in the shade, each with a bottle of whiskey for a bedmate?"

That's how we'all reckoned fiddlers in the Territory of Music. We reckoned them rightly, because we knew their cussed ways deep to the bones and leaders—even deeper, to where their hearts hung red. And we knew them for a breed unfit for winnin' Christian respect.

Just give the Territory of Music some darkness of

night; or put moonlight on the schoolhouse—when there's lamplight inside and the desks and benches have been cleared away from the floor-center. That's when a special chair is put to comfort the King of the World, to receive the royal-rusty of the sweetest human bein' ever born alive, him with a fiddle set snug at his chin; him with his bowstring rosined—with the tappin' foot and the noddin' head, it keepin' time with the tune. Him, that old boy, who turns the square dance 'round.

And next to the fiddler in the Territory of Music comes the feller with the big mouth and leather-lined glottis, with the mind who remembers all the old-time hoe-down calls since the days of Genesis I. The caller, like Uncle Posey Burwinkle, our immigrant out of Bell County, Texas.

So it was that night at the schoolhouse dance, when I felt like a true citizen of my territorial scope. I felt it all by breathin' the smoky air, blue haze with a mixed-in variety of human odors. And it came alive, most of all, when Cousin Drewey reared back and bust a gut at somethin' Hank the Sheriff had said—somethin' that tickled his funny bone. I saw our kinfolks lookin' handsomer than any time since he'd come to live with us Lowdermilks—handsome in his dude-cowboy outfit, in all the drapin's Clyde Skinner and his sister-in-law Lilybelle gave him for a gift, so's to improve his looks while he sawed that square dance 'round and 'round.

I looked at Pap, I gave eyesight to Maw Maw. They looked like two concrete pilin's set perpendicular under a bridge over the Washtaw River. Pap had his focus on Cousin Drewey, he saw how our own blooded kinfolks was actin' friendly with law and order. Maw Maw aimed hers in the same direction, and I could read her thoughts as easy as a chapter in Timothy. Her thoughts were salty, they weren't sweet. Neither moved a hand, they twitched nary a foot. But Pap's jaw moved steady and easy, with an up and down chomp, makin' massacree of the cud he held behind his back teeth. Maw Maw dipped Copenhagen. Every minute or two they'd turn their heads to squirt, to give that can on the bench between them a fraction of an inch more of dark-brown essence.

Cousin Drewey was on his seat, aset and ready to percolate. He nursed his fiddle, he ran some rosin up the bowstrings. Young Buster Prather just held his banjo, awaitin' the high-ball from Uncle Posey. Old Man Lee Bassett stood by the big entrance door, lookin' out to where the automobiles sat parked, for all the world like one of Joshua's sentries atop the walls of Jericho.

"Reckon we got time for a dance, Lee?" Uncle Posey called to that dirt-farmer by the door. He craved no cut-in by lovers.

"Cain't see no headlights comin', Uncle Posey," Old Man Lee said. "Maybe you can set the folks to spinnin'. Damned if I know. Maybe them lovebirds have stopped to spark a little on the way. They might be later than reg'lar. I'll holler 'hogs in the corn' when I see 'em drive up."

Doggone, there was talk for you! When those two fellers talked, every eye looked their way. Not a soul in that room paid mind to us Lowdermilks; they just let us sit. No man, no woman came up to us to stand and quiz us thisaway: "Pap, you reckon you'all's daughter will get here directly?" Or: "Maw Maw, it was you who birthed Verbaline Lou, gave her life. What do you think about tonight anyway? How do you like the way them lovehearts are drippin' from the ceilin'? Ain't you proud how a mossback like Verbaline Lou has done caught an upright young man like Clyde Skinner, hooked him for a husband?" Or: "And you, Newt, why don't you get up and strut a round with us folks? It's your sister we're givin' celebration this night. What you Lowdermilks made of, concrete?"

They just let us set, out of the way.

"Salute your partner!" hollered Uncle Posey; and the dancers fixed to strut, they took their places center of the floor. . . .

So while the music whined, while the dancers circled left, sashayed right, saluted partners, made the promenade—while noise and movement filled the schoolhouse that bright moonlight night—I set my mind to thinkin' back on those three wide scopes of territory. Them that I've got nestled snug, them I take out to think about when I'm alone and peaceful and have no trespassers 'round to mess up the landscape. And because the red cardboard hearts were danglin' from the streamers high above, I got to thinkin' about the best territory of the three—the Mountains of Love, up yonderly, where Clyde and Verbaline Lou reside.

The Mountains of Love—I call 'em the Everywhere Mountains. I call 'em that because they belong to all the souls on earth—are no kin to the Washtaws, or the Arbuckles, or the Kiamish—they're nothin' green and low and sultry like any of the Ozarks. Factways, they're so high you've got to look up; they're foresty with pine and spruce, tender with aspen; their creeks don't run black bass but torrents white and wild. The peaks are coned, their summits solid rock, pure silver against the clean blue sky. And the best thing about the Everywhere Mountains is that they cut the Territory of Music off from the Hank Hudgeons Territory; and factways how nobody lives up there except Clyde Skinner and my sister, Verbaline Lou.

They live up there, them two—maybe in sin, maybe without sin, it's hard to reckon. Cain't tell one way of t'other. But if they *are* sinnin', it's clean sin, like the Everywhere Mountains are clean. What they do ain't nobody's business. There's no need for the preacher.

There's noise in the Everywhere Mountains, but it's

sweet noise. Like this: "You reckon I've got cause to be jealous, Lou? You reckon there's a handsome cowboy down there in Star Valley who's out to grip you by the hand, to take it clean out of mine—to lead you to the preacher and make you his wedded wife? What you say, Lou, you reckon there's some old boy down there who can deal you better love than me?"

That was Clyde talkin', all right. It was him who joshed my sister. Clyde always left off the Verbaline when he uttered ner name. He claimed how it was too mossback. He just called her Lou.

My sister didn't say a damn thing to Clyde's romantic quiz. She just shook her head. The grass was under their rusties, but they leaned against a boulder the size of two automobiles put together, and the rock was clean and rainwashed; except for the north side where moss hung green and silky. It was clean moss; and the grass of that mountain meadow up in those Everywhere Mountains was so clean and dewy that a feller or maybe a girl like Verbaline Lou could run through it in bare feet and have them washed off like they'd've doused them in a galvanized tub.

"What you say, Lou? . . . Who'all's my competition down there in that old Star Valley?"

But Clyde's chosen woman didn't say a goddamn thing. She figgered how Clyde ought to have better sense. Didn't he know how there was just *one* man in all the valley who didn't scare her out of her mossback hide when he got six feet toward her? Didn't he know how until he came along that night at the dance that's when she quit actin' like some old prairie dog next to a hole in the ground, ready to run and hide away if a man said boo? Didn't he know that once a feller got into her britches he was her man for good, and her britches were open to him and no other cuss on earth?

So what Clyde did, instead of quizzin' her some more,

was to reach over and hold her, and *really* put the loveglow to shinin' like nighttime lightnin' in July. To *really* turn on the sparks.

Clyde was full of love; loaded, 'cause he had two armfuls of Verbaline Lou. He couldn't talk. That's the way lovers get, even before they couple. When they couple, that's different. I remember back how more times than once, when I was a teensy kid, say ten or twelve years old, when Pap and Maw Maw figgered I didn't know, that I was too young to know what love was all about; when we all slept in the same room, all of us, even Verbaline Lou—and I'll say how that girl was even teensier than me—how I laid awake listenin' to the grown folks act husband-and-wife. They didn't make much noise at first, which is always natural, but after awhile they cut up somethin' rambunctious. That's when they were in the short rows—just before Pap let her have it. In those days, too—me, I was maybe ten or twelve years old—I'd sometimes see Verbaline Lou when she was all naked, nothin' on, like when Maw Maw told her to get in the galvanized tub. Or maybe when she sat 'round the yard, pantsless, like she figgered nobody was comin' 'round. . . . That's when I got to thinkin' how that's the way it was. Or the time I came on R.J. Woodall floggin' his dummy north side of the barn and he looked like he was havin' a good time. So I went to the south side of the same barn and tried it out myse'f. That's how I got to learn all about it.

And too, the time Uncle Gersh—I was fifteen years old at the time—took me for a ride to Tulsa on the train. And I'll say now how Uncle Gersh was a horny old sonofabitch. A girl knocked on our hotel-room door and Uncle Gersh hollered, "Come in, honey." So she came in, and *was* she a sight for sore eyes! She wore nothin' else but a flimsy dress and a pair of shoes; and her face was painted red like a war-whoop Comanche.

COUSIN DREWEY & THE HOLY TWISTER 145

She was black 'round the eyes, maybe made that way with dabs of paint, and she smoked a cigarette, lookin' tough. "Newt," Uncle Gersh said, "I've done invited this lady to our room so's I can teach you the facts of life. Newt, son, this is your first lesson, and this lady is a goddamn whore."

I said nothin' to Uncle Gersh's invite; I couldn't talk 'cause I was scared. The lady didn't look mean. She didn't scare me that way, but I was scared of my own button-size ignorance. I knew I was in for poontang, that Uncle Gersh was payin' the ticket, but I didn't know what to do. I shook for the fright of it, 'round my ankles, up to my middle-girth, a turnip-sized lump stuck in my throat. I looked over at the bed, and I figgered how *there* it would happen. I was leg-tied; I couldn't run; I didn't want to.

"Sweetheart," I heard Uncle Gersh say, "this kid is a virgin. He's been to school—he can read and write, and he knows how to add the digits. But there's some things in this sweet life he don't know nothin' about; factways, he's most ignorant about *you* when you get your shirt off."

"It'll cost him two dollars," said the painted lady.

"I'll give you three," Uncle Gersh said. "He needs to learn, and the more he learns in his younger life the better a cocksman he'll be when he grows up to be useful. The ladies will love him for it."

I stood lookin' silly while Uncle Gersh gave the lady three one-dollar bills. I must have looked worse when he turned his back on us, and made tracks for the door. He said, "I need some cigars, and it will take me thirty minutes to get 'em. I'll be back, and when I get back I want that kid made into a broke stud-colt." Then he was out in the hall, leavin' me alone with my fateful minute. He closed the door behind him.

The girl went past me and turned the key in the lock.

She didn't need to talk, she just went over to the bed and kicked off her shoes. I liked the way she moved. She moved 'round so pretty. She wasn't heavy, neither was she built like a fence post; but she was more fence post than heavy. She stood barefoot in front of me.

"Ever seen a naked woman?" she asked me.

I blubbered somethin', the best I could do. It didn't make sense; it was no language at all—but when I shook my head she knew how a woman's naked frame had never before shone glorious in front of my eyes. I'd seen Verbaline Lou, but she didn't count. She let me look at her for about half a minute, then she put herself on the bed. She lay with her knees hoisted; and she said, "All right, kid, you know what to do next. This business ain't arithmetic, it don't need no blackboard to show how it's done."

I knew how Uncle Gersh would be back in thirty minutes, after he'd bought his cigars. I didn't crave to have him know how I wasn't busted in. So I did what I figgered was natural.

I liked that girl right smart. I didn't feel my nerves no more. I got down with her on the bed; my feelin' then was just for her, and I didn't give a damn for Uncle Gersh, or Pap, or Maw Maw, and because I was with a whore I wouldn't let myself think about Verbaline Lou. I couldn't, for a fact, think about anythin', only for what I was doin' that very minute. She he'ped me a little, but mostly I did what was right, all by myself. The minutes were movin' along. Sooner than sweetly, I knew Uncle Gersh would be bangin' on the door, pleadin' to get let in. After a while, no tellin' how long, I felt myse'f in the short rows; then I knew how a man has to act when he gets in the short rows. I was shown then why Pap used to make so much noise. And why Maw Maw kept time in the duet. Only that girl in Tulsa didn't make no noise; but she had bronc-action, she nigh lifted me up more than I craved. She made no sound out of her mouth. She was cold that way; she didn't feel like I felt. Since that first, tastiest time I've had a whore under me more times than once. And *never* has she made sound in the short rows. That's the way with whores. And when one talks, she'll say, "Hurry up." That's all she'll say; but the feller don't pay her no mind. Factways, he can't.

Uncle Gersh didn't find the door locked. He just pushed it open and came in. He smoked a big cigar and he wore a grin on his good-natured face. I was sittin' on the bed, with all my clothes put back where they should be. I felt like I'd just run a race. All I craved was to get back my breath. The sweet girl had gone back to her room down the hallway or maybe she was out huntin' another customer. She just got off the bed, put on her dress and shoes, went to the door and passed out to the hall. She left me layin' naked as a jaybird—but the way I felt, I didn't give a damn. She might have told me how I was a done-bred colt, but she didn't.

17

That night in the schoolhouse, while Cousin Drewey made the dance go 'round and 'round, I kept my mind on a different scope of territory. I packed no focus on the Star Valley folks, or on Hank Hudgeons. My ears didn't catch the sweet melodies come off from Cousin Drewey's fiddle, or how Uncle Posey Burwinkle called that old "Captain Jinks" hoe-down. I had my mind on sweeter territory, on the Everywhere Mountains where Clyde Skinner and Verbaline Lou were sparkin' hell-bent, them set against the mighty rock with the soft green grass at its base.

"Listen, Clyde! . . . Do you hear it?"

That's what Verbaline Lou said, all right; and her mouth was so close to Clyde's cheek that her quiz couldn't miss.

Clyde listened. He cocked his ear to the east, toward the Territory of Music. "Doggone!" he said, "if it ain't Cousin Drewey."

Because up the side of the big rocky mountain, like a man ridin' horseback on a switchback trail, the music of Cousin Drewey's fiddle traveled on magic lubrication.

"You reckon it's Cousin Drewey?" said Verbaline Lou.

"Who else!" Clyde said back. "He's playin' 'Big Old

COUSIN DREWEY & THE HOLY TWISTER 149

Tater In The Sandy Land,' ain't he?"

"That's a fact, Clyde. He's playin' that sweet Texas tune; but Cousin Drewey ain't the only fiddler in the Territory of Music who saws out 'Sandy Land' with his bow."

"I know, Lou. But that there, what we're gettin' now, can only come from Cousin Drewey."

"It's sure sweet, Clyde."

"It is for a fact, honey."

"It makes me feel like I love somebody, and I love him 'cause he's a man—and I love him so much I could ache. But I'm proud. Lord, am I proud of my man! He took me out of the mossback. He curried me down from head to toe—and I'm clean and healthy. He trimmed me into somethin' beautiful, and left me just as natural as I've always been. And where he couldn't get to curry me down, 'cause he's a man, he got his sister-in-law, Sonny Boy's woman, that Lilybelle. Lord, I love that man! He got Lilybelle to do it."

"Who's that man, sweetness?" Clyde said, and he grinned that old cattleman's grin. And his arms were full of my sister.

"Who you reckon?"

Verbaline Lou was deep in her man. She couldn't get her face closer to him. He was the strongest in the world; leastways, his arms felt that way. And they were together, clean to the hilt, like never before. And the grass under them was soft like it was made for that there. And their warmths were the same, each feelin' how one skin on a human bein' is like another's. And the fiddle music made time for what Clyde was doin': for the love he was pourin' into Verbaline Lou, with all his doggone might. Old Cousin Drewey just he'pin' a couple of lovers along.

"Clyde."

She said it just as she'd risen from her set; she said it while she leaned against the rock, when she had her dress pulled down, nigh down to her knees again. When she tidied up her hair some. She said it lookin' down on Clyde. That man was still laid out in the grass; 'cause as Uncle Gersh used to say, like he told *me* special on that trip to Tulsa, a man gets pooped.

"What you say, sweetness?" Clyde said, quizzin' my sister.

"Clyde, I fear the wind's gonna change. Look at the clouds up yonder. They're settin' different. Doggone, Clyde, they look kind'a like they're fixin' to make a twister—eastbound, a pure cyclone headin' for the Washtaw Mountains."

"That's natural," Clyde said, gettin' up off his stretch. He knocked away the dried grass that stuck to his knees. He pulled up his pants, he fixed his belt. "Them clouds are settled over the Territory of Music, ain't they? It's in the Territory of Music where Cousin Drewey is at, ain't it? 'Cause, Lou, you know as well as me how Cousin Drewey wouldn't live in the Territory of Music if it didn't have clouds actin' silly; actin' like they're fixin' to build an eastbound cyclone. . . . And when I say eastbound, I mean just *that;* I mean a twister of Houston-size proportions, a *holy* twister, a Frisco Lines twister, with freight waybilled to the Washtaw Mountains."

"Hon," said Verbaline Lou, "it ain't that. It ain't, Clyde. 'Cause I know Cousin Drewey loves cyclones like no man on earth. But if the wind changes its course from west to *east,* and we don't get that blessed east to *west* no more, then we won't hear Cousin Drewey make music. We won't hear his fiddle suffer from the sweep of his rosined bow. . . . Then what you reckon we'll get?"

"Lou," said Clyde, talkin' back at my sister, "what we'll get is too horrible to think about. That's when we'll turn our ears to the west, not east; when we'll cock 'em yonderly to the Hank Hudgeons Territory. We won't hear sweet music; all we'll get will be that sorry

COUSIN DREWEY & THE HOLY TWISTER 151

sonofabitch makin' a political speech."

But the wind hadn't changed just yet. It still went east to west.

"Listen," Verbaline Lou told Clyde, "Cousin Drewey ain't fiddlin' no more. Reckon he'll give us another tune?"

Clyde said, "Lou, Cousin Drewey *had* to end his fiddlin' when he did. He had to 'cause we couldn't keep lovin' on the grass forever, could we? Same way with Cousin Drewey; he can fiddle just so long, then he gets pooped out."

"Listen, Clyde. I think I hear Cousin Drewey again. I can hear him pickin' at his guitar. What you reckon? Does he aim to give us some different kind of music?"

"Likely."

"Does a man get pooped out with a guitar, like he does with a fiddle, or when he has a girl down on the grass?"

"Most fiddlers, yes. They always get pooped out at sunrise, after the dance has been goin' on all night long, when the caller is sufferin' mightily from a dried-out glottis. But with a guitar it's different—with that instrument a man can sing on forever, and before he knows it he's keepin' tune with Gabriel's horn."

Our girl gripped Clyde's hand; she held on real tight, and she said: "Listen, Clyde. The man is singin'. He's singin' a song, he's strummin' that old guitar. . . . You reckon it's Cousin Drewey?"

"If that ain't Cousin Drewey," Clyde said, "my name's Boaz and your name's Ruth."

"Maybe that's who we are, Clyde."

"Cain't be. Them two lovers lived in the Bible, clean back a couple thousand years. Maybe three, maybe four thousand. No tellin'."

"The sweet Lord says we'll get born again."

"Ain't that the truth now. Except I didn't hear the

Lord say it. I hear'd it out of the mouth of one of His saints—the Reverend Sam Hill of the Signal Rock Souls Redemption Center Tabernacle. But like you say, the man down there is sing'in'; and by the song he's sendin' up the mountain—the way we hear it—that man cain't be none other than Cousin Drewey. It's Cousin Drewey, sure enough."

The breeze got stronger; it worked itself into a high wind—but blessedly, it still came out of the east, not the west. And because any song Cousin Drewey sings is a love song, Clyde and my sister got into a clinch again. They heard the song and the more they heard of it the more they loved each other's neck.

> *Honeysuckle Candy Woman,*
> *How come you harass my soul?*
> *I done gave you six-bits.*
> *Now you crave a diamond ring!*

The girl was soft to Clyde's touch. Clyde was strong like Samson; and the grip he held was all she could crave. Blessedly, the wind still came from the east, and they said nary a word while they listened to the guitar-strum and the entire fifty-five verses of "Honeysuckle Candy Woman." And when the song was ended, Cousin Drewey sent them up the sixty verses that belonged to "Job's Boils."

Time sped, and still their nest up yonder was safe from any political interruptions. So safe, thanks to the wind, that Cousin Drewey rendered the short forty-five verse song that told about "The Risin' of Dead Lazarus."

The wind changed directions up in the Everywhere Mountains. That's when the sweetness out of Cousin Drewey's glottis was cut off from the ears of the lovers next to the rock.

COUSIN DREWEY & THE HOLY TWISTER   153

"Hell-fire!" Clyde said. He said that when he raised himself up off Verbaline Lou, when he got a sniff at the new air come over the big wide meadow. "Sweetness," he went on to say, "I don't care to hear that politician make a speech. I don't crave to smell them dead cow breezes come up off the Hank Hudgeons Territory, and I think it's time me and you should be gettin' back to real life, like headin' down to our ranch in Star Valley."

But my sister held tight to Clyde's shirt; she wouldn't let him get shed. If Clyde jumped clear she sure as hell wouldn't let the shirt go with him. So Clyde got down again—he laid hisse'f out on the grass. 'Cause in the Everywhere Mountains there's better things to do than listen to fellers like Hank Hudgeons make promises.

So when Hank Hudgeons made his political speech down west in his territory his talk rose up to the lush meadow. But it fed itse'f to deaf ears. It carried an arid stink. It stank of run-over spittoons in the county courthouse, of the whiskey breath of a country judge while he pounds his gavel and hollers his ignorance. The sonofabitch. And of blood, the red kind that flows off some poor jailed-up bindlestiff beat up first by the railroad dick, then by the city police. And of whores arrested by bastards, caught on the nighttime streets, hustled to jail and thrown in the ladies' section to be gang-shagged by the sheriff, him with his pants down, aided and abetted by his four deputies, each in his turn, to be followed by the jailer-cook, the janitor, the county clerk, the treasurer, the county surveyor, and lastly by the surveyor's flagman. Pure poontang, without a dime for the service; not even a "Thank you, ma'am." And it breaks a whore's heart to give out charity. The speech came up with the west wind; it blasted the rock like a grit-storm.

And I tell you, kind folks, feller Americans, registered voters of this here county, how if you'all will put your X next to my name on next year's ballot, like you did so sweetly on last year's ballot, and elect me for a second term as your dearly beloved sheriff, I promise you I'll make you a man to be proud of, a rounder-upper of all the dirty crooks that ever chance to invade the boundaries of our fair county. I'll tell you now, so he'p me the Lord, and I tell it from the depths of my pure Christian heart—a heart that was raised in Bell County, Texas, there in the Blacklands—how there's crooks roamin' our delicious landscape, and there's honest citizens down on their knees, prayin' to the Lord for justice, for life, liberty and the pursuit of happiness.

There's low, mean, strictly no'count thieves in the night, like that there plumb, honest to God dirty one who rustled Mr. Fats Recknagel's beef; rustled it out of that gentleman's pasture while that gentleman slept in his bed, while he dreamed of high finances like the best grade of gentlemen do when they go to sleep. And folks, that was high-quality Black Angus beef that that dirty thief stole. It was worth five hundred dollars in Denver, Kansas City, or Fort Worth. Mr. Fats Recknagel, that gentleman from way back, that Texan like myse'f, that shinin' light of this county, the lily of the valley, the bright and mornin' star, the dearest of ten thousand to my soul, that there gentleman, that Mr. Fats Recknagel. . . . 'Cause, folks, feller citizens, Christians all, *he* could use five hundred dollars to his sweet advantage, just like me, or you, or the next feller.

Hell's bells, folks, we've got crooks in this county, and to catch 'em we need a sheriff who's pure of heart, just like the Beatitudes say. You need a sheriff who'll get in his prowl car, with the dome-blinker flashin' red, with the siren howlin' like a lean coyote; a sheriff who'll get in that old prowl car and drive up to Star Valley, with a deputy or two by his beautiful side—and when I say beautiful, folks, I mean *beautiful*—and he'll have some handcuffs clipped to his belt, and a Smith & Wesson Police Special ready in the holster; and he'll push that prowl car at eighty, clean up to the shanty where them mossbacks live. He'll run 'em out like rats.

He'll drive his car 'round to Mr. Fats Recknagel's place, and he'll ask Mr. Fats Recknagel to kindly come out. And when Mr. Fats Recknagel, that Texas gentleman, when he sees all what the sheriff has got, them dirty crooks loaded in his car—them sorry mossbacks what stole the beef—he'll throw out his lovin' arms and hug that sheriff's neck. Folks, Mr. Recknagel will kiss that sheriff as a reward for his fine services, just like the sheriff will kiss you'all's babies for the pleasure of your votes—the best sheriff this county ever had, bar-none, none-plus. And after that sheriff, him and his sweet deputies, get Mr. Fats Recknagel's appreciation, plus the promise of a fat bonus, that's when them official boys will run the prisoners down to the county jail. They'll put that dirty old fiddler from the Washtaw Mountains in the coop what had the most cooties, and when they get him inside they'll throw that old sonofabitch who burns automobile tires on top of him. And in the next cell they'll put that sorry boy, that no'count feller; they'll kick him in behind the bars and let him be, let him flog his dummy to his sweet content. They'll give the old lady, that sorry boy's maw maw, a place for herse'f, far enough down the line so she cain't hear her yellin' daughter. And folks, you dearly beloved voters of this here county, that's when we'll take the daughter up to my office and treat her like a pretty girl should be treated. We'll send out for beer, and order sandwiches, we'll tell them to bring up potato chips and we'll put on the damnedest party this county ever saw. We'll invite the police, and the chief of police. And I tell you, with information straight from my heart, how you'll never find a more law-abidin', lady-respectin', Christian-souled, prime upright citizen like a policeman, 'specially a chief of police. And you can bet your pokes, sweet people, how when we get that mossback girl up in our office, after we give her a can of beer, all us boys in law enforcement will politely gang-shag her off. And 'cause of their sins and trespasses against that fine Texas gentleman—and I mean Mr. Fats Recknagel—we'll send them mossbacks up to the State Pen; except the girl, 'cause we like her company. . . . And I promise you fine voters of this county, you'all upright Christians, that I'll beat to a pulp every dirty crook I catch committin' misdemeanors, and I'll show you my loyalty to you'all—how I don't make empty promises, and how I'm the kind of man who . . .

When I say I *woke* up, I mean I *really* woke up. Really! Doggone! I'd done fallen asleep, aset on the bench, and I dreamed all that territorial stuff with Pap and Maw Maw settin' like concrete. There aside me. And what woke me up, out of my dream, was that thing that cut Hank Hudgeons' political speech off so sharp. I mean how the music had stopped and the folks were millin' 'round between sets. But this break was *somethin'* special, because the women were at the long tables, fixed to deal out the vittles.

There they were again, the four of them. Like Cousin Drewey and Uncle Posey, Young Buster Prather and Hank the Sheriff. And nearby stood the big-boy deputy. They joshed, acted the clown, stood aface of each other. They were middle-bent because of so much laughin'. And it was Hank who talked most out of his silly mouth. He talked that way because he was *the* high-mogul sheriff of the county, the kind of man who needs to cut loose with the windies. Natural folks call it politics.

Hank just *couldn't* be insulted; his hide was *mighty* tough. And he showed it, by the way Cousin Drewey cut in on him and made Hank tolerate somebody else's talk. It looked slightly like some brotherly love was gettin' generated between a no'count politician and a pure-D Washtaw Mountain fiddler. Hank was buildin' up that friendship like a construction crew would a skyscraper. It was *that* kind of friendship. But Hank's friendship house was the Bible-parable kind—Matthew or Luke, no tellin' which. It was built on sand, had flimsy foundation and a roof that leaked. And that make of house just can't stand straight. It's bound to topple, and when it does . . .

Lord! Great is the fall of it.

18

Us Lowdermilks are great hands for tendin' our own business. Now it looked mighty like Star Valley was givin' us a dose of our own stuff, for the folks in the dance room were leavin' us mightily alone. We sat stuck to our bench, in dread. All the wooden bits of furniture in that big room had more life to them than we had. Like the teacher's desk and the forty kids' desks that were pushed way to the back and piled in a heap. They had more life and movement than us Lowdermilks. Because what scared us was the possibility of how someone out of the mill-'round crowd might come up to our bench—full of Christian charity, well meanin'—and hand us an invite. Like to say how there was plenty chicken to go 'round for everybody. Lord, did we hate the thought of anythin' like that! And to say, "You'all Lowdermilks get up off your rusties. You look like you need some pie. And that chicken yonder ain't doin' no good, gettin' cold and lookin' golden."

We sat there thinkin, feelin' sorry for any man—or more likely any woman—who'd waste good time handin' us Lowdermilks an invite. Because what we'd do, the three of us, if such would happen . . . Well, hell, we'd just quit chompin' on our quids and dips; we'd look with empty stares to the other side of the room; we'd set so still and stiff that even ourselves would figger the situation lifeless; and we'd pay that kindly human bein' no lick of mind. It was a terrible thought, because it *could* happen.

And yet it riled us slightly while we watched all the valley eat chicken and nary a mortal quiz us for the state of our hunger.

But plenty movement percolated front of the fiddler's throne. I saw Cousin Drewey lead the way to the chicken-table, and Uncle Posey pull Young Buster Prather along next to him—the fat-assed deputy ploddin' at their heels. But Hank the Sheriff stood his ground. His thoughts of chicken might have been sweet, but the itch in his glottis was gettin' primed—and he smiled while he looked 'round, showin' off his white teeth, on the hunt for to kiss a baby.

Old Man Lee Bassett was back at the door again. He had a plate loaded, yellow with chicken and potato chips. Fact was how fried poultry was getting massacreed. But he still played sentry while he held his dish, took potato salad, while he sipped pink drink. He'd throw his eyesight out to the yard. Maybe some fresh souls had come up and parked their cars—no tellin'. Old Man Lee was faithful that way.

If a man aims to make a speech, it ain't right to have fried chicken crammin' his mouth. If a man gets fixed to plead for votes, it's best for him to get high, like up on the fiddler's throne. And that's where Hank the Sheriff got—way up next to the ceilin', where all could see his good-natured face while he called compliments on Star Valley, and to let farm folks know the dire political situation, how "one good term deserves another," how the county *needs* Hank the Sheriff, needs him like Earl the Baby needs a clean change of didies.

There he was, by God, Hank Hudgeons! He'd gotten himself high. Most folks didn't pay him no mind—yet.

Because most folks were milled 'round the chicken tables, loadin' their plates with all the goodies the women were dishin' out. And they said to each other, like this, "I *do* hope the sweet Lord will let us get some of this chicken ate before them lovers drive up outside. Because I *do* love potato salad, and this here macaroni and cheese is plumb larrupin'. Maybe them lovebirds won't get here for awhile yet, though I'd like right smart to love Verbaline Lou's neck. Lord! There won't be no more chicken-eatin' after Old Man Lee hollers 'Hogs in the corn.' "

Us Lowdermilks kept aset; we saw the hand-writ on the wall. The handwrit told how Hank the Sheriff would be taxin' his glottis—and sooner than later my sister, Verbaline Lou, Pap's sugar-tit gal, she and her man, would be struttin' in to make their declaration and get the hugs of the multitude.

"Ladies and gentlemen, grandpaps and widderwomen!"

That was Hank the Sheriff and he yelled his political isms. Folks might be gassin', they might be talkin' crops and livestock—and all the miseries and blessin' thereof. They might have put Hank out of their minds while Star Valley acted sociable with Star Valley. But us Lowdermilks had nothin' else to do but set like we were made of Gunnison granite.

"Kind people, *please*. . . . Unaccustomed as I am toward public speakin' . . . Folks, *please!* I'd be proud of your attention, for just one minute, *please*. I'd be right smart . . ."

Now the folks were movin' away from the vittles table; they were munchin' merrily on all they had on their plates, and all they needed was an earful of politics before they put their dirty plates down, belched in his or her turn, and went to the water bucket for to wash out their mouths with a swig at the dipper. Them who packed toothpicks would sure as hell use them.

"Kind friends of Star Valley, feller Americans, gentlemen, and ladies, sweethearts all . . ."

Hank must have felt good when he saw the folks crowd up in front of where he was at. He had his mouth cleared of spit, he was an old boy primed for action.

I ain't the make of feller who'll blow his whistle, like you already know. 'Cause you know me for the best sheriff this county ever had. You know how I've served you, kindly and true, for the solid year since last election day, which was twelve-month ago come the first Tuesday in November, comin' up. And it ain't more'n six weeks 'til this year's first Tuesday in November, comin' up. But there won't be no election this year. That means I'll have another solid twelve-month to serve you, with all my honest might, from the depths of my lovin' heart. And come the first Tuesday in November, next year comin' up, that's when I'll try to serve you a second term, the best sheriff this county ever had, or ever will have.

You know how you'll have my kind protection from all the doggone crooks, with me in the county courthouse, me and my deputies, me and my prowl-car and the gun on my hip, you'll know how your kids and womenfolks will be safe from thugs and rapers. And Lord, how this Hank Hudgeons loves your womenfolks! You bet! And how can I wrap your darlin' kids in my manly arms and kiss their angel faces! Hell yes! And if their snot-nose countenances needs wipin', it's old Hank Hudgeons who'll wipe 'em. If their didies need changin', it's your lovin' sheriff who'll change 'em.

And you men—you farmers and cattlemen, all you boys who are eatin' fried chicken right now. I tell you for the deacon's truth, with the facts laid down by Saint Paul of Tarsus, and you'll read about 'em in the Bible . . . Gents, I'm talkin', I'm tellin' you straight, upright and perpendicular, how if any doggone rustler—whether he rides a horse, a pickup truck or a mule—ever tries to molest your stock . . . You're damn whistlin'! If he ever tries it then all you need do is sic Sheriff Hank Hudgeons on him, and we'll put him in jail for a goodly stretch so he won't molest your stock no more. So all I ask you sweet people is this, if you'll kindly look up from your potato salad just a minute, is that when the next election day comes 'round, first Tuesday in November next year—not this year like you all know—and when you step with your ballots into the booth, and take up the indelible pencil . . .

Hank's talk made my ass tired. I looked away from him, had to for my own sake; he made me sick. So I gave my eyesight to Pap and Maw Maw instead. They were still concrete except for Maw Maw's dip, and the way Pap's jaw worked on his cud. Once in a while they'd pick up the can and spit. But they didn't get my eyesight for long. I saw how they had theirs glued on Old Man Lee Bassett, him sentry at the door. And altogether, us three, we saw how he was lookin' out to the yard to see what'all. And what'all he saw was car-lights headin' toward the school from off the main road; factways, it was an automobile; double-factways, it came like a bat out of hell.

Pap and Maw Maw were two in cahoots, partners packin' the same thought-of-mind. They figgered how maybe I'd joined the corporation how my mindly figgerin' was slightly kin; and all three of us reckoned how Old Man Lee might be the fourth stockholder; altogether our product was how Clyde and Verbaline Lou—them lovebirds—and the balance of the Skinners would be comin' hell-bent to strut some at the dance.

Nobody but us paid mind to the door. Every soul was up front listenin' to what Hank Hudgeons had to say. Like I say, he made my ass tired. Most part of Star Valley looked up to him on the fiddler's throne. Some farmers stood off from the balance, talkin' serious in bunches, and all about farm-dirt and good four-legged livestock. Then, too, there were boys in a funny frame of mind who liked to hooraw—and they gave it in hecklin' Sheriff Hank Hudgeons.

"Say, Hank, how many mean outlaws have you sent to sparks up in the electric chair, this state and in good old Texas?" That was a plain dirt farmer joshin' old Hank.

"Aplenty."

"Say, Hank, when you kissed our baby did he taste better'n my neighbor's down the road? Did he taste of ice cream and honey, or did he seem like his didies need changin'?"

"Please, friend Orville," the sheriff said back at Orville Klingsinger, "I'll thank you kindly if you just let me plead my cause for reelection next year, 'cause time is fleetin' on the wings of eternity and I need all the minutes from now to that blessed first Tuesday in November next year so's to let you know what a prime sheriff you've got."

The folks hooted at that.

"Ladies and gentlemen, *please!*" hollered old Hank high over the noise. "*Please* let me speak my political speech."

"Prime sheriff, prime bull!" hollered a cowboy feller.

"Please . . ."

So the folks hushed their mouths and let Hank say some more. That's when Old Man Lee faced the congregation, pulled in his wind and let it out: "Hogs in the corn! Hogs in the corn!" Old Man Lee ran for the big table as he hollered, there to get rid of his plate and pink drink. The crowd moved to do likewise, and Cousin Drewey and Young Buster Prather leaped for the fiddler's throne, knockin' Hank Hudgeons off as they hit the heights. Uncle Posey Burwinkle pulled the long-handled ladle off the grip of the Widow Langley, as she stood next to the dishpan half-full of potato salad. The ladle dripped potato-and-onion white, but it made a musician's beat-stick of the finest kind. "Hogs in the corn!" Old Man Lee hollered, for a third and final time.

Now the room was heavin' as the folks stood plateless, them havin' dumped their vittles. They crowded at the door 'til Old Man Lee, the best kind of romance-boss, made them stand to either side, to leave a way for the lovebirds to come through. Hank Hudgeons felt slightly mad, because he figgered the county's political good had been kicked aside in favor of matrimonial monkeyshines. He figgered a prime sheriff was better for the public welfare than a half-assed bridegroom polished like an apple. He was mad; he could have chewed spikes and spit nails, then used his teeth to grind the nails to tacks.

Cousin Drewey was high on his throne, with the bow raised for the ready signal, the fiddle under his chin. He held a keen eye on Uncle Posey, whose hand held the band leader's beat-stick. If the ladle beat-stick dripped potato salad it didn't make the "Bridal March" less sweeter.

There came a human presence at the door. So Uncle Posey gave the down-beat.

Well hell! It wasn't my sister and her lovin' man who came through the door smack into the glory of it but Sonny Boy skinner and his wife Lilybelle, and their mop-headed, bullet-skulled, wet-didied kids. Sonny Boy

COUSIN DREWEY & THE HOLY TWISTER 165

walked with a crook-headed cane. His sprained foot was out of the cast, no more did he need crutches. Old Man Lee hollered "Quit!" And doggone! The music stopped of a sudden.

"Where'all's them lovebirds?" somebody yelled out of the crowd.

Sonny Boy just stood, lookin' slightly silly. Lilybelle made tracks to where some women stood off aways, to the side, like they figgered the show might not be the circus billed to be. My! Lilybelle looked sweet, all dressed up for the dance! And Sonny Boy, still lookin' silly, raised a hand for to get Star Valley's attention.

"Friends and neighbors," he said, loud so every soul could hear. "If you'll let me say a word this romantic night, I'll tell you what'all about Clyde and Verbaline Lou, so that when they get here they won't suffer none from what's popularly called embarrassment. It was mighty kind of you to have the boys play the 'Bridal March,' which is my favorite tune for a fact. But I cain't see the sense of renderin' that sweet melody unless you've got a bride and groom to fit. And we sure as hell *don't* have no bride and groom here at the Star Valley dance this bright and moonlight night."

Lilybelle was explainin' the situation to the women off yonder, and what she said couldn't be heard by the crowd. But the women heard. They clicked their tongues and nodded. What Lilybelle said was all right with them.

"Where's them lovebirds?" somebody quizzed to know, speakin' for everybody in the room.

"You mean Clyde and Verbaline Lou?" Sonny Boy said.

"We don't mean nobody else."

"They're aset."

"Where'all?"

"Outside."

"In the Chivelee?"

"You bet."

"Are they married-up?"

"Cain't say that they be but they're engaged."

"Aw shucks!" said a woman in the crowd, and everybody else got to moanin' and groanin' like the pains of disappointment had caught them mightily. Everybody made a mournful racket, except Cousin Drewey, the man on the fiddler's throne, and us three Lowdermilks down on the far-side bench against the wall. We didn't groan, we didn't mourn. Because we had better things to do, like lookin' at a mob of human bein's primed for somethin' they couldn't get.

Couldn't get what, goddamn it?

No weddin' march, no weddin' ring on the left-hand finger, no weddin' dick down in Clyde's pants, no nothin'. Nothin', the silly sonsofbitches! No romance, no sweet night of love, two in a bed, comin' up, like Uncle Gersh gettin' pooped in the parlor house in Tulsa. . . . Three dollars a throw.

That's when the doorway was suddenly blocked by a mighty sweet sight, somethin' to behold. There they stood, hand in hand, blockin' the doorway and smilin' to beat hell. They beamed at the mob, like to say "Now ain't you'all surprised?" Slightly, they made me sick. The mob gulped for admiration—country folks are simple. Sonny Boy got out of the way so's the picture could be seen by all. There stood my sister; but she wasn't my sister no more. She was a woman, all right, but she wouldn't fit into our shanty-shack. She didn't belong in the home-sweet-home where Pap had his shotgun hangin' on the wall, or where Maw Maw burned old automobile tires in the stove-grate. The girl in the doorway had a name, which couldn't be Lowdermilk. Or if it were Lowdermilk she'd better get shed of it, quick, to match her finery. Pap might have given seed to make her, maybe Maw Maw suffered the pains. But if that girl was on the street, in Signal Rock or anywhere else, and she'd walk up to me and say, "Brother Newt, I'm Verbaline Lou Lowdermilk, you'all's sister, Pap's sugar-tit gal." If she'd meet me and say that there, then I'd be forced to surrender my manly manners and call her a dad-blamed liar. Because *that* girl was high-society, a fact as truthful as any preached by Bible prophets to the Benjaminites.

Both together, she and Clyde were dressed for the square dance Western style. My sister had on a frilled dress of blue and white, shamelessly short-skirted and without sleeves. And spangles, no stockin's and the prettiest slippers. There were blue earrin's at her lobes, 'round her neck was a gold-colored necklace. Bracelets too, at both wrists. But it was the hair-do that caught my surprise, and a teensy slice of admiration. Lilybelle must have fixed *that*. That was the prettiest head ever to top a mortal woman. It was clean-neat, not dusty mossback. It hung like a pony tail down her back, held together with a clip to match her bracelets. And her mouth was red, painted that way, and her eyes sparkled for freedom, for some brand of joy that she'd won, not by work but by bein' just pure Verbaline Lou. And Clyde Skinner, there by her side, was every bit the Cowboy King to match a Western Queen.

I can say so now as I've more-times thought it out with my skimpy mind. Like thisaway: that Lou was never too much like us Lowdermilks. Maybe Maw Maw thought it, and Pap, too. But like me, they kept what they thought to themselves. As a kid, she was gawky; that's natural as milk. Feel her, she was soft; listen to her voice, it was gentle; see her walk, and she didn't carry the mossback slouch. In spite of our eternal pot-likker greens, and our cornbread and fat-back, and the everlastin' can of black syrup aset the lean-to table my sister *never* took on fat. Even in brogue-shoes and Washtaw

Mountain-style gown, under a sunbonnet—times when all she needed was a clay pipe or snuff-dip to be true corn-patch woman—she stayed trim all over, and walked proud like Cleopatra, and never in her earthly days seemed lubricated with grease, like country girls are inclined to get slicked anywhere where there's country.

Folks stampeded to greet her, to love her neck and pump Clyde's hand. Women cackled like hens in a coop, bit farmers roared how they were mighty pleased with Clyde's selection of a woman, and to match her looks, Verbaline Lou paid out good manners. She loved necks, even to Uncle Posey Burwinkle who'd never been loved by a pretty girl before. She looked to the ceilin', she and Clyde. Clyde whooped like a Comanche when he saw the painted red hearts; and I saw my sister get tickled with delight—and she hollered "Who'all?" When Mistress Lee Bassett confessed to makin' them, with the he'p of neighbor-women, Verbaline Lou hugged Mistress Lee's neck. And she danced 'round like this was her *big* night, talkin' to everybody, pullin' Clyde along like he belonged to her, which for a fact he did. And closer and closer, minute by minute, she was gettin' near to the back wall—where us Lowdermilks were aset. And as she moved, the crowd moved with her.

19

It was Sunday again, next mornin' after the dance. Me and Cousin Drewey were high on the wagon seat. We looked down on Signal Rock, a town with the Sunday mornin' blues. Folks down there were not yet up and spry, except maybe those who aimed to take a couple hours at church. That kind shuffled 'round some, maybe; and reckoned themselves sinners all, meat for repentance. Sinners get that way when they feel the flames of hell dustin' their faces, while the feller down the pit keeps honin' his scythe for to reap them to where they belong. That's the way sinners act, and Signal Rock had more of that breed than Old Man Lee Bassett's yard has chickens.

Me and Cousin Drewey were thoughtful in cahoots. We reckoned how just then the Reverend Sam Hill would be sweepin' the floor of his Signal Rock Souls Redemption Center Tabernacle. He'd be dustin' off the pedestal from where he everlastin'ly preached hell-fire. And both of us, me and Cousin Drewey, saw him in our mind's eye. He'd set his hat brimside-up, right front of that place of stance. Because he was bustin' a gut to catch the collection. Reverend Sam was mighty proud of the way his sinners dropped dimes and nickels in the hat. That's why he owned the biggest hat in Star Valley. And it's sweet to think, along with the Reverend Sam Hill, how a hat that size can hold plenty coin to buy lard and sugar and flour, plus a week's supply of snuff-dips. But too, bein' a preacher, Reverend Sam got his fried chicken without money. He everlastin'ly traveled 'round the farmwives to hand out salvation. Because *that* was his stock in trade.

How come we looked down on Signal Rock that Sunday mornin' was because our kinfolks and me were headin' up the San Pablo foothills for to get a wagonload of stove-wood. Old Jeff the mule was strainin' inside his shafts, pullin' on the tugs and single-tree. He made mule-sweat, even though the sun had barely come up. The wagon was empty except for us two humans, and the axe and lash-ropes, and Cousin Drewey's fiddle in its case. All that stuff and his old guitar. Because he aimed to sing some while I cut timber and loaded the wagon. He was *that* kind of musician. Down below, the town and valley were spread out like a pretty quilt on a feller's bed. We could see far and wide.

Just the day before, Saturday, while Cousin Drewey rested on his gunny-sack bed under the box elder, he eased his arm muscles slightly so's to be trimmed for fiddlin'-out the dance comin' up that night. It was before noon and we both ached for dinner. I sashayed over to gas with him a spell. Like always, he was chewin' cud. He sniffed at times toward the house lean-to where Maw Maw was cookin' up some good Cousin Drewey beef, the same that hung down the root cellar. If Cousin Drewey categorized himself as a cattle-rustlin' sinner, it didn't meddle with his appetite. He was the *eatin'est* man.

"Kinfolks," I said, "do you smell them beef-chunks afryin'? Don't your philosophies tell how Maw Maw got 'em in hog fat? . . . And guess what, she's gettin' the heart and tongue fixed to boil in the big iron pot, it settin' in the yard. Maw Maw said to me, 'Newt, you cut some wood and get a fire goin' under that big iron pot, 'cause we're goin' to have mixed heart and tongue for supper. It'll take all day to cook.' "

"If that's the bill o'fare for this bright Saturday it's all right with me," Cousin Drewey said. He was squirtin' cud and lookin' like a man who knew his likes and dislikes. "I like beef hearts, 'specially if the womenfolks stuff 'em with onions and wild parsley, with some hog grease to make 'em slick. I like the tongue cooked down with plenty salt. But I'll confess, Newt, that I don't care to eat no heart or tongue that's been boiled down in the same iron pot that boiled up Pap Lowdermilk's drawers last washday."

I felt like I'd have to comfort Cousin Drewey. So I said, "You won't taste no soap or lye, kinfolks. I've done scraped off the soap-scummin's already. If a little lye can get the sweat out of Pap's drawers, it can tenderize beef-heart too. Maybe it'll give it some taste like you cain't buy at the Hilton Hotel in Tulsa."

"I ain't got the style to eat beef-heart in the Hilton Hotel," Cousin Drewey said.

"Me neither," I confessed. "I just said it from what I hear'd." I got out my Brown's Mule plug like I aimed to set.

"Newt," Cousin Drewey said, all asudden, "when you cut that wood for Maw Maw's pot this mornin', you didn't notice how the supply of cedar is gettin' kind'a low? There's just a few sticks left, and my soul is pained for the thought of it."

"It's low enough," I said back at Cousin Drewey. "And I'll say how my soul is pained like yours. I fear for what the neighbors will say when there ain't no more cedar to burn."

"Newt, me and you will need take old Jeff the mule and hitch him to the wagon and we'll go up to the foothills and get us a load of cedar. You can take the axe so's you can cut that scrub cedar down. And I'll take my guitar and fiddle so's to sing you a song while you work."

"When you reckon we can go, Cousin Drewey?"

"Tomorrow mornin', bright and early."

"Won't you be pooped out after fiddlin' for the dance all night?"

"Maybe," said Cousin Drewey, usin' a sweet smile up-side of his chin-stubble, "but it's you who'll do the choppin'."

"I won't give a damn about you settin' on your royal-rusty," I said. "I won't hold you sinful if you don't lend a he'pin' hand, I won't care, just so long as you sing me a sweet song like 'Job's Boils' or 'Potophar's Sufferin' Woman.' 'Cause, Cousin Drewey, the thought of us gettin' low on stovewood, and the great stink that will happen when we run out, makes me as miserable as a human bein' can get."

"You talk wisdom, Newt," said Cousin Drewey. "Your fears are honest as Bible prophesy. And a fear like that can shake a man 'til he runs for cover and holds a sack to his nose."

The fears and prophesies Cousin Drewey talked about, which made my guts turn sour, was how Pap Lowdermilk, always when we ran out of stovewood, would get to filin' his axe-blace into sharpness, then set to cuttin' up his sacred supply of old automobile tires. He'd do that there in the yard and put the pieces in a bucket. Then he'd take them to Maw Maw for to burn in the cookstove, to make heat and rile every human soul in Star Valley. Lord, what a man! Us three Lowdermilks—me, Maw Maw and Verbaline Lou—would stand and groan while he piled the chunks of rubber in the grate, while he'd whittle kindlin' and strike a match. One sniff of that burnin' rubber and we turned pale like

COUSIN DREWEY & THE HOLY TWISTER 173

we had a sickness kin to death.

That foolish Pap Lowdermilk would put his nose down clean to the stove lid and smell that terrible arome —he'd act like he was smellin' a skilletful of brains and eggs, like it was plumb larrapin'. Then he'd stand up and face us balance proudly and say, "This here rubber makes the best fire. It makes heat like nothin' else. And I don't give a damn what the neighbors think inside their heads or say out of their silly mouths."

There now!

They'd think us Lowdermilks worse than hog-slop. And you couldn't blame 'em.

When we leveled off at the rimrock, high atop the mountain bench, the road made easier pullin' for old Jeff. Upgrade, even an empty wagon can be a burden for an old mule. Nigh all folks in Star Valley owned teams and wagons, not just *one* mule between shafts. Their horses pulled at double-trees and they were mighty in their strength. Which tells a feller how us Lowdermilks were mighty poor. We couldn't get ahead to own better'n a single mule. But we were lucky to own old Jeff. That mule was the best puller, with more sense and love for us Lowdermilks than any other four-legged piece of traction in the sonofabitchin' world. And to pay Jeff back for all he did for us we fed him and loved him dearly. But I know for a fact how none of us loved him more than did Cousin Drewey.

"You know, Newt," Cousin Drewey said to me, one time back when we gassed for nothin' better to do, next to the box elder tree, "I love that mule, I truly do. I love him so much I'd like to have him for my own. I'd like to ride him back to the Washtaw Mountains. Just me and old Jeff, both aset on the cloud, on the big black-and-green spin-'round cloud; I mean the tornado of my dreams, the one that will carry us back to the Washtaw Mountains. How old you reckon old Jeff to be, Newt?"

"Lord, no tellin'!" I said. "I know he pulled us and the wagon out from the Washtaw Mountains, and that was a long time ago. He must be the oldest mule in the valley, and Lord knows what Pap will do when old Jeff falls down in death."

"You cain't kill a good mule, even when you give him a dose of old age," Cousin Drewey said. "Me and Jeff are old together, and if that mule could speak he'd say how he'd love to die in the Washtaw Mountains where water is black and the grass is thick and wet."

"You and old Jeff ain't fixed to die just yet, Cousin Drewey."

"We ain't, Newt," said Cousin Drewey back at me, "and that's because Star Valley ain't the Washtaw Mountains."

We came to a nice place on the bench where the cedar growth was right for cuttin'. That is, there was enough dead wood 'round to load up the wagon. I jumped out, carryin' the axe; and Cousin Drewey slid off the seat with his guitar and fiddle. We'd taken a Sunday dinner along—some hunks of cornbread, cold fried meat, and a glass jar full of factory-made sorghum. It was the kind you buy at the store, sorry stuff for a fact but the best to be found in Star Valley. It was plumb insult to folks who'd come out of the Washtaw Mountains.

And, too, we had stopped at a place where the grass was aplenty; for mules have got to eat. While I cut and piled, while old Jeff gave snout to the bunch-grass, Cousin Drewey sat his royal-rusty on the ground, laid his back against a cedar trunk, took guitar in hand and sang us a sweet song of his own manufacture. He sang "Job's Boils."

While I cut timber and Jeff pulled on grass, I got my mind on the tender categories of life, like my sister's romance with Clyde Skinner and what those lovebirds aimed to do.

The sweet smell of fresh cut cedar made me think of

COUSIN DREWEY & THE HOLY TWISTER 175

that very last night, that Saturday night at the schoolhouse dance, the night before, when Verbaline Lou came in from the dark and Old Man Lee Bassett hollered "Hogs in the corn!"—the signal that told all folks how maybe a bride and groom was there in our midst. . . . Lord, how everybody in that room hollered praises! God Almighty, how we all expected Clyde to shout: "That's right, kind people, me and Lou here have roped ourselves into marriage-joy, and may all our troubles be little ones settin' their blossoms in didies."

But Clyde didn't shout no such thing. He just went 'round shakin' hands with the menfolks while the women ran over to love Verbaline Lou's neck.

Everyone laughed and joshed. And all the while I knew what was devilin' Maw Maw's mind, that which made her talkless, fixed her in a set-down stance kin to death, perpendicular like a pillar of Lot's salt. Poor Maw Maw was miserable while she made essence of a snuff-dip.

Out of her eyes she seemed to say: *They ain't married-up yet . . . Her and Clyde . . . She and her lovin' man . . . Say daughter, has Clyde ravished your virginity, made hash of your bud? And your tubes . . . How are your tubes this bright and moonlit night?*

I looked at Pap, settin' there t'other side, a sour man for a fact. He chewed on his cud, spat juice in the can, and kept mutterin' over and over again, "Here we've got a chippy bitch. She'd done gone to hell. She ain't my sugar-tit gal no more."

Lord, was Verbaline Lou pure Jezebel! I Kings 18, 19. Because her dress and spangles were outlandish, and they showed off her shape beyond reason. It was the way Lilybelle dressed her up. If she wasn't my sister I wouldn't give a damn. Lilybelle looked all right no matter how little she wore. But Lilybelle ain't my sister.

"She ain't my sugar-tit gal no more."

Lord, sweet Jesus . . . Forgive her, sweet Jesus . . . For-

give me, sweet Jesus, for my thoughts . . .

That was Maw Maw thinkin'. She thought as best she could until Verbaline Lou came dancin' up front of us Lowdermilks, bright-eyed and smilin', brazen like her kind of woman was made to be.

"Howdy, Maw Maw," said the shameless girl, bracelets on her wrist.

Maw Maw sat dumb-faced, like Verbaline Lou hadn't talked to her at all, like that get-of-her-loins might be far away in Hale County, Texas, someplace, no tellin' where. But nowhere near us Lowdermilks.

Our girl bent over, fixed to love Maw Maw's neck. But when she got closer she thought better. So she just kissed Maw Maw's brow. A man couldn't blame her, because Copenhagen essence dripped down Maw Maw's chin, and no girl or boy craves to kiss territory like that. But brow or chin, Verbaline Lou's love-show for Maw Maw went thankless. She might as well kissed a lightpole outside the schoolhouse. Maw Maw played like her girl wasn't there; it's the way us Lowdermilks are built.

Verbaline Lou gave a change to her looks, all asudden. She wasn't smilin' now but had the same brightness in her eyes. She could read the writ inside Maw Maw, put there by the Lord's sweet hand.

"You got mighty bad thoughts about me, Maw Maw," Verbaline Lou said. "I can read it like writ in the Book of Judges, and I know you're judgin' me; how you won't let me rest in your mind, and I know how you listen to Pap when he calls me names. Look, Maw Maw, I ain't bad. I ain't what you think I am. You know what, Clyde sleeps out in the bunkhouse where Joe and Odis have their bedrolls laid out, them two cowboys, the fellers the Skinner boys hire. Clyde sleeps in a bed, though, 'cause he don't need to quit like the cowboys do so often. Me and Clyde don't sleep together, because we ain't married up yet. But Clyde and Sonny Boy are buildin' a house, right on headquarters. And when they get it done, that's where me and Clyde will live. Right now I've got a bed in Lilybelle's house, the old Skinner ranch-house, where she lives with Sonny Boy, him and the kids. We'd sure like you and Pap to come up and see the house they're buildin' for Clyde and me. It sure is pretty, because it's got a porch painted with white paint."

Pap sat there next to us, plumb-concrete. The only life he had was in his mind, where he wished he'd brought his shotgun along to the dance. If he'd done that he could have shot Clyde Skinner dead, left him for the piss-ants. So Verbaline Lou paid him no mind. She moved over front of me and put a hand on my shoulder, like sisters naturally do.

"How're you, Newt?" she said, from out of her red-painted lips.

"Tolerable," I said back at her.

I looked down and clasped my hands, held them between my knees, settin' there—feelin' half-silly, t'other half shamed. A feller doesn't know what to do when his sister comes up front of him, dressed like a picture in the Sears Roebuck catalogue and smellin' like a whorehouse.

"When you comin' up to the ranch, Newt?" she quizzed. "You know, t'other day Sonny Boy said to Clyde, 'Clyde, we sure could use Newt up here at the ranch because we need them ponies ridden more than they get. They just eat their fool heads off in the corrals and out on the pasture, and they need a saddle on them and a good man to keep 'em gentled. A quarter horse is that kind of critter and Newt Lowdermilk is the boy to keep 'em in shape.'"

I knew I'd better say nothin' to that, because if I'd hinted how I'd like to, which I *really* did, on the way home Pap would have cold-cocked me with a rock. Because Pap Lowdermilk hated Clyde Skinner worse'n a hound-dog hates a rattlesnake.

"And do you know what Clyde said back to Sonny Boy? He said, 'Brother, that's the best talk I've hear'd for many a day. We *do* need Newt to keep them ponies gentled. We could send to El Paso and get Newt a ridin' outfit clean out of S.D. Myres. We'll get him a double-rigged saddle and a nice Navajo blanket to fit, and a bridle with a set of Crockett bits; and the best chaps money can buy, brown chrome leather with nine-inch wings.' That's what Clyde said to Sonny Boy."

She was temptin' me, like Delilah did Samson, but I still hung my head.

"And you'll never guess what Sonny Boy said back at Clyde! 'Cause Sonny Boy said, 'Brother Clyde, you're entirely right. We need Newt to keep them horses gentled, and we'll pay him wages for it, and he can stay in the bunkhouse along with Joe and Odis. We can measure Newt for size and get him a pair of shop-made boots out of Olathe, Kansas, and he'll need a pair of Kelly spurs, silver mounted with inch-and-a-half rowels. Lord, how the girls will admire Newt when they see him come down Main Street in Signal Rock, wearin' his shop-made boots and his John B. Stetson hat!' And the way Clyde and Sonny Boy talked, Newt, they'd *sure* like to give you a job at the ranch. You'd get the same wages Joe and Odis get."

My Lord!

She'd have talked some more, but just then there came a mighty commotion in the dance room. Uncle Posey Burwinkle suddenly got high on a chair, cupped his hands to make a funnel for his mouth and hollered, "All right, you folks! Doggone, you'all better get fixed to stomp 'cause Cousin Drewey has a hand on the bow and his fiddle ready to give us a tune, and Young Buster Prather's got some ticklin' fingers to his banjo . . ."

Let me say now how it was Clyde who put a quietus to his sweet love's temptation; 'cause he made her quit buyin' me out of the Lowdermilk shanty with the vision of a double-rigged S.D. Myres saddle, it packin' a four-inch cantle and a fourteen-inch swell. He didn't say how I could get the girls on Signal Rock Main Street to admire my good looks, me in a brand-new pair of Hyer's boots out of Olathe, Kansas. It took Clyde Skinner to chouse Delilah out of Verbaline Lou. He came up swingin' on his boots, grabbed our girl like a bale of hay and pranced her out to the dance floor. He didn't pay us Lowdermilks a lick of mind.

Walkin' home that night, us Lowdermilks figgered how it was best not to say a word, 'cause that word might be Verbaline Lou, and when the name of a sinnin' girl is spoken it makes for ire. Pap was ired enough. And if we ired him some more he'd pick up a rock. Now, high over the rimrock on the San Pablo bench, the same Cousin Drewey music pulled my thoughts away from the dance of the night before. I swung my axe and let it bite into the tough cedar, and I stopped choppin' only when I put the stovewood in little heaps, ready to load on the wagon. Only this hour he was strummin' sweetly at his guitar. He'd changed songs, unbeknownst to me. I'd had my mind so dad-blamed set on the remembrance of our girl, and how she acted at the dance, that I failed to hear how Cousin Drewey had changed from "Job's Boils" to "Honeysuckle Candy Woman." I hadn't noticed, even though I'd swung my axe to the tunes—up high, then hit low, and the faster Cousin Drewey gave of his glottis the quicker I cut the stovewood and flung it into heaps.

While Cousin Drewey sang the twenty-fifth verse of his favorite song I figgered I had enough wood cut and split to fill the wagon-bed. So I caught old Jeff and hitched him back to the wagon, and Jeff and me went from heap to heap. I threw on the wood, I packed it down before lashin' it with ropes. Jeff needed a right kind of dinner. For that reason I'd packed a nosebag under the wagon-seat, it loaded with corn-chops. Reward for a faithful mule. Jeff could feed himself once I hung it on, while me and Cousin Drewey rested from our labors and ate our dinner. So we settled down on our hockers, me and that musical man. We bust off hunks from the cold fried meat; it was tough, but made action for our teeth, which we chomped in time with Jeff at the nosebag. We bent over handy to a flat-topped rock, before we blowed off the dust and poured sorghum molasses on the face, enough to take the dips of our cornbread. It made sweet globber. Maybe we ate dirt, but what the hell! A little dirt down the gullet never hurt anybody.

"Goddamn it to hell, Newt!" Cousin Drewey hollered, like a red ant had stung him or somethin'.

I spat first, then said, "What'all, Cousin Drewey?"

Cousin Drewey kicked at the bunch-grass. Because of his forgetfulness he was loaded with ire. "Newt," he said, "I plumb forgot, and it ain't me to forget my generosity. You worked hard at cuttin' that stovewood, and I did likewise at the guitar-music. But I aim to ask you a prominent question, Newt. What the hell did I bring my fiddle along for? You're a deservin' boy, 'cause you sweated like a twenty-unit chain-gang cuttin' down that old cedar scrub. . . . So if you'll oblige me to listen, I'll give you some fiddle-music. I'll play you 'Bull At The Wagon'—it's the tune your Uncle Gersh loved most back in the Washtaw Mountains."

So Cousin Drewey took the fiddle under his chin, after he'd balanced his hat on the back of his head, while I hunkered down and listened. He swung the bow and tapped his right foot; like a pure-D musician he put all his weight on his left leg. And after he'd played his tune

COUSIN DREWEY & THE HOLY TWISTER   181

we packed up and got set on the wagon-seat.

We came to the rimrock and stopped before takin' the downward road. It was a plumb drop-off, the meanest down-trail west of the Railroad Mountains. Here we'd have to fell a tree and rope it to the rear axle of the wagon. We'd need it for a drag, to hold us back as we took the slope, or the loaded wagon would roll down over old Jeff and mash him to death. So I caught my axe and length of rope and slid to the ground. When I had the little tree felled and hooked to the wagon, I climbed aboard again, and we fixed to make the descent.

Leastways, that's what I aimed to do.

"Newt!" hollered Cousin Drewey—a man with somethin' to say.

"Newt, looky yonder! Boy, cain't you see it! Oh, what a beautiful sight, what a salve for sore eyes! On the east horizon, Newt, way off beyond Star Valley. Lord, I love You dearly for sendin' that there for to give peace and contentment to this old man's soul, undeservin' as I am, a sinner since the day I was born. . . ."

I leaned over with my royal-rusty snug on the seat, and I held old Jeff's leather lines loosely in my hands. I couldn't figger the old man out. Try as I might, all I could see was Star Valley down below; and the town of Signal Rock, the dustiest, nastiest huddle of streets and domiciles west of Amarillo. And off yonderly, down on the flats, I could see the Lowdermilk homestead where Maw Maw was out tendin' a stew in the yard, in the big black laundry pot, boilin' the hell out of it. And Pap would be bustin' up old automobile tires . . .

Had Cousin Drewey gone plumb craze?

"Newt, boy, has salvation come at last to this pastsinful, past-iniquitous, whiskey-guzzlin', whoremongerin', past-gamblin', past-ramblin', plumb worthless musical man? Oh what a beautiful sight, praise the Lord!"

"Could be," I said to Cousin Drewey. "But what

make of salvation have you got in your eyesight, kinfolks?"

"Newt, I think I see a tornado cloud."

I looked 'round, but all I could see was sun-yellered earth below and blue sky above.

"Where'all?" I quizzed Cousin Drewey. Old Jeff stood patiently await, wishin' for me to give a flip to the lines so's to head for that good old Lowdermilk place.

"Look yonder at the east skyline."

Now I knew our kinfolks was craze for sure, and how he couldn't tell a cyclone cloud from the planet Jupiter. He *should* know, because he was raised in the Washtaw Mountains and that's where a twister was liable to come upon us any spring or summer day. This was summer, all right, but who ever hear'd of a cyclone comin' out of the east?

I looked in the direction of Cousin Drewey's pointin' hand.

"Hell!" I said. "That ain't no twister. That's just a thunder shower that won't do the stockmen no good; and it won't come nowhere near here. We don't need twisters over Star Valley but we always need rain. Now let's get for home, 'cause . . ."

"Wait, Newt," cried our kinfolks. "Just let me look at that cloud some more from this high place. Let me set here and pretend it's a tornado sent down from heaven. It'll come down from up there like a big black bull bellerin' and pawin', makin' hash of everything it can get its hoofs on—tearin' houses into splinters, pullin' up fencelines, pushin' over trees, liftin' chicken houses clean off the sweet earth and scatterin' the feathers like snowflakes from Muleshoe to the Palo Duro Canyon. . . . Newt, I see a righteous twister, a God-fearin' tornado, a blessin' in the summertime . . ."

Again I figgered how Cousin Drewey must be craze, and there was no cure but to flip the lines to old Jeff and get the victim home to his gunny-sack bed under the box elder tree. But first I had a mighty potent quiz to ask of Cousin Drewey.

"Cousin," I said to that musical man, "how come you're so hepped about them goddamn tornadoes?"

" 'Cause I aim to ride one back to the Washtaw Mountains. That is, if I can catch one eastbound."

"They're all eastbound," I told him. "They come out of the west and make tracks for the east; crawlin' and twistin' like a side-winder rattlesnake, but makin' noise worser'n a buzz."

"Oh, the glory of it!" Cousin Drewey yelled, barkin' and stutterin' and scatterin' spit like he had religion.

"Why cain't you be satisfied with a plain-old summertime thunder and lightnin' storm?" I said. "Like a downpour of rain to put wetness on the ranges and make the grass come out live and healthy, to tassle the corn, to green up the whole world and make the farmers and stockmen sing praises to the Lord?"

"A thunderstorm ain't holy, Newt," Cousin Drewey said. "It ain't got a lick of sweet righteousness about it. I don't need that kind of fuss come down upon us, kicked out of heaven like it wasn't needed there. What I need is an eastbound tornado, one I can ride to the Washtaw Mountains, one that will let me down next to Uncle Gersh's shanty on Pitcher Creek. Then I can tell him all about you Lowdermilks, because I know he'll crave to know how you folks are gettin' along."

"We're gettin' along all right, Cousin Drewey," I said.

"Nothin' else but a *holy* twister will do, Newt," our kinfolks said, shakin' his ashy head, like he had dreams. "The kind of twister I need will sound like a worldful of folks wailin' and groanin' and gnashin' their teeth. They'll wail and groan and gnash in time with Gabriel's horn. That cloud will dance like Salome, makin' juggles of John the Baptist's head; black like a plague of locusts come down on the Land of Goshen. It'll yell like David singin' a psalm, or Solomon givin' praise to womenfolks and crash like the walls of Jericho comin' down, like brimstone fallin' on Sodom, with fury enough to expel Hagar, to turn Lot's wife into a pillar of salt. It'll be Jeremiah callin' doom on the Twelve Tribes of Israel, or Ezekiel makin' a covenant with the Lord or Micah yellin' 'Woe unto thee.' It'll sound like songs of joy at the mourner's bench in the meetin' houses of Rowan County, Kentucky. It'll be Jonah, gettin' swallered up for the salvation of them good hill-country folks. It won't be kindly religion like the Rutherfords or them that make Sabbath on Saturday, or the Assembly of God or the Lutheran brotherhood—never like the Germans 'round Altoona, Pennsylvania. It'll hoot and holler like a freight train on the Clinchfield Railroad, makin' notches through Bandana, North Carolina. Lord, will it pack religion! It won't be no sissy-pretty member of the Church of the Nazarene, or even a God-fearin' Baptist—a Barker Baptist, or a Foot-Washin', or a Forty-Gallon Baptist. Because it will be a Holy Twister, a mile long and a quarter wide, filled with hailstones out of Paradise, from the front cowcatcher to the tail-end light on the yeller caboose. It'll be a pure-D roll-'round Pentecostal Twister. Flashin' lightnin'. . . . Soundin' thunder. . . . Hollerin' tongues."

20

Us Lowdermilks didn't see much of Verbaline Lou after that last Saturday night's dance. She spent all her time up at the Skinner Ranch gettin' fixed for her weddin' day. Which put Maw Maw to frettin' about the state of her bud. Pap didn't give a damn, and he said what he thought about it all. He said so out loud.

"Goddamn it to hell, woman," he said when Maw Maw showed her concern. "She's old enough to be a man's wife, and that means she's woman enough to get caught in a mighty sinful way. Me, I don't give a damn. Before she took up with Clyde Skinner she was my sugar-tit gal. Now I've elected her a candidate for the parlor, in the house in Tulsa, where gentlemen push the button on the front door bell."

Pap had his face aimed toward Maw Maw, and his eyes blazed fire. He meant for Maw Maw to hear what he had to say. "You get what I mean wife?" he said, glarin' like a tree'd cougar-lion.

Maw Maw paid him no mind. But I could see she had a worry on her mind. Then he turned his silly face to me.

"Newt," Pap hollered. "I'd like you to put a bridle on old Jeff, mount his back and go ride among the neighbors. Kindly tell Old Man Lee Bassett how your sister has done joined the whorish sisterhood. Tell Virgie

Klingsinger and Pomona Hobbs how my sugar-tit gal of a year ago is full-blood chippy. Along with them Bible wenches. And you might tell Snookie Hapchester and Shorty Flack to go buy what she has to sell, and do it quick before she ups her price from two dollars to three. . . . I'm tellin' this about my daughter, and I'm aimin' my words at my lawful son, who is a sonofabitch if I ever saw one alive."

In spite of his ire, I noticed how Pap had a hungry look on his face. I tried to think of somethin' I could do, any damn thing to cool him down. I wished how Lilybelle would bring him a chocolate cake, make him sick as a horse, put him to bed so's he wouldn't get up 'til the day after tomorrow. He'd had beef-heart and boiled tongue for dinner just a couple days before, and after that a beef and corn stew. Maybe he needed a change from the beef Cousin Drewey stole from Fats Recknagel.

"Pap," I said. "If you'll loan me your shotgun I'll go out and get us a rabbit for supper. Maybe Maw Maw'll fry it in the skillet."

"Hell yes," Pap said, "and if you run into Verbaline Lou afore you find the rabbit, just shoot her dead. She's a woman taken in adultery and the Pharisees are fixin' to stone her to death. You'll save them Israelites a heap of trouble if you give her some buckshot from her daddy's gun."

That's when I got down the shotgun and fixed to make tracks for the gullies. The two hound-dogs were sleepin' in the shade. I didn't want them chasin' off the rabbits before I could shoot one down. So I let them sleep on. I didn't need their noise.

I thought maybe how I'd better stroll off to Oso Arroyo, where I knew the rabbits ran aplenty and where I'd sure get me a cottontail. That is, if I could shoot straight. That gully was about a mile away. And while I walked I put tender thoughts in my head, about Verbaline Lou and about all the girls in the world.

I can bring to mind a day, once before she even knew Clyde Skinner, how she told me about things she wished would happen to her, things she prayed to the Lord for, things foreign to the likes of us. She was a fool-girl dreamin' up romance. It was an evenin' when she and me were settin' alone on the porch, because Pap and Maw Maw and Cousin Drewey were out in the corn patch messin' 'round, lookin' to see how the crop was gettin' along.

"Newt," Verbaline Lou said to me, "I'm thinkin' somethin', and if I told you what it is you'd say I'm buildin' a kind of mansion in heaven, like the Lord does for them who seek and find, just like Jesus said. You'd say how the Lord would never build a mansion for Lowdermilks. That is, Lowdermilks like us. Because we're the sorriest of all Lowdermilks."

Lord, was she beautiful, settin' there dreamy-eyed! Even the dress she wore was beautiful. It had been made by Maw Maw, sewed together out of cotton print bought from Sears and Roebuck. It was made by that old lady's sorry taste, because Maw Maw had no taste at all. It packed no fashion or style. But it seemed to me a dress more beautiful than could be bought in New York, or even El Paso.

"Do you know, Newt," she said, "I'm seein' somethin', and what I see is really and truly. I see somethin' that's best in the Lord's mansion. You'll never guess what it is, Newt."

"Whatever it is," I said, "it ain't for us Lowdermilks."

"Could be," said the girl.

"We're too sorry for anythin' of the Lord's manufacture," I said.

"Maybe that's true and maybe it ain't."

"It's true all right."

"Guess what I see in my dream, Newt. Just try and guess."

"Cain't, try as I might," I told her. "I cain't guess."

"A bathtub."

I looked at her slanchways, like I didn't believe my ears.

"Say it again, sister?"

"A bathtub, Newt."

Now if there's anythin' us Lowdermilks *don't* need, it's a bathtub. Back in the Washtaw Mountains there were creeks to swim in. If we took along some soap we could call the creeks bathtubs, but most times we swam and got wet, and we just let the water take care of our dirt, clean off the sweat. Most times we got clean, but if some sweat still stuck, like with our feet, then what the hell!

But Star Valley ain't the Washtaw Mountains. The only water here is down two hundred, maybe three hundred feet, deep in the ground; and it's brought up to fresh air by the sucker-rods on windmills, piped into storage tanks, then into troughs for cattle to drink. Ranchfolks and farmfolks alike, they use the same water in their houses. But Pap and me, we have to haul water in barrels. That's 'cause we don't have a well of our own, just the kindness of a kindly neighbor who gives us all the water we need, if we go to get it. Star Valley water is loaded heavy with gyp and a dozen other nasty elements. For that reason it don't mix friendly with soap. It's Western water, it don't pack the goodness of the Ozarks. Washtaw Mountain water is clean and soft.

So I said to my sister, "We got a bathtub. It's the best bathtub, round and galvanized. And it's ours to soap-off in, so long as you or Maw Maw ain't got the dirty wash soakin' in it. Like you women do before you boil it all in the big black pot in the yard. Sister, you cain't find a bathtub better'n that one. Lord God, us Lowdermilks don't need nothin' else."

"I'm not thinkin' of a bathtub like that'n."

"Hell," I said, "it's pure galvanized."

Verbaline Lou laughed at my words, like she figgered my thinkin' was no'count.

"My bathtub is long and white," she said, "and it seems to be built right in the floor, low, shiny and pretty. It's got a faucet at one end. You turn the faucet one way, and it comes out hot water, nice clean hot water. Then you turn the handle t'other way and the water comes out cold. When you mix the two together, it's just right to get down in. You lie flat and naked. Lord, what sweetness I see in my mind! So I get wet and plaster myself all over with soap, and I sing a song of praise because I'm happier there than anywhere else I've been in all my life. Happy and clean, and after I get done I'll smell clean. I won't smell like a Lowdermilk, Newt. I won't smell like a Lowdermilk no more."

"If your name's Lowdermilk you cain't he'p but smell like a Lowdermilk, sister."

"Newt, I'll bet you ain't never seen that kind of bathtub."

"I might be mossback," I said, "but I ain't blind."

"You've seen that kind of bathtub?"

"Why sure."

"Where?"

"In the Sears and Roebuck catalogue," I confessed. "I ain't never seen one alive, but it's all right with me. Like I said, the old washtub is good enough. It's just right for my stance. It's good enough for Pap, 'cause he don't need it much. It's good enough for Maw Maw. And my Christian good sense tells me how it's good enough for you."

Verbaline Lou paid me no mine. She kept a silly smile

on her face while her eyes glistened like two sparks off a welder's torch, and she clasped her hands as she wrapped her arms 'round her knees.

Which put me in mind of the girls in the Sears and Roebuck catalogue. Lord, how us Lowdermilks loved that book!

We kept only two books in our humble home—the Lord's Holy Bible and the Sears and Roebuck catalogue. Us Lowdermilks had no truck with any other, even a book on the history of George Washin'ton. Sometimes a neighbor would give us a Monkey Ward catalog, but I reckoned then, as I do today, that the Monkey Ward girls don't come out pretty like the Sears and Roebuck girls. 'Cause there's a girl on page 34 of the Sears and Roebuck catalogue that I think is the prettiest girl in the world. There's no girl in Star Valley like she is, but Pap said he can remember one just as pretty back in the Washtaw Mountains, and her name was Annie Brightman.

"Pap," I said, "I'll bet Annie Brightman never wore a dress as pretty as this Sears and Roebuck girl."

"Well hell!" Pap said back at me, and he was *sure* ired. "You'd never get Annie Brightman in a dress like that'n, 'cause that girl was a pure-D Assembly of God Christian. Look there, Newt, on page 34, and you'll see a shameless young woman without a lick of morality. Look at that dress, will you! When that girl sets down that dress raises up so you can see her knees. No time in Annie Brightman's young days could a feller see her knees. Hell-fire and damnation, Newt, you couldn't even never see her ankles!"

Pap could talk, but I didn't give a damn. I still loved my Sears and Roebuck girl. She had the sweetest face, and her eyes were brown like her hair. It looked like she must have done somethin' to her eyebrows, but what she did was nice. She had lipstick put on where that stuff belonged and her fingernails were painted white. Gold earrin's drooped on her ears. The dress she wore was called Number 2 on page 34. I loved that girl so much that I tore out the page and kept it hid away, so's to save her from a shameful end. 'Cause you know what happens to Sears and Roebuck catalogues, sooner or later. They end up in the outhouse, where Pap spikes them to the wall with a spike. I got so tenderhearted about that girl that I didn't wish her to end-up like that.

"Newt," Pap said, one day before I tore out the page from the catalogue, "Newt, son, what you reckon that girl has got under there?"

"Pap," I said, "all we got to do is turn some pages and we'll see what that girl's got on under her dress."

So I turned the pages and I came to 179, and there was a girl in a *tricot* slip, which the book said "didn't creep, and has no bulky seams under the bust. It slims your figure."

"Newt," Pap said, "that ain't the same girl as on page 34, but she's just as shameful. But goddamn it, son, she's *sure* pretty."

"That sin't the same girl, Pap. But that slip is the kind my sweetness has got on under her dress."

"Newt, ain't she got better protection than that?"

"Hell yes! So let's turn to page 172; I've looked at that page a hundred times, and I know for a fact what kind of flimsy she's got on down there. It's what Sears and Roebuck says is 'Our Best,' and she gets 'em three for $4.44. They're called "Charmtrique' panties, and my girl orders three at a time, and they got a 'contour crotch panel,' like the book says."

"Newt, if I caught Maw Maw wearin' a thing like that I'd feed her rat poison. Verbaline Lou, well hell! I'd shoot her dead so she couldn't be shameless no more."

Pap reckoned that there long before Verbaline Lou

went up to live at the Skinner Ranch, before Lilybelle dressed her up like my girl on page 34 of the Sears and Roebuck catalogue. It was sometime before that day when Pap shot Verbaline Lou's flimsies off the clothesline, when all the bits fell down on Cousin Drewey's gunny-sack bed, pink panties and brass-seer packed full of buckshot.

The brush was thick along the rim of the gully. Oso Arroyo carried flash-flood water down from the high San Pablo Mountains, and the bottom was sandy and smooth, packed like a paved highway. That is, when it was dry, when it wasn't wild with run-off flood. And while I walked the brushy rim, wishin' for rabbit, a sight came up from down there, like a pretty picture, enough to dazzle sore eyes.

I squonched low in the brush. I asked the sweet Lord to keep me hid, because I didn't need the ire of Clyde Skinner to harass my soul. I liked that old boy, and that old boy liked me. Because what I saw down there on the sandy flat of Oso Arroyo was the Skinner pickup truck, a new and shiny Chivvelee, green. And there down beside it, on the ground was Clyde himself, him and my sister Verbaline Lou.

They had a blanket spread on the sand, store-bought, maybe Sears and Roebuck, full-blood. And atop the blanket was set some plates and bowls, filled with all kinds of baloney, bread and sweetmeats, sandwiches and pickles and the like. And lemonade in a jug, and cake the kind that Lilybelle makes that made Pap sicker'n a horse. All that kind of goodies spread out. But what wasn't spread out, on the blanket, was Clyde and Verbaline Lou. They sat close together, eatin' cake, just like King Solomon and the Queen of Sheba sat close together, eatin' grapes.

They didn't look shameful to me, although Pap Lowdermilk might think different. Verbaline Lou had blue shorts coverin' her hockers, like Lilybelle. Light blue, the color of the sky. Upside of the shorts was a shirt opened at the neck. Below the shorts there was nothin' but shoes, sissy-shoes that wouldn't stand up in a cornfield. She sat with her knees bent, lookin' sweetly at Clyde. And Clyde looked back at Verbaline Lou sweetly, with his hat hung down over the back of his neck.

There was nothin' sinful about that man and my sister. They were havin' a picnic, that's all. Leastways, for the time bein'. I thought about my page 34 Sears and Roebuck girl. I thought how I'd like to be there, settin' beside her on the blanket with the cake and pickles spread out. And we'd talk about things that girls like to hear about, maybe about Cousin Drewey and his fiddlin' music. We'd talk about me gettin' a job up at the Skinner boys' ranch after Clyde and Verbaline Lou get shackled together, man and wife by the laws of this western state.

My sweet girl and me would set like Clyde and my sister, on the blanket. Like them, we wouldn't get unsightly to the eyes of the Lord, sinful in the minds of Pap and Maw Maw, unrighteous to the thinkin' of the Reverend Sam Hill of the Signal Rock Souls Redemption Center Tabernacle. I thought to myself, how sweet!

Until I saw Verbaline Lou reach out and take Clyde's hand in her own. I saw Clyde throw his hat aside, crook an arm and hook it 'round my sister. I saw him take her in both arms and he brushed his hand in her hair, and both together they put lips to lips, like lovers naturally do. Then they lay back, close together, side by side.

I thought just then of the many places I oughtn't to be, where I hadn't no right. But I thought mostly, of all places, I hadn't ought to be where I was *then,* then and there, a hundred yards from where Clyde and Verbaline Lou were laid out on the blanket.

So me and the shotgun, we didn't make a sound. We eased back into the brush, and I got that sweet couple out of my sight and I thanked the dear Lord how they hadn't seen me while I sat there, watchin' what I had no business.

But I thought aplenty as I walked across the gullies, homeward at a more sprightly pace than the one I took outwards. I knew how Pap would hooraw me when I got to the house. He'd see how I didn't pack home a rabbit. He'd tell me how there were more cottontails along the Oso Arroyo than piss-ants 'round the Lowdermilk house. He'd call me a sorry hunter, say how I was like the shaky feller and the constipated owl—how one could shoot but he couldn't hit and t'other could hoot but he couldn't . . .

Well hell! For that reason I feared to go home. I'm human and I've got feelin's. So I put my mind on Clyde and on Verbaline Lou. I pictured them, how sweet they looked. How there wasn't a lick of unrighteousness about them. They just did what lovers naturally do. And I figgered how Pap Lowdermilk was an evil-minded old sonofabitch.

But I figgered rightly, too, how them lovers, Clyde and my sister, had better do somethin' legal—like get married, shackled in wedlock—damn quick.

21

Cousin Drewey sat out by the woodpile thinkin' sweetly about the Washtaw Mountains. He had his guitar by his side, and it was close to sundown. That was the time of day Cousin Drewey loved best, for that was when he felt like he was back again in his kindly mountains, yonderly, eastways.

And he felt his nearness more this summer day, 'cause the air was wet, kind of; and sticky and hot. The weather that day was a sure-fire mystery in this desert climate. It *never* got that way, never. Cousin Drewey sniffed at the air like a man tastes good whiskey. It was soft to his feelin's, air buttered with summer-damp, kin to life-stuff you get in the Washtaw Mountains.

He could smell the slash pine, feel the hickory hardness in his nose, taste the black-gum rosin between his teeth. He sweated; Lord God, did Cousin Drewey sweat! His shirt was wet like he'd doused it in the creek. He worked his feet 'round in his shoes and they were slick, two shoes like engine gear-boxes full of lube oil. And when Cousin Drewey looked to the sky . . .

Doggone!

The blue of the firmament had turned sickly green with streaks of bile-yeller. The clouds were dirty gray. And although there wasn't a breeze below, those clouds were travelin' by the force of the wind. They went faster than clouds are meant to go, in double directions, hittin' themselves head-on like two wild trains, one eastbound, t'other westbound on the same track.

"This," said Cousin Drewey to himself, "is cyclone weather, gospel-pure."

And he thought to himself, *All this minute needs is thunder and lightnin', some rain and hail.* And he figgered, *And a sweet funnel cloud this side of the west horizon, aimed for the sunrise.* He looked westward. *Was there a twister breedin'?*

The answer is: *Hell no!*

But there was one thing certain on Cousin Drewey's mind: *There could come a cyclone to Star Valley.* There *could* and there *will* come a twister to Star Valley, a holy one, a sweep upheaval of the most sanctimonious variety. It was a thought of gladness that Cousin Drewey carried on his mind. It was a hope that put music in his soul.

So Cousin Drewey reached down for his guitar. He aimed to sing a psalm of praise, and he thought for a solid minute, put his mind to all the psalms in the Bible, 'cause his glottis begged for the best he could get. He thought and thought, and he picked King David's hundred and fourth, sung to the tune of "The Birmin'ham Jail."

Bless the Lord, O my soul . . .
Thou art clothed with honor and majesty . . .
Who maketh the clouds his chariot,
Who walketh upon the wings of the wind.

Cousin Drewey strummed the guitar. The heavy air made the tune carry out to the porch where me and Pap were settin', us sayin' nothin', and maybe to Maw Maw who was fryin' supper in the lean-to. Lord that sundown was sticky, like no other evenin' in this western country. And Cousin Drewey sang from a joyful glottis.

COUSIN DREWEY & THE HOLY TWISTER

Pap said, "Cousin Drewey's got religion this evenin'. He must be thinkin' back to the Washtaw Mountains. Maybe he's thinkin' of the day he got made holy in the creek, when the brothers washed Satan off his hide. Did Cousin Drewey ever say to you what kind of Baptist he is, Newt?"

"He never did, Pap. But he acts like a Forty-gallon."

"He's singin' a psalm out of the Lord's own sweet Bible."

"He gets that way when the sky is right, when he's got a holy twister on his mind."

"The sky's that way this evenin', Newt."

"It don't mean nothin', Pap."

"We need rain on the corn, Newt. Maw Maw planted okra and a row of turnips. They need to get wet. If they don't get wet they'll dry up and die. And we cain't have 'em for supper. What you reckon Verbaline Lou's eatin' for supper tonight, up at the Skinner Ranch?"

"No tellin', Pap."

"Maybe fried steak and a mess of okra."

"Likely."

"She used to be my sugar-tit gal. She ain't that no more, Newt."

"She's a goddamn woman, Pap. When the Lord makes a woman, He makes her out of love and meanness, them two mixed together."

"I've known a heap of mean women, Newt. A half-dozen of 'em made me miserable in Tulsa any time I went there. They tantalized me with their charms, then took my money. The second-meanest woman in the world lived in Paul's Valley, and I saw her kill her lovin' man with a bone-cleaver. The judge had me up for a witness, and they sat her in the electric chair. But the meanest woman of all, choice grade, was a gal who lived in Latimer County, Oklahoma. You know who I mean, Newt?"

"Hell yes."

"She charmed me with her sweetness, and made me set in misery. I tried to spend money on her but she wouldn't take it. Lord God, that was the most aggravatin' woman! The worst ever to cross my path, stop, and stay with me to this day."

"Maw Maw's a good woman, Pap."

"You're goddamn right, Newt."

"What you reckon she's cookin' in the skillet?"

"Hog meat. Cousin Drewey's beef's been hangin' down there too long. Right now it's too ripe to cook."

We found out soon enough what Maw Maw had cooked in the skillet, and that was when she hollered out of the door, "You'all come get it. Newt, you holler at Cousin Drewey and tell him supper's ready. It ain't much, but it's the best a woman can do with the kind of man she's got."

Cousin Drewey came into the house, and we could see by his face how he'd been singin' psalms. "I sure like the look of the sky," he said to us all; and he said it while he poured water from the bucket into the washpan. He poured 'cause he was fixed to wash his hands and face.

"It looks like it might stir up some rain," Pap said. He'd done washed and was already aset at the table.

"I was kind'a hopin' for more'n that," Cousin Drewey said.

"The corn needs wetness," Pap said. "If you're hopin' for a twister, Cousin Drewey, I'll remark how we don't need the corn to get lifted up and taken eastbound to Hale County, Texas. I worked on them tassels too hard to wish for that."

Cousin Drewey said 'round a mouthful of greens, "I'm thinkin' of better times and kindlier places, Cousin Lowdermilk. This western country ain't sweet to my feelin's, with the sun never findin' a cloud to get back of, and everybody gettin' down on their knees next to the Reverend Sam Hill and shoutin' in holiness, 'Lord, when you goin' to give us rain? How long, forty days and forty nights?' "

"That's them, all right," Pap said. "These here Star Valley folks is mostly Texans. They cain't move back to East Texas where it rains in Christian style 'cause they've got the hangman waitin' for 'em. They might pray for rain, but they're all afflicted with manifold sins and wickednesses."

Pap and Cousin Drewey gabbed about rain and sunshine, hogs and corn, cornbread and lick, the Democrats and Republicans, and whether or not old Sucky the cow would ever find a calf. I liked the taste of greens with grease on them too much to render an opinion. Maw Maw stood by the stove, lookin' down into the skillet and frettin' her fool head off about Verbaline Lou and her tubes. I'd have worried about Verbaline Lou's tubes, too, if I knew what the hell they were.

Cousin Drewey woke up the next mornin' bright and early, ready for the day. He pulled at his pants to put them on, down from the limb where they hung by the galluses. He put on shoes over crusty feet, then topped himself with his hat. He figgered he was the most joyful, blessed man alive. We all met him at the table, where he claimed he was ready for breakfast; all primed 'cause he'd washed out his mouth with a dipper of water. Maw Maw's rose bush at the lean-to door was wet and drippin' 'cause of us all. Cousin Drewey took vittles to mouth. He blessed Maw Maw with words of comfort after he'd ate his fill. He wished Pap and me the best of luck.

"Lord Jesus," he said, with a psalm on his lips, "I thank Thee for lettin' me live to this happy day."

He went toward the bucket for to wash out his mouth, but somethin' caused him to stop in his tracks. He looked through the open doorway to behold there, on the porch, with a paper in his hand, Hank Hudgeons, sheriff of the county. Hank stood await with his piss-ant deputy there beside him.

"Howdy," said Cousin Drewey, as he stepped out on the porch.

"Howdy, Mr. Stiff," said Hank Hudgeons.

"Most folks call me Cousin Drewey in this here valley," said our kinfolks. "How come you're so goddamn polite, Sheriff?"

" 'Cause I'm here on official duty," Hank Hudgeons said, blowin' on his badge and shinin' it with his coat-sleeve.

I'd followed Cousin Drewey out and faced Hank Hudgeons like a man. He paid me no mind. I figgered rightly how trouble had come to Cousin Drewey and I wouldn't be Newton Lowdermilk if I wasn't there to he'p. Because Pap stayed inside with Maw Maw. Maw Maw said, "Lord, save us!" but Pap hid behind her, bendin' low, so the sheriff wouldn't see him. Pap was a man who didn't pack comfort in the presence of the law. Pap wasn't a sinner. He led a righteous life; even the Reverend Sam Hill couldn't condemn him. You might call the old bastard a coward, if you like. And that's *exactly* what he was.

"I've got here a search warrant, Mr. Stiff. We need to hunt this house and grounds for stolen property. If you resist, or if Mr. Pap Lowdermilk does likewise, or you, Mr. Newton Lowdermilk, me and my deputy will need haul you all off to jail. We'll leave Mrs. Lowdermilk here to keep the house and do up the chores."

He turned slightly sideways, so we could see his holstered revolver. He did that 'cause he was a horse's ass and didn't have better sense.

"Cousin Drewey," said the sheriff, "where'all did you get that beef?"

"That's better, 'cause I don't like your official

COUSIN DREWEY & THE HOLY TWISTER

stance," Cousin Drewey said, with a kindly grin. "I like my friends, and I beg my friends to forget I'm Mr. Drewey Stiff. That's a high-falutin' name, and I keep it handy for use by the President of the United States. Nobody else. I don't like it kicked 'round by a no'count county sheriff who ought to be back in jail in Bell County, Texas, for the crime of various unbecomin' misdemeanors."

"Don't try to be smart with me, Cousin Drewey. I'm the law, and a feller's got to respect the law. Do you want to read this here warrant?"

"No," said Cousin Drewey, "I don't want to read your warrant."

"Why not? I'm tryin' to be kindly with you, Cousin Drewey."

" 'Cause I don't read what you read. I read the Bible, and the Sears and Roebuck catalogue. Sometimes I read the Monkey Ward catalog. I read the words of 'The Star Spangled Banner.' But I don't read search warrants, so I'll be proud if you'll put it back in your pocket and don't show it off no more."

"All right, Cousin Drewey. Where have you got that beef?"

"What beef?"

"The Mr. Fats Recknagel beef what you stole from his pasture sometime over a week ago."

"That's Lowdermilk beef. And I ain't afraid to show you where it is."

The sheriff smiled like he'd won a point, but a man cain't win points with Cousin Drewey.

"What's Pap Lowdermilk's brand, registered with the State Cattle Sanitary Board?" Hank Hudgeons quizzed Cousin Drewey.

"Pap Lowdermilk ain't got no brand, and that's 'cause he ain't got no cattle 'cept old Sucky the milkcow."

"So how come that beef you got hid away is Lowdermilk beef? Tell me that, Cousin Drewey."

"Sheriff, it's Lowdermilk beef for two reasons. One, 'cause it's hangin' up here on the Lowdermilk place. Two, 'cause when it's cooked it's cooked by Maw Maw Lowdermilk, in a Lowdermilk skillet, and it's ate by Pap and Newt Lowdermilk, two pure-blood Lowdermilks if ever two Lowdermilks were born in the Washtaw Mountains."

"Where'all you got it hid?"

"It ain't hid, it's hung."

"Where you got it hung, Cousin Drewey?"

Cousin Drewey made no answer for that nosey potbellied sonofabitch. He just said to me, "Come on Newt, let's git." And he took off down to the dugout where Fats Recknagel's beef hung in the dark. I followed, and behind me came Hank and his deputy.

Cousin Drewey unhooked the latch from the dugout door. He swung the door open. Lord God, how that beef stunk! Somebody should have hauled it off and buried it, but it was too late now. Because Hank Hudgeons had come with a search warrant and aimed to look it over.

We all stood outside the dugout door. The sheriff seemed scared to go down in the dark. Maybe 'cause he didn't like flies. There were teensy little black flies 'round-about the door, and big old blue-bottles. They'd blown the beef and did a job of it, right smart. It's good we saved the heart when we did. And the tongue. Even then we figgered how the taste was slightly over-ripe.

"How come that meat stinks so bad, Cousin Drewey?" Hank Hudgeons said. "How come you'all didn't eat it up before the flies forsook the outhouse and came buzzin' down this way?"

"Because we're in the heat of summer," Cousin Drewey told the sheriff, "and it's ten days since I hung

COUSIN DREWEY & THE HOLY TWISTER 203

up the fresh beef down there."

"Ten days?"

"That's what I said, Sheriff."

Hank Hudgeons looked at his piss-ant deputy. The deputy had his mouth agape like he aimed to trap some flies. But he was only surprised at Cousin Drewey's confession; that's why he had his mouth fixed that way. He winked at Hank Hudgeons, and Hank Hudgeons winked back.

"Ten days ago was when the baby-beef was shot in Fats Recknagel's pasture. That's when Fats's cowboys and me found where some thievin' sonofabitch had cut that critter's throat and let the blood spill out on the green grass. And that's when me and the cowboys and my deputy here saw how that thief had loaded the carcass on a mule. And most of all, Cousin Drewey, them mule hoofs made tracks right down to the Lowdermilk gate. So what you got to say about that, Drewey Stiff?"

"I ain't got nothin' to say to nosey sheriffs of the county," Cousin Drewey told Hank Hudgeons.

The sheriff kicked at the dirt; his deputy did likewise. "Newt," he said to me, "how come this dirt is all dug up, all 'round this dugout? You got somethin' planted here?"

"You bet," I told the sheriff.

"What'all?"

"Potatoes."

"Potatoes?"

"Why, hell yes."

"A feller don't plant potatoes this time of summer, Newt," the sheriff said. "It looks mighty like you Lowdermilks dug up this ground so's to hide somethin'. Maybe like drips of calf-blood and stray hunks of Black Angus hair."

Lord, Lord, was Hank Hudgeons superstitious of us

Lowdermilks! Hank Hudgeons went toward the door but he fell back like the blackness inside was a den of rattlesnakes. Except a man don't spit flies and hold his nose when he's in the company of rattlesnakes.

"I wouldn't go down there if I had all the search warrants a sheriff needs from here to Muleshoe, Texas. Or if all the judges in that wide territory told me to go get Cousin Drewey," Hank Hudgeons said. He choked a little 'cause of the air and we all moved away from the dugout. After we got where we could breathe in comfort, Hank Hudgeons said, "All right, Cousin Drewey, what'all did you do with that there beef-hide?"

We knew for the Baptist-truth how sooner or later Hank Hudgeons would bring up the matter about the beef-hide; 'cause that's where Fats Recknagel's cowboys had burned in that big Texan's registered brand and cut the registered mark on the left ear. If Cousin Drewey got the calf's hide out and showed it to the sheriff, and there against the black would shine the evidence, that's when the law would have the right to send Cousin Drewey up to the State Pen on a rustlin' charge—one to five years, with maybe time off for good behavior.

"You'd be surprised, Sheriff," Cousin Drewey said. Our kinfolks grinned his good old Washtaw Mountain grin. He knew dog-good how the real argument was comin' up.

"Where'd you bury that hide, Cousin Drewey?"

"I didn't bury it."

"Where'all is it at?"

Cousin Drewey didn't say, but he did tell how he butchered that calf about ten days before. He told how he skinned off the hide and hung the head on a fence-post. He cut up the meat and hung it up in the darkness down yonder. He told how he closed the door and let it ripen. But he confessed how he'd let it ripen too much. It got so it wasn't fit to cook in Maw Maw's skillet.

"Where's that beef-hide, Cousin Drewey?"

Cousin Drewey told Hank Hudgeons how when he skinned off the hide he nailed it up on the side of the barn. He said he did that so's to show the sheriff how it didn't wear Fats Recknagel's brand—how it had no brand at all, 'cause Pap didn't pay the state for no mark made with a brandin' iron, or any earmark cut with a case-knife. He didn't have nothin' like that registered with the Cattle Sanitary Board. Cousin Drewey packed an honest man's reputation 'round, and he aimed for Hank Hudgeons to know it.

"Show me that hide."

Cousin Drewey told us how the reason he nailed up the hide on the side of the shed was so Hank Hudgeons and his deputy could see it when they came 'round. They'd see how the hide didn't wear Fats Recknagel's spade brand. Nor was Fats Recknagel's earmark there on the left ear, the same ear which Cousin Drewey had cut off from the head. Cousin Drewey said the sheriff could see how the beef was a Lowdermilk calf, and how it had nothin' at all to do with Fats Recknagel. He figgered how he'd let the sheriff see it for himself. That would be pure liniment for his painful superstitions.

"Let's go look at it," Hank Hudgeons said, leadin' off to the shed that Pap Lowdermilk called a barn.

"If that hide has a spade burned into its left ribs, Cousin Drewey," Hank Hudgeons said, as he walked and as we followed, "you might just pack your satchel, 'cause you'll be headin' for the State Pen just like the balance of calf-rustlers caught by me."

We came to the shed and Cousin Drewey showed the sheriff the spot where he'd nailed the hide to the boards. But it wasn't there.

"Where's the hide, Cousin Drewey?"

"I ate it," Cousin Drewey said.

There were no flies 'round for the deputy to gape at

and no stink that could make Hank Hudgeons hold his nose. But both together, like they were singin' a song in the Tabernacle, the sheriff and deputy hollered, *"You ate it!* What the hell are you talkin' about, Cousin Drewey?"

I let it hang there as long as I could, Sheriff," said Cousin Drewey, "but my appetite got the best of me. I just had to take it down and have it for supper."

"It's too tough," cried the sheriff out loud. "You cain't eat a beef-hide. It's got hair on it."

"That's a fact," the deputy said.

But Cousin Drewey had some facts to tell Hank Hudgeons.

Before you can eat the hide," Cousin Drewey said, "you got to do three things. First you've got to get the hair off, then you've got to soften the meat, then you've got to cook it 'til it's tender. It's best seasoned with salt, pepper and a bay leaf, and if you've got some sprigs of parsley and a quart of hog-grease . . ."

"What are you tellin' us, Cousin Drewey? Are you plumb craze? I ain't never hear'd of anybody eatin' a beef-hide!"

"Me neither," the deputy said.

So cousin Drewey leaned over and faced the sheriff head on, and he pointed a finger straight toward the eyes of the law.

"What I'm tryin' to tell you, Hank Hudgeons, is how to fix a beef-hide so's to cook it for supper."

"Save your breath!" hollered the county law. "Save it for the courtroom when your trial comes up, and come up it will. You can tell it to the judge."

22

So Cousin Drewey's trial was comin' up. Down at the county seat, forty miles south, the sheriff talked it over with the judge. They wouldn't need a regular, pure-D judge, 'cause a Justice of the Peace could do the job of gettin' Cousin Drewey freed of any cattle rustlin' charge against him. And they wouldn't need hunt 'round for a jury that was right smart fond of Cousin Drewey. They'd just select ten fellers and two ladies, each blessed with a solid opinion that Fats Recknagel was strictly no'count. They'd reckon him to be some brand of snake, like a pit-viper. And it was the Baptist-truth that each would raise his hand and declare Cousin Drewey not guilty.

Hank Hudgeons had it all figgered out.

"We the jury of this here county seat, gents and ladies, do solemnly declare Cousin Drewey Stiff, a citizen in our midst, a candidate for the verdict of NOT GUILTY, so he'p us God."

And with such words the jury would smile sweetly on Cousin Drewey.

And the judge would pound his gavel and he'd quiz the jury, "Gents and ladies of the jury, how come you came to that nice verdict, and how come you reckon the defendant to be sinless and righteous?"

"Because he's a musical man," the foreman would

say, with a heap of pride. "If Cousin Drewey rustled Fats Recknagel's beef, his worst crime is messin' 'round with a bunch of snakes—Fats and his cowboys. And you cain't jail a man for messin' 'round with snakes."

And the judge would say back at the jury, "Ain't *that* the Baptist-truth. I could set at this bench for a solid year and never figger out a verdict that way."

Hank Hudgeons lost no time at gettin' that trial into action. It came to pass just two days after Hank came to our place huntin' (if he could find one) a sinful charge against Cousin Drewey; like gettin' stunk up with beef down in the dugout, when Cousin Drewey told how he'd ate the beef-hide for supper. Then, the day after that, which was the day before the trial, the sheriff and his deputy again came up to us Lowdermilks. He craved to tell me that they needed Cousin Drewey the very next day, down at the courthouse. It might be forty miles south, he figgered, but he wanted all us Lowdermilks there for Cousin Drewey's trial—and to bring along the Skinner brothers, Clyde and Sonny Boy and Lilybelle, too, and all their kids. And Verbaline Lou. The kids could *sure* load up on cake and ice cream, and there'll be potato salad and fried chicken if the county seat women can be talked into bein' charitable. 'Cause, as Hank and the judge had it planned, *this* was goin' to be the *damnedest* trial of a criminal ever recorded in the history of jurisprudence.

And for heaven's sakes, don't let Cousin Drewey forget to bring along his fiddle and guitar!

Hank Hudgeons didn't find me at home and he figgered how Pap Lowdermilk didn't have sense enough to give Cousin Drewey the message. And Cousin Drewey was away somewhere for the time bein', out walkin' and thinkin' sweetly about a new song he'd got on his mind, just ramblin' over the solitary flats with the two hound-dogs at his heels.

COUSIN DREWEY & THE HOLY TWISTER 209

Hank Hudgeons found me loafin' on Signal Rock Main Street hunkered down front of the domino parlor. It felt sweet to have my back against the wall and my twin-butts aset on my heels. I chewed cud and spat clean across the sidewalk. I didn't hit no special target but the slickness landed one side or t'other of the yeller fire hydrant. Low down, I had to look up at fellers' faces, them that walked by. Most were ugly faces, and mean. But about fifty percent of the girls who walked by had pretty faces. They had legs that makes a feller want to reach out and touch them, just to see if they're real. That way I didn't look high, like I had to fellers' faces. Girls were a different category. I'm natural, born to this world with a healthy crotch. The sight of girls gives me heavenly thoughts.

Some legs wore stockin's—slick and shiny. Others were naked as jaybirds' legs. The naked legs went by on low-heeled shoes. And it bein' summer, some girls wore shorts instead of skirts; and shirts with their tails out, open at the collars—young girls plump or slim, I loved them both. But most legs that wore stockin's walked on high-heel shoes, stylish, and they looked like they might build up some corns. They let off perfume, those stockin'ed legs. Only the dear Lord knew what kind. You can find it in the Sears and Roebuck catalogue. They wore suits, summer suits, sometimes a hat. Because most of those girls worked at the First National Bank, where you'll find Mr. Wilbur Pruitt in his cage, the horse's titty. And I reckon some of those fancy girls worked in other places, too, out of the sunshine. They walked like they were in a hurry, cravin' to get someplace and then back to the boss. They didn't know hard work; they wrote on pads or punched a typewriter.

That's where Hank Hudgeons found me, me hunkered down.

"Howdy, Newt," he said, comin' up next to me, "how you'all?"

"Of the finest kind," I told Hank.

"You busy, Newt?"

"Hell no."

"You chewin' cud, Newt?"

"Hell yes."

"What kind'a plug you chewin' off, Newt?"

"Brown's Mule."

"I left my plug at the county seat, Newt. You wouldn't he'p a poor lonesome sheriff out by loanin' him a hunk of yours, would you, Newt?"

I gave Hank my Brown's Mule plug, told him to take off a hunk and hand it back. You can never trust the law.

"How come you're so damn friendly all asudden, Hank? You're a sheriff and I'm a Lowdermilk. It ain't natural."

"You ask me why I'm friendly. Well, hell, Newt, why shouldn't I be?" He smiled while he talked. I'm leery of a talk-smilin' sheriff.

"First 'cause you're a country-cop," I said, "second 'cause you're a sidekick of that tolerably-alkalied Fats Recknagel."

"That's what you think, Newt!"

"The hell I think," I said to Hank Hudgeons.

"Look, Newt," Hank Hudgeons said. "We cain't talk here so come over to the prowl car, it with the blinker on top. My deputy is settin' in it right now. But first I'd like to say how I'm friendly for four reasons. One, 'cause I like you Lowdermilks right smart. Two, 'cause I think Cousin Drewey ain't a yearlin'-rustler but a first-rate citizen of this state. Three, I don't love Fats Recknagel worth a damn. Four, 'cause I'd like to talk to you like a friend and after that buy you an ice cream soda down at the Bankhead Drug Store and Fountain."

"I'd sooner set," I said to Hank Hudgeons.

"What flavor ice cream soda do you like, Newt?"

"Strawberry."

"Well hell, Newt. Get high off your hockers and let's go to the prowl car. We'll talk about Cousin Drewey and about one hell of a trial that's comin' up. Main thing is, don't let Cousin Drewey forget to bring along his fiddle."

So I did what Hank craved me to do. My knees felt stiff and the twin-butts of my royal-rusty seemed like they were flattened by shoeheels. It's the penalty for hunkerin' down.

Me and Hank walked two blocks down Main Street and found the prowl car parked at the curb. It was shiny-blue, with a badge of red and gold printed on the door; but the prettiest thing about that car was the red blinker light on top. It wasn't blinkin' then, but even shy of light it was way-high in my admiration. I knew factways how there was a siren on that car, too. I figgered if I got real brotherly with Hank Hudgeons he'd maybe ride us out to the highway and let me percolate the siren. I knew right then how Hank was a good old boy, and if I asked him to do that there I'd put him in the category of the right kind of sheriff.

Hank told me to get in the back seat while he slid himself behind the steerin' wheel up front. Next to him on the front seat was the deputy. And what you reckon the deputy was doin'? He was asleep.

Asleep, by God! He was sprawled out over the front seat, with his mouth agape and snorin' out of his silly face.

I looked out at the fire hydrant there by the curb. It was yeller, same as the one front of the domino parlor. I'll bet all the dogs in Signal Rock hoisted a hind-leg against that instrument. And I remembered back to the day when, right there at that spot, couple years back, when us Lowdermilks hitched old Jeff and the wagon to that fire hydrant while we all went into the bank to get a loan of five thousand dollars from Mr. Wilbur Pruitt.

I came out of my rememberances when I heard Hank

Hudgeons say, "Well, Newt, we ain't gonna put Cousin Drewey in jail."

"How come? He rustled Fats Recknagel's beef, didn't he?"

"He didn't rustle no beef, Newt."

"Maybe they'll send him up for one-to-five years."

"No they won't."

Hank's deputy was too far gone in sleep to know what me and Hank were tryin' to do. So I said to the sheriff, "Cousin Drewey stole that yearlin' from Fats Recknagel, didn't he? That makes him a low-grade stock thief."

"He ain't."

"Then what other category can he be, Hank?"

"He's a musical man," Hank said, "and no musical man can commit a sinful act. He belongs to a breed that respects the Ten Commandments."

"Well, Hank, the way I reckon it . . ."

That's when the sheriff leaned back in his seat and faced me like a man. It seemed he had somethin' to say. He stretched his legs and hoisted his feet up above the dashboard of that old prowl-car. He needed comfort and figgered how that was the best way to get it. He wore shop-made hand-stitched boots, and they rested next to the radio—*it* that brought him talk from headquarters. Just then that radio didn't make a squeak, 'cause Hank had fixed it that way. He didn't need the county seat to cut in while he told me what he aimed about Cousin Drewey.

"Like I said, Newt, me and the judge hates the trailin' guts of Fats Recknagel."

"Hank, you didn't tell me that before. Us Lowdermilks always reckoned how Fats was your sidekick. How he kept you in bribe-money like a kindly man feeds a hungry dog."

"Let me ask you a question, Newt. Why does a kindly man feed a hungry dog?"

COUSIN DREWEY & THE HOLY TWISTER 213

"So the dog won't bite him, Hank."

"Newt, that goddamn Fats Recknagel is the richest man in this county. He's just about the richest a feller can get. But he don't feed scrap to dogs and he don't hand out bribe-money to sheriffs."

"You ought to know, Hank."

"Newt, you don't know the pains a county sheriff has to suffer. You cain't feel the torments."

"You got pains, Hank?"

"I sure got 'em, Newt. They're worse'n La Grippe; they ache more'n a dose. And they come reg'lar every two years."

"What'all you call them aches, Hank?"

"Elections. Runnin' for sheriff. Talkin' folks into givin' me a job."

"Well, hell!"

"Newt, it's plumb grief. 'Cause once a man gets elected sheriff he don't crave no goddamn Republican to take the job away from him."

"You a Democrat, Hank?"

"Worse'n that, Newt, I'm a Texas Democrat. Just as the Lord made Israelites in Genesis He made Democrats in Bell County."

"What you know about Bell County, Texas?"

"Plenty. I know all about it, Newt. Let me tell you somethin'—I was born there. I was born there like the balance of us Hudgeonses. Bell County is the best in the Blacklands, and if you ask anybody who's proud of bein' a Texan he'll tell you how us Hudgeonses are mighty hospitable people."

"I hear'd tell how they ran you out."

"Who ran me out?"

"The sheriff. And I hear'd tell how he called for a lynch mob to come he'p him."

"That's a dad-blamed lie, Newt. Who told you that?"

"Uncle Posey Burwinkle. He comes from Bell County, too. He said how it's the best in the Blacklands, and the people the sweetest in Texas. But he claimed how the Hudgeonses are plumb no'count."

"You know what the sweet folks of Bell County think about that horse's titty? They said he's no good for nothin' . . ."

"The hell he ain't! He's the best caller for a hoedown dance ever come out of the Blacklands. Did you ever hear him call 'Bull At The Wagon'?"

"Hell, yes! And did you ever hear anybody tell dad-burned lies better'n Uncle Posey Burwinkle?"

"Why sure."

"Who?"

"I ain't tellin'."

"Well, Newt Lowdermilk, let me tell you this. It's 'cause Uncle Posey Burwinkle is such a dad-burned liar; and 'cause he's the best hoedown caller west of the Arbuckle Mountains; and 'cause he comes from the worst family of humankind in the Blacklands. . . . All that, bar none, none-plus . . . that gave the court authority to have him subpoenaed to testify at Cousin Drewey's trial. The court needs that noise from his glottis."

"And Young Buster Prather, have you done called him up?"

"You bet, him and his banjo."

"Then it looks to me like Cousin Drewey's gonna have one hell of a trial."

"Newt, it ain't gonna be just one hell of a trial, nothin' so little as that. It's gonna be the stompin'est, most fiddle-whinin', banjo-pickin', old-time hogs in the corn, ladies-go-'round courtroom jamboree ever pulled off in the history of jurisprudence. . . ."

"Where'd you get that jaw-bustin' word?"

"No matter. Wait 'til you meet Eunice and Beverly. We've given 'em a subpoena. This trial needs spark. They're in the ladies section of the county jail. We pulled 'em off the street for the crime of you know what."

"What?"

"And Junior. He's restin' nicely in the men's department. We got him off a freight train down at the yards. He was El Paso-bound."

"A bindlestiff?"

"More'n that, Newt. He ain't only a jailed-up bindlestiff, but he's the best jew's harp twanger ever come out of Tennessee. He got his subpoena 'cause we need him badly."

I was gettin' hungry for the strawberry ice cream soda old Hank had promised me. But right now there was somethin' I *really* needed to know, and I prayed the sweet Lord I'd get it before Hank started up the car, pulled away from the curb, and headed us down to the Bankhead Drug Store and Fountain.

"Hank," I quizzed that man, "how come you don't love Fats Recknagel? I always thought rich men and politicians talk the same language. Maybe I ain't right, but I kind'a figgered how they work together with smiles and get the most they can out of the common population."

Hank the Sheriff bent his head low. He held it down with chin on chest like he had somethin' to think about, and his thoughts were deep 'cause of what I had said. Maybe he asked the tenderhearted Lord for forgiveness. Then he faced me head-on.

"Newt," he said, "I hate Fats Recknagel 'cause of them aches I told you about."

"Them what you said are worser'n La Grippe?"

"Them exactly, Newt, worse'n a dose."

"Them you get every two years?"

"Boy, ain't you talkin'! Every two years."

Truly, my heart pained for Hank Hudgeons. I knew for a fact how he had to make a livin' 'cause he wasn't mossback. He was Texan, a proud man. Besides, he had a wife. Folks claimed how his wife spent his money. Her name was Viola.

"That's right, Newt; I said 'ain't you talkin'.' . . . I get them aches just 'cause of that goddamn election day, *it* which us politicians need like a man needs cornbread and milk. And election days come every two years. Newt boy, you just cain't figger out how hard a politicalman has to work after the primary kicks him head-first, ass-backwards into the campaign. I'd sooner sweat honest sweat behind a team of mules on a Blacklands farm in Texas."

"Then why don't you go back to Bell County, Hank?"

"Cain't, Newt. Me and my loved ones just cain't."

" 'Cause of the Bell County law?"

"Well . . . Newt, maybe it's 'cause Viola loves this county seat better. Me, I've got to go 'round the population usin' up gas to win compliments and wish for votes. It's a hell of a way to beg for a job. Kissin' babies, he'pin' their mothers change didies and heat bottles; tellin' the womenfolks how beautiful they look, and tellin' 'em all how I'll keep their husbands immune from the law."

"What's all that got to do with your hate for the trailin' guts of Fats Recknagel?"

"Plenty, Newt," Hank said with a sigh, like a political-man naturally does. "Mr. Fats Recknagel is a true son of the sweet state of Texas—like me and Old Man Lee Bassett, like Uncle Posey Burwinkle, like ninety percent of the dear folks of this county. If you Lowdermilks and Cousin Drewey came out of Oklahoma, that's 'cause you cain't he'p it."

"We're right proud of bein' Washtaw Mountain Oklahomans, Hank."

"And well you might be, Newt. Some right clever people live in Oklahoma, registered voters all. . . . But Newt, Fats Recknagel is *more* than a Texan—he's a *mil-*

lionaire Texan. You won't believe me, but he's got a house outside Houston that's bigger'n any domicile in this sorry state. That house sets center of a ranch, one that stretches way-yonderly. It's stocked with the best Black Angus cattle and quarter horses—stock so fine that nobody else has got the like, 'specially outside Texas. He's got a swimmin' pool next to his house, its bottom painted blue, and it covers more'n an acre. Center of that pool is statues of naked women, and they're spittin' water-softener out of their mouths. Old Fats says they're Greeks. He gives big get-togethers for three hundred folks at a time, 'round that pool, and they eat shrimps and bits of pineapple cooked on sticks. They drink champagne-wine, and what they do is Texas-style. He's got palm trees growin' all 'round. And do you know what he's got in the garage, Newt?"

"A Cadillac-car."

"Well hell, Newt! You talk like you ain't a Texan, which is entirely right. He's got *five* Cadillacs in that garage, a Rolls Royce and a Jeep, and to fill out the space he's got two or three motor-sickles. And he's got a motorboat in their too, just in case some guest of his wants to sail out on the swimmin' pool and visit the Greek women. I tell you, Newt, everythin' Fats Recknagel does is Houston-size. More'n that, he does 'em up big-D size."

"And that's why you don't love Fats Recknagel," I said.

Hank squonched 'round on the front seat of that old prowl-car, next to his snorin' deputy. "No, Newt," Hank Hudgeons said, "that ain't the reason I don't love Fats Recknagel. I couldn't if I tried, 'cause I come from Texas and in Texas we do things big. Texas bigness is the biggest bigness in the world. We're all made that way. The reason I cain't love Fats Recknagel is thisaway, Newt. Fats Recknagel claims how everythin' in this sorry state is too puny for him to fool with, except maybe the First National Bank and his dear friend Mr. Wilbur Pruitt. Most of all, Fats thinks the politics here is too puny, even if he owns a ranch and lives part-time in Star Valley. Trouble is he owns an air-strip and airplane . . ."

Hank gulped for the sadness in his heart. "But that ain't the worst," Hank went on sayin'. "The worst is that Mr. Fats Recknagel ain't a registered voter in this state, in this county. He don't do me no good. On election day he's always in Texas, votin' Texas-size, 'cause he's that size Texan. He has his pilot drive him there in his airplane. And second, Newt . . . Doggone, you won't believe this . . ."

"What'all?"

"Newt, Fats Recknagel has more money in the First National Bank than all the farmers and stockmen in Star Valley put together, laid end to end. But he don't pack a kind heart. Come election time, every two years, he could hand me out a couple thousand dollars and he wouldn't miss a skinny dime. If I had a couple thousand dollars I could buy the votes of every Mexican in this county, I could put up posters on every telephone pole, each one with a picture of my face. I could even give you Lowdermilks a dollar or two, just to he'p you vote for me at the schoolhouse on that blessed day in November, the day I get shed of my aches one way or another."

"We're mossbacks," I told Hank Hudgeons. "We're too sorry to vote."

"Well hell, Newt. It makes me sad when you say that."

"I never hear'd of a sheriff gettin' sad, Hank."

"Well, Newt, we get sad all right. But them Mexicans. There's a heap of 'em in this county."

"I hear'd you say how ninety percent of the voters in this county come from Texas; the balance from Oklahoma and Arkansas. Where do you fit in the Mexicans?"

" 'Cause they ain't human bein's, Newt. They don't count."

"You sure talk like a Texan, Hank."

"You're damn-tootin'. More'n that, I'm a *Texas* Democrat. The Mexicans are all Republicans, and they'll do anythin' for a dollar."

Silent to myself, I wondered as to what party Fats Recknagel belonged to. Hank would have called him a Republican and I reckoned he'd be right. Millionaires and Republicans go together like hog grease and turnip greens. I didn't quiz it out loud, but I wondered a mighty serious question. If Hank Hudgeons was a Democrat, then what was he in the Lord's sight—a Baptist, a Methodist or an Assembly of God? And if he was a Baptist, was he Foot-Washin' or Forty-gallon?"

Well, now I knew why Fats and Hank weren't sidekicks. But that didn't matter no more. What mattered was a strawberry ice cream soda, like the sheriff promised me. The deputy still snored with his neck snug on the back of the front seat; his mouth wide open, beggin' for flies. I tasted that strawberry flavor in my mouth, and in my dreams pulled it in with a soda straw. But just then the radio over the dashboard got to hissin' like a bullsnake and squawkin' like a turkey buzzard.

The sheriff picked up some kind of microphone. He held it to his fat mouth. "Lee-roy," he said, "is that you?"

Did you ever sit in the back seat of a prowl-car and watch a sheriff talk in his radio to a feller, likely a deputy, at headquarters down at the county seat? That is to say, forty miles south?

You ain't never? Well then, take it from me, it ain't a pretty sight.

The radio squawked and Hank Hudgeons had to fool 'round with knobs so's to clear up the line. He craved to know what Lee-roy had to say. The other deputy, up there in our midst, had shifted some; he'd put his chin down on his chest with the balance of his frame bent over the front seat like a yeller crookneck squash.

"Lee-roy, I cain't hear you, boy. This goddamn radio don't work like it used to; it ain't fit no more."

Squawk! . . . Clank! . . . Clack! . . . Yawp! . . . Blurp! . . .

"Sonofabitch," said Hank Hudgeons, talkin' about the radio.

To clear up a mess like that, some fellers just have to turn the right knob to the right place—no sweat about it, no bustin' a gut.

"Hank! That you? Damnit, sheriff, hold it there!"

"Thank the dear Lord," said Hank Hudgeons. "What you know, Lee-roy? Got any trouble down there?"

"Nothin' but a message for you, Sheriff. Needs to be delivered at a jiffy, 'cause it's worser'n the governor. It's prime authority, Hank. I mean *prime!*"

"What'all?"

"I cain't hear you, Sheriff. I cain't hear you 'cause of all that noise and racket comin' out of the men's department. I cain't . . ."

"What'all's the noise and racket, Lee-roy?"

"It's Junior. He's been twangin' that goddamn jew's harp since midnight, twelve hours back, and he won't shut his music when I tell him to hush. He claims he's practicin' for Cousin Drewey's trial, *it* comin' up."

"Hell, let him make music! What about Eunice and Beverly, are they actin' like ladies?"

"Well, hell no!"

"What'all, Lee-roy?"

"They're makin' more noise and fuss than Junior could *ever* make, and they're wearin' down my poor soul to mush. They're yellin' at Junior for to twang louder and faster, 'cause they're limberin' up for the hoedown,

COUSIN DREWEY & THE HOLY TWISTER 221

for Cousin Drewey's trial, *it* comin' up."

"What are they practicin', Lee-roy?"

" 'Stud Horse In The Clover,' Sheriff. They say they just cain't wait to dance in the courtroom upstairs, and to get a taste of that chicken and potato salad."

"That won't be 'til after Cousin Drewey tells us how he ate the beef-hide."

"They know that, Hank. So does Junior."

"All right, you're doin' your duty, Lee-roy. Elmo is asleep here and he's been that way most of the mornin'. But I've got Newt Lowdermilk in the back seat. I'm turnin' him loose now, so's he can go home and tell Cousin Drewey how he's gonna be tried for a criminal act tomorrow mornin', bright and early. . . . To tell all that, and say for Cousin Drewey to take along his fiddle, guitar, and his singin' glottis. And, Lee-roy . . ."

Quack! Honk! Tweet, beep, puff!

"You hear me, Lee-roy?"

"You bet, Sheriff."

"What'all is that message you said you've got for me?"

"Your wife. She says for you to stop by Charlie's Market when you get back to town. She says to pick up thirty cents worth of onions."

"Thirty cents will buy a hell of a lot of onions, Lee-roy."

"That's a fact, but Viola says you'll need get 'em if you crave onions in your fried okra."

"Goddamn it to hell, Lee-roy! Viola's got an automobile of her own. Why cain't she go over to Charlie's Market for the onions?"

"She ain't got time, she says. It'll take her all day for to primp up to look pretty for Cousin Drewey's trial, *it* comin' up. All that, and she said how a new confession magazine came in with today's mail. But she says she'll take time out to fry the okra if you'll get the onions."

"You phone Viola, Lee-roy, and tell her the onions will be on their way. And tell her, too, to get up off her royal-rusty and quit eatin' out of that sack of chocolate candy, 'cause she's gettin' fat and sloppier'n a hog. And to quit readin' that confession magazine. I cain't live with her at night if she gets ideas out of that book. I reckon that's about all, Lee-roy. Except you *phone* Viola, don't go deliver the message about the onions. You stay away from that there house when Viola's sufferin' from the confession magazine. I don't need no he'p, boy."

Hank Hudgeons switched off the radio before Lee-roy could deal him sass. He reached over and shook his sleepin' deputy like a man does when he craves to bring somethin' back alive. "Wake up, Elmo," he said while he shook. "How you reckon me and you can keep law and order here in Signal Rock if you sleep off your workin' hours?"

Elmo sat up to rub his eyes—and yawn; and say "What the hell!" Then he said to Hank: "Hank, where'all are we at?"

Hank said, "Elmo, we're out by the curb next to the First National Bank. That's Newt Lowdermilk in the back seat and right now I'm gonna send him home so's to tell Cousin Drewey to get set for his trial, *it* comin' up. Then me and you can ride back to town. Lee-roy said how we're needed down there. It's early in the day, but maybe we can find and lift a body somewhere to put in the drunk-tank. Besides, Viola needs onions for the okra."

Hank turned and looked me straight in the face. "Newt," he said, "you'all git."

I slid out of the prowl-car by way of the back door. I knew what to tell Cousin Drewey, just as Hank said for me to do.

"So long, Newt. See you'all folks tomorrow."

COUSIN DREWEY & THE HOLY TWISTER 223

"Wait, Hank," I said, standin' there next to the prowl-car. I looked through the window on the sheriff and Elmo. I had two mighty important questions to ask of Hank Hudgeons before he'd drive away, and right then I could only think of one. But us Lowdermilks never weaken. I trusted the Lord to let me catch the other in my mind right after I quizzed the first.

"Hank," I said, "you reckon Fats Recknagel will be there to call names at Cousin Drewey, him and his lawyer?"

"Fats won't be there, but his lawyer will."

"How come Fats won't stand up and tell Cousin Drewey how he's a low-down cattle thief?"

"Because this ain't Texas, Newt. And any trial we open in this county courthouse is too puny for Fats to mess with. So he's just sendin' a lawyer."

"Who'all? That feller Fats flies in from Houston?"

"Why, Newt! Don't you know better? Our courtroom is too trashy, and Cousin Drewey too mossback for that Houston lawyer to fool with. He wears a blue suit and a jellybean hat."

"You reckon he'll get Shyster Sam Hawkins, Hank?"

"That's the feller who'll condemn Cousin Drewey, Newt."

I said to Hank, "Hell, I saw Shyster Sam just an hour ago, while I hunkered down next to the domino parlor. He had his bag of tools, all primed for a job. I said 'Howdy, Shyster,' and he said back 'Howdy, Newt.' Then he went inside the domino parlor. The toilet leaked and it needed fixin'."

It's like this. Shyster Sam Hawkins studied law from The Postal Legal University and he had a certificate to prove his right. He carried the certificate 'round in his pickup truck. Shyster didn't get many law jobs, just notary public calls and visits. Stuff like that. But even a lawyer has to make a livin', so Shyster Sam did plumbin' jobs. He wasn't much of a plumber, but he *could* fix the leak in the domino parlor.

One time he nearly killed Old Man Puckerdoo Kazort. That's when Old Man Puckerdoo moved down from the foothills and built a new house in Signal Rock. He hired Shyster Sam to fix up the bathroom, 'cause Old Man Puckerdoo Kazort liked to sit in a bathtub and wash off the dirt from his frame. And too, he liked to smoke his pipe while he sat in that receptacle. Well, sir, when the job was finished Old Man Puckerdoo Kazort found out how Shyster Sam had hooked up the pipes wrong. He put the gas pipe on the hot water heater where the hot water pipe ought to be. That was really a terrible thing to do. That night Old Man Puckerdoo went to his bathroom to take a bath. He shed down to his nakedness and sat himself sweetly in the tub. He brought along his pipe and can of Granger, not to forget the matches. Then he turned the faucet and waited for the water to come out steamin'. Nary a drop came out into the tub, but the faucet made a sort of hissin' noise. Old Man Puckerdoo waited and waited, because he was a patient man. He didn't know what to make of it, but reckoned sooner or later he'd find out. So he thought and thought, and while he thought he stuffed Granger tobacco in the bowl of his pipe, 'cause that sort of thing he'ps a man decide.

Well, sir, then he struck a match. The roof over the bathroom went up first, then the bathtub and Old Man Puckerdoo Kazort. They put him in the hospital down at the county seat, and he stayed there just about a month. When he came back to Signal Rock he had to stay at the Blue Bonnet Hotel, *it* run by Mr. Charlie Dwyer, and he had to stay there 'til he got another house built. He slid on crutches for a solid six months and he didn't shed splints for another six weeks after that; and this was claimed to be the Baptist-truth about Old Man Puckerdoo Kazort . . .

Breeze! Not for a solitary minute will I believe that Shyster Sam Hawkins sent Old Man Puckerdoo Kazort sky-high with the gas. Him in a bathtub! Factways, I don't believe Old Man Puckerdoo Kazort ever wet himself by takin' a bath.

Hank backed the prowl-car away from the curb. I watched him head south down the street, hell-bent for the county seat. I figgered how I'd better get home and tell Cousin Drewey to get fixed, and not forget his fiddle and guitar. As I walked southbound down the sidewalk I tried to figger what'all was that second question I'd felt primed to quiz out of Hank. Halfway down the next block it came to me right smack, and it was my nose that put me wise. I'd stopped at the door of the Bankhead Drug Store and Fountain, and the tasty smell of a strawberry ice cream soda made fragrance for my nose. "That sonofabitch, he promised," I said to myself out loud. "He went off and forgot. Or did he forget?"

No, Hank Hudgeons didn't forget. He aimed to pull a fast one on poor old Newt Lowdermilk who's got a trustin' heart and no more sense than a citified hound-dog. Right then Hank was percolatin' the prowl-car back to the county seat, him and that goddam Elmo. They were splittin' their side-guts to the expense of me who took it for truth how the sheriff would spend two-bits at the Bankhead Drug Store and Fountain . . .

23

Well, sir, like the sheriff said, it turned out to be the damnedest trial ever stomped in the courthouse of that county seat. Verbaline Lou stayed away, up at the Skinner ranch with Lilybelle. But it seemed how Hank Hudgeons had talked with Clyde on the telephone right after he left me on the sidewalk outside the First National Bank. He told Clyde for to bring anybody he could down to the trial 'cause it would be the pure-D damnedest. And to give Cousin Drewey and us Lowdermilks a ride down there in his Chivvelee sedan-car. And for Cousin Drewey to put his fiddle and guitar in the trunk next to the spare tire but to leave behind his hog-leg forty-five and his satchel 'cause he wouldn't need either when he stood up in the criminal's dock.

So bright and early, that's when Clyde and Sonny Boy came by to pick up Cousin Drewey and us Lowdermilks. Both together, the Skinner boys sat in the front seat of the sedan-car.

"Where'all's Maw Maw?" Clyde said to us three, as we stood there await outside the porch of the Lowdermilk house.

Sure enough, we stood there dressed up in clean overalls and shirts that Maw Maw boiled in the black pot in the yard, boiled them white before she hung 'em up to dry. She ironed 'em flat. All dressed up we stood

COUSIN DREWEY & THE HOLY TWISTER 227

there, a sight for sore eyes. Cousin Drewey had his guitar leaned against his thigh, but he held the fiddle in its case like a woman holds her child to her bosom.

"Maw Maw ain't goin' down to that courthouse," Pap Lowdermilk said, "'cause she don't crave to hear Cousin Drewey get a dose of sass. She don't need any of that sass come out of Shyster Sam Hawkins' face."

"Well, you boys get in the back seat," Clyde said. "You don't need to put the fiddle in the trunk. The guitar neither. You'all got plenty room back there."

So Cousin Drewey and us Lowdermilk menfolks got in the back seat like Clyde said to do. The old shanty looked mighty lonesome as we rode off down the road. But I knew dog-good how Maw Maw would be hidin' down under the window, peekin' out to see what'all. Maybe she wished she was goin' down with us, even if Shyster Sam aimed to sass Cousin Drewey. 'Cause while we ate supper the night before, Pap quizzed Cousin Drewey. He said, "Cousin Drewey, what'all tune do you aim to play down there in the criminal's dock in the county courthouse?" So Cousin Drewey said back at Pap, "Pap Lowdermilk, I aim to saw 'Eleven Cent Cotton and Twenty Cent Meat.' " That's when Maw Maw said, "Shoot, doggone!" And we knew how she wished she could go along with us, 'cause that old Cotton Belt tune was her favorite for a fact.

There's nothin' sweeter for a man to do than to ride in a Chivvelee. Me, Pap and Cousin Drewey leaned back in the rear seat like we did that thing every day. We smelled of clean attire and outside the sedan-car the sun shone brightly on Star Valley.

"There's Old Man Lee Bassett's corn field," Pap said, lookin' out, "and I'll bet that old buzzard ain't ridin' the sweeps today, 'cause he's got somethin' better to do. I reckon he'll pack some pregnant ideas in that courtroom while they try Cousin Drewey for a criminal act."

"Ain't *that* the truth now," Cousin Drewey said,

tickled silly. Our kinfolks giggled like a kid of fourteen years.

"What you reckon about the jury, Newt?" Pap quizzed me. "Reckon them fellers will send Cousin Drewey off to Huntsville or McAlester? Which of them places, boy?"

I said, "That old jury will say from the heart, 'Cousin Drewey is a righteous citizen, so he stands not guilty.' That's what the jury will say, Pap."

Cousin Drewey sat between me and Pap, gigglin' for the talk that met his ears. He wriggled 'round on that plush upholstery like he needed to go take a leak.

"Amen!" Pap said, snickerin' silly along with Cousin Drewey. "After that, the music will howl coyote language."

Clyde Skinner was eatin' the highway at forty miles an hour, and I was right proud to be in his company. Sonny Boy sat lazy next to Clyde, just lazy like a heavy-set cowboy ought to set. He looked out through the windshield ahead and he said to Clyde: "There's Old Man Bassett's Ford pickup yonder and we'll need pass it if we ever aim to get to the county seat. Old Man Lee ought to have Uncle Posey Burwinkle in there, and Young Buster Prather. Hank Hudgeons begged Old Man Lee, sort'a kindly, if he'd give them two fellers a ride down so's to hear Shyster Sam Hawkins hand Cousin Drewey sass."

Cousin Drewey heard what Sonny Boy said, so he cackled like an old lay-egg hen. Sonny Boy paid him no mind. Clyde stepped on the gas and we went ahead like a bat out of hell. As we passed Old Man Lee Bassett by, that dirt farmer waved a howdy. We could see Young Buster Prather's banjo layin' flat in the bed of the pickup, snug in its case. And while we looked we saw how Uncle Posey Burwinkle had a Baptist-smile on his face.

The road sort of angled off to the east, then turned to make a beeline across a range of hills, southbound. Which put us in the next valley where the county seat shone glory-like in the sunlight. From high up we could see the tin roofs, and the white houses all aset in their yards. High above everythin' rose the courthouse, a block of red brick—gloomy, as if it told how the juries of past years had sent a heap of fellers to the State Pen. I brought to mind that time when Old Man Lee Bassett told us Lowdermilks how before this state put sparks through fellers in the electric chair it hung 'em on the gallows with a rope 'round their necks, and every time the master of ceremonies sprung the trap the poor fellers squealed like stuck pigs. It was the nicest story Old Man Lee Bassett ever told, and us Lowdermilks wished he'd come over and visit us some more. We just liked to hear that old dirt farmer talk.

Maybe my vision of that courthouse, standin' high, was handwrit on the walls of Belshazzar. It looked that way as we came down the hill toward town. What it spelled out for me was doom for Cousin Drewey, miseration for a musical man. Every soul in the county, even Fats Recknagel, knew how this trial would be a circus, an excuse for a hoedown. It had a purpose—planned to make two damned fools out of Fats and Shyster Sam Hawkins. Even Hank Hudgeons knew dog-good-and-well how Cousin Drewey would be made a hero that day. Likewise Elmo and that goddamn Leeroy knew it. But for me, I'll be a dad-blamed liar if I didn't suspicion that someday Cousin Drewey would stand up in the criminal's dock—not this time but the next.

Today Cousin Drewey would saw his fiddle. They'd set him high on the judge's bench and he'd have Young Buster Prather there by his side, pickin' the banjo and makin' sound; and standin' up back, high on the bench, would be Uncle Posey Burwinkle callin' the hoedown, howlin' and gruntin' like a man from the Blacklands. Would the music make circles, 'round and 'round like a cyclone over Kansas? You bet.

But wait! You can't beat big business. They'll get you, those millionaires. They'll suck your blood and spit it out on the dirt. Because if you hurt them once, they're set to get even. Fats Recknagel, he'll get his revenge. Likewise Hank Hudgeons and Shyster Sam Hawkins. You can make clowns of them *once,* but never *twice.* Not today. The next time. In that same courthouse. The next time. You'all kind folks just wait for the next time! I couldn't he'p it, 'cause the sight of that big block of ugly red brick told me so, and I didn't wait long before I got my superstitions.

"Clyde," Cousin Drewey said, all asudden so's to make talk.

"What'all, Cousin Drewey?" Clyde said from behind the steerin' wheel. The Chivvelee purred, and the countryside went by sweetly.

"Clyde, I've done got somethin' on my mind, and it's all about Sonny Boy yonder," Cousin Drewey said.

"What the hell you got about me?" said that heavy-set cowboy sprawled out on the front seat.

"It's about your quarter horse mares, Sonny Boy."

"What about them mares?"

"They need a stud-horse. They need a good-sized weapon so's they can find some colts."

"Ain't you talkin'!"

"Ain't that what they need, Sonny Boy?" Cousin Drewey said. "A stud-horse that's the best west of the cross timbers, one with the best blood a stud-horse can own, the blood of Steeldust, and Peter McCue, and Speed. Wouldn't you like your mares to find colts with that kind of blood, Sonny Boy?"

"I cain't think of a quarter horse man who wouldn't," Sonny Boy told Cousin Drewey.

Cousin Drewey cackled like a lay-egg hen. "Well, folks," he said, "I'm about to tell you somethin' you don't know. When I get shed of this rustlin' charge agin me, I aim to go out and sin some more. I'm gonna give

Sonny Boy a summertime Christmas gift. I'm gonna give him a stud-horse what packs in his veins all that fine blood. More'n that, he's got the most potent weapon in Star Valley."

"Where's your money, Cousin Drewey?" Clyde said. "If us Skinner brothers ain't got money enough to hire a stud of that variety, I'm dog-sure Cousin Drewey Stiff ain't got it. Unless, of course, you can saw your fiddle for a thousand dollars a night for fifteen nights."

"And you'll need travel all the way to Texas to get one," Sonny Boy put in his say-so.

To shame the Skinner boys for their silly talk, Cousin Drewey made an owl-hoot. Then he nickered like a horse.

"Hell-fire!" Cousin Drewey hollered out loud. "I didn't say I was goin' to *buy* that kind of stud-horse, I just said how I aim to sin some more."

"You cain't sin 'round quarter horse men and get by with it," Clyde said.

"There's only one horse with that kind of blood in this county," Sonny Boy said, "and he's owned by a sorry sonofabitch named Fats Recknagel."

"We've tried more times than once to hire that stud, just to service Sonny Boy's mares," Clyde said. "And every time we offered Fats a high stud fee that high-mogul told us to go shovel horseshit."

"That's the stud-horse I'm talkin' about," piped up Cousin Drewey.

"You ain't got enough money," Clyde said.

"Fats will spit in your silly face," said Clyde's heavy-set brother.

"I don't aim to *buy* him, or even *hire* him," Cousin Drewey said, actin' like a man who didn't use good sense, "I am to *steal* him."

Lord! *Cousin Drewey talked that way before two quarter horse men!*

Clyde nigh ran the Chivvelee off the road, so wild was

his amazement. Sonny Boy came out of his sprawl to face Cousin Drewey head-on. Pap Lowdermilk looked at our kinfolks slanchways, not believin' his ears. And I thought back to civilized times; I thought how the lynch mobs used to hang horse thieves in Star Valley.

Sonny Boy held up a big tough hand, so's to halt our kinfolks's talk. "Damn it to hell, Cousin Drewey," he bawled, "you'd better hush your mouth with talk like that."

Cousin Drewey couldn't be fazed. "We'll go out and rustle that stud-horse, *it* belongin' to Fats Recknagel," he said. "We'll chouse that stud yonderly through the gate, and down the road to Sonny Boy's pasture where he's got his prize mares. Because the mares need a taste of that weapon, so's they can find some colts."

Just then, Clyde's Chivvelee hit the edge of town. Clyde slowed down. He steered his vehicle over to the curb. We were in the county seat, and he needed to stop. But just long enough to hand some legal advice to Cousin Drewey.

"Look here, Cousin Drewey," Clyde said, after he'd stopped the car and turned to face our kinfolks head-on. "Me and my brother are both talkin' to you straight. I'll talk for Sonny Boy, 'cause we're brothers of the same mind and tongue. Listen, Cousin Drewey, and you'd better welcome what I say. *Don't you ever, now or anytime, talk horse rustlin' 'round any man, woman or child in Star Valley*. Don't you do it, Cousin Drewey, and I mean what I say. I'm talkin' for Sonny Boy, and for Lilybelle, and for Verbaline Lou who'll soon be my lawful wedded wife, the mother-to-be of my kids, who'll be Baptists every one. Maybe they'll be boys, maybe they'll be girls. I don't give a damn which."

Sonny Boy spoke up. "You listen to Clyde, Cousin Drewey, because he's a quarter horse man and he knows the business from A to Z."

Clyde said, "Cousin Drewey, me and Sonny Boy are Texas-born. We needn't tell you what Texas folks think about horse thieves, 'cause you know already. You come from the Washtaw Mountains, which ain't Texas, but it's the next best thing. Mighty clever people come from the Washtaw Mountains, and they've got plenty sense."

"Clyde's talkin' rightly, Cousin Drewey," Sonny Boy said, speakin' up. "Me and him came west from Montaig County, south of the Red River, west of Nocona. Me and my brother don't need tell you how we reckoned horse-stealers back in Montaig County. We don't need tell you'all how we rated 'em no'count, and how our grand-daddies hung 'em for their misdemeanors. You wouldn't crave the good folks of Montaig County to hang you, would you, Cousin Drewey? And I might add how there's a few Montaig County folks right up there in Star Valley. Like I said, their grand-daddies used to string up horse thieves and cattle rustlers, and they've got what it takes to tie a knot right there in their hands."

"Old Man Ed Jones is one of'em," Clyde added for remark, "and he's got the knot-tyin'est hands."

That kind of talk shamed Cousin Drewey right smart. He went red in the face, and his under-lip shivered like he'd talked somethin' fearful.

He stuttered first like he packed a mouthful of yellerjackets. Then he said straight from his heart: "Doggone my iniquitous ways, gents. I didn't mean to be so bad as all that. All I aimed to do was get a highly-personal *loan* of old Fats's horse, and after he'd used his weapon on Sonny Boy's mares I aimed to sneak him back to the pasture—no harm done. . . . Except make some fine colts, that is."

All us fellers in that car figgered rightly how they were waitin' for us at the courthouse so's they could try Cousin Drewey and shed him of his crime so we all reckoned we better get goin'.

"Just one thing more," Clyde said as he turned frontways so's to start up the Chivvelee, "you ain't told nobody about your fool idea, did you?"

"About rustlin' Fats's stud-horse?"

"You bet," Sonny Boy said.

"Well. . ." Cousin Drewey put a brake on his talk while he started countin' on his fingers. He did that 'cause he'd told fellers aplenty.

"Hell!" hollered Sonny Boy. "You ain't told nobody!"

"Well. . ."

"If you've done told somebody how you aimed to steal that horse, then you'd better take off your necktie and get set for the rope," Clyde said.

"I only told two or three. Maybe half-a-dozen," Cousin Drewey said back at Clyde. "I only told 'em what I aimed, not what I did."

"Who'all did you tell?" quizzed Sonny Boy.

"Old Man Lee Bassett, for one."

"He's a Baptist and a Democrat," Clyde said. "He'll just figger you for a poor old mossback who ain't got better sense. If you told Old Man Lee he'd just make hooraw about it. He'd forget what you said before he went to supper."

"Who else did you tell?" Sonny Boy said.

Cousin Drewey thought for a minute, counted on his fingers and named about four or five.

"No harm," Clyde said. "You cain't think of no one else?"

"Hell yes," said Cousin Drewey.

"Who'all?"

"Billy Beck."

"Good God Almighty!" That's what two fellers shouted, together like Pentecostals.

"Billy Beck!" hollered Clyde.

"That crooked sonofabitch!" grunted Sonny Boy.

"What's wrong with Billy Beck?" Cousin Drewey quizzed. "He seems a right clever feller to my way of reckonin'."

"He's a thief," said Clyde.

"He won't work, but he sets on his hunkers and thinks up meanness," Sonny Boy said, to back up his brother. "He lives in the pool hall, or over at Shorty Flack's Bon Marchee Saloon. He ain't never played an honest game of pool in his life and he'd drink up Shorty's likker stock if Shorty would let him. He's stole and he's cheated, and he don't know what it means to pay for what he gets."

"He's a liar," said Clyde.

"And a bootlegger," Sonny Boy said. "He makes sorry likker, and it comes from the realm of death."

"And worst of all, he's Fats Recknagel's best friend," Clyde told. "He cheats and steals and lies for that high mogul. He gets paid by the politicians."

Well, what the Skinner brothers said was the honest God's truth. 'Cause Billy Beck was just about the most no-good stance of human meat. He was pint-sized and he packed the looks of a cheater at cards. He loved the race track, too, and it's said how he doped horses for pay. He packed a guilty conscience every hour of the live-long day. He could scheme up dirty schemes like no man's business, and folks tell how it was Billy Beck who put Hank Hudgeons in the sheriff's prowl car. He put Hank there every election since the Lord knows how long. He had a weasel's face and he wore his hat brim down to shade his eyes. He chewed on a stogie. He cased his hunkers in pinstriped pants. His necktie was flamin' red, like his hell-bound soul. And his jacket had silver buttons. I don't know much about his boots, but they were the best made in Nocona, Texas, and it was Fats

Recknagel's ill-got money that he'ped him put on dude's attire. His hat was sinful. And like Sonny Boy said, he was a bootlegger.

Billy Beck and Shorty Flack were the best friends. Any man could see that. If Billy Beck wasn't at the race track somewhere, he'd be in the Bon Marchee Saloon. But he never drank his own stuff. Or he'd be down at the county seat, forty miles south, sendin' comets into the spittoons, there in the courthouse while he played dirty politics with Hank Hudgeons. Or with any one or two of the county employees. Or payin' a friendly call at the county seat whorehouse where the girls gave him a cut rate. Or maybe he'd be sippin' coffee and eatin' doughnuts in Fats Recknagel's ranch house kitchen. That's where he'd talk low-down business with that high mogul.

But most times you'd find him in Shorty Flack's Bon Marchee Saloon. For more times than once Billy Beck and Shorty Flack set up their still down by Snookie Hapchester's Lava Lake Tank, way out there where no human bein' could see the white whiskey or smell its rotten odor. Like Sonny Boy said, it *just wasn't* quality whiskey. But it was Snookie hisse'f who told those two to get themse'fs off his place; to take the still with them. 'Cause if they spilled any whiskey onto the grass 'round Lava Lake Tank it might make his cows sick. Snookie said that 'cause he was a cattleman of no small punkins. That way, they had to find somewhere else to set up their still.

It was Billy Beck who got the bright idea." Shorty," Billy Beck said to his crafty brother in business. "Shorty, my boy, I know the best place to set up the still. It's a place where no United States Government Revenue Bureau prohibe can ferret us out." But he wouldn't tell where'all it was 'til Shorty promised on his Texas-honor to take in a third partner.

"What breed of partner you got in mind, Billy?"

Shorty said that 'cause he craved to know. Damn it to hell, he was the boss.

"The best friend a feller could be proud of," Billy Beck said.

"Fats Recknagel? He's your best friend, ain't he?"

"You know better'n that, Shorty," Billy Beck said. "Fats don't need to go in the whiskey business, 'cause he's got Greek women in his swimmin' pool. But it'll need be a three-partner business."

"Who'all and where'all?"

"Reese Blaylock."

"The undertaker?"

"Him and nobody else. And the place is the realm of death."

"Hell!" yelped Shorty, "he don't know how to make whiskey. All he knows is the way to pickle dead fellers."

"And that's exactly what I mean," Billy Beck said. "When you talk about pickle you're invitin' Reese Blaylock into our whiskey business."

"I ain't gonna let no pickle like that get into my whiskey," Shorty said. "It's potent enough. What you tryin' to do, Billy? You tryin' to rustle up some business for the Blaylock Funeral Home? I like to sell my customers whiskey. I don't crave to kill 'em off. What's that pickle called, Billy?"

"Embalmin' fluid."

Shorty Flack poured Billy Beck a shot of Old Jack Daniels and he said from the side of his mouth, "Look, partner, we don't need that there flavor in the whiskey. I ain't never sampled that stuff but folks tell how you can smell it from outside the town limits. The name of it scares hell out of me. One look at Reese Blaylock scares me to my liver, anyway; and I'm scared to go down the street where he's got his funeral business. When I drive my flivver I always take the next street down, even if I go a block out of the way. I'm scared 'cause he might have one of them fellers in there."

Billy Beck blinked his weasel eyes and his mouth twisted into a smart man's smile. So he said, "Shorty, that's *exactly* what I mean. I've already made a contract with Reese Blaylock. If that there funeral parlor can scare you, it can scare the Revenue Bureau prohibes. And the stink of that embalmin' fluid can drown out all fragrance of any kind of bootleg whiskey, even our kind, and our kind stinks mighty awful when it comes out of the coil."

"Hell-fire yes!" hollered Shorty Flack 'cause the words just spoken by Billy Beck had primed him with joy. "There's where we'll run off our lousy booze. We'll set up the still in the embalmin' room, and there ain't a prohibe officer alive who'll be brave enough to make a raid. Factways, Billy, you cain't get a human bein' of any kind to go inside, 'cause there might be a feller laid out. Friend, I'm mighty proud to have old Reese as a partner, 'cause now I can tell Snookie Hapchester to take his tules down by Lava Lake Tank and stick 'em."

Shorty stretched a hand across the bar. Billy Beck took his off the glass, put it in Shorty's open paw, and both together their eyes met. They were drippin' teardrops.

"Flack, Blaylock and Beck, Incorporated, distillers, makers of that fine Bon Marchee brand," said Billy Beck, blinkin' 'cause of the salty eye-wetness. "Let's me and you toast the enterprise; that is, if the toast is free on the house."

"We won't need to move the still, never," Shorty said.

"Only if old Reese needs to bring in one of them fellers," Billy Beck said for a reminder. "When he packs him in, we'll need move the still up agin the wall; when he gets done picklin', we can move back and start the coil actin' pretty. You can believe me, Shorty, it don't take old Reese long to pickle a feller."

That's how Billy Beck and Shorty Flack talked that day and time, and that's how those three bastards got to makin' whiskey in the new location. Reese Blaylock welcomed his share of the money. The undertakin' business in Signal Rock wasn't exactly "land office" like Confucius said. By that I mean the customers didn't come fast enough to keep Reese fed to healthy proportions, and his nakedness covered. By that I mean old Reese's customers were kind'a extra special—not the perpendicular walk-'round, fat-mouthed kind of patronizer, but the horizontal long-gone variety. I mean they were that there breed of loved one. Star Valley folks came from a healthy tribe and they didn't die fast enough to make Reese happy. And when they did die, most folks sent the victims down to the county seat, forty miles south, for boxin' up and puttin' in the dirt. So all Reese Blaylock had to do for to keep in business was get out the rag and polish the hearse; and wipe the windshield and see if the tires needed air. Sometimes he'd go for a nice drive in the country, just to limber up the hearse, and listen to it purr like a kitten, and gun it and see if it would make eighty. And while he drove he admired the looks of Star Valley, and how the birds flew against the blue sky and white clouds; and, if it was sunset, he'd get hisse'f to lovin' its glorious colors—'cause he was a sentimental sonofabitch. But mostly old Reese just drove and wished for stuff to come to his funeral home. But the more he wished for stuff, the more the stuff stayed away.

Soon enough the folks got to know the times when Shorty Flack and Billy Beck were runnin' off a batch of whiskey back yonder. Anytime you'd see black smoke risin' from the coal-oil fired still, *it* comin' out the chimney—that one over the embalmin' room—you could be certain-sure how those two no'counts were down below. You'd know they were drinkin' Jack Daniels Tennessee Sour Mash, the best whiskey in the world, while the coils in the still made the sorriest rotgut in the universe. They'd be tellin' lies about themselves, about their roundin' days and how they'd made plenty money and laid the corn-fed women. In Dallas and Tulsa, in Amarillo and Lubbock. Sweet Texas-Oklahoma towns. In towns like them old Shorty Flack and old Billy Beck, them and gents of that special category, would patronize the downstairs corner saloons; and 'cause they couldn't stay long on the same level, they'd knock with gold-headed walkin' canes on the doors of the upstairs entertainment parlors. That's where the landladies would say, "You'all boys come in." . . . And they'd holler to their crews of burnt-out whores, "Company, girls!"

Always, while Shorty Flack and Billy Beck ran off whiskey inside, old Reese would be outside workin', makin' stink to keep the neighbors away. He'd have Flit-gun in hand, and he'd be sprinklin' the rose bushes with formaldehyde—the pickle-stuff undertakers use on fellers.

What old Reese Blaylock aimed to do was scare off the neighbors. More so, put fear in the United States Government Revenue Bureau of the Treasury Department, and all its low-grade sneakin' prohibes.

Like Floyd Garden, the feller with the badge.

And in that day and time it was mighty public, like all Star Valley knew, how Floyd Garden was more feared of a deadman than any prohibe this side of the sweet land of Texas.

24

Old Floyd couldn't he'p wonderin' how the whiskey-boys got the product out of the funeral home without his catchin' them. Factways, there must have been a sizable supply of full kegs inside, judgin' by the way the chimney pipe gave off coal oil fumes and how Reese Blaylock Flit-gunned the rose bushes. Whiskey stored in the embalmin' room didn't do the drinkin'-public no good. They had to get it somehow.

Floyd Garden talked with Snookie Hapchester down at the domino parlor one day. Old Floyd hung 'round that place in line of duty, 'cause gents made patronage of the pool tables; besides, they bought cigars and cigarettes there. And a heap of the said gents spent their money over at Shorty Flack's Bon Marchee Saloon. Floyd reckoned how if he just lazed 'round at the domino parlor, and acted sociable, he'd pick up some talk about the rot-gut-whiskey boys, news that would he'p him with his prohibe business. That's how come he gassed with Snookie, and Snookie told him what he reckoned.

"Floyd," Snookie said, "I think I know how Shorty Flack and Billy Beck get the whiskey out of the funeral home. But to get my statistics right, I'll need you a question. Floyd, don't you ever watch Reese Blaylock's place? And don't you ever try to catch them fellers comin' out with the whiskey?"

So Floyd said to Snookie, "Snookie, I *sure* do. Like everybody knows, I live in the Blue Bonnet Hotel. And, Snookie, like you know, the Blue Bonnet Hotel is upstairs over the Busy Bee Café. My room is backside of the hotel, and the window gives me a clear view of the next block, slightly yonderly. And backside of Blaylock's nasty place faces my window. It scares me to think about it, Snookie, but that back door is where old Reese parks his hearse and where he loads and unloads the merchandise for his business."

"Like them . . ."

Snookie tried to say "corpses and coffins," but Floyd was so scared of those two words that he cut Snookie's talk off flat, like a preacher hushes a swearin' man.

"Snookie!" Floyd said, duckin' back like he was fixed to get hit. "Don't say what you aimed, 'cause the sound of them words scares the hell out of me."

Well, Floyd," Snookie said, "you'd better get scared if you aim to catch Shorty Flack and Billy Beck packin' out the whiskey. 'Cause that's the way they do it, every damn keg and jug of it—laid out in a coffin and loaded in the hearse. No tellin' where they take it, but sooner or later that sorry whiskey finds its way to the Bon Marchee Saloon."

Old Floyd slapped a hand on the thigh of his pants. "Doggone!" the prohibe said, like he'd heard Snookie make the most valuable statement he'd heard in all his life. "Snookie boy, you're right. Now I'll just need to keep my binoculars fixed out of the window, upstairs in the Blue Bonnet, and aim 'em toward old Reese's back door."

"Anytime you need to hear good sense talked out loud, Floyd," Snookie said, "just hunt me up and I'll he'p you out."

Floyd Garden was a prohibe officer who earned his

wages. He did that by settin' in a chair all day long, at his hotel window with the binoculars by his side. Any time he saw movement over at Reese Blaylock's place he'd hoist the instrument to his eyesight and look to see what'all was goin' on down there. When he wasn't lookin' through the binoculars he'd read the newspaper, or a magazine full of wild west stories, or one of them love-books that pack more kissin' than good sense. Sometimes he'd look down to see Gus Protopapadakis, who ran the Busy Bee Café, come out all covered with sauce stains and grease, to empty garbage in the trash barrel back of his place. Any time old Floyd saw old Gus do that, Floyd yelled for Gus to send up some hot coffee and doughnuts. Old Floyd had an expense account with the United States Government Department of the Treasury, which was Uncle Sam and nobody else; so that prohibe just charged the snacks to the taxpayers. And it looked mighty like the taxpayers paid out plenty for coffee and doughnuts; 'cause Floyd Garden, day by day, was gettin' more and more of a potbelly paunch. It was shameful. And the more he tried to catch the whiskey-boys with booty, the more he drunk-up the wild west stories and the kiss-books, the more he read the newspaper.

But let me say this. Let me make the statement clear for the bad repute of the prohibe business in general, and for the everlastin' prosperity of those three dirty bootleggers. There was one day when Floyd Garden *didn't* read the newspaper, and he damned sure should have! And that was the day followin' the night poor Grandma Sally Anne Kelsey, age ninety-four, coughed up her last spit and laid back and died.

Because before Floyd could pick up the day's copy of *The Star Valley Pinto Bean,* even before he could look at the headline news, he was forced to pick up his high-powered binoculars. The sound of Reese Blaylock startin' up the hearse forced him to do that there. And when he saw old Reese backin' up to the loadin' door behind that fearsome house of last departure, he figgered for certain how Snookie Hapchester was right, and that a coffin-load of bootleg was just about on its way out.

Sure enough, nobody was there next to Reese Blaylock but Shorty Flack, and nobody was there next to Shorty but Billy Beck. They had the funeral house door open, and the back door of the hearse, and it took all three of those sorry humans to pack out the coffin and slide it into the hearse.

"It's right heavy booze," said Floyd Garden to himself, lookin' down on it all by the power of his binoculars.

Shorty Flack and Billy Beck went inside, and with the he'p of old Reese picked out the damnedest heap of flowers, which they piled on top of the coffin.

"They cain't fool me with them flowers," old Floyd said, layin' down the binoculars. He made a bee-line for the hook where his gun belt hung, lawful and ever-ready. Old Floyd swung it 'round his paunch, buckled it up. Then he put on his hat. "Daisies or marigolds, roses and violets, I don't give a damn which. I'm out to catch me three no'count whiskey-boys, and they'll open up and show me what they got."

Floyd took the stairway down-bound—three steps at a time after clearin' the lobby like a bat out of hell. Everybody looked up from the chairs, saw Floyd raise dust. "Well, doggone!" said a guest from East Texas. "You'll reckon that feller's goin' to a fire?"

"Maybe he's goin' to the funeral," said a guest from West Texas, layin' his newspaper down. "I just read about the funeral."

"It's Grandpa Jerry Bob Kelsey's woman, poor old soul," said a feller who knew all about it, "a right clever woman when she had life and breath."

Floyd Garden came out of the Blue Bonnet Hotel. He made a leap head-first into his automobile front seat, behind the steerin' wheel. He was 'round the block in two minutes; and there, praise the Lord, he saw the hearse come slowly and respectfully all by itself, southbound like it was headed for the county seat. Reese Blaylock was drivin', with a white carnation pinned to his black coat. Beside him on the seat sat Shorty Flack and Billy Beck, both loafers dressed up to kill off the calico.

Old Floyd stepped on the gas. He kept about a quarter mile behind the hearse. When the hearse slowed, old Floyd Garden slowed down too. When Reese Blaylock picked up speed, old Floyd pressed a little harder on the gas pedal. After ten miles it looked like they were all headed for the county seat. But Floyd Garden was a government man from way down the line. He figgered the hearse would take off on a side road soon enough, to some lonely and nefarious spot where they'd unload the whiskey from the coffin. But the hearse kept goin' on, and at twenty miles down the highway it looked mighty like they'd all end up in the county seat.

Floyd Garden kept a left hand on the steerin' wheel. With his right palm, which he'd done licked with spit, he polished to a shine the badge that dangled from his shirt. Then he reached down and felt the grip of his six-gun, it holstered on his belt. It would be sweet to know it was there and handy, 'cause them fellers—Reese, Shorty and Billy Beck—would be armed and rarin' to fight, 'specially old Reese who'd need to protect his hearse and coffin. So Floyd stepped hard on the gas pedal, put his blinker light to flashin' red, and howled his siren like a hungry coyote on a moonlight night in the Pease River Valley. And before he could spit out the window he was up against the tail-bumper of that law-bustin' hearse.

Reese Blaylock pulled up along the highway shoulder. There he stopped his mournful vehicle. One thing about old Reese, he was respectful of the law. He got out to see what'all—black coat, white carnation and all. Shorty Flack and Billy Beck came out to his aid, because they knew Floyd Garden wasn't up to no good.

The prohibe got out to meet the bootleggers head-on. He kept his blinker-light to flash red, and held his coat open so the badge could glisten in the sunlight. He looked like the law he was, all right, him with his right hand gripped on his six-gun. Reese, Shorty and Billy Beck squinted like they'd seen a ghost, and they turned their faces to each other and silently agreed that Floyd Garden was behavin' like a silly sonofabitch.

"Fellers," Floyd Garden said, squarely facin' the victims, "I'm here to arrest you'all in the name of Uncle Sam and the Revenue Bureau of the Department of the Treasury of the United States of America."

"What for?" said Reese Blaylock.

"Well, hell!" said Shorty Flack, tellin' off *his* opinion.

"You ain't got no right," Billy Beck said.

It must have been a sight for sore eyes to see the sun shinin' bright on that hearse, and to see the flowers heaped all 'round the coffin inside, and to have Floyd's blinker light spittin' red so's to let the highway travelers know he'd made an arrest. For the time bein' Floyd wasn't scared of the realm of the dead, 'cause he wasn't anywhere near old Reese's embalmin' room. It wasn't the same out on the wide highway, with the Lord's kindly sunshine cheerin' up the scenery.

"All right," Floyd Garden said. "What'all you fellers got in that box?"

"A dear kindly old soul," Reese Blaylock said, talkin' undertaker's language.

"No you ain't, 'cause you've got mighty foul stuff boxed up in there."

"How come you know?"

COUSIN DREWEY & THE HOLY TWISTER   247

"Because I come from Tennessee. I was born and raised there. As I'm a natural officer of the law, I know you've got unlawful stuff packed away under them bouquets of flowers."

"There ain't nothin' unlawful about what we got in there," Reese Blaylock said. "If you follow us to church we'll show you."

"Who says you're goin' to church?" Floyd Garden said, ticklin' the grip of his gun and givin' the victims a squint of his lawman's eye. If old Floyd looked mean, that's exactly the way he aimed himself to look. "Where you're goin' is to *po*lice headquarters down at the county seat. I can scent bad whiskey like a coon-hound smells along a trail. And let me tell you boys, straight from the lawman's mouth, that what you've got in that box under the petunias smells *mighty* bad."

"What we got in there is . . ." Reese Blaylock tried to say; but he was cut off sudden by a pickup truck comin' up behind, headed for the county seat. It was none other than Grandpa Jerry Bob Kelsey, age ninety-eight and spry for his age, Lord God! His brakes squealed when he jammed them down out of high speed. And damned if he wasn't dressed up like to tempt the calico. That is, he wore a clean shirt and Sunday-go-to-barbecue overalls, and his shirt-collar was decorated by a hell-red necktie. It looked like Grandpa Jerry Bob Kelsey was goin' somewhere special.

"Hell-fire and damnation!" he hollered out of his glottis. "I ain't paid you good money to get stopped for speedin' your hearse, Reese Blaylock. We don't need no highway patrol officer to keep you from gettin' to church on time. And we don't . . ."

Shorty Flack cut Grandpa Jerry Bob Kelsey off right sudden. He said, "Grandpa, that ain't no highway patrol officer. It's Floyd Garden, the prohibe, and he just ran us to the side and made us stop."

Grandpa Jerry Bob Kelsey went closer to Floyd

Garden. He stopped and put his chin head-on just two feet and no less from the prohibe's face. He said, "Your business is sorry whiskey, Floyd Garden. You ain't got no right to stop a respectful funeral what aims to get to church on time. How come you made that hearse pull over to the side, flashin' your blinker like it had done a sinful act?"

"Grandpa Jerry Bob Kelsey," Floyd Garden said, "I'm an officer of the law and it's my duty to Uncle Sam for to investigate this crime of unlawful contraband. . . . What them fellers have got in that there hearse, under them roses and gladiolas, is a box—and what that box has got inside it is the dirtiest, stinkin'est load of rot-gut sludge ever made in the history of creation. And you can mark my words, Grandpa Jerry Bob Kelsey, that after we land them three fellers in jail, after we lock 'em up so they cain't commit no more sins, we'll empty the contents of that coffin and pour it in the river, so it won't poison the buzzards. Every goddamn keg and jug of it!"

Grandpa Jerry Bob Kelsey heard enough, so he went over to his pickup truck for to get his thirty-thirty Winchester carbine. Floyd Garden noticed how he had his lights on, like the hearse had its lights on, both wastin' battery juice, but old Floyd didn't aim to be polite and tell those fellers how their lights were on. When Grandpa Jerry Bob Kelsey came back in front of Floyd Garden he had the hammer cocked.

"Please do me a favor, Floyd Garden," Grandpa Jerry Bob Kelsey said, glarin' at the prohibe with all the fire of his ninety-eight-year-old soul. "Just let me hear you repeat the snide remarks you made about the contents of that there coffin."

Old Floyd was fixed to give Grandpa Jerry Bob Kelsey sass, like the low-grade prohibe he was, but somethin' made him look up the highway toward Signal Rock. What he saw was a whole line of automobiles, all

COUSIN DREWEY & THE HOLY TWISTER

with their headlights on, drivin' up and stoppin' behind Grandpa Jerry Bob Kelsey's pickup truck. And within a minute nigh half the population of Signal Rock was crowdin' 'round, so dressed up, all the men with white carnations pinned to their shirts or coats.

"What the hell?" said Old Man Lee Bassett, comin' up close.

Gents and ladies and all the kids in town were standin' 'round, blockin' the highway, even holdin' up some diesel semi-trailer trucks.

"Kindly repeat what you said, Floyd Garden," Grandpa Jerry Bob Kelsey hollered at the prohibe.

"Gladly," said Floyd Garden. "Reese Blaylock ain't no undertaker, 'cause he's a bootlegger. And Shorty Flack and Billy Beck are his partners in crime. And that there coffin is packed with the dirtiest . . ."

Floyd Garden felt the thirty-thirty muzzle come up against his belt buckle. He didn't pull his six-gun 'cause he had respect for old age. But somehow Old Man Lee Bassett was wise and understandin'. He knew Floyd Garden had made a terrible mistake. So he put a kindly hand on Grandpa Jerry Bob's shoulder before he could pull the trigger.

"Grandpa," he said, "this poor prohibe don't mean no harm. He thinks he's doin' his duty to Uncle Sam. And what's more, he thinks that there coffin is full of jugs of lousy whiskey, the kind Shorty Flack and Billy Beck run off in the Blaylock Funeral Home."

"Hell-fire!" Grandpa Jerry Bob Kelsey said, takin' his aim off Floyd Garden's belt buckle.

"He don't know how that box holds the remains of your recently long-gone woman," said Old Man Lee. "And most surely he didn't read the newspaper this mornin', what told about Grandma Sally Anne's funeral. Forgive Floyd Garden, Grandpa Jerry Bob. He's employed by the United States government, and like we all know it's common legend how them kind of fellers make the worst blunders of any human-stance alive."

That was a fact, 'cause all Floyd Garden had done that mornin' was look through his binoculars, or read his kiss-book magazine.

Old Floyd was fit to be tied. So all the mourners—and there must been 'round three hundred in that funeral procession—gathered 'round to watch the prohibe officer make apology to Grandpa Jerry Bob Kelsey. The men took off their hats and the women and kids just looked to see what'all. That's when Mistress Lee Bassett said: "For land's sakes."

So after Floyd Garden made his apology, and Grandpa Jerry Bob Kelsey forgave the prohibe and dealt him a blessin', everybody got back to their vehicles and fixed to follow poor Grandma Sallay Anne Kelsey to her place of eternal repose. Floyd Garden put on his hat and said how he'd better be gettin' back to Signal Rock.

"Like hell you will!" Grandpa Jerry Bob shouted in ire. "You get in that sedan-car of yours and turn off the red blinker. You foller behind the hearse, and I'll be back of you, me and my thirty-thirty. If you try to duck out, I'll shoot the air off your tires."

So they buried our dear neighbor in the county seat cemetery. Reverend Slim Jenkins had some sweet things to say out loud at the grave. And when he bent down to take up some dirt, for to waybill Grandma Sally Anne Kelsey to the yonderly domain, Grandpa Jerry Bob Kelsey stepped out from the mourners with his loaded thirty-thirty short-barrel carbine in hand.

"No you don't, Reverend Slim Jenkins," he said. "'Cause right here I've got the primest sprinkler of that there dirt."

Floyd Garden gave mind to that bereaved widower, saw him come in his direction. Floyd tried to run, but couldn't. No man could, 'cause of the thirty-thirty. And 'cause Grandpa Jerry Bob Kelsey jabbed old Floyd with the blue-steel barrel-point. In two shakes old Floyd was there beside the grave. He felt Grandpa Jerry Bob Kelsey hold the carbine to his back. Lord, what a feelin'! That's when old Floyd bent down, took up some dirt and pitched it over long-gone Grandma Sally Anne Kelsey, she boxed up ready for the end of the line.

"Ashes to ashes," Floyd said, "dust to dust."

That's when Grandpa Jerry Bob Kelsey pointed his rifle down.

The folks all went home. And as they went they tried to think of all of the shotgun weddin's they'd tended but they all agreed how this farewell for Grandma Sally Anne Kelsey was the first and only thirty-thirty funeral ever—and likely enough there'd never be another.

Floyd Garden went back to his room in the Blue Bonnet Hotel. He took off his badge and hung up his gun-belt. He put his binoculars deep down in his trunk and he shut the lid. He looked out the window and saw Gus Protopapadakis emptyin' garbage in the trash barrel back of his Busy Bee Café. So old Floyd called down at Gus and said how he'd be proud if Gus would send him up a jug of hot coffee and a dozen glazed doughnuts. Gus hollered up, "You bet boss." So Floyd pulled down the shade on the window, cleaned out forever his view of the realm of death. He sat down in his chair and picked up a kiss-book. He aimed to read about somebody's livin' granddaughter, and wished prosperity to the distillin' business in the embalmin' room at the Blaylock Funeral Home—Blaylock, Flack and Beck, Props.

All of what happened to Floyd Garden goes to show what a sorry sonofabitch Billy Beck was. That's why, on the way down to the county courthouse, stopped in town with Clyde's Chivvelee sedan-car up agin the curb, Clyde and Sonny Boy gave Cousin Drewey sass for tellin' Billy Beck all about what he aimed, about gettin' Fats Recknagel's stud-horse over to the Skinner Ranch pasture.

So parked there at the curb, down at the county seat, with the big red brick courthouse standin' high just a block away, Clyde made Cousin Drewey promise he wouldn't ever say anymore his intentions of drivin' out Fats Recknagel's stud-horse, and put him over with Sonny Boy's mares, so's he could use his weapon.

Cousin Drewey sulled, 'cause he was a Washtaw Mountain man and didn't take orders from no Texan like Clyde.

"Better promise," Clyde said, "for your sake and for the sake of us Skinners, and for Pap Lowdermilk and that goddamn Newt."

I spoke up for Cousin Drewey, and here's what I said, "Maybe Billy Beck's done forgot what Cousin Drewey said."

"Like hell he has!" barked Sonny Boy, and when I say he barked, I mean he *barked*. "He ain't forgot nothin'. Billy Beck is that breed of no'count low-life who don't forget anythin' said by mortal man that might give him an idea. If he can make ten dollars out of Fats Recknagel by what he hear'd Cousin Drewey say, then you can mark my words how he's the old boy to do it."

"Ain't *that* a fact!" Clyde said.

"You bet," Sonny Boy said back at Clyde.

It was all Texas plain talk, and it shamed Cousin Drewey. We saw our kinfolks hang his head, and he held his chin on his shirt-front for a full minute. When he raised up again, reached across Pap Lowdermilk and spat some cud-juice out the window, he said plain enough, "All right, fellers, I promise I won't talk out loud no more. I won't tell my aim to a livin' soul, no matter who he be. And if you had a Bible in this here Chivvelee, I'd swear like I will before the judge."

So Clyde Skinner reached under the dashboard and pulled out a Bible, claimin' how he was a Baptist and no

Baptist travels without one. And that's when Cousin Drewey made the vow. After he put the Bible away, Clyde drove us all down the block and didn't stop 'til we got to the county courthouse. We saw a woman come 'round the corner, and she packed a basket with a cloth spread over the top, like it held a half-dozen fried chickens and Lord knows how many messes of potato salad. And the little girl that trailed behind her held a gallon jug full of pink drink—just what the court of justice needed.

And we saw Shyster Sam Hawkins' pickup truck parked right next to us, that lawyer who was primed to defend Fats Recknagel against Cousin Drewey. And there were more cars parked in front of that courthouse than you'd see at the county fair, 'cause all Star Valley and the county seat was there to he'p Cousin Drewey clear his good name.

So Clyde got out of the sedan-car and he stretched his legs like they had a cramp. Sonny Boy did likewise, and me and Pap Lowdermilk got our rusties off the back seat and into the sunlight. Cousin Drewey came out last, though he was the primest of us all.

"Let me carry your fiddle," Clyde said to Cousin Drewey. So Cousin Drewey gave Clyde his fiddle.

"I'll pack your guitar, Cousin Drewey," Sonny Boy offered. That's when Cousin Drewey gave Sonny Boy his guitar.

So we all took the courthouse steps like we meant business. First Clyde and Sonny Boy, them with the instruments of a musical man.

That's when me and Pap, us Lowdermilks, got to packin' fears of what'all might happen that day. We feared, but we didn't say so out loud.

And lastly came Cousin Drewey, takin' the steps two at a time, full of piss and vinegar, a feisty little runt. He packed neither fear nor instrument. Except maybe a song in his glottis.

25

Lord, Lord, it was a raucous trial! We'd no sooner took to our seats when the judge hollered off his bench, "Folks, listen to me and my gavel. Let's get this here trial of justice done for quick, 'cause I'm hungry for chicken and potato salad. Pretty to my ears I can hear the fiddle whine, the banjo picked, the jew's harp sound like a freight train comin' to a stop."

It was knock-down, drag-out sure enough. Talk came out of battlin'-faces, mostly from off Shyster Sam Hawkins. That feller strutted up and down like a bantie-rooster, a man full of fire and ignorance. He was a lawyer, all right, so he acted natural. First thing he'd be up front of the jury, handin' sass about Cousin Drewey, then under the judge's bench hollerin' like a Pentecostal. But always he kept a safe distance from Cousin Drewey, about eight feet from the prisoner's corral. He was scared our kinfolks might spit in his eye. And like the judge, Shyster showed he was hungry, that and proud for an earful of mountain music. Because, guilty or innocent, Cousin Drewey was a musical man.

Shyster made so much noise that the judge had to pound his gavel. The courtroom audience hollered and stomped. Cousin Drewey sat his rusty in the corral, bent frontways for the fun of it, holdin' his groin, laughin' to split the tenderloin. And all the while the fried chicken was gettin' dished at the table. The paper plates and cups were set out handy while two women he'ped each other at pourin' more powder and ice in the tub of pink drink.

"Excuse me, folks," a feller said as he went 'round the shoes and boots of the congregation, packin' a bucket of corn meal and sprinklin' the floor.

"You bet," said the folks as they got their tootsies hoisted high, makin' way for that sprinklin' man.

Crash, bang, crash! That's how the judge's gavel went. It seemed to splinter the bench where it hit.

"Who the hell are you?" the judge quizzed, screwin' his gimlet eye at Shyster Sam Hawkins.

"I'm the prosecutin' attorney," Shyster said, brakin' his speech.

"Who says?"

"My client."

"Who's him?"

"Mr. Fats Recknagel, a gentleman of the primest kind."

"Are you fixed to sass Cousin Drewey?"

"I am, your honor," said Shyster. "I've been sassin' him for the past ten minutes, but you ain't given me a lick of mind."

"If you're workin' for Fats Recknagel you ain't worth no mind," said the judge.

Shyster Sam got a hard look on his face, then he coughed like lawyers do.

"Shyster," said the judge, quizzical, "when you ain't a lawyer what'all's your line of work?"

"A plumber, your honor."

"When was the last time you fixed a feller's pipes?"

"Yesterday evenin', your honor."

"Who's pipes did you fix?"

"I fixed for Mr. Gus Protopapadakis, who runs the

Busy Bee Café up in Signal Rock."

"He's of Greek nationality, ain't he?"

"He is, your honor, hundred percent."

"Now tell the court where his pipe leaked."

"Under the sink, your honor."

"Did you win your case?"

"Sure thing, your honor. When I got it fixed the pipe didn't leak no more."

"How come you claim to be a prosecutin' attorney?"

"Because I graduated from a university."

"What'all university, Shyster, son?"

"The Postal Legal University, your honor. I took a six-month course after I saw it advertised in *Wrestlin' Ring Magazine*. I graduated Liberty Come Lordy."

When Shyster said that, folks in the courtroom seats snickered like little old kids.

"All right," the judge said down at Shyster. "If you aim to act the prosecutin' attorney you'd better get started."

Shyster straightened the hide of his hand-me-down suit, picked up his shiney-shoed feet and strutted the courtroom like a Cornish game rooster.

"Your honor, ladies and farmers of the jury, my distinguished opponent the attorney for the defense, gents and calico aset in the audience, witnesses young and old, the court clerk and my friend the janitor, and 'specially you chief cooks and bottle washers yonder at the refreshment table—greetin's, and hear ye, hear ye!"

The judge made his gavel talk. "Shyster," he said, "you've talked enough bullshit. So go ahead and sass Cousin Drewey."

"I cain't," Shyster said.

"Why cain't you?"

"'Cause I've done sassed him, like a Pentecostal. What I need now is praise my client, Mr. Fats Recknagel," Shyster confessed, blushin' cause he knew what popular opinion was ratin' him that very minute. "He's my client, and he's the most respectable millionaire west of West Texas. He's generous with mankind and good in the sight of the preachers, and he's ever ready to forgive any feller what's trespassed agin him—even a sorry mossback from the Washtaw Mountains."

The judge smacked his gavel, the spectators stomped their feet and whistled.

"Shyster," the judge said, when the courtroom gave quietus in favor of racket, "your first statement disqualifies you as a dad-burned liar, and your final statement is the product of your lies. Fats Recknagel ain't a respectable citizen, and that's 'cause he's a millionaire. He ain't generous with mankind, 'cause he's a skinflint sonofabitch. He might be good in the sight of the preachers, 'cause the preachers ain't got better sense. And if he's ever ready to forgive a feller what's trespassed agin him, that lucky feller can only be the president of the First National Bank."

"But, your honor . . ."

"Shut up and set down!" the judge hollered. "You've talked enough out of your glottis. Instead, we'll have the defense pile sweetness on the accused."

And who you'all reckon the defense attorney was? None other than Snookie Hapchester, that young slim cattleman from Lava Lake.

Snookie came out of the grandstand audience when the judge whistled. He blushed 'cause every eye was on his person, but you couldn't see the blush for the tan. He came out wearin' a pink shirt and green necktie, a brand-new haircut and a steer-head belt buckle. And, bein' a bachelor, he was plumb-sure he had the admiration of all in that courtroom.

The judge gave Snookie an invite to set. "Snookie," he said, "you set your rusty up on the witness stand, son. So right now I'll ask you a pregnant question, and I'll quiz it while you raise your right hand. Do you swear to tell the truth, the whole truth, and nothin' else but, so he'p us all God Almighty?"

"You bet," Snookie said, he with his hand hoisted.

"Lord bless you, Snookie," the judge said.

And that's when Snookie set his rusty on the witness seat.

Now, myself, I couldn't he'p notice how Snookie was lettin' his eyesight travel, backwards and forwards and sideways over the audience. I saw him pick out us Lowdermilks, and Clyde and Sonny Boy. I saw him give a nod to Old Man Lee Bassett and the same compliment to Uncle Posey Burwinkle. He gave a swat to a courthouse fly that had come to set on his cheek, and he looked like he was a better man than either Sheriff Hank Hudgeons or his deputy Elmo. He didn't seem to give a damn whether Young Buster Prather was there to hear him testify or not. He saw a feller settin' there wearin' handcuffs, so he reckoned he'd be the jailed-up bindlestiff named Junior, let out for the time bein' so he could twang the jew's harp. He shifted his kindly gaze over to the ladies who stood by the refreshment table, just do-nothin' women 'cause they'd already done dished up the delights. Then all asudden I caught his right eye renderin' a wink, and a sweet cattleman's smile overtake his young sunblistered face. How come? I was certain he gave eye-beam to Eunice and Beverly, the two chippy-bitches the law had pulled off the street, presently residin' in the ladies department. And damned if I didn't catch the girls smilin' back at Snookie.

"Snookie," the judge said, "you better quit your romancin' and get fixed to talk sweetly about Cousin Drewey."

So Snookie changed his glance over to our kinfolks in the prisoner's corral, opened his silly mouth and said howdy.

COUSIN DREWEY & THE HOLY TWISTER 259

The judge banged his gavel twice, then he set back on his bench and faced Snookie and Cousin Drewey head-on.

"Snookie, son, are you highly acquainted with Cousin Drewey?"

"Your honor, I am."

"Have you ever hear'd his music?"

"You bet."

"Can he make his fiddle talk Washtaw Mountain music?"

"He can make his fiddle talk the language of the world from the Blue Ridge of Virginia to the Arbuckles of Oklahoma, then up on the highest peaks of this here western state."

"Then you reckon he's a musical man?"

"Of the finest kind."

"Good enough, and what the court craves to know is how you reckon Cousin Drewey. Is he a low-down thief, or ain't he?"

"He ain't."

"How come he ain't?"

"'Cause he's a musical man."

"That don't mean nothin'. I hear tell how Jesse James played the fiddle but he robbed the Gallatin Bank. Black Jack Ketchum picked a guitar but they had to hang him so's to get him out of the way."

"That don't mean nothin', just like you said. Neither Jesse James nor Black Jack came from the Washtaw Mountains. That's the difference, and that's what clears Cousin Drewey of bein' a low-down thief of the lousiest kind."

"You speak hundred percent patriotic language, Snookie. So get back to your seat while I try the hell out of Cousin Drewey. And keep your eyes off the girls. They're good lookin', all right, but they charge too much. And they hate to give back change."

Snookie went back to his seat in the audience. But he took the long way 'round so's he could brush up agin Eunice and Beverly as he went.

Then the judge turned on his swiveled rusty so's to give Cousin Drewey full aim of his talk. Cousin Drewey giggled slightly like an old man does. But he straightened some when he met the judge eye to eye.

"Cousin Drewey, are you a Christian and a Democrat?"

"Your honor, I vote the Democratic ticket like anybody else in Pushmataha County, and I'm full-blood Baptist."

"Are you a Forty-gallon Baptist or are you a Foot-washin' Baptist?"

"Neither, your honor. I'm a Barker Baptist and I've got the tongues, and I prophesy reg'lar. Uncle Gersh Lowdermilk is a Forty-gallon, but Uncle Gersh Foster is a Foot-washin'."

"Fair enough. Now I'll ask you to swear on your Christian honor."

"I'm ready, your honor."

"Do you swear to tell the truth, the whole truth and nothin' else but, so he'p us all God Almighty?"

"Judge, I *sure* do."

"Then tell me this. Are you a low-down sonofabitch of a cattle thief like Shyster Sam Hawkins says you are?"

When the judge asked that quiz, Cousin Drewey got off his rusty. He turned on his foot-swivels and held his belly for mercy. He couldn't he'p but laugh out loud, like big bearded men do back in the Washtaw Mountains.

"Well, that's testimony enough, so let's go on with the trial before we lose the ham sandwiches to the courthouse rats. More'n that, folks, I'm *hongry*!"

The courtroom spectators whistled and clapped, Cousin Drewey jumped up and down like a tout at the racetrack and the judge pounded his gavel for order.

"Hear ye, hear ye!" hollered his honor, 'cause the racket was slightly out of hand. "We will now call to the stand the star-prosecutor of this here show, who by words from his fat mouth will either send Cousin Drewy to jail for life or over to the table for a he'pin' of potato salad."

Again the racket nigh bust my ear-tackle.

"Hear ye, hear ye!" The judge got down off his bench and made threat to use his gavel on some noisy heads if the whole audience didn't shut up. All asudden the courtroom got hushed. The judge coughed some spit then gave it to the spittoon. That's what they do when they have a life or death message to give.

"WILL SHERIFF HANK HUDGEONS KINDLY TAKE THE STAND!"

Lord, Lord, did we all go wild!

The noise didn't faze Hank Hudgeons a mite. The sheriff took his pot-bellied se'f down the aisle. He said howdy to the judge, took off his hat and plunked his rusty on the witness seat.

"You better stand, Hank, so's I can swear you in. And you better keep standin' so's to sass Cousin Drewey. Raise your right hand. Do you swear to tell the truth, the whole truth, and nothin' else but, so he'p us all God Almighty?"

"I sure do, judge," said the fat-assed sheriff.

The judge told Cousin Drewey to get up and face Hank Hudgeons. "Cousin Drewey, you better take Hank's sass like a man. You ain't got your hog-leg forty-five, but I hear tell how Washtaw Mountain men can kick like mules. Now, let the prosecutor state his case."

"Cousin Drewey," said the sheriff, "you remember that day me and Elmo rode out in the prowl car to the Lowdermilk place?"

"You bet."

"And you and Pap Lowdermilk was there, and Maw Maw. I couldn't see Verbaline Lou, but I reckon she was scared and hid away somewheres. You know how women get when they see the sheriff."

"That's the way we were, all right, and the place stank mightily 'cause Pap was burnin' automobile tires."

"Ain't you talkin' now, Cousin Drewey! That smell wasn't pretty, but the most ugly thing on the Lowdermilk place was your face."

"I ain't never took no beauty prizes."

"That face gave me a confession, Cousin Drewey. 'Cause after I asked you politely if you were a low-down stock-thief, havin' recently shot and butchered one of Mr. Fats Recknagel's registered yearlin's, and packed the carcass mule-back to feed them lousy Lowdermilks, your mouth didn't say, but the look in your eye told how you were guilty—worser'n Sam Bass or any of them Texas rustlers."

"You ought to know, you come from Texas."

"I know where you put that beef, Cousin Drewey, 'cause you hung it in the dugout, it where Pap Lowdermilk stores his potatoes and cabbage. Now, long after that day, can you remember the next question I asked you?"

"I think you asked me if I didn't reckon you a low-lifed no'count out of Bell County, Texas, like most folks in Star Valley think you be, and I told you how I always side in with the majority."

"What I asked you was to produce the hide and prove your innocence. I craved to see a Black Angus yearlin' hide with no brand, 'cause Pap Lowdermilk is too mossback to own any kind of mark registered at the Cattle Sanitary Board in the capital city of this here western state. But more likely you got the black hide which packs Mr. Fats Recknagel's brand—and, let me say, how if it does, by law, it makes you guilty as hell, Cousin Drewey."

"Guilty of what?"

"Of purloinin' from the sweetest, most noble cattleman ever come out of Texas—a bright and mornin' star with more generosity and good looks than you'll find in John D. Rockefeller, senior, who'll give his last dime to he'p out a feller who needs four-bits."

"You crave my testimonial, Sheriff?"

"You bet."

"Well sir, I ain't got no hide. I used to, but it's done gone to glory."

"What'all kind of glory, Cousin Drewey?"

"Down the pit in Pap Lowdermilk's back house."

"Why would a sane man do a thing like that, stuff a good Black Angus yearlin' hide down the hole in Pap Lowdermilk's back house?"

"'Cause I live my life accordin' to the laws of nature."

"Cain't you fish it out and thereby prove your innocence accordin' to the laws of this fair state?"

"I'd sure hate to."

"How come?"

"'Cause it's mixed up with the Sears and Roebuck."

"Cousin Drewey, I'm givin' you one last chance afore the jury declares you guilty as hell. That's when I'll percolate the delightful duty of haulin' you off to the State Pen. Cousin Drewey, I'm askin' you final, plumb on the section line, what'all have you done with that there hide?"

"I ate it."

"What the hell!"

"And I digested it, me and the balance of them Lowdermilks."

When Cousin Drewey made that declaration the whole dad-burned courtroom sounded like a herd of steer-beef gettin' loaded on the cars, fixed to get fattened in Iowa or someplace. That courtroom hooted and hollered and stomped its feet. It rattled the spittoons, it made the shades on the windows shimmy. It was the damnedest racket ever to make sound in that palace of county jurisprudence.

The judge banged his gavel so's to bring order.

"If you'all folks don't hush," he hollered, "we won't get this trial over before the fried chicken dries out. And if you let Hank Hudgeons have his way, and give him right to haul Cousin Drewey off to the State Pen, you won't get no fiddle music for your dinin' entertainment."

"Down with Hank Hudgeons!" the courtroom audience shouted so's to bust its lungs—and the loudest shouters of them all was the twelve gents and ladies of the jury.

"Let this noble trial proceed," the judge ordered, makin' splinters of the bench.

"You say you *ate* the hide?" Hank Hudgeons quizzed.

"I ate it, and it was delicious."

"What can I do with a testimonial like that?"

"Well, you can stick it."

"It's too tough."

"Not when I cook it."

"How'all do you cook it?"

"Well sir, first I soak it in lye. Then you take it out and scrape off the hairs. You put it in lye again, and by that time it's gettin' ripe. You take it to a sawed-off stump and pound it with the blunt side of an axe. Then you cut it up to squares and put it in Maw Maw Lowdermilk's iron washpot. You cook it for three days, simmerin' sweetly. Then you add the salt and potatoes, the pepper and the corn and turnips."

"Did it taste like a Lowdermilk stew, Cousin Drewey, or did it digest more like it was Mr. Fats Recknagel's registered yearlin'?"

"I don't know what the cow's name was that mothered that beef, but it was sure enough Lowdermilk hide-stew when we ate it for supper. You'd never get Mr. Fats Recknagel to eat a stew like that."

Well sir, the court went wild! The racket scared the birds away from the trees outside the windows, it nigh stopped the clock on the wall, and the stompin' feet hoisted more dust off the floor than hogs in the cornpatch.

"Good enough," the judge hollered, poundin'. "Hank Hudgeons can let his fat ass rest while the jury trails off to decide the lawful fate of Cousin Drewey . . ."

The folks wouldn't let him finish, 'cause they snarled at the jury like dogs and shook their fists like they'd give death and destruction if they didn't come back with the right verdict.

"To declare *guilty* . . ." the judge shouted above the ruckus.

The crowd booed and booed at the sorry thought.

". . . Or *not guilty*," the judge made final instruction to the jury.

The audience cheered, hooted, the menfolks tossin' their hats to the ceilin'. Then the twelve gents and ladies went out in single file, like hens and roosters off to the trash dump, for the jury room.

The court sat silent for twenty-thirty seconds. Only Shyster Sam Hawkins kept messin' 'round in front of the judge's bench. The judge paid him no mind, even when he went over to Cousin Drewey to yell how he wouldn't get a dime out of Fats Recknagel if the jury came out with a dirty verdict—*it* that would set Cousin Drewey free to go off and butcher yearlin's and eat their poor black hides. And how it wasn't right, and how jurisprudence wasn't what it used to be back in the good old tree-hangin' days. He told it all in twenty, thirty seconds. And when the jury room door opened, Shyster looked that way to see what'all.

So did us courtroom balance. We saw the twelve of them, men and women and foreman, trail out like that many cockerels and pullets.

"Has the jury come to a verdict?" the judge quizzed, while the ladies over at the refreshment table got fixed to dish out potato salad and sliced pickles next to some joints of fried chicken and a wedge of hot cornbread.

"We have, your honor," said Mistress Stumpy Tutt, the foreman.

Just then two courthouse janitors came in from the hall outside. One packed a piece of lumber from the Valley Ranchers and Farmers and Builders Supply Yard, a two-by-six about ten feet long. The second janitor had both hands full, one packin' a gallon can of roofing tar and the other a feather duster.

"What'all's your verdict, Mistress Tutt?" the judge said, smackin' with his gavel twice.

We didn't wait long to find out.

"NOT GUILTY!" shouted Mistress Stumpy Tutt at the pitch of her Methodist lungs.

Lord!

Every human soul got up and milled 'round like cattle in the feed pens at Clinton, Custer County, Oklahoma. Pap and me watched them act that way, 'cause they were wild with glee—'specially Mistress Stumpy Tutt, who'd have got run out on the rail if the verdict hadn't tasted right. Me and Pap saw a janitor pryin' off the lid on the tar can, so who could the tar and feathers be for? We also watched Shyster give a kindly eye to the sliced ham and pickled beets.

Well, it seemed mighty like everybody was up and 'round except us'uns. We kept our seats 'cause that's the way Lowdermilks are made.

Clyde and Sonny Boy were up among them. Folks were organizin' a chuck-line, joshin' while they waited for to get close where the action was, and right up front was Shyster.

"Newt," Pap said, gettin' close so's to whisper secrets. "Do you see what I see?"

"What'all?"

"Him," Pap said.

"Who'all?"

"Clyde Skinner, the nominated suitor of our sugar-tit gal. He's actin' the whoremonger; he's he'pin' that pretty young chippy, yonder, pour a cupful of Arbuckle's."

Pap licked his mouth like he tasted somethin' larrapin'. First I thought he had his mind on Beverly and Eunice. But I found out different when he nudged me in the ribs—when he said, "Newt, do you see what I see?"

"You bet," I said, 'cause I saw his finger pointed to a chocolate cake about five times the size of any Lilybelle makes. "I see it, Pap, and you're gonna get sicker'n a horse."

A stout cattleman had our runty kinfolks high on a shoulder. Folks fussed 'round while he held out his hands to shake, makin' the rounds so everybody could get a taste of honor.

Shyster Sam had loaded his plate high, and it looked like he was samplin' the lot. He ate as fast as he could and wished he had more time. Four mighty citizens of that county seat town packed over the ten-foot two-by-six, next to the janitors who tended the tar and feathers. They were boys with Fats Recknagel on their minds. But you can't faze the smartness of a prosecutin' attorney, 'cause Shyster saw, and when Shyster sees he gets a hunch . . .

He took a tight grip on his refreshment plate, aimed his direction for the door to the hall, and was outside to daylight like a bat out of hell.

You cain't find nowhere such happy faces as those worn by jailbirds out for the time bein'—time long enough to give salt to a hoedown. There they were circlin' 'round free society, about six of them, pilin' up their cardboard plates and sayin' how the pickled red beets were larrapin'. They'd take the handcuffs off Junior, the bindlestiff. He was there next to the woman wifely-wed to the county school superintendent. Junior had his pants worn out both at the knees and where he sat down, and his shirt was smoked by many a jungle fire. He was bald-headed, and his shoes were laced with balin' wire. They ate, standin', facin' each other, jugglin' a cupful of pink drink nested between the crunchy fried chicken and a mess of pinto beans. Hank Hudgeons walked 'round lookin' over the jail stuff, fearin' they might skip sometime when the shindig got raucous.

'Sheriff,'' said the superintendent's wife to Hank, "you leave us be now. 'Cause this is the potentest man."

Junior said, "Like I was sayin', ma'am, I caught 'em in the jail in North Platte, Nebraska, and by the time my yeller boxcar pulled into Cheyenne, late 'cause it was the Union Pacific, I knew I had 'em."

"Had what?"

"The crabs."

"Oh dear, Mr. Junior, you *are* a caution!"

I watched Pap's face, him there aset. It was full of sadness and his eyes didn't glimmer bright. I knew how his mind wasn't there in the courtroom, but way back to that time Verbaline Lou and Clyde Skinner first got to sufferin' the love-itch, the night of the Signal Rock hoedown when valley women hung cardboard hearts from the ceilin', painted red, to celebrate what'all they'd hear'd tell.

"Newt," Pap said, there in the courtroom. "Do you see what I see? I see two unrighteous men, and they both pack the name of Skinner."

"They're actin' shameful, Pap."

"For a fact."

COUSIN DREWEY & THE HOLY TWISTER

"Nobody seems to give a damn."

"I like Lilybelle, Newt. She's kind to me, she sends me cake."

"She don't aim to get you sick, Pap."

"That's a fact, Newt. That's why I don't like to watch her man actin' the whoremonger. He's sinful for the time bein', like his brother Clyde. Who's that snippity-snap-susan makin' up to Sonny Boy?"

"That Eunice, out of the ladies department. She's the blonde, built like a brick shithouse. And she's *sure* makin' up to Sonny Boy."

"Look at her wiggle her blossom, Newt!"

"She's got it in percolation, Pap."

"Look at Sonny Boy, Newt."

"Don't he look foolish!"

"He's blushin' slightly. Must've been somethin' she said."

"And look at Clyde, Pap. He's got a hand on Beverly's shoulder. When a man does that, that's when he wishes he had three dollars to spend."

"He ain't thinkin sweetly of my sugar-tit gal."

"Not for the time bein', Pap."

We hushed our talk, Pap and me. All we could do was watch a sorry show. Everybody else seemed to be havin' a good time, eatin' and drinkin', joshin' each other, laughin' their guts dry, and every once in a while hollerin' a kindly word to Cousin Drewey.

Young Buster Prather and Uncle Posey Burwinkle were up and 'round the judge's bench, both gettin' set for the hoe-down music. Hank Hudgeons was pushin' his way through the crowd, and right behind him was a feller packin' a guitar. Neither me or Pap knew who he was, but later we heard how his name was Cowboy, a jailbird free of the men's department. Like most folks, he was out from Texas and lately pulled in 'cause he did a criminal act. Like tryin' on a Stetson hat in Culp's

Gents Shop for size—legal enough in daylight, except it was midnight. The door was locked and Bowboy was alone in the store. Then Culp's burglar alarm went off. It was that goddamn Elmo who caught poor Cowboy and hauled him off to jail. He didn't get his Stetson hat. Cowboy was the *worst* crook born in Glasscock County, but he was the *best* guitar-picker in that fair Lone Star State.

Junior was talkin' bindlestiff lingo. He told the superintendent's wife about jungles and reefers, railroad dicks and what'all, about jails and the Salvation Army. He was havin' a good time. But when he saw Cowboy packin' his guitar to the judge's bench, taggin' pretty behind Hank Hudgeons, he quit the superintendent's wife and followed with his jew's harp.

Pap and me directed our view to the judge's bench where the musicians fixed to get set. Cousin Drewey was high-up on the flatness where the judge pounds his gavel, lookin' down on the folks. He was rosinin' up his fiddle-bow as he rested the instrument under his chin. Young Buster Prather tuned his banjo, likewise Cowboy his guitar. Junior the bindlestiff just sat await, 'cause his jew's harp wasn't that touchy. Uncle Posey Burwinkle oiled his glottis with brown, before givin' ambeer to the spittoon. And what you reckon about Old Man Lee Bassett? He was he'pin' the janitors move the seats and benches away from the floor so the square dance could swing the sashay right and docee-do, promenade and go sweetly wild.

"If you two fellers ain't got your concrete set," Old Man Lee said to Pap and me, "we'd be proud if you'll move up agin the wall. We need your bench out of the way."

That's what he said, all right, but before we could get up, we slanted our eyesight toward the big table. There stood Clyde and Sonny Boy laughin' in our direction.

They were bent over like they looked on two prime fools. And before Old Man Lee could shake us, damned if we didn't feel a soft female rusty come plunk—one in Pap's lap, t'other in mine, soft and squashy, wiggly, the warm ends of two gals who knew how it was done.

Eunice for Pap, Beverly for me—and they balanced each a full plate of celebration vittles in their dainty hands.

Eunice said to Pap, "Look Pap! Look what I've got for you. Cake! Sonny Boy says how it will make you sicker'n a mule."

I could see how Pap liked Eunice's fat-end dug in his lap, but he admired the cake a heap more.

Old Man Bassett got hold of our bench and prayed the janitor to give him some he'p. He needed to dump us four onto the floor so's to move the bench over by the wall. 'Cause Uncle Posey Burwinkle was set to holler "Hogs in the corn!"

"Git!" said Old Man Lee. So we got.

Pap and me got hold of our plates. We went up against the wall. Pap snickered while he looked under the big hunk of cake, and damned if he didn't see the pickles and ham. And more, plenty more, even a cup of pink drink. My plate held likewise, but only an itty-bitty piece of cake.

The two whores quit us like we didn't have the price, and Pap said, "Well hell, Newt! They were soft while they lasted, but I'm right proud of the way they think. They knew for sure how this old moss-back loves cake."

We ate like pure hog. We saw how out yonder Beverly and Eunice had caught Snookie Hapchester in the Jezebel-grip, and that young cowman blushed for the sin of it. He liked the way he felt.

Then all hell bust loose. It was Uncle Posey Burwinkle that gave off the racket and Cousin Drewey made his fiddle whine. Cowboy's guitar kept in tune, his lovin' fingers givin' life to the strings; and if Young Buster Prather didn't fire his banjo, sweetly tappin' a foot, then the banjo was born in vain. And Junior—he twanged his melody like on many a moonlight night in the trackside jungles of this prideful nation.

I saw Snookie catch Beverly and hold on tight, while the judge pulled Eunice into the dance. Men wailed like coyotes, just for the hell; calico, young and old, fell in the circle to swish their shirtworks 'round and 'round— to sashay right and how-de-do. . . . Promenade! . . . Swing your pretty girl off the world! . . . Circle right, circle left, circle where the goin's best! . . . Hell-fire, don't you know! . . . This is a trial of jurisprudence in the courthouse down yonder, forty miles south. . . . We're tryin' the hell out of Cousin Drewey. . . . The prosecution gave him sass, the defense sung his praises; and all together we made a prime jackass out of Fats Recknagel. Maybe so, who knows? Maybe Shyster Sam Hawkins has gone to fix his pipes.

Cousin Drewey was makin' music, the blessin' from heaven shone on his countenance—he was the happiest man. He had the whole lovin' world tight in his grip.

26

Now that Fats Recknagel was dealt his punishment there seemed nothin' much to do inside the Lowdermilk house but listen to Verbaline Lou tell all about Clyde Skinner, and what he aimed for us Lowdermilks. That is, what would happen to four crusty mossbacks after he and our girl committed a lawful act of matrimony. Cousin Drewey just sat and took in Clyde's talk anytime that cowman came 'round. Clyde tried hard to make a friend out of Pap Lowdermilk. Clyde came all the way down from his ranch, time after time, to get some sweetness out of Pap. But Pap wouldn't give Clyde sweetness. Clyde would talk kindly to us all. I liked Clyde, so did Cousin Drewey. Maw Maw liked him too. But she couldn't he'p frettin' about Verbaline Lou's tubes, and she feared how Clyde might already have taken her bud. I could see how if any man was to wed up with our girl, Maw Maw figgered how Clyde ought to be that man. But she never said. Women never say much, but they think a heap. They don't talk. You can't find nothin' more silent than a woman. Pap didn't talk much, either. When Clyde said somethin' Pap just whittled and spat. He kept his face down to the dirt. He sulled like a Washtaw Mountain mule.

That day Clyde told all about it. He said how he and Sonny Boy were fixin' to pull us out of our miserable style of life, and give mercy to Maw Maw for a change. The Skinner brothers aimed to he'p me, Newt Lowdermilk, to quit my lazy days; 'cause mostly I sat 'round and did nothin'. The aimed to pull Pap away from his stack of old worn-out automobile tires, which Pap bust up for stove fuel. That's when he stunk up Star Valley with the black smoke of rubber set afire. Clyde said how they aimed to give comfort to Cousin Drewey until our kinfolks saw fit to go back to the Washtaw Mountains.

The Skinners would even give our two hound dogs a new home, that Pee-Dog and that Bitchy Damn. And the cats, and old Jeff the mule. They'd take the milk cows up to their pasture in the pickup truck. And the hogs. We listened to Clyde, all right, and we were mighty proud he aimed to make solid citizens out of us. Except Pap.

"In a pig's ass," Pap said, squirtin' cud-juice.

They had an old unused bunkhouse up at the ranch, which Clyde said he'd fix up to the most liveable fashion. That's where he aimed to plant Pap and Maw Maw and me. And Cousin Drewey, too, if our kinfolks aimed to stay in Star Valley. They'd take Pap into partnership, make him ramrod the farmin' operations. And as for me, Clyde said: "Newt, we'll give you a ranch job, one that pays monthly wages."

"He'll work us to our deathly graves, and starve us to weakness, and we won't lift up our Christian heads no more," Pap said, 'cause he didn't trust Clyde Skinner.

"What you aim to do about Maw Maw?" I quizzed Clyde. "She ain't the kind of wifely-woman who'll set and do nothin'. She's worked all her life. She don't know better."

Clyde said, "When Verbaline Lou 'comes my wife, she'll be my own flesh and blood. Maw Maw gave Verbaline Lou birth, and put her in this world for me to wed. That's why me and Sonny Boy will give Maw Maw a gift of happiness. There'll be plenty for her to do, and

COUSIN DREWEY & THE HOLY TWISTER 275

whatever she does she'll do with a song."

"She cain't sing worth a shit," Pap said.

One thing we knew, Clyde was buildin' a fine new house for himself and Verbaline Lou, and for all the punkin' kids they'd make out of their midnight chores. That's all right. A man can do anythin' with his money, can't he? So long as he pays his taxes and hired hands.

Pap whittled on a stick while Clyde talked sense. He sat his rusty on a sawed-off stump. He didn't look up, but kept his eyes fixed on the brown dirt. His jaw-action massacreed cud, his lips were sticky with ambeer-spit—he looked mean and miserable. He saw no friend in Clyde, and he gave no thanks for Clyde's plan of salvation. If he wasn't whittlin' on the stick (and to lay the stick down would take too much sweat) he'd have risen-up off the stump, took Clyde by the shirt collar and told him to behave.

Clyde said, "How about it, Pap Lowdermilk?"

"How about what?" Pap said, not lookin' up.

"About you folks takin' exit from this crusty shanty."

Talk like that made Pap look up. Pap answered Clyde by gettin' off the stump. He said nothin', he just got up off his rusty. That's when he walked over to the shanty, where his shotgun hung on the inside wall. He took it down and broke the breech, and he did that to see if the two shells were ready for firin' at a two-legged human bein' named Clyde. Then he came out to where me and Cousin Drewey were aset, and where Clyde had shot off his reckless mouth.

"Friend Skinner," Pap said, a man riled, without faith, hope or charity, "you've done ruined my daughter. You made her into a high-society hunk of nothin'. You pulled off her drawers and put her in pink panties. That's a sin listed in Leviticus. Next thing you'll fit her in shorts. You'll make her wear a girdle. You'll lace her up 'round the crotch, you'll spray her with perfume. I know, 'cause I done seen it in the Sears and Roebuck catalogue. You'll tie sparklers in her hair. You think I know nothin' about them things, them lady do-dads. But I'm wise to them, friend Skinner. I'm wise to them all; 'cause like I said, I've studied the mail-order catalogue. Now git! Git your ass off my farm!"

Old Clyde didn't move an inch. He looked at Pap, and at Pap's lifted and aimed shotgun, and all Clyde gave out for answer was a twinkle in his eye.

"Git, goddamn it, git in a hurry," growled Pap like a bear, slobberin'. "And take my shameful daughter with you. Take her for a prize. Put lipstick on her mouth, put shoes on her feet. Take her away. Take her to hell and gone. 'Cause she ain't my sugar-tit gal no more."

Cousin Drewey sat on his hunkers. He said nothin', he just smiled. Clyde got up, stretched, and he didn't smile. He just looked sadly at Pap, and at me, and at Cousin Drewey. And it looked, for the time bein', how Pap's angered talk fixed Clyde. That cattleman acted Texas fashion. He said nothin', but he walked over to his pickup truck. He sat in the cab until Verbaline Lou came out of the house, where she'd been talkin' with Maw Maw. She got in the pickup with Clyde, and they drove away. Where to? The ranch, likely. Or maybe they'd first go to the Bankhead Drug Store and Fountain on Signal Rock Main Street. And Clyde would buy Verbaline Lou a chocolate fudge sundae, another for hisse'f, just to cool the situation down.

Pap Lowdermilk was a man packed with ire. But riled as he might be, he couldn't pull a damper on my hopes for a cozy ranch job out in the Skinner pasture. I did what I had to do on the Lowdermilk place, just to pay for my keep. But come some sweet day when I could leave old Pap backwards of my dust, that's when I'd rein old Jeff up to the ranch. Jeff was a good mule. He packed more sense than most horses. Fair enough, but I did have dreams of ridin' a little pretty-old cowpony of my own, aset in a creaky-new saddle. And I'd ride with arithmetic in my head, of how much I'd be makin' in wages. Maybe fifty dollars a month, but more likely thirty-five. No matter, better ride a Skinner crow-bait at any wage than a Lowdermilk one-mule cultivator. Better smell the grama grass under-hoof than bust up dirt 'round the sweeps. Lord, Lord! I'm Newt Lowdermilk. I'm that kind of feller.

I liked it up at the ranch. Best of all I liked the days we sat 'round, me and the folks, times when I went up to visit. Sometimes out in the shed next to the corrals. Other times in the house-kitchen. That's where Lilybelle and my sister would be messin' 'round makin' cookies or doughnuts or both. The coffee pot was always loaded with hot brown juice. Me, Clyde, Sonny Boy and the girls would set at the table. Sister mine and Lilybelle would nibble dainty on the cookies, but us three gents would gut-stuff the doughnuts. I'll say how Sonny Boy had a high-grade wife in Lilybelle. And I'll say how Clyde would get likewise when he's weld his brass with Verbaline Lou. They were sweet days in the kitchen. I'm proud to remember how Lilybelle's kids acted healthy while they ground up cookies. While they made 'em into hash by the wetness of their little mouths.

Sonny Boy said to me, usin' up a doughnut, "Newt boy, I like the way you treat my kids. I like the way you josh them. I can see how my kids like you, Newt. I can see that plain as hell."

"We'll need to get a woman for old Newt," Clyde said. "We'll need to get him a woman so's he can make kids for hisse'f. A man needs a woman for to make that there; he needs matchin' territory for what the dear Lord gave him."

Lilybelle said, "If Clyde aims to talk raw, I reckon we'd better get these kids out of the way. Clyde's raw talk ain't spoke for the ladies, neither. So let's us get out to the yard, Lou. Let's take these kids out, so Clyde can have his raw talk."

When the gals and kids went outside the walls, us three fellers stretched and ate more doughnuts. We felt more natural. We felt how the Lord didn't give us tassels for nothin'.

"Hell yes," Sonny Boy said. "We might even take old Newt down to the whorehouse."

"Not today, we won't," Clyde said, "'cause I aim to quiz old Newt with a pregnant question."

"What kind of pregnant question?" I said to old Clyde.

"I got two questions, Newt."

"Shoot."

"First question is how the hell are we goin' to gentle Pap Lowdermilk? How we goin' to make him quit that shanty and take domicile in civilized territory?"

"We cain't."

"We'll need to. If we don't the Humane Society will get after us."

"The Humane Society don't care a damn for low-down truck like Pap Lowdermilk. That bunch of fellers gives mercy only to dogs," I said.

"Pap Lowdermilk is better'n a dog," Sonny Boy said.

"Most folks don't think so," I said back at Sonny Boy.

"I think so," Clyde said. "I aim to make him my daddy-in-law, even if it takes a shotgun to make the relation legal."

"He's good with that goddamn shotgun," I said.

All that didn't answer Clyde's pregnant question. What that cowman craved to know was how we'd ever get Pap up to the Skinner ranch.

"Cold-cock him with a board, then hog-tie his hands and ankles. When he wakes up, cold-cock him again," Sonny Boy said.

"Git him drunk 'til he's senseless," I said.

COUSIN DREWEY & THE HOLY TWISTER 279

"I'll tell you what we can do," Sonny Boy said. "We can get us a thirty-foot lariat rope. Then we tie one end 'round that stack of old automobile tires, one tire at a time, them which old Pap likes to burn and stink up the valley. We can hitch t'other end of the lariat rope to the hind bumper of the pickup truck. Then we'll drive up the road, draggin' them stinkin' things. When Pap sees his tires takin' a trip, he'll run out to catch them. But he'll never catch up till we stop here at the ranch. Then we'll have him, by golly! We'll lock him up in the bunkhouse, with his tires, and he won't go back to the shanty no more."

"Hell!" Clyde said. He was shocked speechless 'cause of Sonny Boy's plan. "We don't need them stinkin' things on this outfit."

While Clyde and Sonny Boy joshed about Pap, and about his tires, I didn't say a goddamn thing. 'Cause I had Cousin Drewey on my mind.

I saw that old mossback in my memory. And my memory went back to the winter before, when the dammedest stink came out of the shanty, up the stovepipe. Pap Lowdermilk was firin' up some tire-bits in the cookstove. He did that 'cause Maw Maw aimed to bake some cornbread. Me and Cousin Drewey were aset, over by the box elder tree where he slept of nights, even when the cold nigh hit zero.

I said to Cousin Drewey, "Kinfolks, what salvation you got for Pap Lowdermilk?" That's what I said at that time, 'cause I had a quiz to get shed of.

"Newt," said our kinfolks, "to give salvation to that Washtaw Mountain man ain't the business of humankind. Only the Lord will pull him out of that shanty and set him on high ground, yonder where the decent brand of American society resides. So don't let's me or you, or Verbaline Lou, or them Skinner fellers try. Don't let us waste our time. Talkin' about time, there's a time acomin'. The Lord will do it in His wonderful heavenly way. He'll do it, sure. He'll do it with His might. He'll do it with His wisdom. He'll do it with His lovin' kindness. He'll pick up Pap Lowdermilk and put him on a cloud, a cloud with cushions for Pap to set on. Maybe it'll be the same cloud I aim to ride back to the Washtaw Mountains."

"You always claimed how you'd ride home on a twister-cloud, Cousin Drewey."

"You cain't ride a better wagon, Newt."

"Just like you cain't git Pap back to the Washtaw Mountains," I said.

"Maybe not, Newt. Maybe you reckon right. Only the sweet Lord can figger that pregnant question. And when the Lord figgers the way, and when the Lord does it—that's when old Pap Lowdermilk won't stink up Star Valley no more."

That's how come I thought of the Lord's salvation. I thought of it that day, later, at the Skinner ranch, in the kitchen, after the girls and kids went out 'cause of Sonny Boy's raw talk, when me and Clyde and Sonny Boy sat 'round the table with the doughnuts. I thought backwards, and I told what Cousin Drewey had said. About the Lord and how He in His might would fix Pap Lowdermilk.

"Maybe you're right, Newt," Clyde said, after I told him what I reckoned. "Maybe we'll just wait and see what comes natural."

"I ain't sufferin'," Sonny Boy said. "If Pap aims to live with misery and bedbugs, that ain't no skin off my ass."

I don't reckon how I'll ever forget that day and the doughnuts. Never for the balance of my life. Weeks passed by after that. Then a couple months came and went. Then before a feller could feel the change, it was October. The frost-nip took hold on Star Valley. Time to harvest, time to haul in the year's plunder. We had to get to the pinto beans first. Pap, me and Maw Maw had the speckled crop pulled, threshed and sacked before the frost could give a dose of nip. Now it was time to get the ears off the yellowed corn, stack them away from the rats. Then we sickled down the maize and kaffir corn. Cousin Drewey gave us a he'pin' hand, 'cause he aimed to earn his keep. When we had the harvest done, and when we had the crop stacked away, or put in wooden bins, Pap said a blessin'. He thanked the Lord, 'cause to Him our thanks was due.

Maw Maw was real thankful, like a woman naturally is. Work at a harvest-of-plenty is sweet work for a fact, but sweeter still is when it is done and three fellers—like me, Pap and Cousin Drewey—can set down to rest. Maw Maw was in the shanty, that day, just messin' 'round. Woman-doin's, likely. Us fellers sat out by the woodpile 'cause the October sun was warm and dry, just the kind of weather a man can love. A kindly day.

Kindly, that is, 'til we saw a sedan-car come through the gate, headin' toward us. It was Hank Hudgeons, the sheriff, and he had that piss-ant deputy with him on the seat, that Elmo. Hank didn't flash that dome-light, like a sonofabitchin' law. Neither did he wail his siren. Because he was peaceful as hell, and he didn't aim to worry nobody. That is, worry nobody but Cousin Drewey.
'Howdy, you fellers," Hank hollered out the sedan-window. And he hollered that there when he pulled up in a cloud of dust. "Do you reckon you'll ever amount to a damn?"

Elmo smiled at us out of his silly face, and any time Elmo smiled he looked like he was sick.

"We'll never amount to a damn," Pap said back at Hank, "'cause we're low like the snakes. We can't get no lower unless we fix to run for county sheriff."

Hank laughed that off like Pap was tellin' a funny-windy.

Hank said out of the window, never shiftin' his rusty,

that somethin' frightful had happened in the valley. That's how come he'd driven the sedan-car to see us Lowdermilks.

"Which one of us you aim to take to jail, Hank?" Pap quizzed that law.

"Nobody," Hank Hudgeons said.

He claimed he didn't come out to study Cousin Drewey this time, nor did he crave to be sociable with high-grade folks. But he had to do his duty and ask Cousin Drewey about what he reckoned. Because what had happened in the valley needed the sheriff, needed Hank to get off his fat ass and go to work.

"Somebody stole Fats Recknagel's fine stud-horse," Hank Hudgeons said. "Somebody took him out of the irrigated pasture."

"You mean that special pasture for that special horse?" I said.

"You bet, Newt," said Hank Hudgeons.

"You mean you cain't find that horse nowheres?" Pap said, while Cousin Drewey looked down on the crawlin' ants and said nothin'.

"That's what I mean, fellers. Folks up and down the valley are talkin' some. They don't like Fats Recknagel but they think it's shameful how somebody stole his horse. I'd sure like to see that horse thief git jailed," Hank said.

That's when Cousin Drewey looked up from lookin' down on the ants, when he cleared his teeth of cud-juice. "Don't look at me," he said to the sheriff. "I didn't steal the sonofabitch's horse. I ain't got no need for a stud horse. If I feel I *must* take somethin' off that fat-sized no'count, I'll take somethin' I can use."

"Valley folks are talkin' about who stole Fats Recknagel's horse. They don't like horse thieves, them folks, 'cause they'd like to see that kind of criminal jailed," Hank said.

"Or better hung," cut in that silly-faced Elmo.

"They're usin' your name a heap, Cousin Drewey," Hank said. "They claim you've been talkin' out of your mouth, Cousin Drewey. Me, I like you a heap. I sure wish you hadn't talked like you did. The folks like you, too, 'specially your music. They used to hang horse thieves in Texas, likewise this western state. But until we catch the feller who stole Fats Recknagel's horse, Star Valley folks will have their superstitions."

"They better pull their superstitions off me, sheriff," Cousin Drewey said. "And you, you ain't got no evidence."

"That's the Baptist-truth, Cousin Drewey," Hank said. "We ain't got no evidence. But maybe if me and Elmo look 'round some, that's when we'll bust our asses on it, stumble into it like you do when you're out deer-huntin'. The mostest thing a lawman likes to do is stumble on some evidence. Ain't that the truth, Elmo?"

"You bet," Elmo said.

Hank Hudgeons said no more. He just started up his sedan-car and drove out on the road.

It was the next day when Clyde came by the Lowdermilk domicile. He brought Verbaline Lou with him, down from the ranch. Verbaline Lou craved to talk with Maw Maw, and to deliver a chocolate cake.

Clyde found Cousin Drewey out by the woodpile. He found our kinfolks thinkin' sweetly about the Washtaw Mountains. He had a kind of faraway look. He talked, but he didn't talk to Clyde. He had a heap to say, and he aimed it at someone who wasn't there. Clyde just stood and said nothin'.

"You're damn whistlin'," Cousin Drewey was sayin'. "You can meet me at the depot, Uncle Gersh, 'cause I'll need some he'p with my satchel, and with my guitar and fiddle, and with my hog-leg forty-five. I'll ride the cloud like Saul rode his chariot. I won't give no mind to the Philistines. Nary a Israelite will be skin off my ass. Neither will the Benjaminites, the Jebusites, or the Hittites. 'Cause I'll be ridin' the twister. I won't be on the train, in the smokin' car, where the butcher boy sets. I won't be gassin' with the drummers, I won't be tellin' the conductor how to run the railroad. I won't be payin' my fare. 'Cause with a cyclone to ride, eastbound back to the Washtaw Mountains, I won't need to patronize the Frisco Lines, I won't need to change cars at Hugo."

Just then, Cousin Drewey came out of his fancyland talk. His look got closer than far away, and he snickered some when he saw Clyde standin' next to him. He said, "Well, son, I'll be damned!"

Clyde said, "You love them old Washtaw Mountains, don't you Cousin Drewey?"

"You bet I do," Cousin Drewey said, shakin' his head and shoulders so's to wake up. "I love 'em like a young man loves a young woman. I could wrap them old hills in my arms, nestle my chin in the softness of their slash-pine. Feel the wetness of them when God Almighty gives down His sweet-sap rains. I could dig my hands in her dirt . . . Son, I could never, never leave them mountains again. Never 'til death do us part. And Clyde, son, who you reckon stole that heavy sonofabitch's horse?"

"Billy Beck, who else?" said Clyde.

"That's what I reckon," Cousin Drewey said. "But try and say so to the sheriff. I *do* believe the sheriff thinks the sinner is me."

"You shouldn't have talked so much, Cousin Drewey. Even if you aimed to steal that horse you shouldn't have talked it out loud."

"I reckon," Cousin Drewey said. "I reckon you're right. But you know, Clyde, never for a minute did I really aim to *steal* that stud. All I craved of that prizewinner was the use of his weapon on Sonny Boy's mares. I'd *sure* love to see Sonny Boy's mares git some prize colts. The Lord knows I wanted the *loan* of Fats's stud, nothin' more sinful than that."

Clyde said, "The mostest thing Sonny Boy *don't* need

is the loan of Fats Recknagel's stud. Us Skinners don't need nothin' out of Fats Recknagel."

Cousin Drewey said back at Clyde, "Then that's done cleared my mind for a fact. Now through my days I needn't fret no more about gittin' them Skinner mares bred. All I need think about now is for a happy day, comin' up, and how I can git back to the Washtaw Mountains. I'll leave Billy Beck alone with his sinnin', him and Shorty Flack and Reese Blaylock. And I don't need their sorry whiskey, 'cause I'm a teetotlin' man. When I talked out loud, that's when I only hoped the dear Lord would he'p us git Sonny Boy's mares bred, and Fats Recknagel pay the maternity bill."

"While you're thinkin'," Clyde said, "you might find a way for my sweet wife-to-be to git her silly old daddy out of his shack. We got a reg'lar New York mansion waitin' for him on the ranch. Our sentiments to Pap Lowdermilk go thisaway, us Skinner boys—we don't give a shit for him. But I'd like right smart to reward Maw Maw for birthin' a gal worthy to be my wife, and thank the Lord for makin' me worthy of her. It's a fifty-fifty proposition, like Verabline Lou will tell you, 'cause she trusts mightily in the Lord. We both aim to live a goodly Christian life."

"You're right, son. The Lord ramrods everythin'."

"All right, Cousin Drewey. How we gonna git Pap up to his new home sweet home?"

Cousin Drewey bent down and looked at the ants again. He picked up a stick and made some marks on the ground. He thought and he thought, and after about sixty seconds he looked up—he aimed his eyestraight straight at Clyde's face, *it* shaded by the brim of his John B. Stetson hat.

Cousin Drewey said: "Feed Pap Lowdermilk enough of Lilybelle's chocolate cake 'til he drops unconscious, sicker'n a horse. Pick him up and bind his two wrists together with balin' wire, twenty-strand. Pinion his arms snug to his middle with half-inch rope. Gag him, then chain his legs together. A tow-chain will do. Knock him on the head so he'll sleep awhile longer. Load him in the back of your pickup truck. Then git Maw Maw and Newt, and set them in the seat beside you. Load up the Lowdermilk plunder, that which is good enough to take. You can pack it all in a wheelbarrow. Git one of your horseback cowhands to trail-herd the cow and the mule and the two hounds. You can come back for the hogs and the chickens and the cats. Be good to the mule and them dogs, Clyde, for I love them dearly, and when you pitch off Pap Lowdermilk from the back of the pickup, front side of his new home sweet home, still tied up, give him a sniff from the bottle to wake him up."

"Me and Sonny Boy is both teetotlin' Baptists, Cousin Drewey."

"Like I said," went on Cousin Drewey, "give him a sniff from the bottle; not rum, not whiskey, not gin or brandy—just a noseful of Sir Ashley Pendergast's Revivin' Salts, which Maw Maw will give you if you ain't got none. I can brag on that for a tough case like Pap's."

"What about the old shanty yonder?"

"Douse it with coal oil and fire it to the ground. If Pap tries to run home he'll need sleep in the ashes."

That put Clyde to tell all about the good things and the good life that waited us Lowdermilks up there on the ranch.

"We'd sure love to have you up there with us, Cousin Drewey."

Clyde's invite gave Cousin Drewey a mind to bite off a fresh quid, 'cause he was a cud-chewin' man.

"Sorry, son," our kinfolks said. "This old fiddler ain't gonna be with you'all many weeks more. I'm just waitin' for the storm, the kind that will blow wild and free. 'Cause I'll be headin' home to the green, green hills. I'm goin' where the sweet Lord sets on His slash-pine throne. I don't aim to use the Frisco Lines, and I won't need to change cars at Hugo. I'll be settin' back on the cushions of the tornado, and if that there butcher boy sells me a ham sandwich, I'll just give him two-bits."

"You aim to hunt some, when you git back to the Washtaw Mountains?"

"Son, I sure do, 'cause Uncle Gersh has five of the best hounds in Pushmataha County."

"Do you reckon you'll do some sportin', once in awhile, like pushin' the bell on the front door in Tulsa?"

"No, Clyde, I won't. I like to view a pair of lady-legs at times, just for the sake of admiration. No more. And the biggest town I ever want to see is Antlers, where Christianity is the sport and a good preachin' the wildest thing next to a hoe-down. I'll make music, 'cause that's my reason for life and old age."

"You'll do some fishin'. You'll do that there, won't you, Cousin Drewey?"

"I'll fish the lakes and I'll fish the creeks, and the catfish will love me for hookin' them in. I'll fish for bass and fry them beauties in cracker meal and hot lard."

Clyde said to Cousin Drewey, "You'll be the fishin'est fisherman west of Arkansas and north of Texas, and there ain't none in Louisiana to catch up with you."

"Clyde, son, you're talkin' the most sensible sense."

"Cousin Drewey," Clyde said. "Have you ever hear'd what they say about fishermen like you?"

"No, son, I ain't."

"They say how old fishermen never die. They just *smell* that way."

"Who said that first? Benjamin Franklin or Confucius?"

"Damned if I know, Cousin Drewey."

"Well, let me tell you somethin' about high-smellin' fishermen. I'll say here how I've known a heap of fellers in my day, and they smelled pretty bad. And they never went fishin'."

27

Then it came an evenin', one, maybe two, maybe three evenin's after Clyde talked with Cousin Drewey. No tellin'. It was after sundown, earliest of night. Darkness mixed with silver had struck the valley; the clear moonlight was cool. All of us Lowdermilks had finished supper and done washed our mouths out with water. There was plenty of water in the bucket, so we spat the bits of greens and cornbread on Maw Maw's hollyhock outside the back door. Cousin Drewey did likewise; all of us did except Verbaline Lou. We all figgered she'd done quit us to go live her days at the Skinner ranch. And if she aimed to wed-up with Clyde, it wasn't skin off a solitary ass, none in all Star Valley.

We sort of craved to have a little Cousin Drewey music after supper, so Pap could tap his foot to the fiddlin' tune while we sat on the porch to swat the pesky gnats and flies. But when Pap asked Cousin Drewey to provide, that musical man told us he aimed to walk 'round and think how good the Lord had been to the folks of this humble home.

"When the Lord deals out blessin's," Cousin Drewey said, "the best way to thank Him is to go off in a solitary state of body and mind. It's easy, you just think of good things and act meek and mild."

"Halleluyah," Maw Maw hollered at the whole countryside.

"Amen," Pap mumbled, as he settled on his hunkers.

He was a man fixed to swat flies and curse gnats.

"Look 'round where you walk, Cousin Drewey," Maw Maw said after him, as he took off on a ramble. "You cain't see where you step, and you're fit to get bit by a big old rusty rattlesnake. Them nasty varmints go prowlin' after sundown."

Cousin Drewey said nothin' to that, 'cause he was a Washtaw Mountain man and bein' a good Christian was an Israelite's shield against any one of the whole tribe of rattlesnakes.

So Cousin Drewey walked off, away from us Lowdermilks. But he went only a couple hundred steps. Then he turned 'round and came back. He faced me and Pap hunkered down, and Maw Maw aset in her rockin' chair.

"Folks and Lowdermilks," he said, as he came up to the porch, "I've had a change of mind. I aim to ramble 'round some, but 'cause Pap begged for music, that's what he'll get. The main reason I craved to get off to my quiet thoughts is 'cause Pap Lowdermilk talked too damned much at supper, he just had to shout a mouthful of silliness. He told all he reckoned as what should have happened to them spies, them fellers hidden away by Rahab in the Book of Joshua. What Pap reckoned didn't make sense. So I'll get the guitar and sing you a song. When a man begs music I can't he'p but give it gladly. After that I'll go off on my ramble-'round."

That was a fact. Pap had talked too much at supper. He was feelin' fine after his spell of cake-sickness, after he'd straightened out from sufferin' Lilybelle's kindly gift. And when Pap Lowdermilk feels fine his talk can be pesky enough to stir up ire in anybody listenin'.

Cousin Drewey got out his guitar.

"I feel like a man of peace tonight," he said, gettin' aset on the edge of the porch, ready to sing us "Job's Boils."

The song told exactly as it did the last time, and the time before. It told about Job, and about Bildad the Shuhite, and about Eliphaz the Temanite. It told how they hunkered down to gas about religion. And about politics. They'd talk for twenty-four hours if any one had a potent opinion to give. And when they'd talked enough, and prophesied aplenty, and made each other mad, they'd get out the dice and shoot some craps.

> *Roll, baby, roll!*
> *Come on seven-eleven!*
> *'Cause my name's Bildad,*
> *A Shuhite from down the line.*

And, like always, Eliphaz the Temanite raked in the shekels.

Too, Cousin Drewey would sing about Job, and his dose of boils.

> *He scratched and he scratched,*
> *But they wouldn't come loose.*
> *'Cause the Lord done put 'em there.*

Which called for a change of song, just another before Cousin Drewey would go off on his ramble. So Cousin Drewey gave us that happy ballad, "The Risin' of Dead Lazarus."

> *The sweet Lord said to Lazarus,*
> *"Lazarus, please sir, come forth."*
> *And doggone!*
> *What you reckon!*
> *Lazarus, he done came forth!*

There was mountain music, sweet Washtaw Mountain music. And did Cousin Drewey's song ring clear in the bright moonlight air!

Cousin Drewey got done. He cleared his glottis and rose to his feet. He rambled down toward the gate that sat next to the road. It was where a feller goes out of Pap Lowdermilk's land and onto the public domain. The night was just right for a lonesome man. The moonlight was clear, as clear as Cousin Drewey had ever seen moonlight in all his remembrance. The road was a lonesome one, just like Cousin Drewey was a lonesome man. If it was the highway, he could watch the cars go by. He could admire their headlights and know that some feller was aset in the front seat, and when that feller had to honk his horn he'd do that there. But mighty few cars came along the dirt road front of Pap Lowdermilk's, mighty few. Which was all right with our kinfolks, 'cause he craved to be alone.

He was nearin' the gate, then somethin' dark and slightly movin' came up against his eyesight. Cousin Drewey stopped on his tracks. He looked, tried to see what'all. The brightness of the night told him it was a horse. A foreign horse, eatin' on old Pap Lowdermilk's grass. Pap didn't need a horse, 'cause he had old Jeff. It looked mighty like a horse had invaded mule territory.

Naturally, our kinfolks was nosey of the situation. So he walked up to the horse. It was a saddle-mount, like Sonny Boy ran on his pasture up at the Skinner ranch. He was all meat, had the widest girth Cousin Drewey ever saw on a horse before, and he must have weighed about thirteen hundred pounds by what a man can judge in the moonlight.

The horse had his nose to the grass, and moved only when he needed to reach for a better clump. Cousin Drewey walked 'round the horse which didn't seem to pay him no mind. Then it was that the Lord sent an answer to Cousin Drewey's silent quizzifications. Our kinfolks didn't need ponder his mind no more, 'cause right there, in the moonlight, burned on the horse's left shoulder was a space—Fats Recknagel's official brand, registered in the State Brand Book.

So Cousin Drewey said to hisse'f, "Well, I'll be a sonofabitch."

He looked down under the horse's belly and up below the hind legs, and what he saw was how the victim was a stud-horse, a registered quarter horse stud of the finest kind.

Cousin Drewey thought for a minute, usin' his mind to come to a reason for this horse bein' in Pap Lowdermilk's pasture. He saw how the gate was shut tight, so this stranger couldn't have drifted in from the road. He was puzzled at first, then a flash of truth struck his mind like buckshot hits a rabbit—*this horse was planted here*. He looked 'round and thanked the moonlight. Maybe if he looked some more he'd find Judas Iscariot hangin' 'round.

The first name mindful to Cousin Drewey was that of Billy Beck workin' for Fats Recknagel's wages.

"What the hell?" said Cousin Drewey to himse'f.

What the hell was, he figgered, how Billy Beck was tryin' to get Sonny Boy Skinner in trouble, 'cause word had got 'round that Sonny Boy needed a stud-horse-weapon to use on his mares, so's they could find some colts. Here was a black bastard at work, on the job. Here was trick bein' played on an innocent man, on that Sonny Boy.

"This is *one* blooded horse," Cousin Drewey said, strokin' the stud's back and smoothin' his hand down the withers. "He's used to careful handlin', there ain't an ounce of pissle-tail in him. He's gentle as a dog and sensible like a quarter horse should be. I *do* wish Sonny Boy could see this horse."

Cousin Drewey had to spend some more mind, so he

stood for a minute shackled in thought. "What to do, oh Lord! Oh Lord, what to do?"

So the Lord gave Cousin Drewey an idea; or maybe it wasn't the Lord, 'cause only Satan himse'f could deal with Cousin Drewey in a manner such as it was.

"You bet," Cousin Drewey said, talkin' to the horse. "If anybody catches you in this pasture it won't be funny. 'Cause it'll be sad, Chappo. What we'll do is take you by that fancy halter and lead you out to the road. I know horses like you. You got plenty sense, and of better category than mankind ever packed. Then I'll shut the gate on you, and your good sense will take you home, on your own power, back to Fats Recknagel's pasture."

Cousin Drewey reached for the halter and old Chappo led like a society lady's poodle-dog. They walked together, and nary a balk out of the horse. The gate was only a dozen yards ahead now. Once the horse was outside and headed home, our kinfolks swore he'd go directly back to his guitar. He'd sing a psalm of thanksgivin', and he'd sing it to the tune of "The Birmin'ham Jail."

Cousin Drewey snickered as he thought of Billy Beck. With the Lord's he'p, he'd caught that no'count at his own stinkin' game. What Billy Beck hoped for was for daylight to come, when folks passin' by would see the horse in Pap's pasture, and they'd he'p pin a sure-fire horse theft charge on Pap. Which would make Fats Recknagel smile.

Cousin Drewey let the stud-horse stand while he opened the gate. When man and horse went out to the ruts the moonlight showed the road clear as the hour of noon, like it does in this dry western state. Beyond stretched the grassy flats, wide open, free to the skyline.

They'd already gone down the road about a half-mile. The moon was still shinin' clear. But Cousin Drewey came up against it. A salt cedar clump grew high and wide where a side lane turns south, lookin' like black coal heap against the brightness. It stood maybe twelve, fifteen feet high.

"So long, old horse," Cousin Drewey said, turnin' back hisse'f but lettin' the stud go on. He aimed to trip back to us Lowdermilks. "I'll see you again in the sweet bye-and-bye."

Cousin Drewey put a step in the right direction. But before our kinfolks could take a second step, a flash of light nigh had him blinded, and the flash came from behind the salt cedars. Cousin Drewey jumped like he'd stepped next to a rattlesnake. 'Cause the blindin' beam came from the headlights of a sedan-car parked and hidden, and it lit up Cousin Drewey smack in the road. Truly, that man felt silly to his mortal shame. He jumped on his tracks when he hear'd the siren wail, when the dome light took to flashin' red. And just as sudden he saw a cowboy ahorseback ride out from behind the car, catch up with the stud-horse and put a lead-rope on his halter. It was one of Fats Recknagel's hands, and old Chappo acted like a tame dog while the cowboy led him up to the parked sheriff's car.

"There," said Cousin Drewey to hisse'f, "sets a lowlifed Pharisee. If it ain't Hank Hudgeons I'll eat what's left of my old hat."

It didn't take Cousin Drewey eight-tenths of a second to figger the dirty game Hank Hudgeons was playin', the final innin' of one that would prove our kinfolks to be a horse-thief in the eyes of the law, a proof aided and abetted by polite society. Maybe Billy Beck planted the horse in Pap's pasture, or maybe he didn't. It was a pure-D trap, no matter. After the kangaroo court hoedown trial of justice, when Cousin Drewey made two dad-burned jackasses out of Fats Recknagel and Shyster Sam Hawkins, it was told straight how old Fats hisse'f swore that he'd land our musical man in the State Pen up yonder, and he'd land him pretty-damn-quick. Fats claimed he'd pay out good money to any judge for a

COUSIN DREWEY & THE HOLY TWISTER 295

sentence Cousin Drewey wouldn't get shed of, leastways, not for the balance of the twentieth century. Fats swore it on a stack of Bibles three-feet high; and better yet, he'd swore it on the sacred soil of Texas. That is, if he *had* to. 'Cause Texas dirt is too heavenly for anythin' to do with a mossback like Cousin Drewey.

The car door opened and Hank Hudgeons stepped out. The horseback cowboy stood up front while he held Fats's stud by the leadrope.

"You'd better stand, Cousin Drewey," the sheriff called out. "Don't move a ligament—or else."

As he said "or else," Hank pulled his mighty six-shooter and let it shine in the headlight glow.

"We kind'a figgered it was you who took Mr. Fats Recknagel's horse," Hank said, comin' forward.

Cousin Drewey stood as Hank ordered. Then he raised his hands high; somethin' said how that was the right thing to do. Hank frisked him for his hog-leg forty-five; 'cause, like the old-time hangmen used to say, most horse thieves packed artillery. But our kinfolks was weaponless, and he thanked the Lord for that.

"That's what I reckoned," Hank Hudgeons said. "Now I know my arithmetic is correct."

"You don't know how your ass and your elbow put together makes two, and how that badge on your shirt makes you for one silly sonofabitch," our kinfolks siad to the sheriff. He stuck his chin out for to give a little potent sass.

"I'm a law, Cousin Drewey," the sheriff said. "I'd like you to keep that in mind. Me and my witnesses have done caught you in the act, and we don't aim to let you loose. You've committed a crime agin the finest citizen in the valley, and I dearly hope Mr. Fats Recknagel won't forgive you out of his kindness. His lovin' ways and respect for the sheriff's department is well-known all over Harris County, Texas."

Cousin Drewey didn't say a damn thing. He looked at Hank with fire in his eyes.

"When I say how he won't forgive you, I mean when you git out of the State Pen—maybe one, maybe two or three, maybe four or five years from now."

"Hank Hudgeons," Cousin Drewey said, 'cause of that insult, "I know it now for a fact—your ass sets in blue mud."

That was Washtaw Mountain sass, and it means "You don't know what you're talkin' about, Sheriff!"

But Hank didn't pay that kind of sass no mind.

"How much did Fats Recknagel pay you to compliment his high-mogul personality?" Cousin Drewey kept on sassin'. "You say he's got Houston-sized sweetness, and how it's highly-appreciated in Harris County, Texas? Is that what you're sayin', Hank Hudgeons?"

Hank Hudgeons didn't say, 'cause all he said was, "Any talk from you will be used as evidence against you." He snapped his words like a sheriff should. "When I say evidence, I mean when they try you for a low-down horse thief."

Before Cousin Drewey knew it, old Hank had a pair of handcuffs locked on our kinfolks' wrists.

"Where do we go from here?" Cousin Drewey said.

Hank told him the facts. "Mr. Fats Recknagel will be embarrassed when that cowpoke leads the horse to his rightful pasture. I don't crave to watch that sweet gentleman blush for shame. It would be too delicate a sight to witness. So me and you will be headin' for the county seat. That's where we'll set you in jail 'til somebody goes your bond."

"You need more witnesses than that freckled-faced no'count aset on the horse. Hell, he's sorry like his boss," Cousin Drewey said.

So Hank Hudgeons opened the back door of the sedan car. He told Cousin Drewey to step inside and have a seat. Because he had two more witnesses there aset. They were his two deputies, one that goddamn Elmo. So when Cousin Drewey got in the car, all four

COUSIN DREWEY & THE HOLY TWISTER 297

made tracks for the county seat. Fats Recknagel's sorry cowboy led old Chappo back to his irrigated pasture, where the rank blue grass made spread. Chappo wasn't his rightful name, but Cousin Drewey could respect him a heap more than the four two-legged bastards who thought up and played the dirty game.

Now its natural how the Skinner boys would go Cousin Drewey's bond. They went down to the county seat, forty miles south, and they got Cousin Drewey out of jail for the time bein'. So we had our kinfolks back again, without handcuffs on his wrists, and he made hisse'f at home in that good old Lowdermilk shanty.

But word got 'round Star Valley, and folks began to tell themse'fs, "Neighbor, we told you so . . ." The word told how Cousin Drewey was a low-down horse thief. Even if he only aimed to get the *loan* of the stud-horse, so's to use the weapon on Sonny Boy's mares, do that 'cause Sonny Boy would love to have his quarter horse mares find some colts. But not *all* the folks in the valley were superstitious, or made a disrespectful claim against Cousin Drewey. True, some said how he ought to get hung, like he'd get if he lived back in the early days. Others figgered how, seein' it was Fats Recknagel who made the complaint, that it was the prosecutin' side who was the "low-lifed stinkin' criminal of the horse thief category."

So trial day came bright and early. And this time, at the county court house, there was no sign of a hoe-down comin' up. No fried chicken or potato salad, no pink drink; no Uncle Posey Burwinkle callin' the square dance on. The sheriff hadn't told Cousin Drewey to bring his fiddle and guitar, 'cause he wouldn't need them this time. Really and truly, somethin' seemed to say how there was a change of jurisprudence somewhere.

Fats Recknagel was there in the courtroom. He was dressed up Texas style—in a white cowboy suit and a red necktie, and his big Stetson hat was white as snow before that element hits the dirty ground. His boots cost a hundred and fifty dollars a pair, and they were hand-stitched makin' colors of green and brown. He had a blonde-headed stenographer of his own, a gal who wished she was home in Houston. And he'd called two full-blood lawyers in from that big town, flown them in by airplane. They carried satchels. And they wore suits and they were jellybean dudes if any were ever born to the city. Present was the sheriff and his piss-ant deputies. All three had fat mouths, and they were fixed to witness against Cousin Drewey. Shyster Sam Hawkins sat in the back, but if he tried to make a speech for or agin the culprit they'd tell him to git. The judge was the District Judge, not some puny Justice of the Peace. And the jury —well hell, Nell!—the jury was of the finest kind, hand-picked, unprejudiced, six men and six women. Everyone hated a horse thief more than a normal man hated Fats Recknagel.

"Order!" hollered the judge, smackin' his gavel on oak.

The more the witnesses talked, the more the judge pounded his gavel. The more Fats Recknagel begged the court to send our kinfolks to jail, the more the congregation clapped their hands and scowled hate at a musical man.

"It ain't no use," Clyde said to Sonny Boy. "This lousy court aims to convict Cousin Drewey. There's no talk we can give that will melt the shackles. If he gits off without bein' electrified we might be thankful to the power that is, and the mercy thereof. This is a court of honor, and you know how them things percolate."

Sonny Boy said back to Clyde, "Brother, I've been lookin' 'round some. Try as I might, I cain't see Billy Beck nowheres. You'd reckon, him bein' a gen*uwine* horse thief hisse'f, he'd be here to watch Cousin Drewey git his one to five, *it* with time off for good behavior."

Clyde said to Sonny Boy, "Brother, I've been settin'

COUSIN DREWEY & THE HOLY TWISTER 299

here thinkin' the same thing. Would you like to know where I reckon Billy Beck is? Well sir, he's up 'round Signal Rock doin' one of several nefarious things. He's maybe aset with Shorty Flack, them runnin' off dirty whiskey in the Blaylock Funeral Parlor, right in the embalmin' room where they aim to stretch me and you out some day. They're makin' stink while old Reese is sprayin' the rose bushes with formaldehyde. Or maybe Billy Beck's putin' the money Fats Recknagel gave him in the First National Bank, or maybe he's spendin' it on a good time for hisse'f. It wasn't Benjamin Franklin who said it way back in history, 'cause its Clyde Skinner who's sayin' it now—*most times you can lead a horse to the water trough, but never can you coax a horse thief into the courtroom.*"

The judge instructed the jury, callin' Cousin Drewey for all the worst things he could think of. Then he praised Fats Recknagel for a fine gentleman come out of Houston, Texas. So the jury trailed out of the courtroom, went through a door, closed the door, stayed behind the door five minutes, came out and stood up to face the judge.

"Ladies and gentlemen of the jury," the judge said, "have you folks come to a verdict? What'all do you reckon about the accused, Cousin Drewey Stiff?"

The foreman stood up, a farmer of Star Valley who most citizens claimed to be lackin' in good sense, who whipped his kids and wouldn't let them go to school, who had a woman as sorry as hisse'f. His first name was Cletus and his last name was Jones.

"Judge," Cletus said, "this jury has come upon a verdict."

"I sure hope you'all came to a wise verdict, 'cause Mr. Fats Recknagel is a gentleman and he needs gentleman's treatment out of this court."

"You bet, judge," Cletus said for the jury. "We sure enough came to the right decision about that horse thief. We hear'd the honorable lawyers give Cousin Drewey sass. We didn't hear nobody say sweet things about the criminal, 'cause there wasn't an honorable lawyer who'd dare to hand him compliments. And we hear'd you tell us what stinkin' meat Cousin Drewey was made of, and how Mr. Fats Recknagel is a citizen of the finest kind."

"Then what is your verdict, ladies and gentlemen of the jury?" The judge had his gavel raised, ready to pound the hell out of the bench. "Speak now or forever hold your peace."

"Your honor," said the foreman out of a cud-juiceless mouth, "we find Cousin Drewey Stiff to be a guilty sonofabitch."

The crowd hollered cheers like it was Christmas Eve Night.

"Order!" hollered the judge, makin' splinters with his gavel. "Let's give this poor horse thief one to five years, 'cause it's the humane thing to do. Our granddaddies would have hung him. I hear tell how the State Pen ain't pretty to look at, but they feed fried chicken every Sunday."

Fats Recknagel came up front so's to shake hands with the judge, and Mr. Wilbur Pruitt from the First National Bank danced for joy as he caught Fats with a grip 'round the paunch, then loved the millionaire's neck. Everybody in the audience fought each other so's to get a chance to shake Fats Recknagel's hand, and to wish him more luck. They treated him like they would a dirty politician. Everybody except us Lowdermilks and Skinners.

"Sheriff!" the judge hollered, loud 'cause everybody made such a joyful noise, "take the prisoner away."

Maw Maw wept, so did Lilybelle and Verbaline Lou. Pap Lowdermilk hung his head, shamed 'cause he was a Washtaw Mountain man. He felt bad, right smart, 'cause just then he figgered how he'd never treated Cousin Drewey right. But Clyde pushed his way up to where Hank Hudgeons was holdin' our kinfolks by the arm, ready to push him to where the barred doors and windows shone with sunlight from the outside, and where he and that Elmo would soon give Cousin Drewey a ride in the sedan-car up to the State Pen. I followed Clyde, and right at the heels of us'uns was Sonny Boy, then Maw Maw, then Lilybelle and Verbaline Lou. And all Lilybelle's kids.

Hank Hudgeons blushed for shame when Clyde came up to him. That goddamn Elmo turned his back, 'cause he couldn't look an honest man in the face. Maw Maw loved Cousin Drewey's neck, and the two younger womenfolks dripped tears on his shoulder.

Clyde said to Cousin Drewey, "Kinfolks, what'all would you like us to bring you when you git set up at the State Pen?"

Cousin Drewey thought for a minute, 'cause it seemed like he'd never see us who loved him ever again. "You ask me what'all you can bring me when I git set at the State Pen, dear Cousin Clyde. So I'll tell you how you can bring my satchel, and my fiddle and my guitar. But you needn't bring me my hog-leg forty-five, 'cause they won't let it in through the prison gates. But take good care of it, dear cousin, 'cause I'll need it soon as I get out, need it like I've never needed it before. Treat it like you would a baby girl, keep it polished, keep it loaded, 'cause someday soon old Cousin Drewey will have his trigger finger again, and he'll have some prime targets to hit, and he'll take prime joy when he hits 'em."

He shook hands with Pap and me, and with Clyde and Sonny Boy, and he gave big slobberin' kisses to our calico. And to all Lilybelle's kids.

That's when the sheriff clapped handcuffs on Cousin Drewey, and that's when Cousin Drewey was led away.

"So long, dear hearts," was the last words we heard Cousin Drewey say. "I'll be seein' you'all, in the sweet bye-and-bye."

So they took him away, far away, so's to pay his debt to society.

28

Us Lowdermilks weren't the same after Cousin Drewey went up to the State Pen. We weren't even like we were before that day Cousin Drewey put his blessed presence in our midst. We just sat 'round the house not sayin' much; and when it came time for us to say somethin', that's when we got up and did it. Pap fooled 'round as meek and mild as the prophet Samuel. He didn't show wrath. Factways, he wasn't Pap Lowdermilk no more. Except at times when Lilybelle sent him a cake, and he got sick on it. Sick, but he didn't pack ire. He always smiled while he talked. That's the way Pap was, meek and milk. I saw once how he might be fixed to kiss Maw Maw, but he didn't. A happy man, sweet tempered. Except for the day when Clyde and Verbaline Lou came by to say how they were legalized, man and wife, made that way by the Justice of the Peace.

Lord! That's when Pap threw a conniption. News like that sent him struttin' for his shotgun. Maw Maw screamed bloody hell. She hollered how they didn't need a Justice of the Peace. They needed the Reverend Sam Hill, a preacher, a man ordained to speak the word down from heaven. Pap put some shells in his gun while Maw Maw told how they hadn't committed matrimony in the sight of the Lord, only to fill the docket-books in

COUSIN DREWEY & THE HOLY TWISTER 303

the county courthouse. She put on an act like she'd never done before, yellin' how if they'd already poontanged they'd poontanged in sin. She went to the bed and laid herself down; she took on somethin' frightful, a woman gone crazy.

Clyde and Verbaline Lou stood by, speechless. Clyde held his Texas hat in one hand and Verbaline Lou's hand with the other. Clyde blushed for the misery of it, red-faced with a nigh choked-down glottis. He was that kind of cowboy. And my dear sister looked like she could weep.

"What you reckon, Pap?" I said.

Me and Pap Lowdermilk stood wonderin' what'all to do. Pap held the loaded shotgun in the crook of his arm, like he might use it on Clyde some time in the future. But not for the time bein'.

"What have we got in this poor household, Newt," Pap quizzed, "that will calm that crazy woman down?"

"We ain't got nothin' that will fix her, Pap, unless she faints dead away. Then we can bring her back with a dose of Sir Ashley Pendergast's Revivin' Spirits."

"Looks like she ain't goin' to faint, Newt."

"Not for the time bein', Pap. She's hollerin' too loud to faint."

I turned my face to Verbaline Lou. I said, "Sister, what'all you reckon?"

Pap didn't hear what Verbaline Lou reckoned, 'cause he went to the lean-to to hang the shotgun up on the hook. And while he was gone Verbaline Lou gave us her solid reckonin'. "Folks," she said, "I think it's the sight of Pap that has made her this way. Pap's the devil's own brother when he gets mad." She got loose from Clyde's hand grip and went kindly over to Maw Maw. Maw Maw was yellin' about how it take a preacher to wed man up with a woman. A splice should be tied by the hand of the Lord, not by some paid-by-the-job county no'count like a Justice of the Peace.

Verbaline Lou put her hand on Maw Maw's sweat-wet brow, and said, "There, Maw Maw, don't carry on like crazy. Me and Clyde are *legal* man and wife now, but if you want us to be made *holy* man and wife we'll all go down to the Reverend Sam Hill's Christian tabernacle. He should be there right now—at prayer meetin'."

That calmed Maw Maw down, and I might say did it considerably. Maw Maw just lay flat and breathed heavily, like a hexed man does when he aims to expel the devil.

"There, there. . . . Don't you feel better now? . . . Don't you, Maw Maw?"

All was quiet on the bed. Maw Maw lay like she'd taken on some peace. "It's only your tubes, daughter," Maw Maw said, while Verbaline Lou stroked her cheeks and brow. "I was only thinkin' about the holiness of your tubes."

Whenever Maw Maw got riled in anger about somethin' that happens in the world, she'd get to worryin' about Verbaline Lou's tubes. Whatever the hell *they* are!

So Clyde reckoned how the only way to put Maw Maw out of dire distress was to get married again.

"That's all there is to it," said my sister's legal man. "We all can go down to the tabernacle, but it might be better if we bring the Reverend Sam Hill up here. That way Maw Maw can rest easy on the bed and . . ."

Pap pointed a sassy chin at Clyde. "You're damn right, son," he said, "and that way I can just reach up for the shotgun if you sull about sayin' I do."

I could see by Clyde's eyes how he figgered Pap to be a silly old horse's ass.

"You git goin', Newt," Pap said to me, "and bring the Reverend Sam Hill to this humble home. Keep an eye on Clyde and don't let him break loose and run."

COUSIN DREWEY & THE HOLY TWISTER 305

That's when Clyde and me went out to the pickup truck. Clyde started her up and we both made tracks for Signal Rock. Clyde drove kind'a reckless, 'cause of his ire.

"What you think, Newt?" he said to me. "Do you reckon your sister and me are wedded-up, made that way by the Justice of the Peace, that we're man and wife in the Lord's sight?"

"You bet, Clyde."

"No, honest. What you reckon, Newt?"

I said, "You might be man and wife in the Lord's sight, Clyde, but you ain't in Pap and Maw Maw Lowdermilk's sight. There's been more shotgun weddin's in the Washtaw Mountains than hoot-owls roostin' in the slash pine. Pap was born in the Washtaw Mountains and to him a loaded shotgun carries better sound of blessin' than talk from a Justice of the Peace."

"Then we're doin' the right thing?" Clyde said, gunnin' hell out of that old pickup truck.

He craved to know, so I gave him the fact from my mind.

"Bring on the Reverend Sam Hill," I said. "Him of the Lord's holy ordination. Let him read from the Book of Pious Writ. Let the Reverend Sam Hill put a right hand on your head, and a left hand on Verbaline Lou's head and let him speak the preacher's own words, let him pronounce you'll man and wife. Then, Clyde, *only* then will Pap Lowdermilk lay his shotgun down."

Clyde tried to say somethin' about the talk I gave him from my glottis, but he couldn't. He was in *that* state of a bridegroom. So all he could say was "Well, hell, Newt!"

Like we figgered rightful, they were havin' a prayer meetin' there at the tabernacle and Reverend Sam Hill would be struttin' his stuff. Clyde drove up to the double doors; from inside we heard a song of praise, loud, 'cause when Pentecostals get to praisin', they praise like no man's earthly concern. Not to say that Reverend Sam was a pure-blood Pentecostal. He just acted that way. The pure-bloods craved no truck with that kind of preacher; they claimed he was too noisy and wild.

We opened the door and the music hit us right smack. They were singin' that good old Texas tent-revival camp-meetin' song:

> *Sing Halleloo, sing praises be!*
> *Sing Halleloo, sing glory!*
> *So when we get to heaven*
> *We'll all be hunky dory.*

That was a mighty sweet song for the congregation to be singin', and nary a one saw Clyde and me slip in through the double doors. We just stood in the back. When I looked slanchways to see what Clyde was holdin' in his hand, I caught the right amount of it. It was twenty-five dollars, not a cent more or less. One five-dollar and one twenty-dollar bill. Darcy Jean Kazort, Old Man Puckerdoo Kazort's baby girl, was at the piano up next to the preacher's pedestal, and she yelled her song as loud as she pounded the musical keys.

There must have been thirty human stances in the congregation, which meant that Reverend Sam would get no more than five dollars in his collection hat. It would be all in nickels and dimes. That's how the Signal Rock Pentecostals paid off the preacher. When they hushed their song, that's when a mourner looked back and caught the sight of Clyde and me. And when one mourner looked back, the others did likewise. They scowled at us, to say with their silent faces how they wished we'd stayed outside. They all looked except the Reverend Sam, himself. He couldn't look 'cause he was up there next to Darcy Jean—standin' on his head.

COUSIN DREWEY & THE HOLY TWISTER 307

Let me tell about the Reverend Sam Hill. Any time he gets a dose of religion, that's the way he acts. No man can get holier than the preacher in our midst. The Good Book says to holler, to jump, to make a joyful noise unto the Lord. Sam went by the Good Book, and any time he felt he was ready to take the collection, he took on most frightful. That was the reason. That was how come we caught Sam standin' on his head. And he didn't know just then that Clyde held two bills of United States currency in his hand. He'd have come off that stance mighty quick if he'd known. The congregation had testified before they sang that Texas camp-meetin' Hunky Dory song. They'd all given voice, one by one, and told of their sinful days. They told all about it, then they got to rollin' on the ground. They hollered in tongues. They told of the joys of conversion, how now they could look down on sinners. So thank the Lord for their own heavenly elevation.

While they sang—while Darcy Jean Kazort banged hell out of the piano—the Reverend Sam Hill stood on his head. And there up front of the preacher's pedestal Sam's hat stood brim-side up. It was head-gear rarin' for a collection.

It happened every time, never missed. When Darcy Jean pounded out an end to that song, that's when Sam came out of his holy stance. That's when he got back on his feet again. He got a sudden jolt of religion and shouted slaughterhouse destruction on every soul present. His face went red and his hair seemd to stand on end, and he kicked to the right, then to the left—he knocked over the pedestal, then picked it up again. He set it straight and jumped 'round like a jackrabbit.

If he was hoistin' himself to heaven, he was makin' notches in that perpendicular direction. He hollered like someone touched with a red-hot brandin' iron. He called to the Lord for he'p. Religion caught him first in the toes, then went up his legs like red ants on the prowl. It climbed up his frame, skyward to his pious scalp. There it itched and he had to scratch. It bowled him over where he was at. The weight of it all went down, down, down. Then it rose up again, filled his head with pounds and ounces. Oh Lord, what a blessin'!

Reverend Sam caught sight of me and Clyde. He opened his mouth like to catch some yellerjackets, and he hollered "Halleluyah," 'cause that's what he was up on the pedestal for.

"Dear brethren and sistern," he said to the congregation. "We've got two sinners in our midst. And they're here to be cleaned up white as snow."

It looked like we'd messed up the show. A half-dozen mourners were aset at the bench and a deacon and his wife were fixin' to roll on the ground. Before Sam gave his halleluyah holler, he'd had his hands cupped 'round his mouth so's to shout the holy rollers on. But when he saw Clyde's hand raised high, with the twenty-five dollars shinin' in the light of the tabernacle, Sam changed his mind. He came runnin' up back, so's to love Clyde's neck and call him his brother. The congregation turned 'round in their seats and scowled at me and Clyde. There was hate in their eyes and faces. It's the way some Christians act.

Reverend Sam loved Clyde's neck, then he shook my hand, lickin' his lips for the money Clyde held in his hand.

"Reverend," Clyde said, "we've got a splicin' job for you to do, out at the Lowdermilk place. That is, if you can dismiss these folks and tell them to go home. I got twenty-five dollars, and they're yours if you can make Maw Maw quit fussin' about my wife's tubes. If you can do that pretty quick, old Pap will lay his shotgun down."

Clyde told the Reverend Sam Hill all about what happened, and how badly he was needed. Before Clyde could tell some more, about how the Justice of the Peace had already done half the job, Sam hollered to his congregation.

"Lord bless you all," he said. "Git, you sinners! Git for home you iniquitizers, you who don't know your righteousness from a hole in the ground. Please pass by the hat as you leave this tabernacle, and show the Lord your generosity. Preachers have got to eat, and they need to pay for what they eat. Git . . ."

Nobody shook hands with Reverend Sam that time. The folks just walked out 'cause Sam didn't offer a handshake to them. He had his eye on Clyde Skinner.

"Close up the shop, Reverend," Clyde said, "and let's git out of here ourse'fs. There's holy work in the shanty to do, and you're the man to do it."

"Come back and git saved the next time," Sam called out to the last mourner, just before he locked the tabernacle door.

So the Reverend Sam Hill wedded Clyde Skinner and Verbaline Lou together, man and wife wedded he them. He did it, all right, in our Lowdermilk shack. And if you don't know where Pap Lowdermilk and his shotgun stood, then you don't know mossbacks and their firearms, 'cause Pap stood directly behind Clyde and he had the shotgun pointed in the right direction; that is, aimed where Clyde's liver sat under his skin and behind his belt. If Clyde didn't say what Pap aimed for him to say, that young cattleman would have lost his liver sure enough.

But he kept it, by hell!

Maw Maw wept like a woman, and she told Sam right after the pronouncement that she'd been worried sick about Verbaline Lou's tubes.

"They're the holiest things a woman's got," she said.

"Ain't you talkin'!" said Reverend Sam.

But right then she said what she figered, 'cause Maw Maw told how everythin' was sweet again—'cause the dear Lord's sweet words came out of Sam's mouth and were used to render the splicin' tight. Clyde gave Sam the twenty-five dollars and drove him in the pickup back to the tabernacle.

Cousin Drewey was snug in the Pen when Thanksgivin' Day came bright and early. Clyde and Verbaline Lou came over hopin' to get Maw Maw and Pap, and me, and take us up to the ranch so we could eat dinner—roasted turkey with sage stuffin', mashed potatoes and candied yams, raw salad goo that nobody would want, mince pie and enough chocolate cake to make Pap sick.

Pap stood, he listened, his eyes told how he hated fooferaw. Except for the cake, he didn't crave that kind of dinner.

"Lilybelle cooked it all for you, Maw Maw; and for you, Pap," Verbaline Lou said, her eyes dancin' for joy. She knew how us Lowdermilks had never eaten a dinner like that before. And when she gave the invite she was the happiest girl in Star Valley.

Pap listened to our girl's talk, 'til he figgered she was done. Then he pushed out his chin, put spit in his mouth, and with fire in his eye said: "Git!" Which sent her home without us Lowdermilks.

Well, that was that, Thanksgivin' in the Pap Lowdermilk home. But never mind, I kept goin' up to the Skinner ranch nigh every day that winter. Pap hollered for me to stay home. That was natural, but I didn't pay him no mind. There was little to do on the place, what with Pap just settin' 'round and Maw Maw most of the time at the cookstove. All we'd do was laze until spring should come 'round and the field call for breakin' up into furrows. We'd do that with the he'p of old Jeff and our little single-breasted plow.

Up at the ranch, I talked with Clyde and Sonny Boy a heap. They'd quiz me some. They figgered how it might be sweet to burn down the Lowdermilk shanty for the sake of public decency, and haul Pap as best we would away from the flames. We'd take him up to the ranch where it wasn't so hot. There'd be a new fixed-up house waitin' for Pap and Maw Maw, with a bathroom tub and shower, and place to set without the wind fannin' that act of nature. And a kitchen cookrange run on propane, and an automatic washin' machine for to save Maw Maw some labor. And a nice bed in the bedroom, with sheets and blankets over the mattress. . . . Lord, Lord—but I knew Pap would shoot before he'd flit. He'd aim straight and fire both barrels if Clyde went down to offer the proposition.

I tried to think of a way, but I swore before Amos that even to *think* that way for Pap's civilization would be a waste of time. To get Pap to emigrate would take more misery than Moses ever had with Pharaoh. If Cousin Drewey was down there to he'p, they might tie Pap tightly in rope and Clyde use his pickup truck. But Cousin Drewey was, as all Star Valley knew, he'pless to aid the needy.

After Cousin Drewey was penned up a few months—in fact it was just before Christmas—all us Skinners and Lowdermilks went up to the State Pen, just to see how our kinfolks was gettin' along. We'd already sent his satchel, fiddle and guitar up by parcel post. And the same time Verbaline Lou wrote him a letter to say how we were takin' care of his hog-leg forty-five. And to tell him how Pap said he could buckle it on in the holster when he got out of prison. 'Cause Fats Recknagel would be still hangin' 'round the First National Bank, and Fats would make a prime pistol target if Cousin Drewey could catch him next to the big brass doors. Maybe Mr. Wilbur Pruitt would come out to see what'all, and our kinfolks could plug him too.

They brought Cousin Drewey down from his cell, 'cause they didn't crave visitors from outside up there in the block, as the feller with the badge said. Lord, was that badge-feller big! And he stood by to keep us company while we gassed with Cousin Drewey. Cousin Drewey brought his guitar, 'cause he thought we might like to hear a gospel song. He wore a gray uniform, and he had a big number stamped in paint on his back. Cousin Drewey looked like he'd recently washed his face, and Verbaline Lou said how the uniform made him right stylish.

"God almighty, Cousin Drewey!" Pap hollered when he hugged his neck and asked how he was gettin' along.

Cousin Drewey said he was of the finest kind.

Maw Maw said, "Doggone, if it ain't good to see this old settler again."

I said to Cousin Drewey, "Ain't you hungry for the Washtaw Mountains? Ain't you hungry for a mess of catfish? Wouldn't you love to hunt a rabbit on the meadow in the piney woods? And do they feed you plenty greens in this here State Pen?"

Clyde said howdy to the guard, the feller with the badge. He said, "Officer, I sure hope this old mossback ain't givin' you trouble, 'cause what you fellers in this State Pen don't need is trouble."

So the guard told us Skinners and Lowdermilks that Cousin Drewey was the sweetest inmate in the prison. And how he wished to hell he'd never get out.

Cousin Drewey night split his old groin when he hear'd the guard say that, and he said, "Eulus, you're a dadblamed liar. You know I'm a fussin' sonofabitch, and you put me in solitary every time I make complaint about the fried chicken." Eulus, that was the guard's name, bust a gut laughin' at what Cousin Drewey said.

Cousin Drewey picked up his guitar, tickled the

strings to see if it was in tune. Then he quizzed us all, tried to learn if we'd like some music.

"I'd sure like to hear a Bible song," Maw Maw said.

He primed his glottis and gave us "Potaphar's Sufferin' Woman."

> *Woman, woman,*
> *Sweet Joseph don't need your sass.*
> *He's Pharaoh's favorite slave,*
> *And he he'ped build the pyramids.*

We all liked that song Cousin Drewey made up himself, after he'd read about Joseph and Potaphar in Genesis. The song told about Potaphar's wife, and how she used to get fired on sight of a man, 'specially a handsome man like Joseph. Any time she saw Joseph she got a hankerin' for poontang, 'cause Joseph looked like he could be *that* kind of man and Potaphar acted like he'd been given a dose of saltpeter. When she tried her tricks Joseph took off like a bat out of hell. She grabbed his coat, which was colored like the rainbow, and he had one hell of a time tellin' Pharaoh how he wasn't a sinful man. But Pharaoh took a board to him anyway. He claimed how he could never believe an Israelite. But when Pharaoh had a dream, that King of Egypt couldn't make sense of it. So he got Joseph out of prison, just before Potaphar was ready to brand his ass with a hot-iron. That's when Joseph stood up and told Pharaoh about his dream, and showed himself to be a prophet from way down the line. Pharaoh sent to the harem for Potaphar's wife.

> *Woman, woman,*
> *You ought to go out and set in the snow.*
> *You got too much heat where you need some virtue.*
> *You better don't mess with sweet Joseph no more.*

When Cousin Drewey quit taxin' his glottis, when he laid his guitar down, Maw Maw went over and loved his neck.

"Land sakes, kinfolks!" she said. "If that ain't the potentest song!"

Clyde looked at his watch and said how we had a long ride ahead, back to Star Valley. So we'd better bid Cousin Drewey a sad adieu.

"Cousin Drewey," Clyde said, "before we go we'd like you give us some blessin' words. 'Cause we've got to get home to do up the chores."

Cousin Drewey couldn't think of no final blessin' words, and he said so out loud. So Clyde put a bug into his ear by quizzin' what he aimed. And about how he felt about Hank Hudgeons the sheriff, and about Fats Recknagel and Billy Beck.

So Cousin Drewey opened up. "What I aim," he said, "is to pay my debit to chickenshit-society, and to git out of this buggy jail, so I won't need look at that goddamn Eulus no more. If I stay in the cell block long enough, maybe the chickenshit-folks of society will git to learn how I don't owe them a goddamn thing. As for Fats Recknagel and Billy Beck, just take some lovin' care of my hog-leg forty-five."

We left him there in the big gray prison, which wasn't right for a sunshine-lovin' man. Most times, nigh always, Cousin Drewey wore a sparkle in his eye, but right then at our partin' he had a teardrop instead. "You'all come back," he said to us Lowdermilks and Skinners. Eulus, the guard that stood beside him, said, "You bet." And as Cousin Drewey turned 'round with the guard, to go back to his cell, Clyde had a kindness in his mouth which he'd like to get shed of. He wanted to say "You'all come," as Texas folks naturally do. But he reckoned again and figgered such an invite wouldn't make sense in that place, on that day and time.

Outside the big gate, next to the fire hydrant on the curb, while we all made room for each other in Clyde's sedan-car, I took a final look at the big gray buildin'. I tried to count the many barred windows, I tried to figger where the warden gassed the fellers that needed that kind of patronage. 'Cause there would be nothin' I'd love better, inside there, than to have a guard say, "Come on, Newt, if you crave to see somethin' special." And I'd follow behind him and he'd take me to the gas chamber, where he'd show me the chair where the fellers sit down. He'd let me take hold of the straps they put on the fellers. And he'd let me see the brass handle the warden turns when he gives some sonofabitch zephyrs.

Doggone, what a sight that would be!

Then I got to wonderin' who got the gas bills, the Governor at the State Capital or the Warden of the State Pen. Most likely the State Governor. I kept wonderin' on that category from the time we left the curb, when Clyde stepped on the Chivvelee gas. And I was still wonderin' when I set myself at the same old woodpile where me and Cousin Drewey used to set when we thought out some wisdom apiece. When we talked philosophy straight from the mush of our brains. Lord, them good old Cousin Drewey days! And while I whittled off some shavin's, after we'd all come home from the State Pen, while I spat cud-juice at the axe, I wondered as to who'all got the gas bills—the State Governor or the Warden of that old State Pen. I figgered maybe the Governor. And all the while I thought sweetly about Cousin Drewey.

Cousin Drewey stayed in the State Pen a full year, 'til he got time off for good behavior. And while Cousin Drewey had to keep his presence away from us, that's when the spring plantin' was put in. That's when Pap, Maw Maw and me—along with old Jeff at the plow or planter—altogether we put seed to the dirt. Like corn and beans, kaffir corn and milo maize. Pap and me he'ped Maw Maw put in a garden. We sowed pumpkin and squash and okran, and potatoes and cabbage. We planted plenty cabbage, and that was 'cause we thought kindly about Cousin Drewey. We remembered his prayer, the one he often said out loud to us Lowdermilks: "Lord, when you take my soul to heaven; please Lord, feed me cabbage." Which gave us to know how Cousin Drewey was plumb foolish about that kind of vegetable. But our garden-patch didn't come easy.

Pap and Jeff and me, with a barrel aset in the wagon, hauled water for the garden from Old Man Lee Bassett's well. That patch needed irrigation. We loaded the barrel in a bucket from the windmill tank, and we thanked the Lord when the first summer rains hit Star Valley, when we didn't need haul water no more. And by that time the field was green with crop.

Maw Maw did a lot of cookin' with the garden givin' off its booty, but she had to burn Pap's old automobile tires for fuel. There was just too much work 'round the place for to hunt scrub-cedar on the mesa. It pained me to know how Star Valley got stunk-up pretty bad. Deep in my mind I could hear what the neighbors were callin' us Lowdermilks.

"There go them stink-valley Lowdermilks," they'd be sayin'. "There they go at their no'count ways. And this time they ain't got that sorry horse thief of a Cousin Drewey to he'p 'em at their meanness."

That's what they'd say, but what they uttered was no skin off a Lowdermilk ass. Let 'em talk, let 'em hold their noses and yelp! The Lord was good to us poverty-wrecked humankind. Thank the strength in the dirt, the power in the dirt, thank the rains that fall upon us, thank old Jeff and his harness. Lord, us Lowdermilks were blessed in the sight of heaven. 'Cause it looked mighty like we'd have a fine crop-year for our hard-workin' lives.

COUSIN DREWEY & THE HOLY TWISTER

And thank the Lord for passin' time, a debt against society soon to be paid. For this year would bring Cousin Drewey out of jail.

Fruitful was the name for this year. For the field—for the beans, corn, kaffir corn and milo maize, for the okra and cabbage in the garden-patch. Maybe for old Sucky, too, our milk cow that could never find a calf; for Pee-Dog and Bitchy-Damn, maybe the Lord would he'p them find a litter of pups—and sure as hell the cat might get kittens. We can always hope.

All that increase of animal and field stuff was somethin' to wish for. But there was one thing that was *mighty* sure, a solid fact—and that was how Clyde Skinner would claim it a fruitful year, too. And Lord knows how that man had a right to be proud!

Me, Newton Lowdermilk, I've got pretty good eyesight, and I saw the fruitfulness of Clyde Skinner standin' out before me, plainer than if he'd shouted the news to us Lowdermilks and the world—my sister, Clyde's wife, was walkin' front-heavy!

When did Clyde do it? In the dark of night, or maybe in the bright of noon. 'Cause day by day Verbaline Lou got wider and wider, took on girth. And it looked kind'a how she'd have it on time. She'd run her pregnant days like the Missouri Pacific runs the railroad.

She'd timed it by the clock, timed like the Eagle when it pulls out of St. Louis, hell-bound for that sweet land of Texas.

29

There came a spring rain, wetness from the sky that happens seldom in Star Valley. It sapped down into the dirt and sprouted the seed, 'til the planted rows showed green and pretty. That's when me and Pap got to battlin' the pesky weeds. That's when Clyde and Verbaline Lou kept landin' on Pap to say how the nice modern house was waitin' for him and Maw Maw and for me, too. And how the fields up at the ranch needed our expert jurisdiction. Clyde said how he had a brand-new tractor, all shiny with paint, idle, just waitin'. And a nice little grama grass pasture, just right for old Jeff. 'Cause Clyde reckoned it was the Christian thing to do, to let an old mule graze away his days in comfort. A good mule needs a just reward. Verbaline Lou told how the house had a gas-powered kitchen range, the kind Maw Maw would dearly love. And a pressure cooker, and an automatic washin' machine. . . . And best of all, she told Pap, there was a fine big radio set in the parlor, which gave off country music day and night out of Clint, Texas. And Amos 'n' Andy, and George Burns and Gracie Allen, and a Mr. Major Bowes who says "'round and 'round she goes and where she stops nobody knows"—and all kinds of prachers and deacons, mostly Baptist, who can holler religion so loud it can be hear'd down past the barn. And a refrigerator—no more cooked beans sourin' in the heat, no more dried-out cornbread. Oh yes, sometimes they have prize-fights on the radio.

That's when Clyde would tell how a good ridin' job that paid forty dollars a month was waitin' for me, sleep out in the bunkhouse with the other cowboys, and I'd need a saddle, blanket, bridle and bridle-reins and a nice pair of shop-made boots with silver-mounted spurs to match—'cause I'd be a ridin' sonofagun and when Clyde and Verbaline Lou birthed some kids, those kids would call me Uncle Newt.

Right then I knew Clyde meant what he said, 'cause he was a true man. I didn't say how I already had a saddle, a blanket and bridle and bits. How come? 'Cause only three weeks before that day when Clyde promised the cowboy job, Sonny Boy came by in the pickup. I met him front of the porch and said howdy—and Sonny Boy said back at me, "Howdy, Newt. How are you'all folks this nice bright day?"

After I said, "Of the finest kind," Sonny Boy threw off an old saddle from the pickup, then the blanket and bridle. He started packin' them to the corral, with me to tag along doin' nothin'. Just followin', worthless as hell. Old Jeff was in the corral, pullin' and chewin' at an armful of kaffir.

"Newt," Sonny Boy said, when we got to the corral gate. "This here is a good saddle, a full-blood Porter out of Tucson, Arizona, and the blanket is genuine Navajo. Let's try it on old Jeff, and if Jeff will take the cinch without kickin' and hee-hawin', and he don't pitch you off, I'll give it to you with a Skinner brother's blessin'. 'Cause, Newt, you Lowdermilks can use some muleback transportation."

I he'ped Sonny Boy put the bridle and blanket on Jeff, and together we cinched on the saddle. Jeff stood gentle as a dog, the saddle didn't worry him even slightly. When I led him across the corral by the bridle-reins he acted natural, like a good mule should.

"You get up and see if he'll pitch you off, Newt. If he don't, the saddle is yours, tailormade for old Jeff."

I said, "Sonny Boy, you better ride him. You're a prime cowboy, I ain't."

Sonny Boy said to me, "Newt, you get up there and ride your mule. If we aim to make a cowboy of you, we might as well begin today."

So I mounted old Jeff, got set in the saddle fixed to hunt the horn and hold on for pure hell. I figgered Jeff was that make of prime mule. He'd never had a saddle on his back before. He knew bareback, that's all. But all his life he'd bridle-reined mighty pretty.

I touched Jeff with my heel, sort of gently in the flank. He walked off like he'd worn a saddle all his years. He was the smoothest ride. Sonny Boy opened the corral gate. Me and my mule headed for the corn patch. I trotted him up and down the field. I could see from a distance how Sonny Boy was gut-full with admiration.

"That saddle belongs to Jeff," Sonny Boy said. "It might be you who rides it, or maybe Pap. But that piece of leather belongs to your mule, and when I say that I mean no other quadruped."

So I didn't remind Clyde how I already had a saddle. I sure had my mind on a new one straight from the saddle shop.

"Tell Pap and Maw Maw what we aim for Cousin Drewey," my sister said to her husband Clyde.

So Clyde told how there was a room in the house for Cousin Drewey, waitin' for the happy day when he'd git out. And a porch for him to set hisse'f, on a high stool, where he could sing songs while he tickled his guitar or made musical sawdust out of his fiddle.

Lord, all that and more, and all 'cause Maw Maw and Pap made Verbaline Lou together, so that Clyde could marry up with her and she be his lovin' wife. The Skinners were right proud to call us Lowdermilks kinfolks.

And what you reckon Pap did and said when Clyde and my sister told of that glory?

What Pap did was hang his head low, and when he looked up he said real slow, "Clyde, I love this shanty too much. I don't reckon I can leave it anytime in my legalized lifetime."

Clyde craved to say somethin' to Pap and his talk, but he couldn't 'cause of the womenfolks. It would be too raw.

More times than once the neighbors said how they'd love to see us Lowdermilks move away somewhere. Mainly 'cause of Cousin Drewey, claimin' how they didn't need kinfolks of a horse thief in their midst—how it wouldn't be good for the Christianity of their kids. But too, now that our kinfolks was up at the State Pen it seemed how we didn't go out and hunt firewood anymore. Pap was burnin' cut-up rubber tires again.

After Clyde and Verbaline Lou made a half-dozen trips to our house, and every time got to proddin' Pap for to move up there, Pap began packin' his loaded shotgun everywhere he went. He carried it 'round on the crook of his arm. But he promised Maw Maw how he wouldn't fire the twin shells out of the two barrels at Clyde unless Clyde would just once more pesticate him about movin' up to that foreign ranch.

To that, Maw Maw said, "Pshaw!"

I said, "Bullshit, Pap."

That's when Pap looked sad, just for a minute. Then he squared his jaw, like he was fixed to deliver wisdom.

"Don't say how I didn't tell you," said Pap.

Even though we got a spring rain, with April came the winds that blew and blew and blew up the dust, and they lasted through May and June. June was hot, hotter'n the hinges. Then July came to the valley, still hot and dry. When I say hot and dry, I mean it blazed by the sun. The days packed steel-blue skies. Then toward the month's end, clouds banked on the skyline and thunder made frightful sound. And lightnin' flashed. And the rain fell in fifty-five-gallon barrelloads. Soon, doggone it, it came August, and it rained and rained, and the nights were wild with thunder and lightnin'.

Then, some time back in that last week of July, I'll be a sonofabitch if Verbaline Lou didn't come back from the Signal Rock hospital, the proud mother of a big boy baby.

Well, he was too damned red to be natural.

"What you aim to call him?" I quizzed.

"Sam Houston," Clyde said. "Sam Houston Skinner. But for short, we'll call him SH, which is two letters together and stands for Sam Houston. 'Cause he's his daddy's pride and joy."

Pap said, "Why the hell didn't you name him Clint? That's a right name for a big boy baby."

Maw Maw and me looked each other in the eye, an act which meant how Pap talked sense. Sam Houston was a Texas tag for a big boy baby, potent in Montaig County. But Clyde didn't think how Verbaline Lou was a Pushmataha County girl, and the sweetness from her crotch needed an Oklahoma name. Like maybe Will Rogers, him out from Claremore. That way SH could have been SR instead. . . . Sam Rogers Skinner. Pap could have made somethin' *real* nasty out of SH, but he didn't.

"What'all did you aim to call him if he came out head first and showed himself to be a girl?" Maw Maw quizzed. She held SH in her arms while she talked 'cause the baby was too little to set in her lap.

Verbaline Lou was layin' in her bed, 'cause she'd labored some while she did the birthin' in the Signal Rock hospital. Clyde sat beside her in a chair, right proud by the look of his face.

"If the baby was a girl," my sister said, "we'd have named her LaMoyne. It's a reight pretty name for a big girl baby, a name made in Texas."

There they go again, us Lowdermilks figgered. Texas!

"Anyway," Maw Maw said, "I must say how our girl looked right beautiful while she packed this baby 'round inside her. I think all women are just about the most beautiful they can get when they are in that there condition."

"Hell," I said. "When they're walkin' front-heavy!"

"Damn it!" Pap said after me. "What's beautiful about a woman when she's got a bale of alfalfa stuck behind her belt buckle?"

So Maw Maw said, "Pshaw!" It was somethin' she said most of the time.

"Maybe we'll git a girl next time," Clyde said. "That woman layin' there is my wife, and we love each other dearly. That's the way with Texas folks. So when folks love dearly, that's when we might git another big baby. That's when we might git a girl, and that's when we'll name her LaMoyne."

"That's a sure enough Texas name, all right," Pap said.

"What'all will you name the next baby if he comes out head-first just another boy?" I said.

"We'll name him Rel," Verbaline Lou spoke up and said. "It's a Texas name and the letters stand for Robert E. Lee."

"You bet," Clyde said. He smiled happy 'cause of what his dear wife reckoned.

Pap spat cud into an empty quart oil-can he held in his hand. He spat 'cause he was rambunctious. "That's the second load of bullshit I got unloaded in my ears in five minutes," he said. "I'm gittin' my hearin' clogged from listenin' to names that don't amount to a sonofabitchin' damn. Why don't you name the poor bastard Joe, or Pete, or somethin' like that? I named my boy Newton, or leastways Maw Maw did. He don't amount to a shit, but he's the best we could do. SH, hell! . . . Rel, by golly! Them's the silliest boy-names I ever hear'd tell about."

Verbaline Lou stayed white about the gills for about a week, then she began to pink-up some. Anytime she came to visit, Maw Maw just walked 'round while she held SH. "Doggone," she'd say, makin' noises come out of her mouth that didn't pack sense; but she said the noises just to make that big boy baby giggle and snot-up his nose. "Doggone if this old grandmaw don't love this big boy baby like the glibs off molasses. Sweet! I tell you'all folks how this is the sweetest baby I ever seen in all my days."

Most times SH smelled like peaches and cream, but sometimes he smelled mighty bad. He just didn't seem to give a damn.

"Land sakes, daughter!" Maw Maw would say when SH got to smellin' mighty bad. "Why cain't you change that big boy's didies? He's natural, all right, but he don't make for pretty company."

So Verbaline Lou went to a little satchel and took out a square-didy. She was a wife and mother, and she knew how to wrangle the safety pin.

So it rained all August, one shower after t'other. When September struck us smack in the valley the showers turned into long rains, day-long rains, night-long rains. We pulled the beans when we caught a dry spell, so's to beat the frost to the draw. When October came, that's when we got after the kaffir corn and mile maize. The yellow corn could wait 'til the first week in November.

But just as October pulled out, when November came on the button, the very first week, you'll never guess who came up to the shanty and begged to be took in by us Lowdermilks.

Who'all? Well, he was a man with a satchel. And a

COUSIN DREWEY & THE HOLY TWISTER 325

fiddle in its case. And a guitar slung over his back. It wasn't nobody else.

'Cause Cousin Drewey had come out of the State Pen back home to sleep under the limb of the box elder tree. To eat with us Lowdermilks and wash out his mouth with a dipper of water.

Sonny Boy Skinner was at our house that time Cousin Drewey walked up to the porch. Sonny Boy had come down in the pickup truck, and he brought along a chocolate cake Lilybelle baked for Pap. She'd put PAP in white icin' atop. Pap had his shotgun in the crook of his arm. He was feared it might be Clyde who'd come, and he aimed to scare Clyde if any talk about movin' up to the ranch came 'round. Pap would scare Sonny Boy, too, if Sonny Boy didn't show good sense. But the sight of that cake always tickled Pap plumb to death.

Cousin Drewey came up before us, a sight for sore eyes. The kindly prison folks had given him new clothes without a number writ on the back. He wore new bib-overalls and an Arkansas jumper-jacket of the right fit and shoes made to wear good for a sizeable spell. He wore the same hat as he went to jail with, 'cause Cousin Drewey always claimed how he was wed to that hat, *it* come from the Washtaw Mountains with him.

"Lord, Lord, what a blessin'!" Maw Maw said on sight of that musical man. "How long you aim to stay with us, kinfolks?"

Cousin Drewey said nothin', but he packed a twinkle in his eye. He put the stachel on the ground, and right against it he put the fiddle. *It* in the case. Then he swung the guitar off his back and took hold like he might give us some music. Factways, he tickled the strings so's to put the guitar in tune.

"Where'all did you come from, sweet cousin?" Pap quizzed.

"How did you git here?" Sonny Boy put in his say.

"We're right proud to see you, Cousin Drewey," I said for my part.

So Cousin Drewey cleared his glottis. He did that by spittin' some slick. And he said with the voice of a musical man: "Folks and Lowdermilks, I'm come out straight from the State Pen, where I served a full year out of a five-year sentence. The guards claimed how I needed to git out, and the warden acted in cahoots, which let me out on good behavior. I ain't on parole, 'cause I'm a free man. The state governor gave me a pardon. I'm a musical man, like this wicked world knows, and you cain't keep a musical man shut up for more'n a year at a time."

"How did you git here, Cousin Drewey?" I said. That's what we all craved to know.

"Well," said our kinfolks, "you can go to the depot, and ask what'all to Briggs, the station agent. He'll tell you I came off the train, just like I did a couple years ago when I took up board and sleepin' quarters with you'all Lowdermilks."

"Do tell," Maw Maw said.

"But there's a difference this time. You ain't lookin' at me like I'm a stranger. Pap ain't thinkin' of goin' for his shotgun, and Maw Maw and Verbaline Lou ain't runnin' to the shanty for to hide under the window, like two scared she-rabbits. It ain't the same no more."

"Verbaline Lou's up at the ranch," Sonny Boy said. "She wedded-up with Clyde. She don't live here no more."

"That's right," Cousin Drewey said. "All the time I lived here last time, all them couple years, I asked the dear Lord to give that girl sense. But the Lord didn't need work too hard, 'cause Verbaline Lou had sense aplenty already in her heart and head. That's how come the Lord sent her Clyde Skinner, and that's why she became his lovin' wife."

"Lord bless you, Cousin Drewey," I had to say.

"You bet," Sonny Boy said.

Then Maw Maw spoke up. "Cousin Drewey, you can guess and guess and guess, but you'll never reckon what Clyde and Verbaline Lou's got."

"You needn't tell me, Maw Maw," Cousin Drewey said, grinnin' off his musical face. "'Cause you needn't tell me what them lovers did. They did natural, husband and wife. So what'all did they get? Did they get a big boy, or did that wife birth a big girl?"

"A big boy, and his name is SH," Maw Maw told.

"What do them letters stand for, Maw Maw?"

Pap fixed to open his mouth and say somethin' mean, but Maw Maw cut him off, actin' suddenly.

"It means Sam Houston—Sam Houston Skinner. Clyde comes from Texas, Montaig County, near Nacona, so it's a natural name."

Cousin Drewey snickered a little, at the same time ticklin' the guitar. It looked mighty like he aimed to sing us a song, but he didn't sing. He just tickled and said, "Lowdermilks, and you too, Sonny Boy, I'd like to tell you somethin' straight. I'll remind you'all about that first time I came up to this house, and I tickled my guitar and sang you a song. I disremember what song it was, 'cause a musical man's got plenty in stock. I remember I told you how I was kinfolks out of the Washtaw Mountains, and you'all said, 'Welcome, sweet cousin.' You remember that, Lowdermilks?"

"Land sakes!" Maw Maw said. "How can we forgit that happy day!"

"But I told you, too, how I wouldn't be stayin' with you long, 'cause I'd come to my allotted time, like the Good Book directs. *The days of our years are threescore years and ten, and if by reason of strength they be fourscore years, yet is their strength labor and sorrow; for it is soon cut off, and we fly away.* I was seventy years old then. And it was two, maybe three years ago. Cain't remember which."

Pap spoke up. "I cain't remember neither. Maybe two, maybe three. What I know is you've come to eat up our hog-meat and turnip greens, and to make a bed next to the box elder tree."

"That first time," said Cousin Drewey, "I told you'all how I wouldn't be long among you, 'cause I was fixed to go back to the Washtaw Mountains, and to git there I'd ride the cloud of the first tornado-twister that comes along. Eastbound, by way of Lubbock, Wichita Falls, Sherman; and Hugo, where I change clouds for Antlers. That's when you told me you don't have twisters in Star Valley, 'cause the air is too dry, how clouds don't come reg'lar to your clear blue sky. Ain't that right, Pap Lowdermilk? Didn't you tell me that there?"

"I *sure* did," Pap said, actin' the snotty sonofabitch. "And I'll say it again."

"How much rain did you git this summer, Pap?"

"Aplenty."

"More'n reg'lar?"

Hell, yes."

"Had any rain lately?"

"Last evenin', some more in the night."

"This is November, ain't it?"

"That's what the smart feller says."

"My se'f, I think it's a little warm for November."

"Slightly."

"Should be frosty—nights cold, days bright and dry."

"Should be."

"But the air ain't cold and dry. It's too damned warm and wet, Pap Lowdermilk. This is Washtaw Mountain weather, and it ain't natural for Star Valley. So mark my words. A tornado-twister is fixed to make notches, come this way like a man on a velocipede. And when it hits, this old mossback will do the Good Book says—step aboard and fly away."

"Your ass sets in blue mud, Cousin Drewey," Pap said, plumb sick of hearin' so much mule-talk.

COUSIN DREWEY & THE HOLY TWISTER 329

"Lord! Don't say that," Maw Maw said to our kinfolks.

"We sure wish you'd sing us a song," I said. "Then Maw Maw can fix us some supper, and you can tell us all about your days in the State Pen."

Sonny Boy twisted 'round like he needed to hunt the greasewood, but he knew he just craved to go home. He held back only 'cause Cousin Drewey might sing a song.

"Then I'll need to be gittin' back to the ranch," Sonny Boy said.

So Cousin Drewey tickled his guitar, he opened his mouth and sang from his glottis. He sang us a sweet song, he sang us "Potaphar's Sufferin' Woman."

Well sir, that night at sundown Cousin Drewey sat in his old chair at the Lowdermilk supper table, and Maw Maw fixed him special a mess of greens, so's he could pour hog grease on them and tell Maw Maw how she's a greens-cookin' fool.

"They never fed us fellers greens in the State Pen," he told us Lowdermilks while he ate his supper, before he washed his mouth out with a dipper of water. "They fed us Bluebelly Yankee stuff, like ham and eggs and toast, and orange juice and strawberry jam, and the coffee we drank wasn't Arbuckle's."

"That kind'a stuff would sicken me like a horse," Pap said. "I'd die of starvation afore I'd eat that truck. I'd spit that orange juice in the cook's face, and that *toast!*... Well hell, that light bread ain't fit to feed hogs. They'd git lank on it, and the pork would have no taste at all. That's why the Bluebelly Yankees look the way they do."

"They ain't got nothin' so good as these greens," Cousin Drewey said, shovelin' them into his mouth.

"I'm sure proud you love 'em, Cousin Drewey," Maw Maw said. And she *was* proud, you could see the gladness shinin' in her eyes.

Then Cousin Drewey said somethin' that saddened us

Lowdermilks right smart. I looked at Pap and Pap looked at me. Maw Maw hung her head and looked down at the floor.

"Folks," Cousin Drewey said, "I cain't wait to git out and say howdy to the neighbors. I want to git among them, and show 'em how good I feel. I'll hunt up Old Man Lee Bassett, and when I find him I'll grip his hand and shake it like it was never shook before."

That's the talk that made us Lowdermilks sad.

'Cause of somethin' that happened, right here in this shanty.

It happened thisaway: Back in late September, while me and Pap and Maw Maw got in the crop, Old Man Lee Bassett stopped by the shanty. Us Lowdermilks were eatin' cornbread and greens, some fatback and fried okra. Old Man Lee Bassett came up to the porch and stood there for Pap to come out. When Pap went out, that's when he said howdy to our good neighbor. When Old Man Lee Bassett didn't say a goddamn thing, Pap spoke up, and he quizzed, "What'all's on your mind, Old Man Lee?"

Old Man Lee said, "Pap Lowdermilk, I got plenty on my mind. I'm here to talk with you, and I'm here for a reason. I understand how in the next month or two—maybe October, maybe November—Cousin Drewey will be let out of the State Pen. He'll be back in this house with you'all. Now here's why I've come to see you, and I'm a kind'a diplomat for all Star Valley. I talk for all the solid-minded, Christian folks for fifty miles 'round. What I aim to say is we all aim to club together, fork out a couple dollars each, straight from our pockets, and buy Cousin Drewey a train ticket back to the Washtaw Mountains. We'll give you the ticket, and you can give it to him."

"The hell you say," Pap said, sassily, pointin' an ugly face at Old Man Lee.

"We all reckon how it's the humane thing to do," Old Man Lee said.

Pap's mouth was full of brown slick. He held a chew of Brown's Mule under his jaw so he just squirted a comet of ambeer to the off-side of Old Man Lee. "I sure hate to say so, Old Man Lee, but that's somethin' that won't work with Cousin Drewey."

"It looks to me like it will *have* to work, Pap Lowdermilk," Old Man Lee said.

"Our kinfolks is proud. He won't take charity."

"I hate to say so, Pap, but this ain't charity. Like I said, I'm talkin' for the Valley, for every citizen. Buyin' a train ticket for Cousin Drewey—one way, no 'round trip—is our polite way of gittin' a low-grade horse thief out of our midst. We don't like our kids gittin' next to ex-jailbirds. We don't like the likes of Cousin Drewey messin' 'round our womenfolks. But most of all, we don't want Cousin Drewey anywhere near our horses. We prize our horses right smart."

Pap looked closer at Old Man Lee. He looked like he could spit in his good neighbor's eye. "Cousin Drewey ain't no horse thief." That's what Pap said, and he said it at a three-foot spittin' distance. But Pap didn't spit. He just talked plain.

"He stole Fats Recknagel's stud-horse, didn't he?" Old Man Lee said. "In the very act, like that Bible-woman who was taken in adultery."

"Cousin Drewey didn't steal that horse," Pap told Old Man Lee. "He didn't even take the loan of the stud. He had nary to do with that four-legged sonofabitch."

"Then who stole Fats Recknagel's horse, if it wasn't Cousin Drewey?" Old Man was gettin' red 'round the neck.

"I'll tell you who, nosey neighbor," Pap said, dealin' sass. "Fats Recknagel hisse'f."

"Pap Lowdermilk, you crazy!"

"Him and Billy Beck."

Old Man Lee couldn't believe his ears. There was the stink of burnin' rubber 'round and he suspicioned how it might have clogged his hearin'. No man can steal his own horse.

"Pap, you ain't got a lick of sense."

"I've done named the culprits," Pap said.

"And I've made a generous offer, me and Star Valley," Old Man Lee Bassett said. "We'd like to buy a train ticket, 'cause I've done collected the money. Pap, I'm tellin' you straight, there ain't a man or woman in this kindly valley who craves to see Cousin Drewey come home from the State Pen. We just don't love him no more."

That's the kind of talk that happened back in late September.

That's why we couldn't tell Cousin Drewey about all we knew, about how the folks felt about him, and how they reckoned him a low-life even when he got out of the State Pen. We just couldn't tell him not to shake hands with the neighbors, or sing them a song or a psalm. You just can't tell kinfolks how the neighbors feel about horse thieves when he's eatin' greens with hog grease and a slab or two of cornbread there at our lean-to table.

Lord! What a homecomin' that was!

So us Lowdermilks rode herd on Cousin Drewey. Any time he showed sign for to go ramblin', that's when either me or Pap would catch him and love his neck. We'd beg him to set down and tell us all about doin's in the State Pen, and quiz him if he'd ever seen fellers get hauled off to the gas chamber. So Cousin Drewey would shed all sweet thoughts about neighbors, get them clean out of his mind. Then he'd set down and tell us about the fellers. But soon, too goddamn soon, he'd get away from our grip; sometime when we couldn't stop him, and he'd go off to say howdy, and some silly sonofabitch would hurt his feelin's, call his a low-down horse thief,

COUSIN DREWEY & THE HOLY TWISTER   333

and tell him to git. Git for the Washtaw Mountains and don't come back no more! We saw it comin', the handwrit on the wall.

Then came a day, right after Cousin Drewey came back among us, that Clyde Skinner was settin' in his ranch-house kitchen. He was playin' sweet daddy to SH, and he watched Verbaline Lou stir up some dinner. My sister was over by her stainless steel sink, it with the hot and cold faucets. She was washin' potatoes. Lord, did we all love potatoes. She aimed to boil them. Clyde and Verbaline Lou weren't alone with SH, 'cause I was settin' at the table with Clyde. I drank coffee and it wasn't Arbuckle's.

Then it happened, sweet Lord, it happened!

Sonny Boy came in puffin' and blowing. He heaved and wheezed 'cause of his heavy-setness. And he had a friend with him.

Who'all? None other than that low-grade, highly-alkalied, tolerably no-good Billy Beck! And I'll say now as how when Billy Beck trailed in behind Sonny Boy he made a miserable sight of himself.

He stood hung-head for shame, holdin' his hat in his hand. There was a smell about him—formaldehyde! Which told for truth how he'd just come away from the whiskey still in Reese Blaylock's funeral parlor, and maybe old Reese got some of that stinkin' stuff on Billy Beck while he was sprayin' the rose bushes.

"I need two witnesses," Sonny Boy said. He went over to the table next to Clyde and me. Verbaline Lou came close to Clyde, so she wouldn't get poisoned by closeness to Billy Beck.

"Where'd you pick him up?" Clyde said.

"Down the road," Sonny Boy said. "I was drivin' up this way in the pickup. Comin' home from town, and damned if Billy Beck wasn't headin' this way too. So I picked him up."

"What's on his mind, if he's got a mind?" said Clyde.

Clyde had come out of Montaig County, Texas, so he was polite by nature. He showed Billy Beck a chair at the table and told him to go set. Billy put on his hat, went to the table and plunked his rusty. Clyde told Verbaline Lou to get Billy Beck some coffee, to pour him a cup.

"Doggone," Billy said. "This coffee is just what this old sinner needs. It'll he'p me make adjustments with the Lord."

Sonny Boy spoke up. So he said, "We'll need witnesses, all right. Like I said. You can be one, brother Clyde; and Lou, you can be another. Old Newt, here, he can keep his ears open."

"What's Billy Beck got to say for hisse'f if we need two witnesses in this here house?" Clyde said.

Verbaline Lou gave Sonny Boy a cup, and it was brown with coffee. We all had coffee like in a kangaroo court.

"All right, Billy Beck," Sonny Boy said, "go ahead and tell these fine folks your history. The sooner you confess your sins the sooner the Lord will forgive you."

So Billy Beck gave a cocky angle to his hat and fixed to open his mouth. "Clyde," he said, "I'm a shamed man, and it ain't whiskey in the funeral parlor that's makin' me that way. I'm shamed 'cause the millionaires and politicians kicked me down and made me into a low-down no'count."

"You were no'count before they kicked," Clyde said.

"You'all folks tellin' me?" Billy Beck said, a humble man made that way by his misdemeanors. "I never was any good. All my kinfolks can tell you that, mostly my old dead daddy and long-gone mother."

"We believe you," Sonny Boy said. "Now tell these good folks what you told me, like what you said when I stopped for you on the road."

"Well," Billy Beck said, "I was headin' this way when Sonny Boy picked me up in his pickup truck. I ached all over, mostly in my heart. I didn't have a heart attack, I just ached for the dirty trick I played on Cousin Drewey, for me and my dirty partners sendin' an innocent man to the State Pen."

"It was a dirty trick, all right," Clyde said.

"Well, I was walkin' on the road, so when Sonny Boy picked me up I told him how it was me who stole Fats Recknagel's horse, me and old Fats hisse'f. I told all that to Sonny Boy, told him so's I could confess my sing."

"You'all maybe need testify in the courtroom, Billy," Clyde said.

"You bet, if it will ease-up my burdened heart."

"Go on," Sonny Boy said.

"Well, it wasn't only me and Fats, 'cause it was them three dirty politicians too. I mean Hank Hudgeons, the sheriff, and his two piss-ant deputies—that Elmo and the other sonofabitch. We're five in all, no-good horse thieves. We sent a righteous man to the State Pen, gave him a dose of hell and misery, and the gent who paid out the money was Fats Recknagel. I need to git shed of my sin, 'cause of my Christian conscience. I cain't sleep at night. I need some shut-eye mighty bad."

"Deep in your heart, you're a good man, Billy Beck," Clyde said.

"What made you turn all asudden?" Verbaline Lou said, speakin' up for the first time since she asked Billy Beck if he liked milk and sugar in his coffee.

"What made me!" Billy Beck said, pushin' his empty coffee cup toward my sister. "What made me see my sinful ways is the way the sorry Star Valley folks are thinkin' about Cousin Drewey, like buyin' him a train ticket to the Washtaw Mountains, so's to git his sinfulness out of their midst. Cousin Drewey ain't no sinner. It's old Fats and Hank, and me and that goddamn Elmo. It's us'ns who's the sinners."

Clyde said, "You're a just and noble man, Billy Beck, if you can feel your sinfulness. The Lord will forgive you, even Cousin Drewey hisse'f will forgive you."

"Them's the sweetest words, Clyde."

"What happened?" Sonny Boy said. "How'all did you sin?"

"Well, one night about a year ago old Fats sent a feller to Shorty Flack's Bon Marchee Saloon, and the feller came in a Cadillac-car, 'cause the feller was Fats's own chauffeur. He found me and Shorty in the saloon that night, 'cause Reese Blaylock had some merchandise to tend, and he needed the embalmin' room. . . . 'Billy,' the feller said, 'Mr. Recknagel says how he'd like to see you, and to tell you how there's money in it.' Well, it stood to reason how I couldn't turn money down, so I went with the feller to Fats Recknagel's house, out on the ranch, and there I found Hank Hudgeons and the two deputies. They were all at the big dinner table, and they were eatin' a feast to fill up the Sultan of Bulgaria and his fifty concubines."

"Well, hell, do tell," said Clyde.

"Well, while we were eatin' ham old Fats made the proposition. He said he craved to git square with Cousin Drewey, 'cause that mossback got free in the courtroom after rustlin' one of his best registered Black Angus calves and takin' it off on the mule for to feed them Lowdermilks. Cousin Drewey got free 'cause he couldn't show the hide, and the brand on the hide, 'cause he said he'd done ate it with the balance of the meat."

"You're talkin' like an honest man," Sonny Boy said.

"Well, so I went in cahoots with old Fats, after he said how I should take his prize stud-horse down to my place near Signal Rock and feed him hay and mixed corn-chops and oats, and to hide him in the barn for a week. One of his cowboys would haul the horse down, in the horse-trailer in the black of night. Well, that's what I did, like Fats directed, and after a week I took the horse and planted him in Pap Lowdermilk's pasture, after talk had gone 'round Star Valley how some no-good bastard had stolen Fats Recknagel's stud-horse, and everybody got to thinkin' about Cousin Drewey."

"That's right, Cousin Drewey talked too much," Clyde said.

"Well, the valley folks said to each other, 'That's that wicked Cousin Drewey again, and he's done stole old Fats's horse.' That's exactly what Fats craved them to say. So when Cousin Drewey went for a ramble that night, in the bright moonlight, he found the stud in Pap Lowdermilk's pasture. That's when Cousin Drewey kindly tried to lead the horse back to Fats Recknagel's gate, when Hank and the deputies, and that sorry Recknagel cowboy, caught him in the act, chousin' stolen property down the road."

"You said there was money in the deal," Sonny Boy said.

"Well, you're damn right. Fats gave me fifty dollars for my part. Next day he went down to the courthouse in the county seat, forty miles south. He found the sheriff in his office, and the two piss-ants, and he talked to them again. 'Cause Fats was feared how his dirty scheme might git talked 'round the valley, and Cousin Drewey wouldn't git chastised, 'cause folks would always favor a musical man."

"He's musical, all right," I spoke up in favor of Cousin Drewey.

Billy Beck nodded like I had it down pat. And he was primed for a genuine confession.

"Well, that's what Fats was feared about. So he made a second proposition with Hank Hudgeons, and with the deputies, 'cause he couldn't trust the dirty politicians. A dirty politician is worse than any sonofabitch you'll find at the First National Bank. Fats offered Hank a hundred dollars, and Elmo and his sidekick fifty dollars apiece, for to keep everythin' quiet; and when it was time to arrest Cousin Drewey with the stolen goods, for Hank to do his duty like a gentleman."

"Did Hank and the deputies take the money?" Clyde said.

"Well," Billy Beck said, "did you ever offer county politicians money when they didn't take it? That's what they got their hands out for, day and night, even when they plead for votes and kiss the babies. So Fats gave Hank two fifty-dollar bills, and the deputies a fifty apiece. I already had my fifty; so that's when Fats got nigh to weepin', sayin' how two hundred and fifty dollars don't grow on trees and how all us lousy crooks should be grateful to him."

"Did Hank Hudgeons pledge hisse'f to be Fats's friend, that time when he got the money?" Clyde said.

"Well," said Billy Beck, "like hell he did! Hank accused Fats of bribin' the law, and how he had Fats in his grip hook-line-and-sinker. Hank said how bribin' a sheriff was a serious felony, and how he could send Fats to the State Pen just as easy as droppin' his hat. That scared hell out of Fats, 'cause Fats feared how maybe Hank needed more money. You'all folks know how feared millionaires git when they've got to pay out more money."

"I didn't think nothin' could scare Fats," Clyde said.

Sonny Boy said, "You bet. Millionaires get scared like anybody else."

Me and Verbaline Lou just listened.

"Well, Fats was scared but Hank Hudgeons treated him kindly. The sheriff said how if Fats would he'p him in the up-comin' election he wouldn't prosecute for bribery, how he'd go ahead and catch Cousin Drewey. He'd do that sure as hell and send that mossback to the State Pen. 'Sheriff,' Fats said to that, 'I'm your dutiful servant. Just he'p me convict Cousin Drewey and I'll git you elected sure as hell.' "

"But that was more'n a year ago," Clyde said. "The election ain't comin' up 'til next week, this comin' Tuesday. Why'all did Hank need to git Fats to workin' for him so soon? Anybody in Star Valley knows how no campaignin' politician can flush Hank Hudgeons out of the sheriff's office. It just cain't be done."

Billy Beck pointed at Clyde, and it was the hand of wisdom for a fact. "You're correct, friend Skinner," he said, "but you know how them candidates be—they need three hundred and sixty-five days to hand-shake and kiss the fryin'-size, and to finish the job of lies and temptations."

"Who'all's runnin' agin Hank Hudgeons?" I quizzed.

"Mike Stover, he wants to be sheriff," Clyde said.

"A right clever man, and honest," Sonny Boy said.

I'd forgot how there was an election comin' up. Us Lowdermilks never cast a ballot, which stands to reason. Mossbacks just don't give a damn. Sheriffs don't do us no good; they just arrest us and make us miserable. So what's the need for us to he'p put them in office? Clyde and Sonny Boy never failed to mark a ballot. That's 'cause they run a cow-outfit, and be the best of Democrats and Baptists.

"Go on, Billy Beck," Clyde said. "Tell us more about your nefarious doin's, and about the sheriff and the millionaire."

"Well, I hate to talk about wickedness," Billy Beck said, "but I'll sure talk loud if it will clear my good name."

"You ain't got a good name," Sonny Boy said.

"No I ain't, and I ain't proud of what I got. So Fats said to the sheriff, 'I fed you ham and oysters up at my ranch last night, and right now I gave you a hundred dollars. But I hate that mossback Cousin Drewey so much that I'd pay even more out of my bank account for to get him in trouble. So name it, sheriff, 'cause I'm your friend and admirer."

Me and Clyde and Sonny Boy whistled for amazement.

"Well," Billy Beck went on, "that's when Hank named his price—he craved no money but a heap of compliments, said how him and his deputies were the best officers the county ever had, loyal to the people and how they'd never take bribes. And for Fats to he'p him in his campaign for reelection. What Hank needed out of Fats was praise where praise was needed—like at the First National Bank, and 'round the county commissioners, and most of all among the big farmers who hated mossbacks and loved Fats 'cause he was a millionaire. 'That way,' Hank said, 'I won't arrest you for offerin' me a bribe. Is it a deal?' When Fats said, 'You bet,' that's when they all shook hands. And that's my confession. You'all know how Cousin Drewey got caught with the horse and got sent to the State Pen."

Now all of us folks in that kitchen, even Verbaline Lou, looked each other in the face. Each of us menfolks said, "Well, I'll be a sonofabitch!" But Verbaline Lou said, "My!"

"You're the best scoundrel as ever lived, Billy Beck," Clyde said.

"Maybe so," Billy Beck said back at Clyde, "but I tell you fellers I'd *sure* hate to git sent to the State Pen for my misdemeanors."

"You needn't fret, Billy," Clyde said. "You needn't give a damn, and you won't go to the State Pen—not even to the county jail. All Fats did to you was pay you forty-five dollars for a week's keep of his horse in your barn and he even supplied the grain and hay. That there, and a night's wages of five dollars for puttin' the horse in Pap Lowdermilk's sorry pasture."

"When they git me in the courtroom they might think different," Billy Beck said.

"You ain't goin' to the courtroom, 'cause you're actin' state's evidence right here and now, enough evidence to shed this county of three spittoon politicians and one Texas-size millionaire. Them three fellers we won't see no more, and Fats Recknagel will operate his ranch by remote control from Houston."

"You Skinner boys ain't makin' mock of me, are you?"

"No, Billy Beck, we ain't," Sonny Boy said. "By sundown of tomorrow all Star Valley will be grateful to you. They'll love you dearly, 'cause you put the terminal stop to a sorry politician's time in office. You saved 'em a heap of trouble. You saved 'em from votin' Hank Hudgeons out. Lord bless you, Billy Beck."

"You gave a chance to put a good man in his place," said Clyde, "without waitin' for election day. And most of all, you'll make the president of the First National Bank weep like the fire hydrant that sets front of his big brass door. He'll do that there 'cause his best customer has gone back to Texas, and he won't see Fats Recknagel's face no more."

Billy Beck heaved a mighty sigh, and he shook his shoulders for the relief to his anxiety. He snickered slightly, and he said to Verbaline Lou, "Mistress Skinner, I ain't had nothin' to eat since I hear'd Cousin Drewey got home, 'cause my sinful ways were troublin' me right smart. I'm hungry like a coyote. You ain't got a piece of apple pie, have you?"

"No, we ain't," my sister said, but she gave him a hunk of Lilybelle's chocolate cake, the kind that makes Pap Lowdermilk sick.

Clyde got up off his chair and went to the telephone that hung on the wall next to Verbaline Lou's shiny stainless steel sink. He got down the receiver and pleaded with the operator, asked her kindly to get Old Man Lee Bassett, and said he hoped the weather was pleasant 'round the telephone exchange.

"Hello, that you, Old Man Lee?" Clyde said into the telephone. "This is Clyde Skinner. We got Billy Beck in my ranch-house kitchen. He's eatin' cake now, but when you git here as soon as you can he'll be ready to open up and make you a confession, one that'll . . ."

It seemed like Old Man Lee Bassett didn't wait for Clyde to talk anymore. He hung up the telephone.

"He says he's on his way," Clyde said.

We waited, and while we waited we talked about horses. Clyde quizzed Billy Beck—how he reckoned about quarter horses, 'specially stud-horses. Billy Beck didn't have a yellerjacket in his mouth, but he stuttered that way. It seemed like he craved to get stud-horses off his mind, leastways for the time bein'.

Then Old Man Lee put his presence in our midst. He was rarin' to hear a confession.

"Billy," Clyde said, "you just go ahead and tell this fat old man all you told us here in my kitchen. Tell it all, then you can go home and give your Christian soul some shut-eye."

So Billy Beck gave Old Man Lee Bassett the details of the nefarious doin's, the same as he gave us'ns. It took him ten minutes to tell it all, but he did right smart of a sweet job at talk.

"I don't think we'll need fool 'round with a trial for bribery, or even agin Fats Recknagel for stealin' his own horse," Old Man Lee said. "Just leave it to me and the talk from my glottis."

The next day Old Man Lee Bassett went to say howdy to Fats Recknagel. He found Fats aset in the sunshine, out by the swimmin' pool, which hadn't any water 'cause it was November. He told Fats about Billy Beck's confession, and how he'd turn state's evidence if the case came up to court.

"By today's sundown," Old Man Lee said, "you'll be branded a horse-stealer, a briber, and an all'round no-good no'count by every man, woman and child in Star Valley, and you know how country folks hate the guts of horse-stealers, bribers and no-good no'counts. You needn't put your ranch on the market, Fats, but you can

COUSIN DREWEY & THE HOLY TWISTER 343

keep your hide and tripe out of this decent community. Do you hear me, or are you deaf?"

"I ain't deaf," said Fats Recknagel, "but I'm a man who cain't live for his health's sake anywhere but Texas."

Like Old Man Lee told us later, by sundown that day he'd gone to every ranch and farm in Star Valley, and given the folks back the cash they gave to buy Cousin Drewey a train ticket back to the Washtaw Mountains. Some fellers said how they might all get a rope and lynch all the crooks except Billy Beck. But Fats said there'd be no chance to catch up with them, 'cause they were long gone.

Old Man Lee had to wait another day before drivin' down to the county seat, to make notches in his pickup truck. He went to the courthouse for to say howdy to Hank Hudgeons and his deputies, but the sheriff's stenographer said how Hank had all of a sudden quit his job and gone back to Texas. She said how Hank claimed the climate there was better for his constitution. And how the deputies took off in the opposite direction—to Arizona, and they went in a hurry. They loved Texas, the stenographer told, and would like to go home, but they decided agin it. For health reasons, just like Hank. You see, they were wanted by four sheriffs there in four different counties in that good old Lone Star State.

"Then it looks like Mike Stover won't have no opposition come next Tuesday," Old Man Lee said to the girls in the office. "Maybe he's as good as our new sheriff right now."

"That's the way the boot fits, Mr. Bassett," said the blonde-headed stenographer, and Lord was she proud! "He's pinned on his badge and chosen his deputies. And he'll make the best sheriff this county ever had, 'cause he's already told us girls how we can keep our jobs."

30

November got itself half-way through on Friday, that year Cousin Drewey came home to us Lowdermilks; that is, the fifteenth hit on that blessed day of the week. Cousin Drewey hadn't got out among the neighbors yet, but we could feel in the air how Star Valley was mighty shamed for the way folks suspicioned our kinfolks for bein' a low-grade horse thief.

Fats Recknagel, back in Houston, wrote a letter to *The Star Valley Pinto Bean,* sayin' how he reckoned us all on this flat to be a gang of horse-stealers, yarlin'-rustlers, and how we all ought to get hung. That ired us all, when folks saw Fats's letter in the paper, which made every farmer and stockman with sense and muscle vow to find a rope if Fats ever came back to Star Valley again. He hauled off his fine quarter horses and registered cattle and put them on his South Texas ranch, that place where there's Greek women in the swimmin' pool, naked, pretty statues spoutin' water from their mouths, 'cause that's the way millionaires do.

First thing Cousin Drewey noticed when he got back from the State Pen was how our stack of cedar stovewood was down to the last dozen sticks, and how Pap's pile of old auto tires would play out in a week—judgin' by the way Pap loved to bust them up with the axe, burn them in the cookstove and stink the neighbors into hollerin' how they wished Pap Lowdermilk was dead.

COUSIN DREWEY & THE HOLY TWISTER 345

That way, when Cousin Drewey saw what he did, he filed the axe to sharpness and whistled in my direction.

"Newt," he said, when I went to his whistle, "let's me and you get out old Jeff and the wagon and go up to the bench for a load of wood. We need to do that afore Pap gets a dose of old dead Atlases and Goodyears on his mind."

We made two trips right after election day, after we thanked the Lord for Mike Stover. Both trips brought down the damnedest stack of mixed cedar and piñon, the best firewood in the wide world, sweet to the nose and clean to the stovepipe. We admired what we'd hauled down; so did Maw Maw. But Lord, Pap, he was ired. "Damn it to hell!" we hear'd him shout, when we saw him stop by the new woodpile.

He didn't open his silly mouth all that day, but the next mornin' we saw how he'd put on clean overalls and a shirt, washed clean of his daily dirt, dressed to kill off the calico or maybe visit Mr. Wilbur Pruitt at the First National Bank. We couldn't think what ailed Pap, 'cause he kept his silly mouth shut. But when he put the harness on old Jeff and hooked him to the wagon, we knew for sure how he was fixin' to head for town. Then, when he loaded on five hundred-pound sacks of pinto beans and the same of shelled corn, we knew he was ridin' off to do somethin' foolish.

"Newt," Cousin Drewey said, after Pap drove off to town. "Son, are you reckonin' the same as me?"

"Cousin Drewey," I said, "I can smell the stink already, and the neighbors will moan and groan and dress theirse'fs in sackcloth and ashes. The wrath of Moses will be on the Lowdermilk name."

And sure enough. When Pap got home we saw how he'd gone tradin' off beans and shelled corn at Dwight's Auto Wreckin' Yard, and what he threw off from the wagon was black and sinful, enough to dull the best brand of axe. But Pap wasn't ired no more. He walked 'round smilin' to hisse'f and actin' proud for what he had done.

Cousin Drewey sat out a heap of time under the limb of the box elder tree, where he laid out his pallet and hung his pants when he went to sleep. He'd whittle a stick, like he did by the woodpile. But he didn't spit cud-juice at the axe 'cause there wasn't an axe thereabouts. He just hit the ground and covered it with slick.

Outside of chores there wasn't much to do after the crops were hauled in, so I spent some hours with Cousin Drewey next to the box elder tree. I leaned back against the trunk, kicked away the ants when they got close and listened to Cousin Drewey gas about the State Pen.

But I had to say it, somethin' about myse'f. "Cousin Drewey, it wasn't only Pap's hands that shelled the corn and pulled the beans that got traded off for old Dwight's nasty tires. It was mine and Maw Maw's, too, and I don't crave my labor to get hauled to town and come back shaped like somethin' everybody on earth hates but Pap."

"Newt," Cousin Drewey said, "that's what the Bible calls *injustice*. You find it here on Lowdermilk land, just like sweet Joseph found it in the Land of Goshen."

Which put our kinfolks in a mind to sing "Potaphar's Sufferin' Woman." So he reached up the limb to get his guitar.

While Cousin Drewey sang his song I looked over to the off-side of where he hunkered, and damned if our two hound dogs weren't laid out in slumber right up against Cousin Drewey.

The sight pleasured me right smart. Nobody since Verbaline Lou left from under our roof, to wed-up with Clyde, paid mind to those old dogs, except to pitch them scraps. And us Lowdermilks were never burdened-down with scraps. Old Pee-Dog, and old Bitchy-Damn, they were huntin' fools and kept alive on the rabbits they ran down. But my sister loved them, showed it by the way she made cornbread for them, and after she matrimonialized herse'f with Clyde, it was my Christian duty to love them too. But I never made cornbread. So when Cousin Drewey took a shine to Pee-Dog and Bitchy-Damn, it did somethin' good to my heart. A Washtaw Mountain man needs a pair of hound dogs next to him, like he does a fiddle and a song down his glottis, a twelve-gauge shotgun and a fishin' pole. All them, and lazy lonesome nights and days.

Later that very same day Old Man Lee Bassett stopped his pickup truck in our yard front of the shanty. It looked how he left someone in the seat when he got out and yelled howdy. Who'all that someone was neither me nor Cousin Drewey could figger. When Old Man Lee came our way, with a big Texas smile on his face, I could see how Cousin Drewey was plumb silly to see his old friend again.

That's when he laid his guitar down, got up off his hunkers and loved Old Man Lee's neck.

That's when we three got down to hunkerin' and spittin'.

"Cousin Drewey," Old Man Lee said asudden, "I've come to beg you a favor."

"You bet," said our kinfolks, "what kind of favor do you crave, sweet neighbor?"

Old Man Lee said, "Cousin Drewey, instead of takin' your hog-leg forty-five to Billy Beck when you meet him first time, like you threatened you'd do, I'd be proud if you'd put a hand on his humble head and give him your Baptist forgiveness."

"Well. . . ." Cousin Drewey tried to say.

He couldn't say 'cause right then our dear neighbor got up off his hunkers. He went to the pickup truck and hauled out a feller from the seat, and damned if the feller wasn't Billy Beck!

If Cousin Drewey ever had a mind to shoot Billy Beck

he shed hisse'f of the meanness there and then. 'Cause Billy Beck stood next to us lookin' runtier than ever before, lank like he'd packed no appetite since the day our kinfolks went to jail, sadness makin' cloud of face, hat in hand, head bowed, a humbled man sure enough.

Cousin Drewey said, "Friend Billy, kindly raise your face and look me in the eye."

So Billy Beck did what Cousin Drewey craved.

That's when our kinfolks put his right hand on Billy Beck's head. That's when he forgave the horse thief for sendin' him up to the State Pen. That's when he called on the Lord for he'p, so's he wouldn't show ire on sight of this no-count. Billy Beck leaked from the eyes 'cause his heart was heavy. 'Cause he'd done Cousin Drewey wrong just to he'p out Fats Recknagel, for goin' into cahoots with Hank Hudgeons. That's when Billy Beck turned on his swivels so's to give Cousin Drewey his back, 'cause he couldn't look an honest man in the face. And that minute, the minute when Cousin Drewey saw the seat of Billy Beck's pants shinin' in his direction, when he asked the Lord's he'p for a second time—to save him from temptation.

Temptation! To kick the ass of Billy Beck's pants.

For the good man he was, Cousin Drewey got heaven's he'p.

Soon after that, no more than a week, it came to the ears of us Lowdermilks how Star Valley folks were fixin' to give Cousin Drewey the biggest barbecue and hoedown ever held west of the Cross Timbers. They'd build a dance stage and everythin', a high-up platform for the musicians, a pure Solomon's throne for Cousin Drewey and his fiddle. Old Man Lee Bassett would give a yearlin' for the barbecue pit, Snookie Hapchester another, and enough pink drink in tubs to float the Hungarian navy. We hear'd how about three hundred eager folks were gettin' primed to strut and sashay, to circle right and how-dee-do, all to the whine of Cousin Drewey's fiddle, and to Young Buster Prather's banjo, and to the call from Uncle Posey Burwinkle's glottis. Like in the days afore Cousin Drewey's sad incarceration. Only bigger, even happier. With more action and hooraw. Only this time they'd hold the shindig in Old Man Lee's open space next to the barn—the right place to barbecue two beef-steer-yearlin's down a pit. All to celebrate Cousin Drewey's blessed presence come back to the dirt where he was appreciated most.

We waited on the day, which we figgered might be another week, maybe about the time all this great nation will be shoutin thanks to the Lord. Me and Cousin Drewey hunkered by the woodpile. The cedar smelled good, perfumed like Potaphar's wife, and the split piñon hunks oozed pitch. So what us Lowdermilks had to be thankful for was the stack that would feed the cookstove and keep us warm when the cold weather started to plague us, *if* it would ever happen our way. But like I said the night before, gassin' with Pap, I said, "Pap, can you think of a November as warm and sticky as this one? Can you think of any like it since we left the Washtaw Mountains?"

Pap said, "Newt, I cain't. I disremember any time this month ever got so hot before. Maybe it's them Germans, or them Jaypans that are settin' a bug on us, 'cause they're smart and hateful of us fellers. November in this western state comes cold and dry, the right kind of daylight for haulin' in the crops. But it ain't so this year, Newt."

I said to Pap, "It's like we sometimes got back in Oklahoma. . . . Too much rain, crazy weather. Cousin Drewey gets mighty wet on many a night, lately, sleepin' under the box elder tree. . . . Pap, I sure *wish* it would get cold."

"It's pitiful, son."

"Sure hope it clears for the hoe-down, Pap."

Pap said, "You bet."

"You aim to strut some, Pap?"

"Maybe, if I can pull an armload of calico."

"Young Buster Prather will make his banjo sing."

"And Cousin Drewey will percolate the instrument, make it whine and whine and whine."

"Uncle Posey Burwinkle will holler 'Hogs in the corn!'"

"Too bad we ain't got Cowboy to tickle his guitar, Newt. Maybe Mike Stover will let him out of jail, just for the shindig. . . . Lord, he'll tickle 'Bull at the Wagon'!"

"He ain't in jail no more, Pap. Hank Hudgeons let him out."

"Where'all you reckon he went, Newt?"

"Back to Texas, Glasscock County. He's got kinfolks there."

"And what you reckon about them two chippies, son? You reckon they're still in the ladies department?"

"Beverly and Eunice?"

"Hell yes. You reckon they're still down there?"

"Hell no."

"How come?"

"Hank Hudgeons let 'em out. They both took turns and gave him a charity-piece. That's how come Hank let 'em out. A tolerable time ago it was, Pap. It's been over fourteen, fifteen months since Cowboy tickled."

Pap said, "That's right, Newt. Fool me. Them folks tickled and poontanged a long time ago. That day of the kangaroo court. Time before Cousin Drewey went up to the State Pen."

Pap and me talked like that the night before, and we talked it 'cause of the way November was actin' up. . . . But right now I was out at the woodpile with Cousin Drewey. We both chewed cud; and the two hounds had their snouts restin' on Cousin Drewey's feet 'cause they loved him so. I spat a comet in the other direction, then I quizzed him about what he reckoned.

"Kinfolks," I said, "do you reckon you'all put on your fancy cowboy fiddler's outfit, it with the boots and spangles, come the day of the barbecue shindig?"

Cousin Drewey said, "Newt, I cain't.... I just cain't, Newt.... I might be a musical man, but more'n that I'm a Washtaw Mountain man. And a Washtaw Mountain man don't need spangles and cowboy boots. He needs bib-overalls and an Arkansas jumper-jacket, and the same hat that sat on my head that day I first said howdy to you'all Lowdermilks. I'm that brand of feller, Newt."

Pap was in the shanty while me and Cousin Drewey talked about fiddler's attire. And while we were aset, Maw Maw made dinner at the cookstove, for the sun was gettin' up-amiddle. And it seems mighty like everybody in the world comes 'round us Lowdermilks when me and Cousin Drewey are at the woodpile. 'Cause just then we saw Clyde Skinner gunnin' his pickup truck into the yard, to park front of Pap who was hunkerin' on the porch.

We saw Verbaline Lou get out packin' SH high against her neck, that big baby done up in sissy frills of pink and white. Pap got up off his rusty so's he could love SH's neck, he'd talk coo-coo language while he slobbered Copenhagen down his chin-bristles. Verbaline Lou went inside to where Maw Maw sweated at the stove, cookin' greens. Pap set his rusty down again. He looked at Clyde who still sat in the pickup, and the way he pointed his face showed how he didn't care a damn for his fine and bright son-in-law.

"Friend Skinner," Pap yelled out at Clyde, "ain't you comin' in to give respects to kinfolks? Look at us crusty Lowdermilks, friend Skinner. We're mossbacks and we don't amount to a dime's worth of hog-slop in your high-up-society reckonin'. But me and Maw Maw is kinfolks, you silly bastard, and it's us'ns who birthed your wife, my sugar-tit gal. So come pay respect to your daddy-in-law, friend Skinner."

Clyde just sat in the pickup truck, waitin' for Verbaline Lou to come out from gassin' with Maw Maw.

"You hear me? You deaf?" Pap kept yellin' at Clyde. "I need respect. I'm king of this castle."

Clyde, bein' a husband, figgered how Verbaline Lou might spend a sizeable spell inside the shanty, gassin' with Maw Maw and changin' didies. So he got out of the pickup and walked straight over to where Pap sat actin' the impudent sonofabitch. But he kept goin' and passed Pap by about ten feet. He didn't go into the shanty, but aimed his direction our way, to me and Cousin Drewey. He said as he came up next to us, "Do you reckon you fellers will ever amount to a damn?"

Both me and Cousin Drewey grunted our howdies.

"Newt," Clyde said, hunkerin' down on his hockers, "Sonny Boy and me talked last night, after supper, and we need a hand pretty quick. I mean maybe next week. We've got some old fence to take out and new wire to staple on, and after that you can ride pasture. We'll pay forty-a-month, with chuck. You'll need some real good cowboy's gear, not mossback stuff, and we'll lend you the price, Sonny Boy and me."

"That's mighty sweet language," I said to Clyde.

"You'll live in the bunkhouse with the bunch, and we'll need you right soon, maybe after the hoe-down barbecue. My wife will be proud to have her dear brother up at the ranch."

So I said you bet to Clyde.

Cousin Drewey sat on the chop-block, his guitar snug and handy. Clyde and me, we hunkered down facin' each other. We could see Pap on the porch, a man with an ugly face. His chin was pointed yonderly, but we knew for sure how his eyesight was aimed at us three.

"Look at him," Clyde said. "He's coyote-bait, if any was ever mixed in a barrel and left to rot. The barrel stinks 'cause Pap Lowdermilk's in it. Try to fish him out and he'll hate you for it. I cain't savvy that sonofabitch."

But Cousin Drewey knew that old mossback better than Clyde could savvy in all his wisdom-packed days. "Pap thinks he belongs here, Clyde," Cousin Drewey said. "And it's gonna take more'n you Skinners, or Maw Maw, or me, or old Newt there, to tell him different. The only satisfaction I can give your philosophy, Clyde, is that old Bible-truth, a truth popular with mankind clean back to the Book of Exodus—*the Lord will provide*. That's the honest truth—*the Lord will provide*."

Clyde knew how nothin' temporal or mortal could get Pap to change his mind about immigration. They'd just need wait for the Lord to provide.

"That's what I'm waitin' for too, dear kinfolks," Cousin Drewey said to me and Clyde. "I'm settin' on this here stump ready for Divine Provision to come my way. And when It comes I'll beg to be waybilled to the Washtaw Mountains. I'm waitin' to be put aset on a big old cloud, one with a tail like a horse. . . . I'll ride atop a roarin' twister, eastbound. . . . I'll go non-stop 'til it lets me down. . . . Gently down on a cushion of green pasture, next to where the water lays still and sweet, deep and dark. . . . Water thick with catfish, bass and carp. . . . Mankind! . . . While I set on this here stump next to you fellers, I cain't he'p but think how I could do with a mess of fried catfish right now."

Clyde said, "You love to eat, don't you Cousin Drewey?"

And Cousin Drewey said back at Clyde, "Dear nephew, that's *exactly* what they told me up at the State Pen."

So Clyde took my sister and the big boy baby back to the ranch. He thought us Lowdermilks waitin' for the Lord to provide. He figgered if he had the Lord's he'p, Pap wouldn't sull. How we needn't tie him up and lash him down in the bed of the pickup truck. With the

Lord's he'p Pap would look without ire at the fine house Clyde and Sonny Boy fixed up for him and Maw Maw, while I stayed with the cowboys in the bunkhouse. And with the Lord's prime blessin' Pap would come to know what time and expense Clyde had gone to make life sweet for his dear wife's manufacturers. For the granddaddy and grandmaw of the big boy baby named SH.

Then came the day of Cousin Drewey's glory! They timed the hoe-down for a Saturday late in November, when the kids were out of school and farm business was finished for the week. And how Sunday would give the hoe-downers a day of rest before Monday sunrise yelled for a day of labor and sweat.

Clyde came by that mornin' for to take us Lowdermilks to the big shindig of glory. And for Cousin Drewey and his instruments. He came in his Chivvelee-sedan, and he was alone. He'd already done dropped off Verbaline Lou at the Bassett farm so she could he'p the womenfolks, she with an armload of SH. Clyde gunned the Chivvelee in our direction, and told us how there was room for us all—for me, Pap and Maw and Maw, for Cousin Drewey and his musical plunder. Cousin Drewey claimed how he would saw the fiddle while the folks went 'round and 'round, while they pranced the docee-do. But he'd need the guitar when he's sing his songs.

Maw Maw dressed herse'f in a clean print dress and Sunday sunbonnet. She wore shoes she'd bought at Sears and Roebuck. Lord, was she a dream! Pap had on clean overalls that were boiled with lye in Maw Maw's big iron pot. His shirt was likewise but slightly faded in the sun. He's shaved his bristles so's to look like a Christian for a change. And me, I packed the same cover for my nakedness as Pap. When Maw Maw said how me and Pap looked right handsome, Pap said, "Wife, that's the damnedest load of bullshit I hear'd in many a day."

But Cousin Drewey didn't make fuss about cleanin' up for the day, even if he was prime reason for the hoedown. He wore his Arkansas jumper-jacket, and the pants and shoes he'd gotten from the kindly State Pen folks. And the hat he'd worn that day when he first came into our yard.

Pap wouldn't set next to Clyde on the front seat because of how he carried no love in his heart for that fine young Texan. So Cousin Drewey piled in next to Clyde, with Pap and me and Maw Maw in the back, us'ns and the instruments. We took the road and headed in the right direction. Clyde and Cousin Drewey gassed some, and I hear'd Clyde say to our kinfolks, "Cousin Drewey, how come you ain't got on your musical-cowboy outfit? It with the spangles and green high-heeled boots? Don't you know how this is a celebration in your honor?"

We could see how that cattleman was shocked when his eyesight saw how Cousin Drewey wasn't duded-up.

Cousin Drewey snickered like a little old kid, and said back at Clyde, "I'm dressed this way 'cause I'm fixed to go home to the Washtaw Mountains. And because I ain't no jellybean out of Hollywood, California."

"Cousin Drewey, you craze! You'd sure look handsome in your musical-cowboy outfit," Clyde said.

"I'm musical, dear nephew Clyde, but I ain't no cowboy," Cousin Drewey said back at Clyde. "I got my fiddle and my guitar, and I got my satchel packed. Under my Arkansas jumper-jacket is hid my hog-leg forty-five. 'Cause tonight or in the mornin' I'll mount my transportation, and me and my friends will travel eastbound to the Lord's own slash-pine heaven."

"You sure of that, Cousin Drewey?" Clyde said.

"Sure like the Book of Romans."

"Who'all are your friends?"

"Old Jeff, the mule, to name one. He was my pardner in crime, and Fats Rechnagel hates him like he does me."

Clyde said, "And your other friends? Not Pap Lowdermilk, or he'll make your trip not worth the price."

"Hell no! You can have him, up at the ranch, and you'll have him no later than tomorrow evenin'. I'm takin' old Pee-Dog and Bitchy-Damn. They're the best hound dogs come out of a litter, and they don't belong here. They'll hunt with me in the Washtaw Mountains, and we'll run the 'possum up a tree."

"You better tell Briggs," Clyde said, "him at the depot. Tell him to flag the eastbound down. He'll sell you a ticket that'll take you as far as Amarillo. But I don't know if they can take Jeff and the hound dogs. Maybe they can stuff old Jeff in the baggage car. Damned if I know."

To that Cousin Drewey said, "You're talkin' fool-talk, Clyde, 'Cause this old Ozark cracker don't need no baggage car."

Clyde said nothin', he just pressed that old gas pedal down.

"Clyde, son," Cousin Drewey said, "I know you're a Christian, so you read your Bible. Now you can tell me this, have you ever read ought about baggage cars anywhere from Genesis to Revelation?"

"Cain't say as I have," Clyde confessed.

"They had plenty transportation back in them holy days, like chariots and camels and backs of asses," Cousin Drewey said. "So what I aim to ride back to the Washtaw Mountains is a vehicle that's Bible-pure, the holiest kind of transportation, the sweet Lord's own provision."

"A chariot, a camel, or the back of an ass?" said Clyde, "You might find a jackass in Star Valley, but no camels or chariots."

"None of them there," Cousin Drewey said. "But you'll read about my vehicle in Job, chapter one, verse nineteen."

"They didn't run the Frisco Lines back in the Book of

Job," Clyde said, steerin' the Chivvelee. "And they didn't need change cars at Hugo."

"That's right, Bible truth," Cousin Drewey said. "So my vehicle ain't no Frisco Lines, and I won't need change cars at Hugo. Just smell the air. Look at the sky —the clouds are green and the sun is weak, and the sky looks sickly like it's got La Grippe."

"It's too warm for November," Clyde said in agreement. "It's wet and sticky when the days should be cold and dry. It feels like tornado weather, like we used to have back in Montaig County."

"*That's* my transportation, son," Cousin Drewey said, "eastbound—me and my gear, me and my mule and hound dogs, waybilled for the Washtaw Mountains. Me on the cushions of a twister, that big gray funnel fresh out of Job, chapter one. A Bible twister, a holy twister of the holiest variety."

Clyde would have said somethin' to that, but he had to give mind to the Chivvelee. We'd done pulled into Old Man Lee Bassett's yard. And Lord, what a sight!

There must have been a hundred, two hundred, three hundred folks packed like sticks in a matchbox, all millin' 'round Old Man Lee Bassett's yard. They were gassin' and joshin' and laughin' because the day was sweet for a hoe-down barbecue. But maybe a little warm. And damp. Folks would sure sweat their skin-pores when the dance got to percolatin'.

The men had finished the dance platform. The barbecue pits were dug and smokin', and Old Man Lee and Snookie Hapchester tended the beef that was piled on the iron grids, sizzlin' its goodness over the coals. Mistress Lee Bassett had cooked the sauce all night in the kitchen. It smelled like a mess hall in heaven where sinners ain't allowed. And while the beef-yearlin's browned in the sauce, about two dozen valley women tended the big long table covered from end to end with oilcloth and enough vittles to feed the American army on parade. Pies, there must've been a hundred; potatoes and yams and beans by the tubful, okra and greens, and cornbread stacked like the Pyramids of Exodus. Pink drink—what a kindly sight! Cake and coffee, lemonade for the kids! And most beautiful of all was the throne the menfolks built for Cousin Drewey, high so he could stand way over the world while he percolated the bow and made sawdust of his fiddle. On either side, east and west, was a chair apiece for Young Buster Prather and his banjo; and another chair, empty—an invite to any old boy who'd volunteer to he'p out with a guitar. Uncle Posey Burwinkle would call the square dance, and he'd call it standin' upright in front of the throne.

As soon as we stepped off the Chivvelee our combined eyesight met somethin' that made our hearts glad—us being Lowdermilks, kin to Cousin Drewey. Mistress Lee Bassett, with valley ladies he'p, had made a big old welcome flag out of a white double-bed sheet, and they had the menfolks hang it on a wire over Cousin Drewey's stand of honor. On it, the ladies had painted:

WELCOME HOME COUSIN DREWEY
BACK FROM UP YONDER
STAR VALLEY'S NUMBER ONE CITIZEN

We got off the Chivvelee at five minutes to twelve and they started the hoe-down at high noon straight on the button.

Old Man Lee Bassett called for order, standin' high on Cousin Drewey's fiddler's perch. He cupped his hands to his jowls and hollered like an auctioneer. He let the folks know that we'd have a square dance first, up on the platform, then we could stuff our guts. The women were lovin' Cousin Drewey's neck, the men banged his back in good cheer like they needed to knock out somethin' from inside. Old Man Lee had to holler loud, and stay at it a long time. The noise of the crowd was *that* potent.

COUSIN DREWEY & THE HOLY TWISTER   359

When the folks let Cousin Drewey go, our kinfolks took up his fiddle and went high up the stand. Young Buster Prather followed with his banjo, and Uncle Posey Burwinkle shed his Copenhagen dip so's to clear his glottis. He was fixed to call "The Ocean Wave." A ring of dancers got up on the stand, young and old alike. There they were, the prime muscle of Star Valley—country folks all, each in his or her own way. They were fixed to dance for a mess of dinner, to satisfy their own rumblin' bellies and the gullets of one hundred, two hundred, maybe three hundred citizens watchin' 'round the platform. Sure thing, some were no'count, some were full of hate, ignorant of that thing called the golden rule. Some figgered money was the only thing in the world that matters, others liked the dirt they lived by better than money. And some thought a feller's only duty on earth was to praise God. They stood, ready for "The Ocean Wave"—they watched, fixed to listen, to admire. All the categories of Star Valley were there. It was the old Texas cattleman who talked in wisdom, for his mind was bright from close friendship with horses, cattle and all breeds of men. He once said how if they divide all human bein's of the world into bunches of a hundred, you'll find that each bunch holds one saint, one sonofabitch, and ninety-eight sheep.

The dance went 'round like the drivers on old 9999, that engine on the Frisco Lines; or "Big Boy" on the Union Pacific. The fiddle whined a long coyote howl, like them critters, but more like the whistle on the Warren and Ouachita Valley road, makin' notches across Calhoun County, Arkansas. Young Buster Prather tickled his banjo to Cousin Drewey's swing of the bow, in time with our kinfolks' tap of the foot. Uncle Posey Burwinkle called "The Ocean Wave," and he called so loud the sea next to Port Sabine, Texas, ached to stir up a hurricane.

Wave that ocean, wave that sea,

> *Wave my true love back to me.*
> *Circle eight 'til you get all straight.*
> *Swing them ladies!*

All through the evenin' after folks had stuffed their guts and whittled the vittles down, the music sparked our warmer-than-natural November air. The dance platform thumped like fifty carpenters hit it with hammers, 'cause the foot-action was that potent. There were men wearin' boots, the cowboy breed. There were men shod with farm-heavy shoes. There was the dainty tap of the women's heels.

> *First by the right, then by the wrong,*
> *Now your partner and carry her along,*
> *Wave the ocean, wave the sea.*

Over by the skyline we heard the thunder rumble. Thataway west, where the big storms come from.

The dresses were bright, the finest the ladies owned. The frills were there. There was red and green, white and blue, yeller and eye-dazzlin' orange. There were young and younger, middle aged, slightly elderly, mothers and grandmaws, girls and boys from the high school. Chasin' 'round were little old mop-heads, feisty-pants bullet-heads. And standin' 'round were fellers' sweethearts, with the fellers holdin' on tight for fear they'd get away.

> *Wave 'em up and wave 'em down,*
> *Wave 'em all the way 'round and 'round,*
> *Wave the ocean, wave the sea,*
> *Wave my true love back to me.*

There were men's wives and widows. There were men bound to matrimony, others free like wind from the west. And of the west they were, wearin' western re-

COUSIN DREWEY & THE HOLY TWISTER 361

fineries, westerners measured by the most exact digits. They wore big hats, monstrous of crown and far-reachin' brim. Their belts were alive with neat's-foot oil, the buckles glistenin' in the weak sunlight. Their pants were tight-legged, their shirts so neat, their neckties bowed or danglin'. They were cowboys, stockmen all, not a jellybean in the pack. The farmers were fat or lean, tall or short in their clean-laundered overalls. Some were droop-seated like farmers' overalls sometimes get.

The sky, not so bright, stretched high above the square dance.

The music plastered the quiet country air.

And Uncle Posey Burwinkle called the circle right and circle left, promenade and how-dee-do. Cousin Drewey's fiddle talked plains and mountain language— and Young Buster Prather kept his banjo in tune.

But, doggone it, they needed a guitar, or best a hand to tickle Cousin Drewey's guitar that lay atop the musician's stand. Idle, silent, 'cause there wasn't a man in the whole three hundred who could make that instrument speak. And the guitar-picker's chair was empty of any kind of joyful enterprise.

Us Lowdermilks were standin' by ourse'fs, Pap and Maw Maw and me. We were watchin' the dance-bugs circle the platform, we hear'd Cousin Drewey give his fiddle some percolation. Of a sudden Pap looked up at the sky, then down to the level of the earth. He said, "Newt, do you see what I see? Do you hear somethin' loud and raucous?"

I said, "Pap, I can see them pretty girls swish their skirts while they make livin' glory of their legs, I can hear Cousin Drewey make sawdust of his fiddle."

Then we both saw Maw Maw look to the gate into Old Man Lee Bassett's yard. And we heard her say, "Praise the Lord! He taketh away, and doggone if He don't give back again."

He came in ridin' the prowl-car, old Mike Stover, our

new and upright sheriff. He had his siren howlin', his dome light flashed red like the brimstone of Sodom and Gomorrah, his brakes squealed as he stopped on a dime and scattered the crowd next to the dance platform.

He was the sheriff, all right, newly elected. And he had some plunder to deliver.

When Mike Stover got out of his prowl-car, folks caught his blessed presence and ran over to see what'all in heaven's name he had on the seat next to him.

Mike Stover's face beamed like a waxed apple under his John B. Stetson hat. He kindly opened the prowl-car door, and. . . .

Hell! Anybody with eyesight could see who Mike had with him . . . All the way from Glasscock County, Texas! So everybody said "Doggone!"

Old Man Lee Bassett pushed his way through the folks and he pumped Cowboy's hand like a long-lost prodigal son, slapped that no'count's back before he'd slid halfway out of the door. Cowboy smiled happy at everybody, then choked after swallowin' spit from so much back-slappin'.

"Hell-fire, Cowboy," Old Man Lee gave his greetin', speakin' for everybody in Star Valley. "What'all you doin' down this way? We figgered you'd gone to ticklin' a guitar up and down the North Concho, or up pleasin' musical customers in Big Spring. What you doin' on my farm, Cowboy, son?"

Cowboy didn't say, so the sheriff said for him. "He came back to the county seat, down yonder, forty miles south. I didn't know he was in town 'til he went to tryin' on shoes in Culp's gent's outfittin' store. Which was all right, except Mr. Culp was nowhere 'round. It was midnight, and Cowboy got in through a skylight. That's when the burglar alarm went off."

When Cousin Drewey saw Cowboy in our midst, he kindly laid his fiddle down, jumped off the stand and ran to love Cowboy's neck.

"Lord bless you, Cowboy," our kinfolks said. "I reckon old Mike let you out of jail for the time bein', so's to he'p us out with the guitar."

The sheriff cut off Cousin Drewey's talk. He said, "And that ain't all. You just wait and see what's comin' up the road. I caught 'em in town just as they were fixin' to move on to Hollywood, California. I told them how you folks were stompin' out a hoe-down. They're hellbound for a contest out yonder. They said how a hoe-down in Star Valley would be mighty fine practice. 'Cause they come all the way from Lubbock in the good old Lone Star State."

And Mike Stover had no sooner finished his talk when a big yeller school bus came rockin' into the yard, it piled with baggage atop. And on its side was painted with black letters:

SOUTH PLAINS OLD TIME
FIDDLERS ASSOCIATION

Well, the fellers emptied that bus like so many honey bees out from a hive. There were two dozen, some packin' fiddles, others guitars. Five of them fellers had French harps in their hands, another four jew's harps. They were really and truly a happy busload of musical men.

"I told you'all people how Mike Stover would make the best sheriff this county ever had," shouted a lady in the assembly. "I told you, and that's all there is to it."

Cowboy filled the empty chair after Cousin Drewey gave him his guitar. The Texas boys took their places and the music went 'round and 'round. The tunes went up, the tunes went down—and punishment of the dance floor went on and on.

Who'all was in the dance? . . . Well, Clyde and Lilybelle, Sonny Boy and Verbaline Lou. They were there to match the folks for good looks. Old Man Lee

Bassett pranced like a Percheron, his wife did her best for a heavy woman. There was Orville Klingsinger and Virgie, Shorty Flack and Snookie Hapchester, Venus and Zenus Langley, old Rooster, and Tobe the cowboy from Shingle Butte. They were the good folks of valley and town, not a sonofabitch on the floor, 'cause the First National Bank stayed away.

And where was us Lowdermilks?

The prophet Amos spoke the truth, so I'll speak the truth of Amos. We weren't aset in the sidelines, lookin' sour, glum, mean, bashful, full of hate. 'Cause we were *up on the floor,* where Pap led off the docee-do.

And who was his armload when Uncle Posey Burwinkle called the promenade? Maw Maw, that's who, that old gal whose shoes put dents in the pine dance floor. Neither had square-danced, or danced at all, since the time long ago when they blessed Oklahoma with their rural citizenships.

Pap pranced and bowed to the ladies; he'd make a half-right here and full-left there, while Maw Maw's skirt swirled 'round her hockers. Under the visor of her sunbonnet folks could see how she was right proud.

And where was I? Well, I had an armload of pretty girl, and Lord, was she proud of me!

So the hoe-down went on, straddlin' sundown into the night. The vittles table got emptier and emptier, and Pap made hash of the cake Lilybelle made specially for him, it with PAP writ in icin'.

Virgie Klingsinger, who hashed alongside Mistress Langley at the table, who fed Pap hunks of cake one after t'other, whispered in Mistress Langley's ear, "He's gonna git sicker'n a horse." But Pap didn't get sick that night. 'Cause he was havin' a good time, never miserable like he was in the shanty, and 'cause his shotgun was five miles away.

Never before in Cousin Drewey's remembrance did he saw his fiddle as he did—what with the South Plains Old

Time Fiddlers Association to he'p him out, and Cowboy, and Young Buster Prather, and the powerful glottis of Uncle Posey Burwinkle. . . . Altogether, eleven fiddles, six guitars, one banjo, five French harps, four jew's harps, made the potentest musical assembly ever to percolate melody west of Yell County, Arkansas. In the light of twenty coal-oil lanterns we stomped "The Ocean Wave," chased the "Chase That Rabbit." The young folks hug-danced some, the fiddlers sawed and the guitars got theirse'fs picked, Young Buster Prather did the best he could. We wished for moonlight, but there was no moon that night. As any musical man knows, there's nothin' sweeter than five French harps and four jew's harps playin' in the moonlight, that's how come we all wished for moonlight.

To ease our feet and he'p us to josh some, Snookie Hapchester stood up next to Cowboy's guitar and sang us "The Strawberry Roan." Like that rounder named Rooster said to Shorty Glack how Snookie had better stick to ridin' the pissle-tails and leave singin' about them to Jimmie Rodgers. About midnight the fiddlers gave us "Oklahoma Farewell," and in the dark before daylight the whole dad-blamed force nigh burst our hearin' with "San Antonio Rose"—that in honor of the big state shaped like the horn of plenty, home ground of ninety-five percent of the whiskers and sunbonnets there at Cousin Drewey's farewell hoe-down.

Farewell, did I say?

The dance broke up and everybody loved each other's necks. It was still dark, soon to dawn. But there'd be no dawn that day, not like most mornin's in old Star Valley. The air was thick and wet 'round us, and it looked like we'd quit just in time. The sprinkles were settin' in. When we all pulled out for home the world 'round us was as black as the tail-end of a coalie. Cousin Drewey smelled the air like it was cherry wine.

It took Clyde's Chivvelee and Sonny Boy's pickup to

haul us Lowdermilks home to the shanty. Pap and Maw Maw and me rode with Clyde, also Cousin Drewey and his instruments. Only this time we had Verbaline Lou and SH with us. Sonny Boy followed with his wife and kids. It was still dark when we pulled up front of the porch—so shy of light that it seemed like a warm wet hell was there to punish us Lowdermilks for our sins, right on our own home ground.

Sonny Boy was ready to pull out for the ranch, hollerin' for Clyde to keep close behind him, old Clyde with my sister and the baby. Factways, he'd already yelled "You'all come!" But somethin' held him back, even forced him to shut off the motor.

It was a somethin' that knew the situation. . . .

Was feared by it—for us Lowdermilks and the Skinners. . . .

Was filled with glory by it. . . .

For it was his joy and salvation. . . .

And that somethin' was Cousin Drewey.

We could see by the headlights how Cousin Drewey had jumped out from Clyde's car and run out to the drizzlin' rain like it was his own breath of life. He faced the east, the skyline toward Texas that was as black and blank to the Lowdermilk vision as nothin' else in the world. We all said to ourse'fs, "What the hell!"

Then he turned to the even darker west and drew the dirty air up through his sniffers. In the light, like the brightness was tailormade for him, we saw him raise his arms like a preacher in benediction. We could see the happy gleam in his eyes, brighter than the headlights. He looked like some feller in the Bible while he prophesied in the Land of Judah. Then he turned to us folks still in the cars, he beckoned us to come out, like to some feast of goodness and plenty.

"I tell you folks," Clyde said as we all got out in the mud, "I *do* believe Cousin Drewey is plumb craze."

But we watched and listened to Cousin Drewey. We watched him point to the east, then to the west, we saw him dance for the joy that was in his heart, for the thankfulness to the Lord for the salvation that would be provided this day. SH, the baby, was asleep in Verbaline Lou's arms, but the balance of us was highly awake, gapin' at Cousin Drewey, not believin' our eyes or ears.

"Smell it, it's beautiful," he yelled to us through the wet fog. "I've smelled it before, back in the Washtaw Mountains, once down by the Cross Timbers, another time near Wewoka in Seminole County. This is twister weather, it belongs in Oklahoma, that dear sweet heaven of the Lord. Soon you'all folks will hear it comin', a plume out of dark cloud, roarin' like a stampede of bulls. It will pack waybilled freight for Pushmataha County, where two Uncle Gershes will claim it, wagon it to the Washtaws from the depot in Antlers, fiddlin' as it goes. . . ."

"He's crazed like a hoot-owl," Pap said.

But Cousin Drewey paid no mind to Pap, his ears weren't open to doubtful talk. It was time to get ready, to saddle Jeff and fix him for the trip. To pick up his satchel and call the hound dogs to come get a feed of glory. He had his fiddle in the case, he could swing the guitar over his back and he'd already done buckled on his hog-leg forty-five.

"Give it two hours, no more," Cousin Drewey prophesied. "It's acomin' from the west, on time. It's a tornado, a holy twister. . . .

"Straight out of the Book of Job. . . .

"Chapter one. . . .

"Verse nineteen. . . .

"Amen, kinfolks."

Amen.

31

Maw Maw and Verbaline Lou went into the shanty, packin' SH. Lilybelle and her kids followed, leavin' us menfolks outside with the automobiles to gas about the weather, to say out loud how Cousin Drewey didn't know a twister from a dose of lightnin' and rain. But I did confess how the lightnin' was gettin' closer, the thunder rumblin' like a big old bear. It was brightenin' in the east. Sonny Boy said: "Look, you'all, it's daylight breakin' as sure as hell."

We got in Clyde's Chivvelee, us five, just to wait and see what'all. One thing you can say about Lowdermilks, we've got sense enough to come in out of the wet.

"It's gettin' daylight, all right," Sonny Boy said. "It's a Montaig County daylight if I ever saw one. It's fixin' to stir up somethin'; and if that somethin' ain't powerful enough to blow us over to Thackerville, then I ain't the kind of man born in tornado country."

"It's sunup of a sweet holy twister day," Cousin Drewey said. "It's the day when this old mossback aims to wish you Skinners and Lowdermilks a kindly fare-you-well."

"Lord save us," I said.

"All you fellers got asses," Pap Lowdermilk said. "And you all set in blue mud. You don't know nothin'."

It was still dark, but through the lamplit window of the shanty we could see Maw Maw fussin' 'round next to my sister and Lilybelle, and Lilybelle's kids. I knew what she was sayin', though I couldn't hear a word.

She was sayin', "People, I know a twister when it's comin' our way, Cousin Drewey says so, so you better mind his words."

Myse'f, I took some stock of what we had on the Lowdermilk place, what we'd lose if the twister struck us smack-on. There was the shanty, its porch and lean-to. Our beds in the big room, though it wasn't so mighty big. There were three of 'em, with blankets and all. There was the heater and the coal-oil lamp, the Bible and Sears and Roebuck catalogue. The trunk that held our Sunday clothes. Four rickety chairs—a shelf of do-hunkuses, like purgatives, ointments, a clock that didn't work anymore. Me and Pap's razor and strop, and a hair-comb we all used.

Verbaline Lou had taken all her plunder up to the ranch, so the Lord was good to her that way. In the lean-to was the table where we ate, four chairs, the cookstove, the stand where sat the face-wash basin and soap, the water bucket and dipper, the roller towel that dried all us Lowdermilks and Cousin Drewey. And the shelves and covered barrels that kept the vittles away from the bugs. Away from the pesky ants and scorpions. Maw Maw had pictures on the wall that Verbaline Lou once ordered from the catalogue, like a lonely wolf in the snow. There was nothin' on the porch except two rockin' chairs. Their seats and skids had seen better days. And I knew dog-good how the two cats were asleep on the beds, 'cause even Samson wasn't strong enough to keep them off. It's the way cats act.

Yonder was the corral where old Jeff stood droop-necked over a low stack of fodder. The barn was packed solid with milo maize, kaffir, bean hay. The cribs were loaded with corn, shelled or still in the ear. The two milk cows were nowhere about. I figgered they were out in the patch pullin' on the corn stubble. Or maybe off aways on the grass, down where the gate opened to the road.

Cousin Drewey's box elder tree had, set 'round it, his satchel and musical man's spangled cowboy pants. It and the fancy jacket. They hung from a limb, gettin' wet. The green-topped boots were wrapped in a blanket, rolled against the tree trunk. The two hound-dogs stayed mostly 'round Cousin Drewey's pallet, but now they knew how their best friend was in Clyde's Chivvelee. So they came up and smelled 'round. Jeff's harness and my saddle hung in the barn. Yonder was the woodpile of cedar, juniper and piñon that Cousin Drewey and me had worked so hard to bring in. And Maw Maw's big iron wash pot.

Pap's stock of old automobile tires was front of the shanty up agin the porch. Prime love-junk for Pap. The axe and file sat close by. Yonder was the dugout that stored Maw Maw's garden truck—potatoes, turnips and cabbage. A mighty slim supply this year. And back of the dugout was the hogpen where two old pigs grunted and squealed while they fussed at each other. Any man knows how hogs *do* fuss.

So it stood plain to me, as I sat thinkin' in the Chivvelee, how even if the twister took all we owned up to the sky, swirled it 'round and dumped it on Muleshoe, Texas, us Lowdermilks would have nothin' much to lose. We hoped naturally that we'd get our bodies and souls out of the way.

The rain quit when daylight took over Star Valley. Now we could see all 'round us, for mile after mile. Cousin Drewey pushed open the Chivvelee door, got out on the Lord's naked dirt. It took him five seconds flat. He looked west, cupped his hands 'round his eyesight.

COUSIN DREWEY & THE HOLY TWISTER

He looked west like a man at the Signal Rock depot, when a train is headin' in and he knows he's there to meet and greet an old friend. Cousin Drewey was talkin' to hisse'f, sayin', "Thank you, Lord, for this great sunrise. And may Your lovin' friendship be with me every mile of the way."

In less time than it takes to spit a comet, Clyde and Sonny Boy was out there with him, lookin' west. That's when Sonny Boy hollered, "Good God Almighty!"

Sonny Boy said that 'cause the sky was a mess like we'd never seen it before. Sickly streamers of gray clouds mixed up with yeller-green sky, and big heavy black clouds bumped agin the other. It was the damnedest sight a man could witness.

Clyde made tracks for the shanty. He had to fix somethin', somethin' to do with the womenfolks. 'Cause Lilybelle and Verbaline Lou were in there, and the kids, both Clyde's and Sonny Boy's. All the love two cattlemen could have was packed there in that shanty. But before Clyde could make the porch, Maw Maw was out to render speculation on the sky above.

"Lord save us!" she yelled in a womanly way. Then she said in our direction, "People, I was raised in the Washtaw Mountains, and I know a twister when it's on its way. I do believe we'd better go sleep 'til it's over, and we'd better take that shut-eye in the dugout."

While Clyde fussed 'round the shanty, Pap came out of the Chivvelee, onto the mud. He was dancin' 'round like a wild Comanche fixed to raid the settlers in the Pease River Valley.

"I've done changed my mind," he ranted like a silly old coot-rooster. "There's a cloud makin' funnel yonder. I cain't see it, but it's somewheres. And I reckon that somewheres is near."

My sister and Lilybelle followed Clyde out of the shanty. The kids hollered and danced for fun. Verbaline

Lou was scared out of her flimsy britches, she held onto SH like the wind might take him away. . . . But there wasn't any wind yet.

"Brother," Clyde said to Sonny Boy. "You better take the womenfolks up to the ranch, and do it in a hurry. You drive the Chivvelee and Lilybelle can take the pickup. Divide the kids the way you like. I know a twister when I smell one, like you can, and there ain't no tellin' where this one will hit. So git, dear brother, and make it sudden."

Clyde yelled to round up the womenfolks. Lilybelle showed sense by runnin' for the pickup-truck, the kids pilin' in the back. Sonny Boy was already in the Chivvelee, callin' for Maw Maw and Verbaline Lou to come quick with SH.

"I know these meddlesome things from Montaig County," Clyde said to Sonny Boy. "I'll stay with Pap and Newt. When the twister hits, it will pass in no time at all. It might hit here or anywheres else. We'll be snug in the dugout, with the door shut. Watch where we are from the ranch, and when it's passed come down with the vehicles and pick up our remnants."

Verbaline Lou was gettin' into Sonny Boy's car, but all sudden she stopped in her tracks. She looked at Maw Maw and decided different. She looked at Clyde. She said nothin'.

"I ain't goin'," Maw Maw said. "I'm stayin' with my man."

Maw Maw stood her ground with folded arms under her sunbonnet strings.

"He's my lovin' man," she said.

Verbaline Lou stayed outside the Chivvelee, lookin' silly. SH yelled bloody hell 'cause she squeezed him too much. None of us knew what the hell to do just then, until Cousin Drewey stepped up among us from his admiration of the sky. He had somethin' to say.

He said, "Lowdermilks and Skinners, you'd better git in your own direction. If Maw Maw cain't be made to go, then let her stay. Verbaline Lou, she can stay too. I talked of my admiration when I put the Recknagel beef in the dugout that day after old Fats hurt my feelin's. I knew the glory of it when I got even with him by feedin' you Lowdermilks the best supper you ever had. That's when I said it from the wisdom in my head, how that dugout is the best cyclone shelter west of the Oklahoma line. They ain't got none better in Tulsa. But take the advice of a musical man, do what you got to do and do it quick. I can smell the twister but I cain't see it comin', yet. It's only when you *hear* it; that's when you pray for the preservation of your mortal bodies. That's when you go in the dugout and shut the door."

"I'm stayin' with Maw Maw," Verbaline Lou said, with SH yellin' like he needed a change of didies. "And I'm stayin' with my man."

Then all hell broke loose in the Lowdermilk yard. Pap had the dugout door open while Lilybelle and Sonny Boy drove off with the vehicles, after Cousin Drewey unloaded his guitar and fiddle. Verbaline Lou made a bed for SH down in the dugout and gave him a pacifier. The big boy baby cooed like the nearest twister was east-side of Kansas. Maw Maw rescued the Bible and catalogue from the shanty, Pap got down his shotgun.

We couldn't see Cousin Drewey nowheres, but we figgered he was doin' what he had to do. I got the axe and file from the woodpile, and picked up Maw Maw's black wash pot on the way. Maw Maw was comin' out with an armload of woman-things, like a change of dresses and drawers. Pap was dancin' 'round his stack of automobile tires, askin' the Lord what to do. Verbaline Lou came out of the shanty with the cats. I looked 'round for Pee-Dog and Bitchy-Damn, but they were nowheres to be seen. The chickens, all six of them, had come out at daylight to scratch up some business, but Maw Maw was chasin them back in the hen house. In no time at all she came out with them kickin' and squawkin' in a gunnysack.

Factways, all we could pick up in a hurry was stashed in the dugout—cats, shotgun, axe, file, woman-do-dads, chickens-in-a-sack, the Bible and Sears and Roebuck. Now it was time for Pap and me to grab a hog apiece and wrestle them into the dugout. After that I'd go get my saddle and ridin' gear, 'cause I didn't crave to have the wind take it all away.

And to go find Cousin Drewey.

'Cause we couldn't see Cousin Drewey, the hounds or the fiddle anywheres 'round. Or the guitar. We all wondered where'all Cousin Drewey was at.

Pap hollered to Maw Maw and Verbaline Lou. "You'all ladies, get next to that big boy baby sweetness down the shelter. Newt and me are fixin' to chouse old Jeff and the milk cows t'other side of the corn patch. They got cow-sense and mule-sense, so they'll know how to git away from that big old black twister."

So Maw Maw and Verbaline Lou did what Pap said to do.

I made hasty tracks to the corral so's to chouse old Jeff out the gate and tell him to use his mule-sense. Mules like Jeff can always duck tornadoes. We figgered the two milk cows were out in the corn patch. Bein' cows they didn't aim to be took away. Pap was next to me on the run. He craved to he'p. I had to pee mighty bad, 'cause I'd drunk too damned much pink drink at the shindig. I was fixed to tend the low rail of the corral, with an ache like I was ready to drown, when Pap got to the corral-gate first. I heard him yell, "What'all you doin', you old mossback? Ain't you got a lick of sense?"

It was talk that got me out of the pee-notion. I didn't even get down to unhookin' my fly. I just gave mind to Pap.

COUSIN DREWEY & THE HOLY TWISTER 375

"Look there, Newt," Pap called to me. "It's Cousin Drewey."

We went through the gate. In the corral was our kinfolks, and he was saddlin' old Jeff. He pulled the cinch and buckled the latigo with *my* saddle aset on the back and girth of *Pap*'s mule. The two hounds were next to him, waitin'. You can tell by a hound dog's face what he's got on his mind, and these two were rarin' for a hunt of some kind. Cousin Drewey had his satchel aset next to the barn, and his fiddle in the case, and the naked guitar. Pap and me knew for sure how he had his belt and hog-leg forty-five under his jumper-jacket. He held Copenhagen behind his under-lip, 'cause it dripped some. He said nothin' while he saddled the mule. But just for the time bein'. He was a musical man, so he sure as hell had a mountain song ticklin' his glottis. But the song stayed down in his glottis.

"You gone craze, Cousin Drewey?" Pap said.

"Ain't craze," our kinfolks told Pap.

"Where'all you goin', old settler?"

"I'm goin' home to the Washtaw Mountains."

"Ridin' old Jeff?"

"Part of the way. After we get let off the cloud at Antlers. We'll ride the twister from here to that Kiamishi town, but me and the hounds will need old Jeff to haul us up t'other side of Crum Creek, where we'll say howdy to the Uncle Gershes, good Democrats both."

Pap said, "Cousin Drewey, I once knew two fellers who took their own lives 'cause they didn't have better sense. One used a shotgun, t'other a hang-rope. Now I'm lookin' at another silly sonofabitch."

Cousin Drewey didn't say a damn thing. 'Cause he'd finished saddlin' the mule. I had to go to the corral rail 'cause I'd took on considerable pink drink. Cousin Drewey did the same thing; he had to go or drown.

"Newt," Cousin Drewey said while we wet together that old pine pole. "I ain't craze, 'cause I'm goin' home.

I hate to take your saddle, but I hear'd the Skinner boys tell how you'd get a new one when you ride for them on the ranch. I ain't makin' no excuses for Pap's mule or the hound dogs 'cause Pap don't love them nohow. But I love them, and they'll be ridin' with me to the Washtaw Mountains."

So I hooked up my fly and Cousin Drewey did the same.

Pap stood like a sull mule while Cousin Drewey picked up the guitar and tied it to the off-side saddle-string. Pap stayed sull when our kinfolks made his satchel tight on the near-side saddle-string. And he kept sull with ire when Cousin Drewey hooked the fiddle in its case over the saddle horn. All that, and he didn't recover sweetness when Cousin Drewey led old Jeff out the corral-gate. The two dogs trailed at the mule's heels.

"Where you headin', you prime lunatic?" Pap called after Cousin Drewey.

Cousin Drewey paid him no mind. He just kept leadin' Jeff up next to the dugout. Me and Pap kept behind. Pap marveled at our kinfolks' silliness, but deep in my mind I knew Cousin Drewey knew what he aimed to do. Clyde was workin' on the dugout door, fixin' it to stoutness, makin'g sure the storm wouldn't tear it away. Maw Maw and Verbaline Lou came out to see Cousin Drewey stop front of where they were at.

Our kinfolks didn't talk, and the women only gaped for surprise. Clyde said, "What the hell?" And all together we watched Cousin Drewey drop Jeff's bridle-reins, to let the mule stand while he went to the shanty. He came back packin' a chair, one of them we sat on when we ate supper in the lean-to.

"You ain't goin' off with my chair," Pap hollered, dancin' like a coot slobberin' Brown's Mule, a man so loaded with ire that his mind packed scant reason.

Cousin Drewey put down the chair next to Jeff and

COUSIN DREWEY & THE HOLY TWISTER 377

the dogs. Jeff stood quiet, full of sanity. The dogs just waited for the trip, sparked-up with their tongues hung out.

Cousin Drewey spat Copenhagen so's to clear his glottis. Not for a song, but to give us Skinners and Lowdermilks a sweet fare-you-well. He stood facin' us like a preacher front of a lovin' congregation.

"You'all kinfolks," he began sayin'. "I stand here like a man, humbled and grateful, with all the gear I own packed on this mule, with the love of two dogs at my heels, with my vehicle bound for the Washtaw Mountains comin' closer by the minute, black and crawlin', tearin' up the dirt, full of wind and destruction, the Lord's own wrath in a funnel of His holy might. Let Him be, people, 'cause this old mossback is gettin' a promise fulfilled, an exodus like the Lord gave Moses out of Egypt, across the Red Sea with a herd of trailin' Israelites headin' for the Land of Canaan. And like you know, sweet Skinners and Lowdermilks, the Washtaw Mountains is really and truly the slashpine and clear creeks of Canaan."

When Cousin Drewey talked Canaan it put sparks in Pap's he'pmeet.

"Praise the goats of the Tribe of Reuben!" Maw Maw hollered, a woman caught with a dose of religion.

"I'm leavin' you now, like I said I'd do two, maybe three years ago," Cousin Drewey said. "That evenin' I first saw your sweet and dear faces, when I first gave you a Washtaw Mountain song, when I sawed a tune on the fiddle. I told you then how I was three score and ten years, the right days and years allowed us humans by the Lord's command, 'cause after that age we're like the flowers of the field, we just dry up and fade away."

"You're goin' to live with us a long, long time, Cousin Drewey, 'cause we love you so," Verbaline Lou said. She had one eye on our kinfolks and the other aimed at

SH, that big boy baby done gone to sleep in the dugout.

"I aim to live six, maybe seven years more," Cousin Drewey went on. "Or maybe ten or fourteen if the Lord says it's all right with Him. But I don't need any more of your Star Valley, of your dry creeks and yeller grass, of your clouds that don't make rain—except for just this time so's the Promise can be fulfilled. I'm takin' along this chair, it which I sat on when I ate greens and okra with you'all Lowdermilks. I aim to set it on the deck of the cloud, right over that big old funnel. Old Jeff, saddled and ready, will stand drop-reined aside me, and the two hounds will snuggle their noses up agin my knees. I'll set in the chair and fiddle my way, or sometimes I'll tickle the guitar; and once I might sing 'Job's Boils.' But main thing, me and mine will be ridin' the twister for Pushmataha County."

Clyde said, "You bet."

But Pap was ired, and he said, "He's crazed like Nebuchadnezzar when that poor man ate grass."

Cousin Drewey picked up the chair and held it with his left hand. With his right he took hold of Jeff's bridle-reins.

"I aim to leave you now, dear kinfolks," he said, and I knew how a tear might be leakin' from his eye. Like Maw Maw and Verbaline Lou, who wept and hugged each other's necks. "But I leave you with love and happiness, 'cause I know you're goin' to a better life, just like me. We can hear the twister now, and it's tearin' up the ground slightly to the west. It's a holy one for sure."

Lord! Was the sky black with fury in the direction to where Cousin Drewey said the storm should be. The clouds were collidin' one agin the other, the lightnin' was scarin' us out of our wits, and the rain made cloudburst. But most noise came from the funnel that lifted the earth, tossed it 'round like a man forks hay. It bellowed like a thousand black bulls.

But all that raucous was goin' on yonderly west. Where we stood it was quiet like nothin' would happen. A cloud leaked some sprinkles, but not enough to wet a jackrabbit.

"Farewell, Cousin Drewey," Maw Maw said after she'd got loose from Verbaline Lou's neck, when we all watched Cousin Drewey take off for the corn patch with his mule, dogs and chair. Went like he aimed to get in line with the tornado. "Farewell, and may the Lord set you down near Antlers. May you ride old Jeff up the Kiamishi into soft green hills. And tell them Uncle Gershes how we love them both."

Clyde had his eyesight west. "That cloud there," he said to us Lowdermilks. "Yonder's the one that's gonna drop a funnel."

We watched and saw Cousin Drewey stop just about middle of the corn patch. He sat the chair down so's to face east, took time to get the legs straight on the dirt; like a man does when he looks 'round for a seat in the chair-car on the Frisco Lines. He led Jeff 'round so's to look east, a mule drop-reined and waitin' for a ride. Lord, it broke our hearts to watch! Then Cousin Drewey reached up to the saddle and got his fiddle out of the case. He rosined the bow and called the hound dogs to set at his feet. It's sweet to look at a mountain fiddler with hound dogs asettin' at his feet, rosinin' his bow. After he pocketed the rosin Cousin Drewey put the fiddle to his chin. He got set in the chai, and he sawed, and he sawed, and he sawed.

No tellin' what his tune was, but it could have been "Old Dan Tucker."

Clyde said, "Skinners and Lowdermilks, you'all better take a look at this old place afore we go in for cover. Look 'round, and bid it a fond fare-you-well. 'Cause we won't see the Lowdermilk shanty no more."

So we all looked 'round. The shanty stood ready for

wreckin', and next to it was Pap's stack of automobile tires. Behind the shanty was Cousin Drewey's box elder tree, with his pallet rolled up agin it and his spangled musical-cowboy's outfit hangin' from the limb. Then down apiece ran the barb-wire fence. T'other side of the patch was where Cousin Drewey sat and fiddled.

But up the slope aways was the dugout which would be our salvation, next to which we stood at the time; and the woodpile where us menfolks used to set and gas. And the barn and corral, and all our farm do-hunkuses like the wagon, plow, middle-buster and go-devil. And the hog pen empty of the two pigs. And the chicken house. And the place with the pit, where we sat of cold nights and hot days, *it* with the rickety door.

"So long, old place," Maw Maw said, weepin', "we'll see you in the sweet bye-and-bye."

"It makes me feel sad," I said to Clyde.

"It makes me happy," Clyde said, back at me. "Lou wants her daddy and mamma up at the ranch, so's they can know what civilization feels like afore they die. Only a tornado has power enough to move Pap Lowdermilk up that way."

Verbaline Lou choked of sadness. She couldn't say anythin'. She kept her eyesight mostly on Cousin Drewey.

Old Pap Lowdermilk was too mean and ugly. He just growled like a bear and spat some cud.

Down in the dugout we could hear the damnedest racket. The chickens squawked in the gunnysack, the cats yowled like cats do, the pigs squealed like they were gettin' stuck. And above the entire hullabaloo SH screamed out his lungs for he'p. He needed his pacifier or a change of didies.

The women made tracks to he'p SH out, duckin' down the low doorway to the space underground. That left just me and Clyde and Pap outside. All three, we

COUSIN DREWEY & THE HOLY TWISTER 381

gave a look at Cousin Drewey. Out there our kinfolks fiddled music with his chin, hand and bow. He didn't pack mind for us'ns.

"Here she comes," Clyde hollered of asudden. "She's makin' funnel. And may the Lord have mercy on Cousin Drewey's soul."

All three, we watched the cloud's tail come down to hit ground, while over our heads it began to get dark as night. Never in my days have I hear'd such a roarin', hell-fire bust-up of the world, while the twister ate its dinner of Star Valley earth. Too, we knew how all Star Valley, even the folks in Signal Rock, were lookin' our way and they said while they looked, "Them Lowdermilks, they're gonna git hit by that old twister."

Clyde, Pap and me, we took one last look at Cousin Drewey and the mule and the hound dogs. Then we ducked for the dugout and shut the door behind us.

Maw Maw had rescued the coal-oil lamp from off the lean-to table, and now it lit up the dugout. It was settin' on a wooden box next to the turnips. Verbaline Lou had shut up SH's hollerin' by swingin' him in her arms agin her motherly breast. Soon she'd haul out a bubby and give him dinner. And the pigs and chickens didn't squeal and squawk so much now that they had human company. The cats got off someplace where it was dark and hid like cats naturally do. Only the storm outside was actin' like a bunch of Comanches in the Pease River Valley.

Lord!

"I know these here twisters," Pap said, hunkerin' on his hockers. "This one ain't hit yet. When it does we'll know it."

That's a fact, I reckoned to myse'f, we'll know it all right.

Maw Maw said to me, aset on the dirt floor, "Newt, what you reckon Cousin Drewey's fiddlin', him out there alone with old Jeff and the dogs?"

"He's fiddlin' a tune, Maw Maw. Maybe the one they sing up there in the Missouri Ozarks, and it's sad and full of love and murder."

"You reckon it's about that jealous lover, Newt?"

"You bet it is, Maw Maw."

"You cain't sing like Cousin Drewey," Maw Maw said, "'cause you ain't a musical man. But maybe if you'll sing it to us the best you can, it'll limber our tight feelin's some. By the time that jealous lover cuts his dear one's heart from out her ribs, the twister will've passed and the storm long-gone."

So I did the best I could. And only Maw Maw paid me mind. The song was the best to sing in a tornado.

Down by yon weepin' willow,
Where the violets gently bloom,
There sleeps our young Florilla
So silent in the tomb.

Like I said, only Maw Maw paid me mind. Verbaline Lou was dancin' SH up and down in her arms, and swayin' him yonderly and thataway, like a Hawaiian hoochie-coochie dancer, only slower while she percolated her rusty. She was tellin' her big boy baby how he was so sweet she could eat him up. Clyde was hunkered down next to Pap while they gassed about tornadoes.

Clyde said, "I once got caught in one on the Pease River, north of Vernon. It was s sure-enough Texas big-un. It had five funnels, all doin' duty. Lord, was the world black! They took ten people to the hospital in Wichita Falls, and one old man was dead when he got there. He didn't know what hit him. They counted twenty-nine hurt ones. It put seventy-five people out of house and home so they fed 'em and bedded 'em down in the Baptist church. Pap Lowdermilk, you cain't tell what an old twister will do."

"You sure cain't, Clyde," Pap said. "I seen aplenty in the Washtaw Mountain country and none of them acted natural, 'cept to leave dust and wreckage. Once I got caught in a twister on the Clear Boggy near Tushka. That old twister picked up a straw stack and sent it asail in the sky, and it landed in the trees 'round the courthouse in Atoka. Was it spread out on the ground like you'd put hay to dry? Like hell it was! 'Cause all them bits of straw were stuck in the tree trunks like pins in a pin-cushion. It was the damnedest sight, and every sonofabitch for miles 'round came to see. If I was rich, I'd have bought them trees and took 'em 'round in a carnival. I'd be a millionaire today if I'd done that there. I wouldn't be settin' in this dugout talkin' to a silly horse's ass like you."

The wind was tearin' up the world outside. The dugout roof was so heavy with dirt that we couldn't hear its punishment, but the way the rain pounded the door it seemed like the Lord was ridin' over Egypt.

'Twas on a Sunday evenin'
When early fell the dew,
Up to her cottage window
Her jealous lover drew.

Down on her knees before him
She pleaded for her life,
But in her snow-white bosom
He plunged the fatal knife.

Maw Maw choked for grief when I finished my song, so I had to smack her on the back.

"It's done hit!" Clyde hollered. Lord save us Lowdermilks and Skinners! "Lou, cover that big boy baby with the blanket, and everybody lie out flat."

"Lord save us," Maw Maw prayed, and in the lamplight I could see her hands hoisted to heaven, just before she went flat.

Just as quick as the tornado hit us—maybe fifteen seconds, no more—it passed over the dugout and set the weather to actin' civilized. "Well," Clyde said, as we all got up from the dirt floor, "I reckon that's that."

He was the first to go frontways to open the door. Clyde pushed, me and Pap he'ped him, but the door wasn't easy to open. The wreckage of a mile 'round seemed laid on top. We bust it with our triple strength and daylight shone through. First Clyde went out, then me, and lastly old Pap. The country stank, and what we saw wasn't pretty.

We saw the good old Lowdermilk shanty gone to splinters; worse than splinters 'cause splinters stay where they are. Our home wasn't there any more. It was entirely swept away—porch, settin'-'round room, lean-to, tin roof and all. Lord knows where the cookstove went to.

Maw Maw came out from the dugout; and Verbaline Lou, holdin' SH against her motherly bosom. I hear'd Maw Maw say, "Land sakes!"

Pap said, "The shanty was no good no how. The roof leaked and the rats were gettin' worser."

"But it was our home," Maw Maw said.

Clyde said, "It was the teensiest little-bitty old cyclone I ever seen in my life. This ain't Montaig County, so we cain't expect Texas-size twisters here."

"It's done enough damage," I said. "Enough to get Pap ired, and when Pap gets ired he don't know mercy for humankind."

"I ain't ired," Pap said. "We can build it back again. Seems like the twister hit only the house and Cousin Drewey's box elder tree. It's left the barn and corral like nothin' hit em. And the woodpile yonder. And the wagon and the farm do-hunkuses."

"That's the way twisters do," Maw Maw said. "What

we got left is a blessin' down from the Lord. I say that from my heart, and that's all there is to it."

The skyline west was brightenin' up, and it looked like the kind of November we knew in Star Valley comin' our way. Black clouds were banked along the east, movin' fast and wouldn't stop 'til they hit Amarillo. There wasn't a funnel cloud trailin', 'cause the cyclone was long-gone. And I reckoned how maybe a half mile east we'd find some remnants of lumber and tin roof, maybe the cookstove. Or better still, maybe nothin' of what used to be home for us Lowdermilks.

"Looks like maybe the worst of it went over the corn patch," Clyde said. "It made a dirty sweep there. Look for yourse'f, folks. You'll see what I mean."

So we looked, we saw, and we gave thoughts to our minds, and we didn't say a damned thing. Cousin Drewey wasn't there any more. He wasn't set in the chair, facin' east toward the Washtaw Mountains while he made sawdust of his fiddle. Old Jeff wasn't there aside him, droop-headed like mules get. Or the hounds, or the empty fiddle-case and the guitar settin' naked, both tied to the saddle strings. Or the satchel that never held anythin' but a pair of socks and a change of shirt, that there what I saw Cousin Drewey take down off the saddle and put beside the chair just before he went to fiddlin', before the balance of us ducked into the dugout. No sirree, Cousin Drewey wasn't there, 'cause he'd done mounted his transportation and rode away.

We bowed our heads for the thoughts on our minds, for the sudden ache come to our hearts.

Maw Maw said, "Lord, take Cousin Drewey to Your heavenly kingdom, and when it comes time for supper feed him greens and catfish."

"Damn the sonofabitchin' luck," Pap said. "The twister took him away. No tellin' where his remnants be."

Maw Maw looked at Pap, and she looked him

straight in the face. She gave him full power of her eyes —eyes cold or warm, no tellin' which. She talked soft but I knew she meant to be hear'd by us all. She said, "It don't matter where Cousin Drewey's lifely-leftovers be. They might be scattered over the prairie a half-mile east, or he might already be come to the Washtaw Mountains. Right now he might be fiddlin' 'Cattle in the Canebrake' for the pleasure of the Lord, dressed in a white gown pure as snow, with an angel pickin' a guitar and another twangin' a jew's harp. Folks, it don't matter where Cousin Drewey's remnants be, but where his *spirit* is . . . Well, that's a mighty fine place to be."

Clyde reached for Verbaline Lou and put an arm 'round her middle. He did that after Maw Maw took the big boy baby to hold for herse'f. That lovin' man said to his wife, and to us all, "Well, it's all over now, folks. So I reckon we'd better get fixed to go up to the ranch. It's the only place left for you Lowdermilks. Sonny Boy and Lilybelle will be here directly. Lilybelle will drive the Chivvelee, and Sonny Boy will wrangle the three-ton truck. Maw Maw, Lou and the big boy baby can go up in the Chivvelee, and us menfolks can follow up when we get the plunder loaded in the truck—like what's down in the dugout, cats and chickens and hogs and all. We can pick up the woodpile some other time."

When Clyde made mention of the woodpile Pap went into conniptions. He broke away and ran like a dog to where the shanty used to be, to where the stack of old auto tires once made pleasure for him in front of the porch. He hollered bad language, worse'n any he'd used before, while Maw Maw and Verbaline Lou finger-lugged their ears. He danced like a wild man covered with hair, with big feet like the Giant of the Hills in the canebrakes along the Saline River. He flung his arms skyward, he kicked at the empty dirt. Then he bent over, stilled his wildness. He put a brake on his ire. We all had good eyesight, we saw how tough old Pap Lowdermilk was cryin', leakin' tears like a big boy baby. 'Cause the twister had taken the tire-stack clean away. Pap's prime love had gone eastbound with the wind.

He came back to us like a whipped dog, humbled, shakin' his head and wipin' his eyes with a shirt-sleeve. He was Pap Lowdermilk, all right, but he didn't act right.

He stopped, he stood facin' Maw Maw. She saw somehin' in his eyes, so she gave the big boy baby back to Verbaline Lou. Pap walked up to Maw Maw and he did somethin' he'd never done before. He loved her neck. Lord he'p us, he slobbered kisses all over her face. And his frame shook for the love of it, for the tears that were wettin' the shoulders of Maw Maw's dress.

He broke away from his grip on Maw Maw, 'cause all tender things must end. Verbaline Lou was lookin' off to the road t'other side of the corn patch. Off to where the gate gave way out of our place. Like us all, she thought maybe Lilybelle might be comin' with the Chivvelee, Sonny Boy with the truck.

"They'll be here directly," Pap said.

Then he said to us balance, "Clyde, and you too Newt, we'd better pick up the pieces. We can get the plunder stacked for loadin', ready when Sonny Boy gets here. Maybe we can find a box for the cats, or Verbaline Lou can hold them in her grip up to the ranch, she and Maw Maw in the Chivvelee. The chickens are sacked, but we'll need all hands to load the hogs."

Then he said with a twinkle in his eye, "Maybe Lilybelle will make a chocolate cake for this old settler, just to celebrate our migration to a better world, one without the misery we all had here. And that cake will have PAP writ with icin' on the top."

"It'll make you sicker'n a horse, Pap," Clyde said.

So we all got to messin' 'round, pickin' up what we could.

"Newt," Pap said, "what you reckon happened to old

Sucky, the cow that cain't find calves, and t'other one just as sorry? You reckon the twister took 'em away?"

"No tellin', Pap," I said.

So Pap looked across the corn patch, and doggone if he didn't point out two specks of white and brindle yonder by the gate that sat next to the road. "Newt," he said, "you better get out and bring them two no-goods this way. We might need to get them to the ranch on another trip."

So I went to drive in the cows while the balance got ready for the comin' of Lilybelle and Sonny Boy. I stopped at the place where Cousin Drewey fiddled while he waited to get off by the tornado. There wasn't a remnant 'round of man, mule or hounds.

I walked on and the cows were gettin' closer. The gate was gettin' closer, soon the Skinner folks would be comin' through that gate. The dirt under me was swept clean, like a broom had done a sweet job. No sign of anythin' but natural dirt. Everythin' was wet after the rain. My shoes squeaked while they made tracks. I came by a couple of scrub cedars; atop one was Cousin Drewey's chair, among the limbs of t'other was his satchel. I just kept on walkin', thinkin' how it was the Lord's will, and how our kinfolks had done the will of the Lord.

The cows and gate were just a piece-aways now. I'd soon have old Sucky and her sidekick up to the corral, where we'd feed 'em milo maize. Now the ground looked natural, a hundred yards beyond the path of the tornado. It was grass all over, like nothin' had happened there. Then I looked down, and, damned if I didn't see them, I saw them plain, as freshly printed tracks planted clean in the wet earth—the hoofprints of a mule trottin' toward the gate and the paw-tracks of two hound dogs trailin' behind.

I said to myse'f, "Doggone, that crafty old bastard!

The Washtaw Mountains are seven hundred miles away, but he'll make them, him and his mule, and his hounds, his fiddle, his guitar and his hog-leg forty-five."

I kept on. Lilybelle came through the gate first, drivin' the Chivvelee. She'd left her kids up at the ranch. She called out, "Newt, did the twister leave you Lowdermilks in one piece?"

I said, "You bet, and we're all fixed for a migration, even Pap."

That tickled Lilybelle to death, and Sonny Boy followed her with the three-ton truck.

I went to the gate and onto the road. The mule and dog tracks turned east, just ramblin' along.

I knew somethin', a secret for myse'f. What I knew was how soon as we shut the dugout door and got clear of the tornado, when we couldn't see out and trusted only to the Lord, Cousin Drewey just quit his fiddlin', put his instrument in the case, mounted old Jeff and whistled the hounds to trail along. He left the chair and satchel for the twister to take away. He might've talked about ridin' that there cyclone, but he had a better and slower way of gettin' to the Washtaw Mountains. Unless the rider be the Lord, a mule is better'n a cloud anytime.

"I won't tell 'em 'til you're out of the way, Cousin Drewey," I said out loud, lookin' the way he had gone. "So far gone that they won't crave to catch up, or aim to bring you back."

So I got behind the cows and started drivin' them to the corral, across the corn patch. As I went I could see him like he was next to me, him on his mule with the hound dogs trailin'.

High on the saddle, pointed for Tucumcari, then for Lubbock and for roads and towns that are full of lovin' people in that dear old Lone Star State. In my mind I saw him come by Seymour and stop in front of the white stone courthouse. He was set in the saddle, up on Jeff, and he'll fiddle a tune 'til the folks come 'round. He'll fling his hat on the ground, brim-side up, 'cause Texas folks are generous with their dimes and two-bit pieces. He'll switch from fiddle to guitar, give them a song, and his kindly voice would gladden their hearts.

> *Honeysuckle Candy Woman,*
> *Where did you get them eyes?*
> *They're mean like a cat's,*
> *And they match your mouth for lies.*

He'll come to Bowie in Montaig County, homeland of the Skinner boys, where the Rock Island crosses with the Fort Worth and Denver City. While there he'll go to the depot, sing "Potaphar's Sufferin' Woman," and say howdy to the Rock Island fellers, and to the Fort Worth and Denver City fellers. He'll ride by Forestburg and Gainesville—mighty clever people live in Gainesville. At Whitesboro he'll sing a song:

> *Honeysuckle Candy Woman,*
> *Fry them pork chops brown . . .*

At Sherrman he'll give out some fiddle tunes, like "Cornbread and Clabber," "Midnight Breakdown" and "Soldier's Joy." The folks will hear and whoop and holler, they'll pitch dimes into Cousin Drewey's hat and a kindly man will say, "You'all come stay all night, Cousin Drewey; you and old Jeff and the hound dogs. We got cornbread and hog-jowls and black-eye peas for supper. Don't you know it's New Year's Day?"

He'll cross the Red River at Denison, get off old Jeff, hunker down and kiss the dirt of Texas a sweet fare-you-well. He'll cross the bridge and meet the dearest land in the nation, Oklahoma, the Sooner State, where the world's best fellers get born, live and die.

COUSIN DREWEY & THE HOLY TWISTER

At Durant they'll say, "Well hell-fire, it's Cousin Drewey! Where you been all these years, Cousin Drewey? They're lonesome for you up in the Kiamishi Mountains. They need your sweetness in the Windin' Stair Mountains, and up next to the Jackfork."

So Cousin Drewey will thank them kindly, ride north-aways to Caney, and at Caney come to the Clear Boggy. And there he'll sing a song:

> *He scratched and he scratched*
> *But they wouldn't come loose,*
> *'Cause the Lord done put 'em there.*

It will be late February when Cousin Drewey pulls into Antlers and he'll snicker with thankfulness when the folks there tell him how both Uncle Gershes are feelin' of the finest kind and how they aim to welcome Cousin Drewey like mountain men do. So Cousin Drewey will mount old Jeff and call the hound dogs to come get behind, and all together they'll make tracks for the Kiamishi Mountains. Northeast of Nashoba he'll come up to a pine-slab cabin and he'll holler howdy, and when the two big white-bearded fellers come out he'll quiz them if they reckon they'll ever amount to a damn. So Uncle Gersh Lowdermilk and Uncle Gersh Foster will catch Cousin Drewey when he slides down from the saddle and they'll take turns lovin' his neck. Uncle Gersh will say, and it don't matter which, "Put old Jeff out in the pasture, dear cousin, and you'all come in for supper—you and Pee-Dog and that Bitchy Damn. We got cabbage and turnips."

So Cousin Drewey, that night, will eat supper with his dearly beloved kin, and while he eats he'll reach for the rhubarb. 'Cause Cousin Drewey is slightly silly about rhubarb.

"Tell us all you know about them Lowdermilks," Uncle Gersh will say, and it don't matter a damn which Uncle Gersh. So Cousin Drewey will tell them all he knows about Pap, about Maw Maw, about me. He'll tell about Clyde, about Verbaline Lou, and about that stinkin' SH.

And while he talks he'll think, and his mind will dwell on the good years ahead, of the sweet life the Lord will ordain for him in the soft green world of the Washtaws. Of huntin' with the hounds, fishin' in the creeks, whittlin' the hardest wood in creation, and gassin' with the best fellers a man could hunker with. And, maybe, win a prize at the watermelon-seed-spittin' contest at Tuskahoma come June.

But until then he'll just ramble along, across Texas and over the Red River with old Jeff and the hound dogs, with his fiddle and guitar, and his hog-leg forty-five.

With love in his heart and a song come off his glottis:

Honeysuckle Candy Woman,
I ain't got a dime to my name.

There are a lot more where this one came from!

ORDER your FREE catalog of ACE paperbacks here. We have hundreds of inexpensive books where this one came from priced from 75¢ to $2.50. Now you can read all the books you have always wanted to at tremendous savings. Order your *free* catalog of ACE paperbacks now.

ACE BOOKS
P.O. Box 400, Kirkwood, N.Y. 13795

DON'T MISS THESE OTHER FICTION BESTSELLERS FROM ACE!

☐ **BORDERLINE** Keener 07080-9 $2.50
A fast-paced novel of hijacks and hijinks!

☐ **CASINO** Lynch 09229-2 $2.50
Blockbuster in the bestselling tradition of AIRPORT and HOTEL!

☐ **CHARADES** Kelrich 10261-1 $2.50
A yacht-filled marina is a private pleasure oasis for the rich and beautiful, where survival depends on how well they play the game.

☐ **DIARY OF A NAZI LADY** Freeman 14740-2 $2.50
Riveting confessions of a young woman's rise and fall in Nazi society.

☐ **FLOOD** Stern 24094 $2.50
Riveting suspense adventure story about a disaster that could happen. By the bestselling author of THE TOWER.

☐ **THE WATCHER** Smith 87357 $2.75
Glimpse into the unknown corners of the human soul in this spellbinding novel of unrelenting suspense.

ACE BOOKS F-01
P.O. Box 400, Kirkwood, N.Y. 13795

Please send me the titles checked above. I enclose _____.
Include 75¢ for postage and handling if one book is ordered; 50¢ per book for two to five. If six or more are ordered, postage is free. California, Illinois, New York and Tennessee residents please add sales tax.

NAME_____

ADDRESS_____

CITY_____STATE_____ZIP_____